"SHE'S GONE COUNTRY is a celebration of a woman's indomitable spirit. Suddenly single, juggling motherhood and a journey home, Shey embodies every woman's hopes and dreams. Once again, Jane Porter has written her way into this reader's heart."

—Susan Wiggs, *New York Times* bestselling author of *The Summer Hideaway*

Praise for the Novels of Jane Porter

EASY ON THE EYES

"Porter just keeps getting better and better. Timely issues and realistic characters propel the story."

—*RT Book Reviews*

"Touching and unpredictable, *Easy on the Eyes* is a real winner."

—*Fredericksburg Free Lance-Star* (VA)

"Entertaining, gratifying chick lit distinguished by a realistic look at aging in a business that values youth and beauty above all else."

—*Booklist*

"A great summer read...Porter doesn't disappoint in this novel."

—ANovelMenagerie.com

"[Jane] Porter ensures that *Easy on the Eyes* is fortified with a stimulating intellect and emotional message, strong conscience, and pure heart."

—*Honolulu Advertiser*

"Jane Porter is a master of the buoyant, blissful read, often incorporating issues that almost all women face in a highly readable way...this is a breezy read about the entertainment industry and its never-ending fascination with youth and beauty."

—BookReporter.com

"An entertaining tale."

—*Bellevue Reporter* (WA)

"Delightful women's fiction with strong romantic themes."

—AmySueNathan.com

"Jane Porter writes endlessly entertaining and yet deeply thoughtful novels. *Easy on the Eyes* is a perceptive, tender page-turner—a joy to read."

—Laura Caldwell, author of *Red Hot Lies*

"A page-turning novel about love, loss, friendship, aging, and beauty (not necessarily in that order). I couldn't put it down."

—Karen Quinn, author of *Holly Would Dream* and *The Ivy Chronicles*

"Jane Porter knows a woman's heart as well as her mind. *Easy on the Eyes* is a smart, sophisticated, fun read with characters you'll fall in love with. Another winning novel by Jane Porter."

—Mia King, national bestselling author of
Good Things and *Sweet Life*

"Witty and observant—Tiana's search for love and meaning amidst shallow celebrity will stay with you long after you've finished reading."

—Berta Platas, author of *Lucky Chica*

"A fun, poignant story about searching for life and love on the other side of forty."

—Beth Kendrick, author of *The Pre-Nup*

MRS. PERFECT

"Great warmth and wisdom...Jane Porter creates a richly emotional story."

—*Chicago Tribune*

"Porter's authentic character studies and meditations on what really matters make *Mrs. Perfect* a perfect...novel."

—*USA Today*

"Porter scores another home run."

—*RT Book Reviews*

"Fans will appreciate Ms. Porter's strong look at what happens to relationships when the walls come tumbling down."
—*Midwest Book Review*

"More poignant than the standard mommy lit fare."
—*Publishers Weekly*

"Compulsively readable...a delicious treat."
—BookReporter.com

"Real life hits trophy wife right in the Botox, in Porter's empowering page-turner!"
—Leslie Carroll, author of *Choosing Sophie* and *Play Dates*

ODD MOM OUT

"Jane Porter nails it poignantly and perfectly. This mommy-lit is far from fluff. Sensitive characters and a protagonist who doesn't cave in to the in-crowd give this novel its heft."
—*USA Today*

"With a superb sense of characterization, a subtle sense of wit, and a great deal of wisdom, Jane Porter writes about family and friendship, love and work."
—*Chicago Tribune*

"Funny and poignant...delightful."
—Stella Cameron

"*Odd Mom Out* is an engaging tale that examines important issues of today's world. Behind the entertaining, witty prose are insightful observations about real life."
—*Woodbury Magazine*

"Marta is an intriguing heroine."
—*Publishers Weekly*

"Keenly emotional and truly uplifting."
—*Booklist*

FLIRTING WITH FORTY

"A terrific read! A wonderful, life and love-affirming story for women of all ages."
—Jayne Ann Krentz, *New York Times* bestselling author

"Calorie-free accompaniment for a poolside daiquiri."
—*Publishers Weekly*

"Strongly recommended. Porter's thoughtful prose and strong characters make for an entertaining and thought-provoking summer read."
—*Library Journal*

She's Gone Country

Also by Jane Porter

Easy on the Eyes
Mrs. Perfect
Odd Mom Out
Flirting with Forty
The Frog Prince

She's Gone Country

Jane Porter

NEW YORK   BOSTON

5 Spot
Hachette Book Group
237 Park Avenue
New York, NY 10017

www.5-spot.com

5 Spot is an imprint of Grand Central Publishing.
The 5 Spot name and logo are trademarks of
Hachette Book Group, Inc.

Printed in the United States of America

First Edition: August 2010
10 9 8 7 6 5 4 3 2 1

Library of Congress Cataloging-in-Publication Data
Porter, Jane
She's gone country/Jane Porter.
p. cm.
ISBN 978-0-446-50941-1
1. Self-realization in women—Fiction. 2. Chick lit. I. Title.
PS3616.O78S54 2010
813'.6—dc22
2009042990

For my boys
Jake, Ty, and Mac
You own my heart

Acknowledgments

I couldn't have done this one without the girls—the girls in this case being my friends, my family, and my fans.

This past year was a challenging one as I juggled my passion for my career with my desire to add a baby to the family.

Grateful thanks to my editor, Karen Kosztolnyik, and my agent, Karen Solem, for being so patient and supportive during the process. Big thanks to Emily Cotler and the Wax team for always making me look good even when I didn't know which end was up. Massive thanks and love go to Jamette Windham, Lee Hyat, Alaia Davies, Emily Lanfear, and Kari Andersen for the hours of help, encouragement, and TLC.

To my Bellevue friends Lisa Johnson, Lorrie Hambling, Janie Lee, and Kristiina Hiukka for feeding me and checking on me and making sure I knew I was loved. To Sinclair Sawhney for believing there was one more baby, and giving me all those shots to make the miracle happen.

To my sister, Kathy, and all the incredibly smart, successful women in my family. You make me proud to be a member of the Porter/Lyles family.

And finally to my writer friends who are always there for me and help me remember what's important in fiction and in life: Megan Crane, Liza Palmer, Lilian Darcy, CJ Carmichael, and Barbara Dunlop.

To all my readers—you really are the best.

And one last shout-out to my four boys—Surfer Ty, Jake, Ty, and Mac. I love you all so much.

She's Gone Country

Chapter One

"Shey Lynne, you've been here three months now and not once have you taken those boys to church."

I look up from the bacon frying on the 1950s-era Sears stove to see my mother standing in the kitchen doorway with her blue wool coat over her arm and her ancient black vinyl purse on her wrist. It's hot out and humid, yet Mama's got her coat—and it's an old coat, not one of the gorgeous ones I've given her. My mother has a closetful of designer pieces she's never worn. I don't know why she won't wear them, but I swear, it's as if she takes pride in rejecting everything nice I give her.

"No, I haven't, and I'm not," I answer, grease sizzling and splattering the back of my hand. Mama's been here eight days, and it's been a power struggle from the moment she arrived. But she's going home later today, and I can keep my cool for another few hours. "You know I don't make the boys go to church. If they want to go, great. If they don't, fine. It's their choice."

But my mother, the daughter of a Southern Baptist preacher, fixes her cool blue gaze on me in silent rebuke. "If you went to church, then maybe they'd go."

The grease splatter burns, and I press my hand against my side. I don't want to argue with her, not today, not after the fight my son Bo and I had last night. "I know it shocks you, Mama, but I haven't gone since you sent me away to St. Pious to finish high school—"

"Then I failed you, Shey Lynne."

I shake my head. My mother can do guilt like no other. "You didn't fail me, and God's not going to blame you for whatever mistakes I make. But I'd be a hypocrite to make the kids go to church now when it's something I don't even do."

"I'd call it being a good role model. Your boys could use some religion along with some serious attitude adjustment."

I grit my teeth to keep from saying something I might regret. I love my mother, I really do, and I appreciate everything she's done for us since we moved back home after Cody's funeral last June—loaning us her house here in Parkfield, giving me Pop's old truck. But I'm not a kid anymore, I'm a woman with children of my own, and I'm going to raise my kids my way.

Mama sees my silence as a chance to press her case. "The Bible commands us to come together and worship—"

"I *know* what the Bible says!" Impatiently, I turn the heat down beneath the cast-iron skillet before reaching for the chipped ceramic bowl with the waffle batter. "I grew up going to church every Sunday and youth group every Tuesday night and Bible camp every summer. That's how you raised all of us, but John and I chose to raise our boys differently—"

"And maybe that's why you're in this mess, Shey Lynne. Maybe that's why your boys are out of control."

Oh, those are fighting words. They are. I face her, bowl clutched to my middle, one hand on my hip. "They're not out of control!"

"I've been here a week, Shey Lynne. I've heard plenty."

It hurts biting my tongue this hard, but I do it for the sake of peace, as well as the preservation of my sanity. It's been a rough year. It pretty much broke my heart, but things will improve, things are improving. "Mama, go to church. Brick and Charlotte will be here any minute. You'll feel better once you're out of the house and heading to the service, and frankly, I'll feel better, too—"

"Shey Lynn!"

Great. I've offended her *and* wounded her.

I set down the bowl, but I don't go to her. We're not a touchy-feely kind of family. Stiff upper lip. German-Irish-Scandinavian stock. "I'm sorry. I don't want to fight with you, and I don't want to be disrespectful. But I'm trying so hard and I don't feel like you even care—"

"Of course I care! I'm worried sick about you all. I lie awake at night, unable to sleep with all the worrying."

"I don't want you to worry. Worrying won't change anything. The only thing that will get us through is getting through, and we're doing it, Mama, one day at a time. It might not be pretty, but it works, and I'm lucky. My kids are good kids. Yes, they're having some problems adjusting to all the changes, but they're twelve, fourteen, and fifteen, and boys. Life's not easy for them right now."

"You aren't the only one to raise boys. I raised three, too…" Her voice cracks, and she falls silent. We're both suddenly, achingly aware that although she raised three, we just buried Cody, the brother closest to me in age and my best friend growing up.

The loss is still too new, the grief too raw. It was hard enough losing my brother. I can't even fathom losing a son.

My mother has paled, but she finds her voice. "Boys need discipline. They need a firm hand."

"And I'm trying." I feel a surge of fury. Fury at John for falling in love with someone else. Fury at the economy that went south just when I had to become financially self-sufficient. And most of all, fury at me for coming home. I don't know why I thought coming back to Parkfield would be a good idea. I don't know how I thought moving back to Texas after Cody's death would help anything. It hasn't. I'm the first to admit that I shouldn't have left New York. Don't know what I was thinking. Don't know that I *am* thinking. But I don't need Mama rubbing it in my face. "I have a different relationship with my boys than you had with yours."

Mama's chin lifts, hands clasped prayerfully together. "You don't think Bo was disrespectful last night? Shouting at you? Cursing at his brother? Slamming doors?"

"I think he's fourteen and he melted down. He lost it. It happens."

"Your brothers would have never shouted at me, or slammed a door in my face."

I throw up my hands. "You're right. My brothers wouldn't have talked back to you, not with Pop around. But my boys' dad isn't around, and I have a different relationship with them than you had with Brick, Blue, and Cody. I want my kids to talk to me—"

"Talk back, you mean."

I never fight like this, never raise my voice, and I hate that I feel so out of control now. "I've never been able to please you. Nothing I do is right." My eyes burn, but there are no tears. I haven't cried since last December, when I discovered John wanted out. I couldn't even cry at Cody's funeral. "But I'm not useless, Mama. I'm smart and strong, and I'm going to get my boys through. You just watch me."

I'm saying the right things but I've used the wrong tone of voice, and my mother's lips press tight. She's not hearing anything I'm saying, only the way I'm saying it.

Mama, Louisiana born and educated, is a true southern mama, and she throws back her shoulders. "God doesn't like your tone, Shey Lynne."

That's when I give up—arguing, that is. She's going to win this one. But then she always wins. I don't know how to fight with my mother. "No, He might not, but maybe today when you go to church you could remind Him that I'm doing the best I can considering the hand I've been dealt."

With the faintest shake of her head, she marches out of the kitchen, back stiff, silvery blond head high, down the paneled hallway for the front door, where my brother Brick is probably waiting to take her to church.

I lean my weight against the counter, eyes tightly closed as I gulp a breath, and then another.

This is not the life I wanted.

This is not the life I planned.

But this is now the life I have, and I'm going to make it work, so help me God, I am.

Eyes still closed, I hear the front door open with a squeak and then shut. Mama's gone. I exhale, and sagging with relief, I reach for the waffle batter.

Ladling the buttermilk batter onto the sizzling iron, I hear an engine and see a flash of blue as Brick's Chevy passes on the way down the drive.

Thank God she's gone. And thank God for Brick. Firstborn, eldest son, he's always done his best to take care of Mama. But I know it's not easy. He hates going to church. He goes only because it makes her happy, and when she's in Jefferson at my grandmother's, he doesn't attend.

A few moments later, Cooper, my youngest, slinks into the kitchen, shoulders hunched. He's only twelve but already five ten, and it's a body he can't quite figure out. "Gramma gone?" he asks, still in the rust-colored T-shirt and jeans he wore during his morning ride.

"Yeah." I rescue the bacon from the frying pan and line up the pieces to drain on a stack of paper towels. "What do you want to drink for breakfast, milk or juice?"

"Juice."

"Then go ahead and pour it, and call your brothers to the table. Breakfast is almost ready."

He fills his glass with orange juice and drains half before even bothering to shut the refrigerator door. "Gramma doesn't like us much, does she."

I'm pulling off the first waffle and am about to ladle more batter onto the griddle when I hear him. It's not a question, it's a statement, and it makes my chest squeeze. "Grandma *loves* you," I say fiercely, looking at him over my shoulder.

Cooper at twelve has my height and pale complexion, along with a smattering of freckles across his nose. He and Bo could probably have handled being tall and thin if they'd escaped the Callen red hair. But both of them inherited it, and being a redhead is about the worst thing they can think of.

Coop's shoulders hunch further. "Doesn't sound like she loves us. She makes us sound like we're the spawn of Satan."

"Her daddy was a preacher, Sugar. Grandma was raised in the church, going to church, and she's just worried about us."

"'Cause we don't go to church?"

"That, and Daddy's and my separation, as well as Uncle Cody's death."

"And going to church will change all that?"

"No. But it'd make her feel better." I drop a kiss on the top of his head. Another few months and he'll be taller than me. And he's my baby. "Go get your brothers. Breakfast is ready."

Brick calls me on his cell about an hour later. "That was the most boring sermon ever, Shey. You owe me."

I grin at the misery in his deep voice. He might be the oldest and I might be the youngest, but we've always been tight. "You don't have to pretend to like church just because she's here," I answer, taking a step outside the house to stretch and stand on the screened porch with its view of the oak-lined drive. More oak trees dot the pasture between the house and the six-stall barn. There's not a lot else to see but trees, cows, and land. Mama and Pop lived here for fifty-some years, and Pop's parents before that.

"It makes her happy," he says.

"That's why you'll go to heaven and I won't." I laugh and ruffle my hair. I've always gotten along well with all my brothers, but I enjoy teasing Brick most, probably because he takes his job as the oldest so damn seriously. "You all on your way home now?"

"No. We're going out for breakfast. Mama's still worked up, and Charlotte thought a good hot meal would put her in a better mood, especially since she's driving back to Jefferson this afternoon. Don't want her on the road when she's in a mood."

"No, we certainly don't. So where are you going, and are we invited?"

"Um, Shey, you're the reason Mama's in a bad mood. You're probably better off staying at the house."

"Gotcha." My lips twist in a rueful smile. My mother and I have a funny relationship. Given that I'm the only daughter and the baby of the family, you'd think we would have been close. Only it didn't work out that way. Mama prefers boys. But I can't complain. I certainly wasn't neglected growing up. I had three brothers to chase after and always was the apple of my daddy's eye. "We'll see you later, then, and don't rush your meal. We'll be here when you return."

I pocket the cell phone in my snug-fitting jeans and push through the screen door to step into the yard. Now that I'm back on the ranch, I wear only jeans, T-shirts, and boots, which makes getting dressed every morning easy.

The heels of my cowboy boots sink in the muddy drive as I walk from the shade of the house into the sun. We've had a few days of rain, which is good for the land but not so great for the property. The driveway is more mud than gravel these days, and the mud sticks to everything.

The Sleepy Acre Ranch hasn't changed since I was a

little girl. Pop never saw the point of spending money to fix up the house or yard—this is a working cattle ranch, after all—and when Brick married Charlotte twenty-five years ago, they built their own house on our family ranch, and that's where Charlotte's energy and design skills go.

Now kicking around the scraggly front yard, I wonder yet again how I could have thought the answer to our problems was moving back home.

How could I have imagined that Parkfield, Texas, population sixty-seven, would solve anything?

But then I am a Texas girl, born and raised on our ranch—literally born on the ranch, since for the birth of her fourth baby, Mama didn't even bother going to the hospital—and when I came home last June for Cody's funeral, I felt better than I had in a long time. I'm crazy about all the fields and oak trees and big sky, and I love the relaxed pace as well. Even the boys seemed happy to be out of New York, and they're East Coast, private-school-educated, field-hockey-and-lacrosse-playing kids.

But three months into our new "adventure," I'm beginning to question my impulsive decision to relocate us all here. Cooper has settled in fine, but Bo and Hank are struggling. They miss their friends and their sports—no one here plays lacrosse or field hockey—and I can't help wondering if maybe I shouldn't move us back to New York.

But my husband, John, is in New York. And John's no longer in love with me. He's living with his new partner—a man—and I can compete with another woman, but how on earth do I compete with a man for my husband's affections?

I can't.

My heart sinks and I dig the toe of my beat-up boot into the mud, watching the reddish brown earth ooze around the scuffed, pointed tip.

We would have been married seventeen years this year. I was happy with him. We'd had a good marriage, and at times a great marriage, until this.

I've known for nine months now that John's in love with someone else, but it's still bigger than I can get my head around. I'm mad. Confused. But maybe the worst part is that I still love John. I don't know how to stop loving him. Don't know if I should. I don't want a divorce, but I sure don't want to share him. Thus, we've filed for divorce, but it all feels so hideously wrong.

The phone in my pocket vibrates and I fish it out, grateful for the distraction, and see Marta's name and number. Marta. One of my buds. "Hey, Ta," I say, taking Marta's call. "How are you?"

"I'm good. Eva's at a birthday party and the other three are all napping, so I thought I'd call you, check in, see how things are going."

Marta's one of my two best friends from boarding school. We met in Monterey, California, when we were attending St. Pious. She lives outside Seattle now, although for nearly ten years we both lived in New York. I've missed her ever since she moved away.

"You're an answer to a prayer, girl," I admit, crossing the sticky muddy drive to sit on the open tailgate of my dad's old truck. "I think I'm losing my mind."

"What's wrong?"

I push my long hair from my face and discover that my

hand is trembling. It's just stress and fatigue, but I don't like it. "My mama's been here a week visiting us, and living with her is like attending a church revival. It's Jesus this, and Jesus that, and nothing I do is ever right or good enough. Why didn't I remember this before I moved us all home?"

Marta laughs on the other end of the line. "Moving home always sounds so idyllic until you do it."

"It did seem idyllic—empty ranch house, no rent, free schools, Pop's truck—but Mama keeps showing up on the doorstep, and my brothers seem to think I'm still sixteen, not thirty-nine!"

"If it's any consolation, I was miserable when we first moved back to Seattle, too. Eva was lonely. I despised the wealthy stay-at-home moms. You were the one who gave me the big lecture about how I needed to make more of an effort to fit in—"

"I didn't!"

"You did. On the ferry coming back from the San Juan Islands."

My brow clears as I remember our weekend away three years ago. "That wasn't a lecture, Ta. That was a pep talk."

"The point is, my first year I was really unhappy in Bellevue. I was missing New York. Missing you. Missing the life I'd left behind."

"But you had a reason to stick it out in Bellevue. And you didn't move back because you were running away from anything." I swing my legs and soak up the autumn sunshine. After the past two days of rain, I'll take every bit of sun I can get. "I've never run away from anything before. Why am I running now?"

"You didn't run away from New York. You just wanted change. There's nothing wrong with that."

"But Parkfield? The ranch? I pulled my kids out of the best private boys' school in the city and dragged them out to the sticks. And they hate it, at least Bo and Hank do. Cooper's a country kid at heart and loving life here. He and my brother Brick have totally bonded, but my older two...they're unhappy. They don't know what to do with pasture, tractors, and cow patties."

Marta stifles a laugh. "Can't say I blame them. I'd hate being stuck in the country."

"I don't think Bo and Hank are really trying, though. It's like they think if they fight it long enough, I'll eventually cave in and take them back to New York."

"Will you?"

That's when I lose steam.

I don't want to return to New York. It feels good to be out of the city, away from the traffic and noise and stress. I love having a horse again and going riding every day and waking up to the crowing of our rooster. After sixteen years of living the high life as a glamorous fashion model, it's a hoot bouncing around in Pop's ancient work truck in my boots and jeans and cowboy hat. I might complain about my overprotective big brothers, but I adore them. I also happen to think it's good for my boys to have their uncles around, especially in light of their father's recent identity crisis.

"If I had to," I say slowly, "I would. But I'm not ready to throw in the towel. Not by a long shot."

"Can you afford to buy a new place on the Upper East Side?"

"I could. It'd be smaller than what we had before, but

I'd rather sit on my little nest egg instead of purchase real estate, because it's not long until the boys go to college and that's going to be expensive."

"So you're okay financially?" Marta asks.

"I'm good. I've always been careful with my money, and since John and I kept separate checking accounts, it was relatively easy dividing our assets." I pause, think of John now living with his boyfriend, Erik, try not to cringe. "John's hurting financially, but Erik's supporting him so I guess he'll be okay."

"Why are you still worrying about John? He was the one who wanted out, not you."

"I can't help worrying about him. He was my partner, my husband—"

"Was," she interrupts flatly. "And you need to move on and focus on you now. Which leads me to my next question. Are you working?"

"Brick's hired me to do the ranch books, but that's only a part-time job."

"I meant modeling."

I swing a leg, flex my foot, and study my scuffed boot. These are my favorite pair. They're so comfy that they feel better than slippers. "I signed with Stars of Dallas but haven't been booked for anything yet."

"They'll call you. You're still gorgeous."

I flex the other foot. "I think I'm getting lazy, though. The idea of commuting to Dallas isn't appealing."

"How long a drive is it?"

"Ninety minutes or so."

"That's not lazy, that's being real. It's hard enough working without spending hours in the car."

"How about you? Working a ton?"

"Not as much as I used to. I can't, not with Zach and the twins. I don't know what happened to me, Shey, but I'm beat. Tired all the time now."

"That's because you have babies. The twins still waking up at all hours of the night?"

"Unfortunately."

"Sorry, Ta," I commiserate, lifting my face to the sun, concentrating on the warmth against my skin. I can't get enough sunshine. I need it, crave it, depend on it. "I remember those days. Couldn't do it now. Need my sleep too much."

"This is why women are cranky, you know that, don't you? We're tired. Our bodies are trashed and we're seriously sleep-deprived." Marta hesitates. "So how are your three? Coping better with John's lifestyle, or is that still an issue?"

I sigh and open my eyes. "They don't really talk about it, but I know it's a struggle, especially for Bo. He doesn't want to get on the phone when his dad calls, and he definitely doesn't want to hear about John's life with Erik."

Marta digests this. "And Bo's depression?"

I feel a swift, hot shaft of pain. Bo's the one I have to watch. Bo's my worry. "Seems okay for now. But I'm keeping an eye on him. Determined to stay on top of it this time."

"Sounds like we've both got our hands full." Marta's voice is full of sympathy. "But we can do this. We're strong. Damn tough. And besides, you've got the best heart, Shey, you really do. No one loves more than you do."

My eyes suddenly burn, and I'm glad she can't see me because my lower lip quivers. I bite it, hard. "We are tough. And Bo's going to be fine. We're going to get through this. It's just going to take some time."

"Love you, Shey-girl."

"Love you, too, Ta. Let's get together soon."

And then, ending the call, I jump off the back of the truck and walk a brisk, fierce circle around the yard, my heart thumping like mad.

Bo isn't crazy. Bo isn't like my brother Cody. Bo is going to be okay.

I walk another frenzied circle, and another, and another, until some of the suffocating fear in me fades and my pace slows and my pulse returns to normal. It's only then that I head for the house.

This is life. Life is full of ups and downs. We're going to be fine.

And my boy Bo is going to be fine, too. There's no way I'll let him become another Cody.

Chapter Two

———— ✳ ————

Later that afternoon I see my mother off, and the moment she's in her car, heading east for Jefferson, I feel a weight lift from my shoulders. Sounds mean, but hosting Mama for a week felt like a root canal without anesthesia. I'm just glad she's gone and won't be back until Thanksgiving, which is still—thankfully—over nine weeks away.

In the house I strip the sheets from the master bedroom bed, which is where Mama slept, before starting a load of laundry. I contemplate what to make for Sunday night dinner (usually it's beef, beef, beef, since we are a cattle ranch), but nothing in the freezer looks good. The sun pools on the kitchen floor, and I want to get out. Go do something. Something preferably fun.

That's when I decide to track down the boys and see if any of them are up for a matinee movie.

Cooper and Bo enthusiastically endorse the idea. Hank, my oldest, declines, says he has homework he needs to finish. I suspect it isn't true, but I don't push it. I've learned the hard way that you can't make someone enjoy being with you. Instead, I go online to check movie listings at Fandango. Because we're in the middle of nowhere, everything's a drive, and the question is whether we can make do with one of the movies showing at the Brazos in Mineral Wells, a twenty-minute drive, or do we have to make the trip all the way to Weatherford, which is a forty-five-minute drive.

Fortunately, the boys find a movie they want to watch in Mineral Wells, and if we leave now, we'll just make it in time. We arrive as the previews are showing, and since the movie's been out a few weeks already, the theater is almost empty and we have no problem finding good seats.

It's not my kind of film, but as the only female in the family I'm used to our diet of action-adventure thrillers. I sometimes miss the days of Disney and Pixar films, but there are also advantages to having bigger kids. I don't have to take them to the bathroom. I don't worry (as much) about them being kidnapped. I know they can cross a street and navigate traffic and drop and roll should their clothes catch fire.

Still, they're my kids, my boys, and I glance at them once, twice, during the film, as enamored of their faces as I was when they were newborns. These two, my youngest two, look so much like my brother Cody that it's uncanny. Cody was a redhead, too. And funny. And brilliant. And bipolar.

And just maybe schizophrenic.

But I don't know if that's true. My brother Blue called Cody a schizophrenic at Pop's funeral four years ago, but Mama says Cody was just a lost soul. Brick said he was a drug addict. The truth is probably somewhere in between.

Bo leans over, hisses in my ear that I'm supposed to be watching the movie.

"I like watching you better," I whisper back.

"Wow. Scary," he answers before turning back to the big screen.

Emotion tugs at me, and it's bittersweet. Bo has no idea

how much I worry about him. And I do worry, because Cody wasn't always a lost soul. Cody was once my best friend, the brother who never left me behind, the brother who gave me rides to the games and then out to pizza or burgers after.

If I loved Cody as much as I did, and it couldn't keep him together, what does that mean for Bo?

Bo grabs my hands, gives a squeeze to my fingers. "Watch. The. Movie. Mom."

I lift his hand to my mouth and kiss the back of it before letting it go so we can watch the movie. All remaining fifty-six minutes of violence and mayhem.

We leave when the credits roll, and Cooper is enthusiastically reliving every detail of the big fight scene. In his mind, he's part Jackie Chan, part John Cena, and more badass than the two of them put together.

While Coop's on a high, Bo's mood has turned and he's angry, and particularly angry at Coop for being happy. "You're so stupid," I hear Bo tell Cooper. "You couldn't fight anyone. You're the biggest chicken I know."

"No, I'm not!"

"Yes, you are."

I face Bo. "What are you doing? Why are you being mean?"

"I can fight," Cooper protests.

Bo is oblivious to everything but making his point. "You can't even play sports. How do you think you could fight?"

"I play sports—"

"You still don't even know how to cradle the ball," Bo interrupts scornfully. "Why do you think you were always on defense?"

"Because I was good at defense."

"Because you couldn't play offense. Defense is where they stick the losers."

"That's it. That's enough." I step between them, hands pushing them farther apart. "I'm not in the mood for this tonight. If you're going to fight, let's just go home and we can skip dinner and you can fight to your heart's content. But if you want to eat tonight, you'll shut your mouths now."

And then Bo—damn him—opens his mouth. "I played better at eight than you do at twelve—"

I grab Bo then, seizing his upper arm hard, and haul him toward me. I know the parenting books say we're not supposed to manhandle our kids, but Jesus, there's got to come a point when they *listen*. "Did you not hear me, Bo Thomas Darcy? I said not one word, and yet you had to—"

"It's true. He can't play. He doesn't practice—"

I let go then, disgusted. Biting back curses, I reach into my purse for my keys as I walk away. "You boys better get in the truck now," I call over my shoulder, because I'm done. Done arguing. Done pleading. Done being nice. Today has been exhausting from beginning to end, and all I want now is some peace and quiet in my own room.

"Now look what you did," Cooper mutters as they follow after me. "If you'd just shut up!"

Miraculously, Bo doesn't answer, and silently they climb into the truck, scooting as far from me as they can on the seat.

I don't even look at them as I drive. I'm too mad.

Hank's at the breakfast table when I enter the kitchen in my flannel shorts and T-shirt the next morning. He's already dressed and eating the toasted, buttered bagel that's his breakfast every morning before school.

"Morning," I greet him, kissing the top of his head. "What are you doing up so early?"

"Studying."

I pull out a seat at the table and sit across from him, my head as thick as cotton wool. "Are you having trouble in school?"

"No. But the PSATs are next week and I want to do well."

"Right. College." Can't believe college is just a few years away. Can't believe Hank is already a high school sophomore. Where did the time go?

"You know, if I were at Dyer, they'd have us doing all kinds of tutorials and test study sessions," Hank says, looking up at me. "Here they don't do any of that. Nobody cares about college, not unless they're going to go on a football scholarship."

"That's not true."

Hank holds my gaze. "I want to return to Dyer."

"Hank—"

"They'll let me back in. I already called the admissions office. My class has always been small, and they haven't given my place away. We just have to send the tuition and I'm in."

I blink, dumbfounded. "You called the school?"

"You weren't going to."

I just keep staring at him. He's tall and broad through the shoulders, with the faintest stubble shadowing his jawline. Even at his thinnest, he was never as lanky as his younger brothers. Instead, he takes after John with his muscular build and darker coloring. John, a brunette with olive skin, is still strikingly handsome, and it's becoming increasingly evident that Hank's going to look like his dad when he's an adult.

Lucky Hank.

"I want to go back to New York, Mom."

He isn't a boy anymore. He's becoming that man who'll head off to school one day and not come home.

He's going to have a whole life apart from mine.

He's going to have other people to love. Other people who will matter more.

It's the strangest realization, and one that hurts. I love my boys. I've loved being their mom. Nothing—not modeling, not marriage, no amount of traveling or fine things—has ever come close to the joy I get from being Hank, Bo, and Cooper's mother.

"You want to leave?" My voice shakes. I could use a strong, hot cup of coffee.

"I'd miss you," he admits gruffly.

But he still wants to leave. Me.

My head pounds, and I push away from the table to make a pot. I drink too much coffee—three, four cups each day—but it keeps me going, occupies my hands, and keeps my belly warm. It's either that or back to smoking, and I don't need to smoke.

"I'd still see you," Hank says to my back as I measure out the grounds. "I'd come visit for holidays," he adds, "and you could always come to New York and see me."

"What about your brothers?" I ask, turning on the machine.

He doesn't immediately answer, and keeping my expression blank, I face him. But Hank's not looking at me. He's frowning at the table and nudging what's left of his bagel around the perimeter of his plate. Finally, he shrugs. "I was going to go away sooner or later."

Later being the key word.

I battle to keep my voice neutral. Don't need to put him on the defensive. Don't need to draw party lines. "You only just turned fifteen, honey."

His head lifts, and he looks at me, his eyes more gold than brown. "You went away to boarding school at sixteen."

Yes, and I never came home again.

I want to go and wrap my arms around him and tell him if he goes, I will miss him every day he's gone. I want to tell him that he's not just my oldest son, but my heart. I want to tell him that I've just lost his dad and I'm not ready to lose him, too.

But I don't. I can't.

I can't cry and can't cling because I'm raising boys, boys who must become strong, independent men.

"True." I force a smile.

"You made good friends," he continues. "Aunt Marta and Tiana."

I nod.

"And you ended up getting into Stanford, something you wouldn't have done if you'd stayed here in Parkfield instead of going to St. Pious."

I nod again.

He stands up, carries his plate and milk glass to the sink, and then looks at me. We used to be the same height. Now he has a couple of inches on me. "So can I?"

My heart is so heavy, it's a stone in my chest. "Have you talked to your dad about this?"

"Yesterday, when you were at the movies."

Of course. "And what did he say?"

"That he'd love it. That he misses us kids."

I'm stunned by the wave of anger that shoots through me. He misses the kids, just the kids. Not me. Not his wife. Not his partner of seventeen years.

But why should he?

He's come out of the closet. Discovered he's gay. Discovered sex with a man is more fulfilling than sex with me. Jesus Christ. I grip a damp sponge in my hand and squeeze for all it's worth.

I am so mad and so confused, yet according to Dr. Phil and every other relationship expert, I can't say a word about it to the boys. Can't speak against their father. Can't show how shattered I am, because kids of divorce already carry around enough guilt as it is.

"So when could I start?" Hank presses. "After Christmas? At the start of the second semester?"

I take a slow, deep breath. "I don't know."

"Mom."

"Do we have to do this now?" I joke weakly. "I haven't even had my coffee yet."

"Be serious. This is important." Hank's brow furrows. "It's not that I don't love you," he adds gruffly.

"I know that."

His expression turns pensive. "Do you?"

I wrap him in my arms then and hold him tight. Who knows how many more chances I'll have to do this? "I do," I whisper. "I've known every day since you were born."

He returns the hug, and for a moment I'm at peace. He is mine. Everything is good. And then we let go and step apart, and Hank disappears to brush his teeth as Cooper enters the kitchen, complaining bitterly about Bo using up all the hot water. Again.

"Morning," I say mildly, pouring my coffee.

"Hate mornings," he grouses.

The edge of my mouth lifts. Cooper is not a morning person. "How'd you sleep?"

"Fine. Until I had to wake up."

The corner of my mouth lifts higher as I throw a packet of sweetener into my coffee. "How old are you again?" I ask as he grabs a box of cereal from the cupboard and a bowl and spoon from the cabinet.

He scowls at me, and the freckles dusted across his nose dance. "Twelve."

I blow on my coffee. "Good."

The morning news said it was going to be another scorcher today, with temperatures hovering in the mid- to high eighties, and I believe it as I step outside to drive the boys to school. Even though it's the end of September, north central Texas is still warm, and the humidity in the air sets my teeth on edge. I shouldn't be wearing jeans. I should put on a skirt and sandals and at least be cool. But putting on a skirt means shaving my legs, and that's the last thing I feel like doing.

The fact is, I am thoroughly enjoying country life and dressing down and easing up on my beauty routine. In New York I spent a lot of time on maintenance, but it's exhausting work and boring besides.

Brick's blue truck appears in the driveway, bouncing over the deep ruts worsened by last week's rain. I stand on the top step as his truck pulls up next to me.

Brick's a big guy, and a good-looking guy, if you like rugged men who don't believe in doing too much to themselves other than basics like hair and teeth and a once-a-day shave. I remember how a couple of years ago John tried to convince Brick that he should use some moisturizer and eye cream, said it'd really help with all Brick's sun exposure, and Brick looked at John as if he were a freak. Moisturizer, eye cream? Not on this brother.

The truck idles and Brick rolls down the passenger window. He's got his straw cowboy hat pulled low, and the brim shades his eyes. "You might want to check your cell phone and make sure it's not dead, 'cause I got a call from your agency in Dallas. They want to book you for a shoot today. Said they'd been trying to reach you since last night."

I walk around the truck to the driver's side. "How'd they find you?"

"I guess I'm an emergency contact. Anyway, you need to call them and then hightail it into Dallas."

"I've got to take the boys to school."

"I'll take them. You need to do this. It's always great money, and it'd be good for you to get off the ranch for the day."

"I'm okay here—"

"Mama's thinking about moving back home."

"*What?*"

Brick tips his hat back. "She thinks you need her, that you're in over your head and can't handle the boys—"

"That's ridiculous! I'm doing fine. Everything's fine."

"That's not what she says."

"Because Mama's a busybody!"

Brick gives me a long look. "Yes, she is. And if you don't want her taking up residence with you in the next couple weeks, you better pull it together and look like you actually enjoy life."

"I do."

"Aw, Shey, you've always been thin, but you're downright puny now. The only thing I ever see you put in your mouth is coffee. If I didn't know better, I'd say you were smoking again—"

"I'm not."

"You're not taking any pills? Calmers, tranquilizers like Valium, Xanax, anything?"

"No!" I cross my arms over my chest and glare at him. "I've never taken anything. You know how I feel about stuff like that, especially after Cody's problems with substances."

He reaches out, pushes a long blond tendril from my face. "Do you know you shake, hon? You can't even hold a pen without your hand trembling. Mama noticed. Charlotte's noticed. Even I've noticed."

His protectiveness touches me. "I'm just tired, Brick. I don't sleep like I used to."

"Maybe we need to take you out of the office and away from the books and put you in the barn instead. A day or two of hauling hay and mucking out stalls might help you with the sleep problem."

I crack a smile. "Maybe."

The front door opens and the boys come tumbling out of the house, voices raised in anger. "They're at it again," I groan.

"You can't be soft," Brick answers.

"I'm not."

He gives me another long look before laying on the horn. The horn shuts the boys up. "Get in," he orders, "I'm taking you to school today. Your mom's got something to do."

My boys look at me with surprise. "What are you doing, Mom?" Cooper asks, at my side for a good-bye kiss.

I kiss Cooper's cheek and answer that I might have a modeling job.

"Modeling what? Tractors?" Bo snorts.

"You're such a jerk, Bo," Hank mutters as he climbs into the truck to ride shotgun.

Cooper grimaces at me as Bo jumps past him to get into the cab's backseat. "Have a good day, Mom."

"I will. You too."

I lift my hand in farewell as the truck door closes and Brick drives off. Cooper turns to wave good-bye from the back. I shake my head. My boys. Hellions, each of them.

With the boys gone, I go in search of my cell phone and find it on the floor of Pop's old truck. As Brick suspected, the battery is dead, and I have to plug it in in the kitchen to retrieve messages. One from Mama and three from Joanne at Stars.

I call the number Joanne's left for me, which must be her cell since the agency doesn't open for another two hours. Joanne answers right away. "You finally got my message?" she asks.

"I did, sorry, the phone was in the truck."

"Are you available?"

"I could be. Where do I go, how long is the shoot?"

"It's for a Dillard's newspaper insert the day after Thanksgiving. They'll pay you your hourly rate. You're to be on location in Highland Park in an hour—"

"Oh, then there's no way. I'm two full hours from Highland Park. My brother lives there and I've never made it in less than two hours, and that's without traffic."

"I'll tell them you'll be there as soon as you can." And then she rattles off the address, and I'm fairly confident I know the house since Blue lives on Beverly Drive, too.

"Make sure they're okay with me being late," I say.

"They'll be fine. They need you."

Glad somebody does, I think, ending the call.

I shower and leave the house with my hair wet. I've also shaved—laser hair removal treatments aren't completely permanent—and am now racing to Dallas. I'm flying down Highway 180, cell phone connected to car charger, and I dial my brother Blue's cell phone.

I end up getting his voice mail and leave a message: "Blue, it's Shey, and I'm doing a photo shoot in Highland Park today on Beverly Drive. I'm thinking it's the big red-brick Georgian-style mansion down the street from you. Not sure how long I'll be working, but it'd be great to see you and Emily before I head home if there's time. Call me on my cell."

I hang up and concentrate on driving. And trying to quell the butterflies. I haven't done a lot of modeling in the past ten years, just a couple of jobs a year, but at least I knew most of the photographers in New York as well as the stylists. This, though, is my first job since returning to Dallas and my first job working with the Stars agency. I hope it goes well. I need it to go well. I don't know why it wouldn't. I've been modeling since the early nineties, appearing on my first U.S. *Vogue* cover in 1994, and then three years later making back-to-back covers for the *Sports Illustrated* swimsuit edition.

But modeling is different now. I'm older—thirty-nine—and not as toned or fit. My face is different, too, and when I lived in New York I kept up with all the skin treatments and fillers and injectables. But since moving home this June, I've concentrated on the kids, not on my appearance.

Turning the rearview mirror toward me, I steal a quick look at my reflection. Eyebrows need to be waxed. Eyelashes should be dyed. Hair should be colored and cut. Skin cries out for dermabrasion or a chemical peel.

Irritated, I snap the rearview mirror back into place and focus on the road, trying to pretend that my hands aren't clammy and my stomach isn't in knots.

Lord, I'm nervous. What if I arrive and they're disappointed? What if I'm too big for the clothes? What if I'm too old? Sweet Jesus, maybe taking this modeling job today wasn't such a good idea after all.

I reach Highland Park in exactly two hours and make only one wrong turn before finding the right house. It isn't the Tudor brick mansion I was thinking of, but it's similar in style, and U-Haul trucks and cars line the quiet street, with cameras and lights set up outside the house in front of the arched front door. The dark-stained door boasts a huge wreath, and a decorated Christmas tree is visible through the living room's leaded glass window.

I park the truck down the street and head for the house. My palms are still damp, but I walk the catwalk walk, the one I first learned in Milan and then perfected in

New York. It's a strut that looks confident and careless and hides the fact that I feel like an impostor.

Members of the crew look up as I approach. One of the men has a light meter around his neck. He must be the photographer or the photographer's assistant. Another man has tools and duct tape hanging from his belt. The thin, graying brunette with closely cropped hair and a clipboard has to be the stylist. She eyes me critically as I join them. I know the look. She's a woman who feels she has to be a bitch to be taken seriously. She also thinks that Dallas is the big time and she's the big cheese and I'm lucky to be here on her shoot.

"Good morning," I say, feeling the sun beat down. It's not yet ten and it's already muggy hot. If we're shooting outside today, wearing winter coats, it's going to be miserable. "I'm Shey Darcy, and I'm looking for DeeDee."

The graying brunette gives me another slow once-over. "You're late."

I open my mouth to protest, as Joanne had assured me she'd handle this part, then snap it shut and smile tightly instead. "DeeDee?"

She rolls her eyes at the men and then gestures for me to follow her. "Let's get you to hair and makeup."

I follow her to a small trailer tucked between a U-Haul truck and a white equipment truck. The trailer is already too crowded with models in various states of dress and undress. It's also noisy, thanks to the chatter of half a dozen voices and the air conditioner chugging out cool air.

DeeDee introduces me to Marna, who apparently is doing hair and some makeup. "This is our model, the one we've been waiting for."

Marna frowns as her gaze sweeps me up and down. "*This* is our grandmother?"

DeeDee shrugs. "It's who the agency sent. Age her. Put a wig on her or spray some gray on the hair. Do what you can."

My heart sinks as DeeDee exits the trailer. I'm not a young adult or a young mom. I'm playing Grandma today. Lucky, lucky me.

Chapter Three

———— ✹ ————

It's one-thirty in the afternoon and I'm standing on the bottom step of the Highland Park Tudor-style mansion holding a stack of brightly wrapped Christmas packages, dressed in a silver turtleneck, black pants, a black merino wool jacket, and black leather boots, with a long black wool coat on top. And despite the packages crammed in my arms, tight wig on my head, and the scratch of itchy wool fabric, I'm smiling up at my adorable grandchildren, who are running out of the house to meet me.

Unfortunately, the adorable grandchildren can't smile in the same frame, which means we reshoot again and again. And the sun's a little too direct overhead, which means we keep repositioning the lights and reflector screens. And heck, it's only eighty-nine degrees without the wig, turtleneck, jacket, coat, boots, lights, and silver reflectors.

A bead of sweat slides down my rib cage. And then another.

The photographer pauses to check his camera and then the light meter. DeeDee sends the little boy and girl back onto the top step. I close my eyes and count backward from ten. I am not hot. I am not sweating profusely. I am not suffocating.

DeeDee and the photographer talk, and then DeeDee claps her hands. "Let's do it again," she calls. "And Shey, a little more expression. These are your grandbabies, and it is Christmas."

The sweat slides down the small of my back. My cheeks feel tight, like a papier-mâché puppet's. "You got it, DeeDee."

I finish just before three-thirty, but it means I won't be in Mineral Wells for another two hours and I'll need Brick to pick up the boys. I call him and start to apologize for needing the favor, but he cuts me short, saying he'd planned on picking them up and was already in Mineral Wells at a feed store, so everything was under control.

"But how'd it go?" he asks. "Did you knock their socks off?"

I'm just starting my truck, and it's hotter than hell inside after baking in the sun all day. I pause to scoop up my hair and twist it into a knot on top of my head, using one of the boys' pencils to secure it in a bun. "They want me back tomorrow. We're doing the making-holiday-cookies-with-Grandma shots then."

"Holiday cookies with Grandma?"

"Yeah." I clear my throat. "I'm Grandma."

Brick barks a laugh, and I make a face as I pull away from the curb and head down the street. Blue's house is just two blocks from here, and I'm not sure if I should swing past it to see if anyone is home or just head back to the ranch. "Do you know if Blue is out of town? I called him earlier to let him know I'm in the neighborhood but never heard back."

"I don't think he's gone anywhere."

"Think I should stop by?"

"Only if you want to listen to Emily moan about how hard her life is, and how Blue hasn't amounted to anything."

Brick likes everybody, but even he finds Blue's demanding wife exasperating. Emily comes from old Dallas money, and although Blue has made some serious dough during their marriage, it's still not enough for her. She wants Blue to be like her daddy, and unfortunately he's not. Blue's just a millionaire, not a billionaire.

I stretch, try to get more comfortable as I'm still wired from the shoot. "I'll head home, then. I should be there around five if traffic isn't too bad."

"You might want to stop somewhere and do some shopping instead of coming straight back."

"Why?"

"Because once I get the boys home, I'm going to have them help me with some chores. They probably won't like it and they'll probably bitch and you'll get all worked up. Better you let me handle it."

My anxiety returns. "What kind of chores?"

"Basic ranch chores, Mama Bear. Stacking hay bales. Unloading feed sacks. Shoveling manure. Cleaning out the water troughs. Nothing that will hurt them, but jobs that need to get done."

He's right. The boys won't like it. The boys hate farm-work. But at the same time, we're living rent-free on the ranch, not even paying utility bills, and it's not right that Brick works his ass off while my three boys sit around and play video games. "I think I will make a little detour and let you handle this one."

"They'll probably call you and complain."

They probably will. My brothers wouldn't have dreamed of trying to get out of chores, but my boys don't have the same sense of responsibility or work ethic. In their mind, the world revolves around them: their sports, their entertainment, their needs. Guilt and unease gnaw at me. "I won't answer my phone."

"Smart."

Off the phone, I lean back against the seat, aware that if the boys are spoiled and self-centered, I have no one to blame but myself. I'm their mom. I've raised them to be who they are. Which is lazy and quite often selfish.

It's a sobering thought, and far from flattering.

Traffic already clogs the South 75, and I'm grateful I have to be on this freeway for only a couple of miles. I can't imagine 30 West will be much better, though, and I have forty-eight miles on that freeway.

And then tomorrow I'll do this again.

I probably shouldn't have agreed to return tomorrow. Today was horrible. The models weren't friendly, and the crew kept to themselves. I was treated like an outsider, and I suppose I am. In New York I knew everyone, but I'm starting over here, and starting as a senior.

Grandma in today's Dillard's shoot.

The corner of my mouth lifts in a faint, wry smile. And I was worried that I'd look too old.

I end up making better time than I expect, and seeing that it's only five now and Brick told me not to come until six, I stop at the Brief Encounter Café on the edge of Mineral Wells for a jumbo iced tea and a turkey club sandwich.

I sink into the vinyl booth with a grateful sigh. I'm hot

and tired and definitely hungry. Brick's right: I probably
don't eat enough. But sometimes it's hard to eat when I'm
surrounded by the boys and all they do is bicker and fight,
which Dr. Phil would also say is my fault.

For the second time today, I'm aware that my parenting skills are lacking. Were they always this bad, I wonder
as I snag a piece of crisp bacon from the sandwich to
munch on, or have I lost control since separating from
John?

I'm still puzzling over the situation when the café's
glass door opens, sucking in the hot, heavy heat of Texas.
The white glare of late afternoon sunlight floods the
brown linoleum floor, and as I glance up to see why the
door is so slow to close, my curiosity gives way to
shock.

Dane.

Dane Kelly.

Oh, my God.

I wondered when I'd finally see him—he didn't attend
Cody's funeral—and I choke on a breath, the air catching
inside my lungs just the way it used to when I was sixteen
and hopelessly in love with Dane Kelly, bull-riding champ,
neighbor, and my brother Brick's best friend.

I stare at him, drinking him in, drinking him as if he's
water and I'm dying of thirst.

He hasn't changed, not much. He still has the same
thick head of hair that's neither blond nor brown, but a
little of both. He's well over six feet and still fills a doorway
with those shoulders that are a little too broad and legs
that are a little too muscular and long. He's wearing the
tight, faded Wranglers cowboys prefer and a short-sleeved

T-shirt that hugs his chest. And even if I didn't know him, I'd think it's a *really* nice chest.

The glass door finally shuts behind him, and as the little fan on the corner cabinet coughs and whirs, Dane takes a step, heading for the long counter. That's when I see his cane and notice his limp.

Dane limps now. The champion bull rider got hurt.

I know I'm staring, but I can't help it. I have to look, have to watch him, as he takes a seat at the coffee shop counter and slowly stretches his right leg out and then rests his cane against his denim-clad thigh.

My gaze travels from his thigh and then up, over his chest, to his mile-wide shoulders, and finally to his face.

Sweet Jesus, he's good-looking. Even better looking at forty-something than twenty-something. He's all man now. There's no boy left in that face.

"Ma'am?" the waitress at my elbow repeats.

Startled, I jerk my head around, look up at her. She's holding a plastic pitcher. "More tea, ma'am?"

I hear what she's saying, but I'm so shocked that it requires an effort to respond. "Uh, yes, please. Thank you."

She fills my huge plastic tumbler and then moves on. I steal another glance at Dane, who's ordering the barbecue beef brisket dinner plate.

Oh wow. Dane. Here. Dane. After all these years, and it's been a long time since I last saw him. Eighteen years. I'd just graduated from Stanford, and he'd just won his second national bull-riding championship. He was also newly engaged to Shellie Ann, a girl I went to high school with. It made me so mad. I felt physically sick from jealousy, love, and longing. So sick I couldn't even be in the same room with him, and he was at our house, in our kitchen.

Brick said I acted like a bitch that day, but Brick didn't understand. I loved Dane. I'd loved him for years, and I'd hoped that once I finished school, once I was twenty-one and finally old enough to be with him, we'd be together. Instead, he proposed to a pretty girl from my high school class whose only accomplishment in life was being crowned homecoming queen.

Appetite gone, I reach into my purse for cash to pay the bill and escape before he sees me. It's being a chicken, I know, but I don't want to talk to him. My feelings are still too strong—and not in a good way. Seeing him again just makes me mad.

He knew how I felt.

He knew I adored him.

He knew I wanted him.

But maybe that's how it is with first loves. Maybe it's natural to carry a torch. And let's face it, I didn't fall for him just a little bit. I fell hard. So hard that my folks sent me to California to boarding school just to keep me away from him.

In hindsight, no sixteen-year-old girl belongs on the professional rodeo circuit, and as a parent, I can say it was the right thing for them to do. But at the time, it broke my heart. I loved him. God, I loved him. I don't think I've ever loved anyone like that since, not even John. And looking at Dane now, feeling what I'm feeling, I know I didn't make up those emotions.

I might have been a teenager, but it was love. Crazy love. The kind of love that breaks you open and makes you someone else.

Someone harder.

Someone stronger.

It's then that Dane turns his head and looks straight at me.

It crosses my mind that he doesn't recognize me, and I don't know if I'm more relieved or disappointed, but I'm the one to look away first. I drop my gaze to my half-eaten sandwich even as heat rushes through me, from my collarbone up my neck to my cheekbones.

He still has those eyes.

He still has it, that energy, chemistry, whatever it is that made me crazy all those years ago.

I hate him. I do.

I leave fifteen dollars on the table, far more than I need to, but I don't have change and I don't want to wait. I have to get out of here, have to get away.

On my feet, I'm heading for the door, but I can't get there before Dane does. He cuts me off before I reach the door.

"Shey."

It's all he says, and I tilt my head back and look into Dane's green eyes.

"Dane," I say in reply, my voice just as cool as his, although my pulse is racing as if I'm running for my life. And in a way, I am. I chased this man for over a year. I mailed him letters. Made cookies. Left notes beneath his truck's windshield wipers.

I was a fool, such a fool, and so out of my league. But I had to let him know how I felt. Had to let him know how much he mattered, and how much he mattered to me.

Dane's expression is peculiar. "Home on vacation?"

"Not exactly. We're living on the ranch right now."

"We?"

"My boys and me."

Dane's eyebrows lift. He doesn't need to add anything else, but I do. "'We moved back after Cody's funeral," I blurt out. "We're trying to figure a few things out, and with Mama gone to Jefferson to be with Grandma, Brick could use some help on the ranch, so here we are."

Flustered by Dane's silence, I add, "I looked for you at Cody's funeral."

"I called your mother. And sent flowers."

I feel a lash of anger. "It's not the same thing."

"No, it's not." He shifts his weight. "But I was in a hospital in Houston, rehabbing after my last surgery. I wanted to be there. I would have, if I could have."

My fury subsides, and I feel just loss. "Brick doesn't talk about you anymore," I say, hating the sadness that's replaced the anger. "What's happened between you?"

"It's a long story."

I frown and am about to press him for a better answer when I notice he's not wearing a wedding ring. My thoughts jump, abruptly changing direction. Is he divorced? Or is he just not wearing his ring? Lots of ranchers and cowboys don't wear their wedding ring when working, because it can get tangled up in ropes and machinery, but Brick's always worn his. But that's Brick. He's rock solid and after twenty-five years of marriage still completely devoted to his wife, Charlotte.

The waitress sets Dane's steaming plate on the counter. "Your food's here," I say to him, aware of the awkwardness and hating it.

"You take care, Shey."

"Thanks, Dane. You too."

And then I'm outside, where the sun's just beginning to sink on the horizon, painting the sky layers of lavender and red.

For a moment I'm lost, filled with emotions both bitter and sweet.

He was the last person I expected to see, the last person I wanted to see. My legs feel wooden as I head for the truck and climb behind the steering wheel.

Starting the engine, I feel the most ridiculous urge to cry.

The past once hurt so much. The present is a mess, and I can't even see a future.

Can't even imagine where we're supposed to go from here.

The red sky and rolling countryside stretch in all directions as I leave historic Highway 80 and take the turnoff toward our ranch. The oak trees look like hulking giants in the twilight, and meadowlarks warble from their nests in the lavender-shrouded fields.

Usually I love this drive. Usually I find the landscape with the hills in the distance beautiful, but tonight I feel cornered. Empty. Trapped.

The problem with a small town is that everyone knows you.

The problem with a small town is that you know everyone.

I slow down as an owl swoops low over the road in front of me. I turn my head and see a jackrabbit running. Poor little jackrabbit. Hope it makes its way home.

*   *   *

It's quiet when I pull up in front of the old brick-and-clapboard ranch house. The house is dimly lit, and Brick's blue truck is still parked out front. I open the front door, and the living room is empty. No sound comes from the back. Maybe everyone's still in the barn.

And then I hear voices coming from the kitchen. I shut the door, set my purse on the table next to the sofa, and head to the kitchen, where I see Brick sitting at the oak table next to Cooper with Cooper's math book open between them. But they're not doing math. The kitchen's warm, and I can smell something savory cooking in the oven.

It's a tranquil scene and touchingly domestic.

"Hi, guys," I say, leaning over to kiss the top of Coop's head. I ruffle Brick's short hair, the sun-bleached strands just starting to gray. "Something smells good."

"Charlotte sent dinner over. She knew you were working, and since she had to attend a hospital fund-raiser, she made us all dinner."

"You do know you have the best wife," I say, opening the oven and peeking in. Pork chop casserole, and the sauce is bubbling and the chops are just starting to turn golden brown.

"I'm a little fond of her," Brick admits.

"Me too." I straighten, open the fridge, note the four chilled beer bottles that have been in the door for the past three weeks. No one in our family is much of a drinker, but Mama still had a fit when she saw the beer in my refrigerator. "Are you thirsty? Want a beer?"

He shakes his head. "No, I'm good, and Coop here has just one more problem and then he's done."

I put together a salad while Brick finishes helping Cooper. As soon as Cooper finishes his math, he packs up his books and binders and takes off for his room, where I'm sure he's gone to play his PSP. The boys have been begging me to buy an Xbox or a Wii since we moved here, but I've refused. They each have a PSP, and that's all the electronic games they need.

"How did it go with the boys?" I ask once Cooper's gone.

"Fine." Brick extends his legs and folds his arms over his deep barrel chest. You wouldn't know he's forty-five by looking at him. Working the ranch keeps him in great shape.

"They didn't give you too hard a time, did they?"

"I've raised two kids, Shey. I can handle yours."

So they did give him a hard time. I grimace, feeling guilty all over again. The last thing I want is for my boys to be disrespectful, much less to a member of the family. "I'm sorry—"

"Not looking for an apology, and not wanting you to feel bad. I'm glad you and the boys are here. You're a big part of this family, and I want to do what I can to help. So does everyone else."

Thus the casserole and the babysitting and the tutoring help...

I feel a wash of deep, inarticulate gratitude. "Thank you."

"Whatever I can do, hon, I'll do."

My chest grows tight. It's a bittersweet thing being home. I wouldn't have moved home if Cody hadn't died. Two years my senior, Cody would have been forty-one this month. "It was Cody's birthday on Friday," I say now. "Mama didn't say a word about it."

"Did you say anything to her?" Brick asks.

I shake my head. "She gets so upset every time his name is mentioned that I just thought it was better to leave it alone."

"You know that's why she was here last week."

I look at him, surprised. "Was it?"

He nods. "She's having a hard time accepting that Cody's gone. She told me she keeps having dreams where he's alive and she just has to find him and everything will be okay."

I feel a stab of guilt for not being more patient with her. "Poor Mama," I say, opening the refrigerator once more to retrieve a bottle of ranch salad dressing. Suddenly I remember my conversation with Dane. "Oh! Guess who I bumped into at the Brief Encounter Café in Mineral Wells?" I ask, drizzling the dressing over the torn-up greens.

"Dane Kelly."

My head jerks up. "How did you know?"

"Ricky saw him at Miller's Feed and Grain today." Ricky is Brick's foreman and has worked on the ranch for over ten years. "Apparently Kelly just got back from Brazil, where he's been working with a breeder there."

"I thought he was in Houston rehabbing."

Brick shrugs. "I honestly wouldn't know. We don't stay in touch anymore."

Brick sounds strangely detached, especially since Dane was once his best friend. I shoot him a swift side glance as I grab the tongs and begin tossing the lettuce. "How'd he get hurt?"

"In the ring."

"Ah." The questions bubble up. There's so much I want to ask Brick about Dane. About the accident. About his wife. About his life. "Why don't you talk?" I persist, knowing that Dane and Brick met on the first day of kindergarten and had been tight ever since.

Brick doesn't answer immediately, and I can tell he's picking his words with care once he does. "Dane and Blue got into a feud. It turned ugly and eventually forced me to take a side."

I pause, salad tongs in midair. "Blue and Dane fighting? I can't believe that. Blue always looked up to Dane—"

"Twenty years ago. Things have changed. Dane's just a rancher now. Blue's a big city developer. And they blame each other for what happened to Cody."

I shoot my brother a quick glance, thinking he's joking. But his blue eyes aren't smiling. He looks tired and dead serious. "How are either of them responsible for Cody's problems?"

"It's a long story."

I grab pot holders from the drawer and lift the simmering scalloped-potato casserole out of the oven and set it on the stove. "That's the same thing Dane said, but I have time and I'm interested."

Brick goes to the fridge and retrieves a beer. He pops off the cap and takes a quick drink. "Blue tried to get Cody help a couple years ago—it was kind of a tough love program for addicts—but Dane didn't agree with the tough love approach, got involved, and scared Cody off. Now Cody's dead."

I freeze. "You don't blame Dane, do you?"

"Dane should have minded his own business," Brick answers gruffly. He's not comfortable with conversations like this. He's never been able to criticize our parents, his family, or his friends. It's disloyal, and Brick's loyal to a fault. "And now the bad blood between Blue and Dane has spilled over into other things, like Blue's development of the McCurdy property. Folks around here are taking sides, and quite a few have taken Dane's side..."

His voice drifts off, but I hear what he doesn't say. Out of family loyalty, Brick has taken Blue's side.

I lift five plates from the painted cupboard. "I guess I've been gone too long. What's Blue doing with the McCurdy ranch?"

Brick takes a long time to answer. "Blue's company bought McCurdy's property and is developing it into fifty ranchettes. Ten houses have already been built. Forty more are to come."

I'm just reaching for glasses and stop. Appalled, I face him. The McCurdy ranch was one of the bigger ranches in the area and had been family owned all the way back to the 1880s, when the first McCurdy moved here and established his sheep and cattle ranch. "The McCurdys sold to Blue?"

Brick nods.

"And Blue's putting fifty home sites on the property?"

He shrugs. "Blue got the zoning. The county thought it'd be good for the economy, what with the population still shrinking. But Dane's property lies next to McCurdy's, and he hates the development right next to his place."

For a farmer or rancher, this is the worst thing that could happen. Land is precious. Land represents pasture, fields, crops, grazing, important acreage that's lost once you build on it. "Has Blue's development impacted Dane?"

"There have been problems with ATV riders and hunters trespassing, riding off-terrain vehicles through fields and pastures."

"Wow."

Brick's expression is grim.

"You'd hate it if someone built a condominium right next to our place," I add.

Brick's lips press tighter. "I hear that."

I lean against the counter. "So you and Dane aren't talking at all anymore?"

"He sent me a note after Cody's death, but otherwise, no. We don't have any communication."

"For nearly forty years he was your best friend."

Brick exhales, shrugs. "Blue's my brother."

And blood's real thick around here, I think, reaching for the glasses again.

Chapter Four

———— ✳ ————

Brick leaves after dinner, and I finish washing up dishes while the boys scatter into different rooms. Kitchen clean and lights out, I crash on the couch to watch CNN news for an hour, and Cooper comes in to snuggle with me on the couch. He might be as tall as a man, but he's still very much a sixth grader and hungry for love.

"Can we see if there's any bull riding on?" he asks. "They should be showing last night's results from Nashville."

I hand him the remote, and he immediately pulls up the Versus channel, which is indeed replaying last night's highlights.

"Just another five weeks until the finals in Las Vegas," he says a few minutes later as they go to a commercial break. "Wish we could go. Is there any way we could go?"

"To Las Vegas?"

"It'd be so cool, Mom. The best of the best will be competing. Guilherme Marchi, Kody Lostroh, Zack Brown, Chris Shivers, Ryan McConnel. They'll all be there."

"What about J. B. Mauney?" I ask slyly, fully aware that J.B. is Coop's favorite rider on the Built Ford Tough tour.

"He'll be there for sure. And he could win it all, too."

"It'd be fun, but expensive—"

"I'll save my money!"

"Honey, we're talking hundreds of dollars."

"What about for an early Christmas present?"

"You already asked for your own horse."

"Oh. Right." He slumps lower to rest his head against my shoulder. "But I really, really want to go," he says in a small voice.

I remember how I used to love attending the rodeo with Pop and my brothers. Mama never went, but Pop would load us all up in his truck and we'd head to Fort Worth or Weatherford or Beaumont for the weekend. If the weather was good, we'd camp. If the weather was bad, we'd stay in a little motel room. Dane would sometimes go with us, and those were my favorite trips. Even from a young age, I would watch him with equal parts fascination and adoration. But ultimately it was Pop's love of the rodeo that got Brick hooked on riding roughstock, and now it seems my youngest has inherited the Callen love affair with broncs and bulls.

"We'll see," I tell him. "No promises. But I will look into costs and the dates. Okay?"

He flashes a huge grin up at me, and I hate how I fall for his killer smile every time. I'm such a sucker, I really am.

Determined not to be late for the shoot, I leave the next morning as soon as Brick and Charlotte arrive to get the boys off to school for me. I hadn't expected Charlotte, but she said she was better at handling sleepy boys than Brick. I give her a grateful hug good-bye on my way out the door.

The sun is up and glowing pink and yellow as I head toward Mineral Wells. I drive with my window down, soaking up the still cool, fresh morning air, listening to the warble and cooing of meadowlarks, starlings, and rock doves. I love the early mornings best, when the earth still smells fragrant and the sky is washed in the sheerest shades of pink and yellow and blue.

Pop's favorite work truck, now a very rusty red, lacks power steering, power windows, and a fancy sound system, but it does have an old cassette player and an even older radio that no longer works. As traffic continues to get heavier now that I've hit U.S. 80, I drum my fingers on the open window.

I don't want to return to the photo shoot. I don't like being made to feel incompetent. And I definitely don't enjoy playing Grandma.

But it's a job, and it pays really good money, money I definitely need.

I draw a deep breath and exhale slowly, then do it again. I'm marginally calmer. I can do this. I'm good at this. No reason to stress.

My phone rings just then, and I think it might be Blue, finally returning my call. Instead it's my husband, calling from New York. "Morning, John."

"You got a minute?" he asks.

"At least sixty of them," I answer as traffic slows to forty. "I'm driving into Dallas right now. I was booked for a shoot yesterday and we wrap up today."

"That's great. Good for you. Did Liza find you work?"

"No, I've signed on with a Dallas agency. It's the first time they've done anything with me since I arrived. So, what's up? Everything okay there?"

"Fine. I was just curious about Thanksgiving and Christmas, wanted to nail down the kids' plans and book their airline tickets if you haven't."

Thanksgiving without the boys. I've never not been with them during the holidays. "I haven't. No."

"They are still coming to see me, aren't they?"

"Of course."

"I'll go ahead and make the travel arrangements, then. I'm going to use Erik's miles, and I can get a better deal if they fly out Saturday before Thanksgiving and then back on Sunday following Thanksgiving."

"That'd be nine days, and they'll miss school—"

"I haven't seen them in six weeks, Shey."

I bite my lip, chagrined. He's right. "They can miss school. That's not a problem. They're coasting here."

John hesitates. "I was going to talk to you about that. They're not real happy in Parkfield, and Hank's worried about not getting into a top university if he stays there."

"I know."

"Maybe they should come back to New York. Live with Erik and me—"

"No."

"Erik and I are looking for a bigger place—"

"No! No. You can't take the boys from me, John. Absolutely not."

"You took them from me! You moved them to Timbuktu."

"Because you left. You left our home, our marriage—"

"I left the marriage. I didn't leave the kids. And I've always been a good father, a hands-on dad, and you know it."

Emotion rushes through me and I hold it back, my left hand gripping the steering wheel for all it's worth. I do know it, but it doesn't change the way I feel, and I feel betrayed as well as abandoned. "You and I made these kids, John, not you and Erik, and I won't have you and Erik raising them."

"Then come back to New York—"

"With what money? We have no money. You have no money. If it weren't for Erik, you couldn't afford to be in New York either!"

He doesn't immediately answer. John's not a hot-tempered guy, and he and I weren't ever fighters. But then, when we were together we didn't need to fight. We always agreed on everything.

"But I do have Erik," he says finally, "and Erik was the one who suggested we have them come live with us—"

"Of course he would. He's not a parent. He doesn't know what it's like to lose your kids—"

"Shey, I miss them."

The sadness in his voice makes me feel guilty, which just makes me angry. "These are things that should have been considered before you turned our world upside down, John."

"So you're never coming back to New York. Is that what you're telling me?"

I want to punch him. I do. He makes it all sound so simple. Just come back to New York and everything will be fine. But it won't be fine. I won't be fine. I'll be surrounded by constant reminders of the life we had and the life we lost. "I loved you, John. I loved being married to you and sharing a home with you. And maybe you've moved on, and maybe you're okay, but I'm not! I'm still struggling to figure out what the hell happened to my life. Never mind what happened to you."

"I'm gay—"

"Hooray. So glad we found that out."

My bitterness silences him. Finally he sighs. "I'm sorry I've hurt you. I wish I hadn't, wish I hadn't ever had these other feelings, or doubts…" His voice drifts away. I guess there's not much else he can add, because he did have the other feelings, the ones that made him desire a man instead of me.

I still don't understand it. I don't know how he could be with me, attracted to me, make love to me, live with me, and then realize it was all wrong, that he wasn't heterosexual but homosexual and that Erik was his true soul mate. "I'm sorry, too." He's trying to make me feel better, but I actually feel worse. It'd be easier to accept this if we hated each other or we weren't happy together. It'd be easier if he'd fallen in love with another woman. Then I could rage properly. I could shout and throw things and feel victimized. But the way it is now, with John miserable for hurting me and lost without the kids, I feel like the bad guy.

"Go ahead and book the Thanksgiving tickets," I tell him, desperate now to just get off the phone. "I'll work on Christmas."

"The twenty-sixth to New Year's Day, yes?"

"Yes."

"Great. Hope the shoot goes well."

I hang up and brake yet again as traffic thickens. My head pounds, my hands shake, and I'm dangerously close to throwing up.

I shouldn't have taken his call. I shouldn't try to have these horrendous conversations where he's pleasant and I'm not.

The car in front of me has come to a dead stop. I apply the brake hard, jerk to a halt. Hear brakes squeal behind me, pray I don't get hit.

Highland Park is still fifty miles away, which means this is going to be a very long day.

Turns out my day isn't as long as I'd thought it would be. In fact, the modeling part is very short. I arrive in Highland Park at nine, go to check in with DeeDee, and discover I'm not needed after all. The model I was substituting for is back—apparently recovered from her flu or food poisoning or whatever ailed her—and I'm free to go home.

I'm seriously annoyed, but this is the business. So instead of protesting, I simply present my voucher book to DeeDee. She looks down at the basic information I've already filled in. Three-hour minimum. Five hundred dollars an hour. Additional four hours' travel time, although that's prorated at 50 percent of my hourly rate.

"Twenty-five hundred dollars?" DeeDee says, jaw dropping.

I don't even bat an eye. "Yes."

"We don't pay five hundred an hour—"

"It's my rate—"

"For models we don't use."

I smile serenely as I fish into my purse for my phone. "Let me give Joanne a call at the agency. You two can sort this out."

Once I have Joanne on the line, I hand over the phone and walk away, heading to the catering table, where I pour myself a big Styrofoam cup of coffee and add several packets of sweetener. I calmly stir the Splenda into the coffee as DeeDee's voice grows louder. She's not happy. She's been ripped off. This isn't New York. I can't charge New York rates here.

Joanne must be speaking because DeeDee falls quiet for a long time, and then it's a low, tight "Mmm-hmm" from DeeDee and then silence.

A moment later, DeeDee walks my phone back over to me. "I'll sign your book," she says tersely, not even looking at me.

I hand the book to her, knowing she'll never request me, never want to work with me again. Knowing that no one might want to work with me again. But I don't bat an eye as I watch her scribble her name and signature in the book, because rates are rates and business is business and I'm not a nineteen-year-old on a first job. This has been my career for nearly twenty years, and I've earned my rate and earned my success.

"Big New York model," she mutters, ripping out a copy of the voucher to keep for their files.

My silence must frustrate her further, because her head jerks up and she gives me a withering look as she shoves my book back into my hands. "This isn't New York, you know."

"I know," I answer as gently as I can, "because in New York stylists and creative directors are professional."

And then I take my voucher book and my coffee and leave.

It's not until I drive away from the tree-lined neighborhood of multimillion-dollar homes that I realize it's only nine-fifteen. And even after paying my agency's commission, I've just earned two thousand dollars. Not bad for a day's work.

Once again, I debate whether I should stop by Blue and Emily's house. It's strange that Blue never called me back yesterday. That's not like him. He's definitely more materialistic than Brick, but he shares my older brother's values in terms of family and loyalty. He and Emily haven't had the easiest marriage, but he never complains and he dotes on his daughters, Megan, sixteen, and Andrea, fourteen. His daughters, interestingly, don't dote on us. They're beautiful girls—already as polished and sophisticated as their mother—but they treat the boys as if they're country hicks.

Maybe it's because my boys are a bit in awe of their glamorous cousins.

Or maybe it's just that my boys aren't movie-star beautiful. They're pimply and gangly and geeky...well, not Hank. Hank so far has escaped zits and ghostly pale skin. But let's face it, boys at this age aren't as cool as girls. Girls mature faster, and they never let you forget it.

I end up driving by Blue's sprawling Georgian brick mansion. A tall wrought-iron fence encircles the property, but Emily's huge black Mercedes sedan is in the driveway and the wrought-iron gates are open, so I pull in behind her car.

Climbing out of Pop's truck, I'm dazzled by the sun glinting off the Mercedes's chrome bumper. Emily's car is always spotless. Blue told me once that Emily has her car detailed every four weeks and hand-washed a few times a week. I can't imagine even having the energy to care about keeping a car that clean, much less spending the money on such meticulous maintenance. But then I'm not overly obsessed with details. It's the big picture I worry about, the big picture that gets my attention.

After stepping around the clay pots of clipped topiary standing sentry on the front steps, I knock on the door. Blue and Emily's maid, Yolanda, answers. Yolanda has met me half a dozen times but never seems to remember me. Or maybe she's just never happy to see me. Not that it matters.

"Good morning, Yolanda. *Buenos días*. Is Emily home?"

She nods sullenly, motions for me to step into the grand marble entry, but leaves me standing next to the door while she goes off in search of Emily.

It takes Emily so long to appear that I check my watch twice, just to make sure I'm not imagining the wait. Three minutes. Seven minutes. But then she appears, regally descending the curving stone staircase, immaculate in black slacks, an ivory silk blouse, and a little gold chain around an even smaller waist. She always wears staggeringly high heels, and today her dark hair is pulled back in a pouf of a ponytail, teased at the crown to give it height. With her dark hair, blue eyes, and liberal use of eyeliner, she reminds me of Priscilla Presley in her Elvis days. Only I have a feeling Priscilla was a whole lot warmer.

"Why, Shey, what a lovely surprise," she says coolly, reaching the bottom step and moving toward me even though nothing in her expression reveals pleasure.

I have to smash the wave of regret I feel for stopping by impulsively. I should have known better, but I'm here now and we air-kiss, a fake smooch just off each cheek.

As I bend down to reach Emily—she's only five feet four, if that—I get a whiff of hairspray, cloying perfume, and something else, something far sharper, almost medicinal or metallic.

"Sorry to drop in on you like this," I apologize. "I was in the area and just wanted to say hello, let you know I was thinking of you."

She smiles, her teeth small but exquisitely white and beautifully shaped. "How sweet of you."

She doesn't mean it, of course, and I feel as though I've somehow interrupted something, only I don't know what.

Emily glances at my faded jeans, boots, and green lace-edged T-shirt before forcing a smile. "Shall we sit?" she suggests, gesturing to her living room, which is crowded with chintz and imported English antiques.

She leads me to the living room and we both sit down on opposite yellow-and-white-striped silk love seats. Emily plumps a pink-and-yellow chintz pillow and smiles at me. I push a matching pillow out of my way.

"Would you like a glass of sweet tea? Yolanda just made a new pitcher," Emily offers.

"No, thank you. I had some coffee on the way."

She smiles at me.

I smile at her.

Our conversation seems to end there.

Emily and I have never had the comfortable relationship Charlotte and I share, but it doesn't keep me from wanting it. I love my brothers. I want to love their wives. Aware of the strained silence, I rack my brain for a suitable topic. "How are the girls?"

"Wonderful." She sits as straight as if she had a yardstick

down the back of her blouse, her hands resting lightly on one leg. "How are the boys?"

"Still settling in."

Her smooth forehead struggles to register concern. "Public schools aren't always the best option."

"I agree, but there aren't many options in Palo Pinto other than public schools."

"We warned you," she replies regretfully.

Yes, she did. Many, many times. "My brothers went to school in Mineral Wells. They turned out fine."

She doesn't look as if she believes me. In fact, her lips press and compress a moment before she speaks again. "I heard that Mother was visiting from Jefferson. How is she?"

"Mother" being my mama. Emily and Mama have perhaps the strangest relationship of all of us. They're almost fond of each other, although they rarely see or speak to each other. But Mama has long respected Emily for being a regular churchgoer, and Emily admires Mama's devoutness.

"Mama's doing well. I think it's an adjustment living with Grandma, but at the same time, they were both lonely and now they have each other."

"Mother said she'd be joining us for Thanksgiving dinner. Will you and the boys be coming, too?"

I flash back to my conversation with John this morning and shake my head. "The boys will be in New York with their dad."

"Oh, I'm sorry." But she doesn't appear sorry in the least. She's relieved. Pleased. "But you will still be joining us, won't you?"

I'd already said yes a month ago when the subject

came up, but now I'm not so sure. Thanksgiving at Blue's house without my kids sounds like the most depressing Thanksgiving I could imagine. "I might be away that weekend," I fib, hoping it just might be true. "I'm still working on some plans."

We change topics, moving from the holiday back to her girls and then finally to Blue.

"Your brother is entertaining prospective buyers Saturday and Sunday on the ranch," Emily announces with a disapproving sniff. "I think it's a waste of time, but he doesn't listen to me. Never has."

It takes me a second to realize she means the McCurdy ranch. Blue's development property.

A sick, sinking feeling hits my gut. I still can't believe Blue is taking some of the most beautiful land in Palo Pinto County and turning it into fifty ranchettes.

Emily squares her thin shoulders. "My daddy would have never thrown a lavish party for people who hadn't even committed to a purchase. It's a waste of money, and yet one more example of Blue's lack of business acumen."

I'd like to defend Blue, but how can I, when I know nothing of his plans or how much he's investing into this weekend?

"So we'll see you this weekend?" I ask, feeling unusually evil, as I know that Emily would rather run naked through the streets of exclusive Dallas suburb Preston Hollow than spend a weekend with us in the country.

Emily is not a fan of rodeos, farms, or livestock. She visits Brick and Charlotte on the ranch as infrequently as possible, which usually amounts to once a year, and even then the visit is timed to last two hours precisely.

"Oh, I wish I could," Emily answers with admirable sweetness, "but this weekend is dedicated to my cookbook committee."

"You're writing a cookbook?"

"Compiling." She bestows a painfully gracious smile in my direction. "It's for the new *Dallas Junior League Cookbook*. The cookbook is one of our most successful fund-raisers, and this weekend we make the final recipe selection."

"Ah."

Her dark arched eyebrows wing so high, I'm reminded of a bird in flight. "I told all the girls last year that I wouldn't chair the committee again. I made it clear that it was to be my last year, but my dear friend Sidney Sterett, who was chairing the committee, was diagnosed last spring with breast cancer and I had to step forward. I couldn't have Sidney worrying, and the fund-raiser is just too important to leave to chance."

"Well, we'll miss you," I say, getting to my feet. I have no idea how long I've been here—twenty minutes? thirty?— but I'm so uncomfortable, I feel as though I'm about to pop out of my skin. "And if you change your mind, I know the boys would love to see you and the girls."

"How sweet."

We walk to the entry, and we air-kiss again, and this time as I lean over Emily, I know what it is I smell. Vodka.

It's only ten in the morning, but my proper, church-going sister-in-law has already been drinking.

Chapter Five

————— ✦ —————

As I drive home, I puzzle over my exquisitely dressed, vodka-scented sister-in-law. Why is Emily drinking at nine-something in the morning? And what does Blue think of it? Because he has to know. She wasn't slurring or anything, but she reeked.

It wasn't just her breath that smelled like alcohol. Her skin smelled bitter, too.

Maybe I'm just imagining it. I hope I'm imagining it. I come from a tough family, heavy on testosterone, and while we have our problems, alcohol has never been one of them. But John's mom was an alcoholic, and a mean one when she drank (which was nightly), and I wouldn't wish a dependence on alcohol on anyone.

Thirty miles from Mineral Wells, my phone rings. It's Blue. He must have heard I stopped by the house. "Hey, Blue," I say, picking up. "I'm sorry I didn't get to see you when I was in Dallas, but I understand you're coming our way this weekend."

"I just hung up from talking to Brick. He couldn't have called you already," he answers.

"Emily told me. I saw her car out front this morning, so I stopped by to say hello."

"You saw Emily today?"

"Yeah."

There is a moment's hesitation on the line. "But I thought you were in Highland Park yesterday."

I note the confusion in his voice. "I was," I answer. "And back today to finish the job. Only it wrapped up a lot sooner than I expected. So I stopped by to say hello, and now I'm heading home."

There's another odd beat, as if he's struggling to decide what he's going to say next.

"How was Emily?" he finally asks, and I sense it's not a casual question.

I know my brothers really well and have been pretty tight with them since I was little. Even when I lived in New York, I talked to them every couple of weeks. Well, Brick and Blue. Cody's another story. "Are you worried about her?"

He sighs, and the sigh adds to my unease.

"She's a perfectionist," he replies almost defensively. "And the girls keep her busy. They're involved in everything."

I feel for him. I do. He knows something's wrong, but he's not going to talk about it. Maybe not even deal with it. But that's how we were raised. Family matters are private. They're not things you discuss. Not even with other family members.

"Emily didn't sound too happy about your plans for the weekend," I tell him. "You're entertaining prospective buyers?"

"A developer friend did it in Kauai, and it was a huge success. So I thought I'd try the same idea for the ranch. I'm putting everyone up at the Cliffs Resort over at Possum Kingdom and then busing them in for the day and evening activities, including horseback riding, fishing on the Brazos, a guided bird-watching tour—"

"No ATV wheeling?"

He groans. "Very funny. God knows I don't need Kelly going ballistic and shooting my buyers."

"Dane's pulled a gun?" I ask, finding the idea impossible. Dane's not a violent guy. He's a big man, a strong man, but he also has patience and tremendous discipline, which is one of the reasons he became a champion bull rider. Dane controls the bull, not the other way around.

"Of course not. But it got pretty ugly when some of my new owners rode vehicles onto his property. They did do a fair amount of damage, and the kids weren't exactly remorseful."

"Blue!"

"In all fairness, they couldn't tell a crop from a pasture. And I've paid for the damages to the crop and paid to repair the fence the kids ran over, so Kelly has nothing to gripe about."

I don't agree, but I hold my tongue. This isn't my feud. I don't want to get into the middle of it.

But Blue isn't content to leave me out of it. "Of course you're taking his side."

"I didn't say that."

"This development is the biggest thing I've ever done on my own. I'm going to see a very satisfying return on my investment, and maybe Emily will finally see I don't need her daddy's help to be successful."

I can't help thinking the whole thing is such a mess. Blue alienated Dane over the development. Emily hates the development. And Blue just wants to prove to Emily that he's a man and worthy of her respect. "I just wish you and Brick and Dane could patch things up. You were all such good friends for so many years—"

"Cody's dead, Shey, and I do blame Dane."

I picture Dane and just shake my head. It's not right. None of this is right. Growing up, Dane was considered part of the family. He spent so much time at our house that Pop gave him chores to do. My earliest memory is trailing after Brick and Dane as they headed for the barn. I remember it was hot outside and I was wearing nothing but a diaper and my boots with my fuzzy pink blanket under my arm. Brick kept telling me to go back to the house, but I wouldn't. Finally Dane, all of eight years old, picked me up and carried me back to Mama so I wouldn't get run over by the work trucks or horses.

But Dane wasn't protective just of me. An only child, he was that way with Blue and Cody, too.

"Well, I don't hold Dane responsible for Cody's problems. If anything, I blame Mama and Pop for not getting Cody help when he first started exhibiting signs of manic depression."

"You're still in love with Kelly."

The contempt in Blue's voice makes my stomach churn. "Gotta go, Blue. Don't want to do this." And I hang up before I can say something I would regret. Because yes, I probably am still a little in love with Dane and probably always will be. Even though I was never his girl, I always wanted to be.

I'm ten minutes from the ranch when my phone rings again. It's Blue calling back, and he's quite conciliatory. "Sorry," he says roughly. "Don't want to fight with you, especially as I was calling to ask a favor. I'm putting together a sales brochure for the development, and this weekend I've got one of Dallas's best photographers coming to take the photographs and I need you. You're my model."

I need you. Ah, Blue. "Of course I'll help you. I will always help you. Tell me about the brochure."

"It's to mail to prospective buyers and will be eight and a half by eleven, six to ten pages, glossy. There'll be horseback-riding shots, campfire shots, fishing on the river shots, plus photos of the completed home sites."

"Are you working with an ad agency, or is someone in-house?"

"I've got an agency overseeing it, and they're the ones who recommended the photographer. He's been out to the ranch already to select his locations."

"Sounds good. Shoot me an e-mail with the details and I'll be there."

"Will do. And tell the boys I'm expecting to see them at the party I'm hosting Saturday night. It'll be a proper barbecue with a chuckwagon grill and smoker, live band, and sawdust-covered dance floor. I think they'll have a good time."

"We are so there."

"You don't have to check your calendar?" he drawls, aware that I was once attached at the hip to my Black-Berry, having spent the past ten years perfecting my multi-tasking skills. I didn't just co-own a modeling agency, I still modeled occasionally, while developing a show for the Oxygen channel as well as coauthoring a book on beauty and self-esteem for teens. "Blue, I don't even own a calendar anymore."

"Well then, you might just enjoy having somewhere to go after three quiet months on the ranch."

I'm smiling as I hang up. Blue's the most social of all of us and knows how to throw a party. Even back in high school, Blue was the big man on campus. Although recruited to play quarterback, Blue wouldn't stay in the pocket and ended up running all over the field in a West Coast offense that didn't fly with the old school Texas coaches. After a couple of intense discussions, Blue ended up doing what he always wanted to do—catch, run, block, and make plays. He graduated from Mineral Wells High as the most celebrated tight end in school history, earning a full scholarship to Texas Tech, where he dazzled again until he blew out his ACL his junior year, ending his sports career.

But by then Blue had caught the eye of Emily Thornton, daughter of Roger Thornton III, oil baron and pillar of Dallas society. She'd grown up in exclusive Old Preston Hollow, a two-square-mile neighborhood dotted with Texas celebrities and Dallas power brokers, and she knew what she wanted—and she wanted Blue Callen, as much for his athletic prowess as for his dark blond hair, deep blue eyes, and square chin. She knew he came from a ranching family. She knew he didn't have a flashy car or big bank account. But he was handsome and driven and proud, and she liked that, too.

They enjoyed a fairy-tale courtship, followed by a formal black-tie wedding the *Dallas Gazette* called the most extravagant of the decade, and then the birth of their first daughter.

Roger Thornton, now a doting grandfather, rewarded them with their first little house in University Park—a five-thousand-square-foot cottage—which they outgrew two years later when daughter number two arrived. Again Grandpa Thornton stepped in, surprising them with the Georgian mansion on Beverly Drive in Highland Park.

When I lived in New York, I thought Blue and Emily lived a charmed life. Now I'm not so sure.

After pulling off the highway, I stop in Weatherford at Bealls to do some shopping. Hank needs new shoes for PE, Bo could use some new boxers, and Coop needs jeans.

I end up buying more for the boys than boxers, athletic shoes, and jeans. I spot some T-shirts I think they'd like and purchase a heavy sweatshirt for each.

An hour later, I've turned off the highway and onto our private lane. I brake as I cross the metal cattle crossing guard and breathe in deep as the gravel road cuts through gold-and-brown fields with the hint of green hills in the background. I love this stretch of road. As a little girl, I never wanted to live anywhere else. I was always going to live here. I had big plans for myself, too, plans that included marrying Dane Kelly—yes, even at seven I had my sights set on him—and having a bunch of kids and spending all day making cookies and strawberry jam.

Five minutes later, I've left the fields and pastureland for the grove of big oak trees that shield the house. I turn the corner slowly in case one of Brick's mongrels might be wandering around. He has three dogs—all abandoned mutts, including one that has only three legs—and they're spoiled rotten. They also tend to view our house as an extension of Brick's.

But there aren't dogs in front of the house. There's a truck, a big black shiny truck with fancy gold script painted on the side. Kelly Bucking Bulls.

My pulse does a funny little jump.

Kelly, as in Dane Kelly?

I hope. Hope not.

Hope.

Not.

My hands tremble as I park Pop's rusted truck between the house and shed. My legs feel stiff but not very steady as I walk the distance to the house. I see where the white paint is peeling from the siding on the enclosed porch, and in the sunlight tall green weeds pop up around the brick steps. I'm suddenly embarrassed by the ranch's run-down appearance. Not sure why I feel this way. We've never been a fancy family, never lived in a fancy house, and Dane knows that. Dane knows who we are, so I don't know why I feel this sudden need to impress him.

I'm climbing the steps two at a time when the front door opens and Dane appears on the threshold. He moves forward far enough that the front door can close behind him.

He's wearing jeans and a white western button-down shirt. Even though his cane rests near the outside tip of his right boot, he looks rugged and virile. And because Dane's so big and solid, there's no room for both of us on the stairs, and I quickly step back down.

"I found one of your boys walking along the highway," he says bluntly. "Brought him home."

I don't know what I thought Dane would be doing at my house, but this is the last thing I expected. "Who?"

"Bo."

My heart sinks. All the boys should be in school. I don't know why Bo wouldn't be. I squint against the sun as I look up at Dane. "Where did you find him?"

"A couple miles outside of town."

"He was walking back to the ranch?"

"I didn't know he was yours when I stopped. I just knew he was a long way from anything." Dane hesitates. "He sure takes after Cody."

I feel the pinch in my heart again. So much pain and worry for this middle son of mine. "I know."

Dane looks as if he wants to say something else, but he shakes his head instead and carefully climbs down the steps toward me, his dark cane supporting his weight. "It's going to look worse before it gets better," he adds, fishing his keys from his pocket. "I don't think anything's broken, though—"

"What do you mean?"

Dane and I are just a foot apart, and as he looks down at me, I see a flash of something in his eyes. It's there only a moment before it's gone. "He's been in a fight." There's the briefest pause. "He didn't win."

"A fight?" My voice rises. "Bo's never been in a fight before. He doesn't know how to fight—"

"So he's learned." Dane's voice is deep and calm and hard. It's so Dane, too. Dane has never been one to show fear or emotion, much less vulnerability.

I start up the steps, anxious to get to Bo. But Dane reaches out, snags my wrist. "His pride's hurt worse than he is, Shey."

For a moment, I feel only the warmth of his fingers against my skin and my pulse leaps in response. He's always had this effect on me, has always stirred me up, made me feel hot and sharp and bright. My head jerks up and I look into his eyes. They're so very green and full of anger.

"He says he asked Brick to teach him how to fight," Dane adds, "but Brick said you and your husband don't believe in fighting. That's a nice sentiment, Shey, but your boy has to be able to protect himself."

I don't like his tone or his expression, and I pull my wrist from his grasp and press it to my side. The skin at my wrist is so hot and sensitive, it feels as if I've just burned it again on sizzling bacon grease. "I didn't know he needed to protect himself," I say roughly.

"Maybe you need to spend more time talking with him—"

"I talk to him every day!"

"—because he's not a happy kid."

Hurt washes through me. Hurt for my son and hurt for the young Shey who fell in love with this beautiful, hard man.

"Like I said, he reminds me a lot of Cody," Dane adds gruffly, before tipping his head and walking to his truck.

His words echo within me, making me ache. Dane glances at me as he climbs into his truck, the sunlight turning his thick honey hair to bronze and burnished gold. Our gazes meet, lock, and he looks at me so long that my chest grows tight and my throat seals shut.

How can he make me feel so much? I haven't seen him in eighteen years, yet I'm right back where I was when in high school. It's those eyes of his. That energy he has. The way he looks at the world.

The way he looks at me.

Scared that I'm so open, scared that I'm still so attracted, I dash into the house to find my son.

*   *   *

Bo isn't in his room, he's in the boys' small spare bathroom. I try the door. It's locked. I knock lightly. "Bo, it's Mom. Can you open the door?"

"No."

His voice is low and muffled, but I can hear the tears. He's been crying.

I tip my head against the door. "Honey, let me see you."

"No."

"Please, Bo."

"Just go away, Mom." But the harshness of his words is softened by the raggedness of his voice. He's crying harder.

Bo never cries.

I press my palm against the door, wanting him, wanting to reach him, needing to comfort him. It makes me feel crazy that my child hurts and I can't even help him. "What happened, honey?"

"I got beat up. I got my ass kicked. Okay? Feel better?"

No.

No, baby. You getting hurt makes me crazy. You getting hurt makes me want blood and vengeance. "Why would it make me feel better?" I ask thickly.

He doesn't answer, and my eyes burn so much that I squeeze them shut, will them to water. I wish I could cry. I want to cry. "Did you go to the office, honey? Did you tell anyone?"

"Mom!"

"What?"

"Just go away—" His voice breaks. "Please just go."

*   *   *

I do, if only out of respect for his feelings.

In the kitchen I make a fresh pot of coffee, and my hand trembles as I pour the water into the back of the machine.

I want to call John. John's a man. John would know what to do. But then I remember John saying this morning how he wants the boys to live with him, and I picture my sons being raised by Erik and John. I don't pick up the phone.

These are my sons. I can figure this out. I can do this. I don't need a man to fix this. I don't need a man to fix anything for me.

Yet my heart is heavy as I pull the coffee can from the shelf. I think about calling the school. I should call the school. They should know. But I picture that call and am filled with fresh dread. School policy for fighting is a three-day suspension. Does Bo need the humiliation of being suspended on top of everything else?

Coffee started, I pace the kitchen, trying to calm down. But I can't. I'm absolutely sick and still pacing when the back door opens and bangs closed. Brick comes walking into the kitchen from the screened porch. "Saw Dane's truck leave. You and he—"

"No!" I practically hurl the word at him.

"Whoa. Easy, Shey." Brick stops midstep. "What's the matter?"

"There's nothing between Dane and me. There's never been anything between us. We went out a couple times when I was sixteen, and that was it. Yet you all freak out whenever I'm around him—"

"Nobody's freaking out. I just wanted to know why he was here."

"He was here because he found Bo walking alongside the highway. Dane picked him up and gave him a lift home."

"Bo skipped school?"

"Bo was apparently beat up at school this morning."

Brick drags a chair out from the kitchen table and sits down, his eyes on my face. "How is he?"

"I haven't seen Bo yet. He's locked himself in the bathroom." I swallow hard and, suppressing a shiver, fold my arms across my chest. "But Dane said he got it pretty good. And I guess the bruises will keep getting darker, because Dane said Bo's going to look worse before he looks better."

Brick nods. Growing up, he was considered a good fighter. He was tough. Strong. And unlike Blue, he could fight when he wasn't mad. Blue fought only when upset, but Brick could fight anyone at any time, and when he was around, no one messed with his sister or his brothers.

He now shifts in the oak ladder-back chair. "Bo asked me to teach him, you know. I wouldn't out of respect for your feelings—"

"I didn't know he needed it." My eyes burn and my throat is raw. "I didn't know someone wanted to beat him up."

"Is anything broken?"

"Dane says no. I just wish I could see him, but he won't let me. He's...crying."

"He's licking his wounds," Brick says flatly, but I can see from his grim expression that he feels guilty. He wishes now he'd taught Bo how to defend himself. I do, too.

The ancient Mr. Coffee hisses loudly and spits out a cloud of steam as it finishes brewing. The coffee machine's at least fifteen years old but just keeps going.

Brick rises to his feet. "I'll go talk to him."

"He probably won't open the door."

"He will."

Chapter Six

———— ✳ ————

Brick doesn't return, and after a few minutes I carry my mug down the hall to check on the situation and discover that Bo's no longer in the bathroom but in his bedroom, where he and Brick are talking.

I stand outside Bo's bedroom, wishing I were inside. I want to be the one talking to him, and it kills me not to know the story behind the fight.

I try to listen to the conversation, but Brick's and Bo's voices are too low and muffled. So after an indecisive moment I return to the kitchen, where I wipe down the counter and then water the little herb pots on the windowsill and finally just head outside through the screened porch.

I'm kneeling next to the house, savagely pulling weeds, when Brick emerges, his boots thudding on the steps.

The sun's hot and sweat trickles at my nape beneath my heavy hair, but I don't stop weeding. "Well?" I demand.

Brick hooks his thumbs around his belt. "A kid challenged him to a fight and Bo said yes."

"But Bo doesn't know how to fight!"

"He thought he might. He told me he likes watching wrestling on TV—"

"WWE wrestling." I sit back on my heels, rub the dirt from my fingers. "But that's not real. It's staged."

Brick grimaces. "He thought if he just grabbed the other guy around the middle, he could throw him down."

"In a wrestling move."

"Right. Only this was a fistfight, and in fistfights you fight until you draw first blood."

"First blood?"

"That's usually from the nose. This other kid seems to be an experienced fighter. He got Bo in a headlock and went at his face, saving the nose for last."

I press my dirty palms to my thighs. "How does he look?"

Brick's expression gentles. "Rough."

"He's got a black eye?"

"Two shiners." He takes a breath. "And more. He's going to look pretty bad tomorrow. Just be prepared."

Sickened, I reach for another weed and yank it out by the roots, dropping the clump on the pile I've been building, and then another. "So this other kid," I say when I can trust myself to speak, "why did he want to fight Bo?"

"He has a problem with Bo."

"How? Why?"

Brick shrugs. "He thought Bo had attitude."

I yank another weed from the ground, breaking it off midstem, and fling it at the ground. "Bo doesn't have attitude. He has a history of depression!"

"Kids don't know that. And I feel bad for Bo, but this is life, this is how it is for boys. He's in eighth grade. He'll be going to high school next year. He can't hide behind Mama's skirts."

Rage rolls through me, rage and frustration, and I want to grab all the weeds I've pulled and throw them, just throw them. Why do boys have to fight? Why do they have to be so goddamn aggressive? "So what happens now?" I ask, climbing to my feet. "You're a man. You used to fight. Tell me what I'm supposed to do. How am I supposed to handle this? What do I say to him? Do I get mad? Do I call the school—"

"You do nothing. You leave it alone. If you get involved, it'll just make it worse for him."

"But shouldn't the school know? I'd think they'd want to know."

"If you get the school involved, I guarantee there'll be more fights and name-calling. Kids know what happened today. This kid who fought Bo had a whole group of friends around. Some were keeping watch, keeping an eye out for teachers. Others were there to watch the fight."

"So kids just watched Bo get beat up?"

"That's a typical fight."

I lift my hands in surrender. I don't want to hear more. Can't hear more. "You're not helping."

"Think of today's fight as a rite of passage."

"Still not helping."

"That's because you're a woman."

"I'm beginning to think testosterone's overrated."

Brick tugs gently on my long ponytail. "Go see Bo. He probably could use some TLC about now."

"You didn't give him any?"

"Hell, no. I told him next time go for the nose. Draw first blood. It's the only way to win a fight."

"*Next* time? Great. Can't wait for that."

Brick's sympathetic laughter follows me into the house,

where I wash my hands with soap and water at the kitchen sink before heading to Bo's room.

I knock on his door. "It's Mom."

"Come in," he answers, his voice cracking. "It's not locked."

I push the door open and see him sitting on the side of his bed, shoulders hunched, but his head is turned toward me, waiting judgment.

I suck in a breath, shocked. Brick wasn't kidding about the two shiners. Both of Bo's eyes are already black-and-blue. His lip is cut and swollen. His nose shows where it bled earlier.

My fury returns, and I slide my hands into my back pockets to keep from making fists. "Hey, sugar."

"Hey, Mom."

"You okay?"

"Yeah."

Yeah. I stand next to his bed and battle the emotions rushing at me. He's beaten black-and-blue, but he's okay. "It's past lunchtime. You hungry?"

He shakes his head.

"In an hour I'll have to go get your brothers from school. Want to come?"

He twists his head, gives me a look like I'm crazy.

"Didn't think so," I say on a sigh.

I'm not sure what to say or do next when he abruptly leaves the bed and moves into my arms and hugs me tight. "Mom—" His voice cracks, and he shudders against me.

"I'm sorry." My hand comes up to cup the back of his head, and he buries his face against my collarbone. I feel something wet against my skin. He's crying. I stroke his head, his hair thick and wavy beneath my fingers. "I really am."

"I thought I could fight him—" His voice breaks. "Thought I could, but I didn't know anything."

"Was it bad?"

His chin digs into my collarbone as he nods. "It hurt. It hurt a lot more than I thought it would."

"Fighting's not a lot of fun, is it."

"No."

I just keep holding him. Being a mom is so hard. Loving this much hurts. "You sure you don't want to go with me? We could stop on the way back, get ice cream—"

"I don't want anyone to see me, not right now, not like this."

I lift his face to kiss his forehead, but he winces as I touch his jaw.

"Sorry," I apologize, placing the lightest of kisses in the middle of his forehead, which doesn't appear as bruised.

"It's okay." He yawns a little and slides carefully out of my arms. "I think I'm just going to chill out. Maybe take a nap, if that's okay."

"That's a good idea. Sleep, and I'll see you when I get back from picking up your brothers."

Charlotte's heard about the fight and stops by the house on her way home from the hospital. "How is he?" she asks, giving me a hug.

Charlotte's an extraordinary sister-in-law, loving and generous to a fault. "Better," I answer, hugging her back.

"How about you?"

I grimace and lead her to the kitchen, where I pour two

glasses of iced tea. "Don't like my kids getting hurt."

"I'm with you." She takes a sip of tea, swallows, then casually asks, "Heard Dane stopped by. Was he still using a cane?"

"Yes. Why? Shouldn't he be?"

"He was scheduled for another surgery last June to repair old injuries. He was hoping after he finished rehab he'd be able to get around without one. I just wondered if the surgery was successful."

"I don't know if the surgery was successful, but he still has the cane and the limp."

"That's a shame. That man's been through a lot."

I plunk a couple of ice cubes in my tea. "You mean getting hurt?"

"That, and the divorce, and losing Matthew."

I hate how my pulse jumps. "He's divorced?"

Charlotte gives me an incredulous look. "You didn't know?"

I shake my head. "Dane isn't exactly a popular person around here."

"I know, and that's wrong because Dane doesn't have any family left. His parents died a couple years ago, and Shellie Ann moved to Austin with her boyfriend."

"Don't make me feel sorry for him. He married the girl he wanted. He pursued a career he desired. He's not even fifty, and yet he's rich and famous and still ridiculously good-looking." But I'm not unmoved. I don't like that he's suffered, but isn't that part of life? You take risks and sometimes you win and sometimes you lose, but that's just the way life is.

Charlotte heads home, and I start dinner for the boys.

Our meal is subdued, and for a change, Hank, Bo, and
Cooper try to get along. Cooper and Hank obviously feel
bad for Bo, and I can hardly look at Bo without feeling
sick.

It's a relief when everybody goes to bed, and I climb
into mine with the latest issue of *Harper's Bazaar*. I'm leaf-
ing through the issue when there's a knock on my door.
Coop opens it and peers at me from the hall. "Can't sleep,
Mom."

"You've only been in bed fifteen minutes."

"I'm not going to be able to sleep. I'm too mad about
Bo's fight. I hate that he got beat up by some jerk kid."

I have to squelch my smile. Cooper is so mellow until
his family is threatened. I put down the magazine and pat
the mattress next to me. "Sit down. Talk to me."

He shuts the door and stretches out on the bed next to
me, his long legs hanging off the end. "I'm so mad at what
happened to Bo today. Bo's been afraid of this guy for a
long time, too."

"You knew, then?"

"Yeah. I tried to tell Bo how to fight, but he didn't listen
to me. He thinks he knows everything, but I do know how
to fight. I've been in two fights already. And I won both,
too."

I gaze down at him. "You've been in fights? When?"

"New York. Last year." He looks up into my eyes. "Are
you mad at me?"

"No. I'm just surprised."

He shrugs and folds his thin arms behind his strawberry blond head. His hair is thick and has a slight wave
and an impossible cowlick at the front. When he was a

little boy, he looked just like a kid from an old-fashioned comic strip—all freckles and reddish blond hair, with an enormous gap-toothed smile. John and I used to grin just looking at him. How fast even the baby grows.

"I don't like fighting," he answers, "but I'll do it if I have to."

"Why did you fight?"

He stares up at the ceiling, studying the pale blue light fixture. "Because someone told me Dad was a faggot." He turns his head, looks at me. "And that was pretty much what happened the second time, too."

My heart falls. I knew it was just a matter of time before the boys experienced some backlash for John's new sexual orientation. I've worked with brilliant gay men ever since I became a model—many of the industry greats are gay—but unfortunately it can still be a source of fear and phobia in the mainstream population. "You should have told me."

"It doesn't matter. I handled it. And now we're here and nobody knows."

"You like that."

"I like living here." He hesitates, studies me. "You're a beautiful mom. No one else has a mom as pretty as you."

His sincerity touches me, and I realize all over again how lucky I am to have my boys. I love my children, and even though things are hard right now, I love my life. "You're just biased 'cause I'm your mom."

"But you are beautiful. You're still a model. No one else's mom is a model."

I lean down, kiss his forehead. "As long as I'm beautiful to you. That's all that matters to me."

He's silent a moment, thinking. "Yesterday I heard you and Uncle Brick talking. It was about Dane Kelly." He pauses, turns his head to look up at me again, and his bright blue eyes hold mine. "I know who he is. He's a bull-riding champion. Won three championships—'91, '92, and again in 1999. He was leading the rankings in 2000, too, but then got hurt and was forced to retire."

Dane again. It seems like now that I've run into Dane, I can't escape him. It was easier being back in Parkfield before Dane reappeared on the scene. But I don't say any of that to Cooper. There's enough drama going on without dragging Coop into the middle of it. Instead I reach down to smooth his cowlick, which of course doesn't work. The hair at the front grows straight up. "How do you know so much about Dane?"

"The school has a plaque on the library wall. He went to my school, you know."

"I know. He was Uncle Brick's best friend."

"But not anymore?"

This is the most adult conversation Coop and I have ever had. It seems as if he's grown up almost overnight. "They're not as close as they used to be."

"Why?"

"People change. Life happens—"

"Like Dane Kelly's accident?"

"Yeah. Like that."

Cooper looks back up at the ceiling, expression pensive. I can tell he has something on his mind, but I'm not sure what. There seems to be a lot I don't know about my boys these days.

"Uncle Brick was a bull rider like Dane Kelly," he says

after an endless moment. "And I want to learn to ride, too."

"Bulls?"

"Not just bulls, but all roughstock."

He's referring to bull riding, bareback riding, and saddle bronc riding, and I suppress a shudder because they're all dangerous, but bull riding is by far the worst. "Bull riding is one of the most dangerous sports in the world, Coop, and I'm glad your uncle Brick gave it up before he got seriously hurt—"

"I'm not afraid."

"Maybe not, but you're not built to be a rodeo cowboy. You're going to be too big. You're already five ten, and the top professional cowboys are smaller, leaner—"

"Dane Kelly's big. I read his biography at school. He's at least six two. And Owen Washburn was big, too."

"Yeah, but bull riders like Dane Kelly and Owen Washburn are the exception, not the norm."

He sits up. "I can be the exception, too."

I'm sure he could, but he doesn't realize that the great cowboys all start young, really young. Cooper's twelve, and yes, he's comfortable in the saddle and getting proficient at roping, but that's a far cry from riding a bucking animal. "You'd discover there's a pretty steep learning curve, Coop. Kids your age have already been competing for years."

"I know." His jaw tightens, and the freckles on the bridge of his nose darken against his flushed skin. "Ty Murray rode his first calf when he was two and his first bull at nine. But I want to try. I think I could be good. No, I know I could be."

This is a new Cooper, one I've never met before. "Why this now?"

Agitated, he plucks at the black threads of the heirloom quilt covering my bed. "I want to be good at something. And I want to be important. So important that people won't be mean to Bo or say things about Dad." He looks at me, blue gaze piercing. "Can you talk to Dane Kelly? See if he can't teach me? I want to learn everything. I want to ride and rope. But most of all, I want to win."

"Honey, I don't know that Dane's the best one to teach you—"

"Why not? He's one of the best bull riders in Texas."

"Things are tense between your uncles and Dane, and it'd feel awkward to ask him."

"But you don't have a problem with him." His gaze is so blue and steady. Bo might remind me of Cody, but Cooper is all Brick. "You could at least ask, Mom."

But I don't want to ask Dane for favors or be in his debt. I have no desire to think about him or depend on him or risk getting hung up on him again. It's bad enough that he rescued Bo from the side of the road. I'm not going to involve Dane in Coop's life, too. "I'll think about it."

He frowns. "That means no."

He knows me pretty well. "I just don't think it's a good idea approaching Dane now. But if you really want to ride, I'll do some research and see who else is teaching."

"Mom."

I shake my head. "Don't push, Coop. You're just going to make me mad and then I won't find anyone to help you."

Wisely, he drops the subject and returns to his room. I turn out my light to try to sleep, but it's hard to relax. I think about Bo's fight. And then I think about Dane bringing Bo home. And then I think about Dane on our doorstep and how he's now single and Shellie Ann's in Austin. Yet I feel no satisfaction knowing they're no longer together. It just makes me mad. He should have never married her in the first place. He was supposed to marry me. That was my dream. It was my only dream. And now I realize what a silly dream it was.

Dane Kelly is no hero. He's just a man. A man like any other man, albeit a hundred times more gorgeous than most—which means I have to remember he's a problem, not a solution to a problem. And I don't need more problems.

I can cope with my boys' teenage angst and attitude. I can survive my mother's preaching. Endure my brothers' overprotective nature.

But Dane?

Can't deal with Dane. Won't deal with Dane. He had his chance and he blew it. Big-time.

Because of the bruising, I decide to let Bo stay home the next couple of days from school, which Brick immediately says is a mistake.

"You let those boys walk all over you," he tells me after stopping by the house early Wednesday morning to check on Bo and discovering that Bo is still in bed asleep. "And you can't reward them for getting into trouble."

"I'm not rewarding him. He's tired and he was beaten up. He even has bruises on his back and chest. That kid did more than punch. He must have knocked Bo down or kicked him—"

"Probably both, but it's not going to kill him. And you can't baby him, or every time there's a problem, he'll come running to Mama."

I roll my eyes, top off my coffee. "I can't believe you were this tough on Tyler," I say, referring to his twenty-year-old son, who is a junior at Texas A&M. Tyler's an amazing kid. Good-looking and bright, he grew up helping his dad and Pop on the ranch and is studying to become a big-animal veterinarian.

"Shey, Tyler learned early that Charlotte wasn't going to save him when he screwed up. And screwups are part of life." He pours the rest of the coffee into the mug he brought from home. "Now, are you getting that boy up or am I?"

I spend Friday cleaning, organizing, and pulling together my wardrobe for Blue's photo shoot tomorrow—jeans, vests, skirts, cute tops, boots, silver-and-turquoise necklaces—and then return to Mineral Wells to pick up the boys from school.

On the way home, Hank reminds me it's Mineral Wells High School's homecoming tonight, and he wants to attend the football game and the dance afterward. I hadn't planned on driving back into town today, but Hank rarely attends the games and I think it's great that he's interested in going, so I agree.

Bo immediately chimes in that he wants to go, too, and although I've allowed him to tag along with Hank in the past, I say no now. "You've just missed two days of school. You can use tonight to catch up on your homework."

"Homework on a Friday night?"

Here comes another argument, I think, pushing my hair back from my face. Everything's an argument lately. "School comes first, you know that."

"But I don't have anything."

"How is that possible? You missed two days of school. You've got to have homework, classwork, something that needs to be done."

Bo flushes, making the purple-and-yellow marks on his brow, temples, and jaw darken. I hate the bruises. I can't wait for them to fade completely. "I did it at school today," he says. He sees my expression and groans. "It's the truth, Mom."

"Okay, fine."

"So can I go to the game tonight?"

"If your work is really done."

"It is."

"Then yes, you can go."

The boys have been home only an hour when Blue arrives in his silver Range Rover. It's the newest super-charged model, a car that cost well over one hundred thousand dollars, and every time I see it I want to throttle Blue. Why does he need a car that costs that much money? And why is he already looking at ads for the 2011 edition, a car that doesn't officially hit the market for another couple of months?

But the car's forgotten as soon as he steps into the house. Blue is handsome and charming, and as the father of girls, he enjoys my boys. It also takes him only one look at Bo to know what happened earlier in the week.

"Whoa, gunslinger," he says to Bo, "no one told me about this."

"Got into a fight," Bo answers, crashing onto the living room sofa.

Blue takes Pop's old leather chair, stretches his legs out on the matching ottoman. "I hope the other guy looks as bad."

Bo grins, the first real smile I've seen from him in days. "Worse."

Blue laughs appreciatively and then asks the boys, who've now gathered in the living room, if any of them are planning on playing basketball. "Especially you, Coop," Blue says. "With your height you'd totally dominate."

Cooper flushes. "But I don't want to play basketball. I want to learn to ride. I want to be like Uncle Brick and compete on the circuit." Cooper glances around the room as if expecting to be ridiculed.

"Brick told me you've been doing a bit of riding and roping," Blue answers. "I didn't realize you were serious about it."

"I am. And Mom's going to get me lessons. Maybe even from Dane Kelly."

Cooper really has Blue's attention now. "Dane Kelly?" Blue repeats.

Coop doesn't even blink. "Uncle Brick's friend."

"I know who he is," Blue answers before glancing at me as if to say, Did you put him up to this?

"I told Coop that it probably won't be with Dane, but yes, I am looking into hiring someone to work with him."

Blue's narrowed gaze still rests on me. "Probably not with Dane?"

"Don't bully me, Blue," I flash.

"I just think your loyalties would lie with your family, Shey."

I roll my eyes but am saved from answering by the ringing of the phone. I jump up and head to the kitchen, where the mustard yellow corded phone hangs on the wall near the back door, stuck in the same sixties time warp as the rest of the house. "Hello?"

"Shey, it's Dane."

Speaking of the devil. My stomach does an impressive nosedive, and I marvel at his impeccable timing. "Hey, Dane," I answer coolly, my nonchalant tone masking the fact that everything in me has just gone weak and wobbly. "Thank you for bringing Bo home Tuesday. I appreciate it."

"No problem. How is he?"

I lean against the counter. "Better. Thanks."

"How's the bruising?"

"He's in that yellow-and-purple stage."

"I wanted to stop by and say hello to him, if you don't mind."

My chest constricts again, making breathing harder. I don't know why Dane has that effect on me, but I've got to get a grip. "Bo would love it," I answer.

He laughs softly. "Just Bo?"

I flush. "Cooper, too. He'd like to join your fan club."

He laughs again. "I just picked up hay from the Sorensens and am still in the area, so I'll be there in fifteen."

My pulse leaps and I dig a hand into the back pocket of my jeans. "Sure. But, uh, Blue just arrived for the weekend, and he's here now..."

"Oh."

That one syllable says it all.

"In that case, Shey, I won't stop. But let Bo know I called—"

"Dane."

"What?"

The hardness of his voice undermines my courage. I gulp a breath before blurting, "You, Brick, and Blue used to be such good friends, friends for nearly forty years. Can't you guys work this thing out? Can't it be like it used to be?"

Silence stretches across the phone line, and then he sighs. "Darlin', I wish it was."

There's loneliness in his voice. Regret, too. A lump forms in my throat. I don't want to feel this much or care as deeply as I do, but it's too late for that. "Then talk to Blue," I beg. "And then maybe Brick will feel like he doesn't have to take sides."

"I've tried talking to him. Believe me. It doesn't help. Maybe if Cody hadn't died..." His voice drifts off.

Because Cody did die, and apparently my brothers do blame him. I close my eyes, shake my head, finding this all so impossible. *"Dane."*

"Darlin', I wish things had turned out differently, I do, but there's no going back now. What's done is done. What's said is said." He hesitates. "And unfortunately for all, a lot was said."

And then he hangs up, and the click of the phone has never sounded quite so final.

Off the phone, I return to the living room fully expecting to be hassled by Blue, but he and the boys have headed outside and are in the Range Rover. I think Blue's showing the car off until I see Hank slide behind the wheel.

Blue is teaching him to drive.

My lower lip catches between my teeth. Blue was the one who taught me to drive. And Dane was the one who taught Blue to drive. We're all so connected. Too connected.

Filled with bittersweet emotion, I watch Blue show Hank how to stop and start, reverse, and park. Blue is exceedingly patient, just as patient with Hank as he was with me.

But Hank isn't the only one to get a driving lesson. Bo and Coop each get a turn behind the wheel, and by the time the boys are done, the driveway is cloudy with dust from all the zooming down the drive and jerky reverses.

The lesson ends, and the boys climb out of the dust-covered SUV. Blue checks his watch as he approaches me. "I was thinking I might drive Hank and Bo to tonight's game. I haven't been to one of the high school games in years, and homecoming's always a lot of fun."

I love the idea of not driving any more today. "That'd be great. It'd save me the trip into town."

"Perfect. We'll head out now. And are we still good for tomorrow?"

"I'll be at the McCurdy guesthouse bright and early."

The two older boys take a quick shower and change and then leave with Blue, while Cooper heads to the barn to practice, which means riding the blue barrel he's strung up between two posts. Coop rides this practice bull every day, and after a half hour I walk down to the barn to watch him train. Inside the barn, I find him leaning back on the barrel, knees clamped tight, heels down deep, left arm high in the air. His brow is furrowed and he's concentrating hard, as if imagining the next direction the bull will buck.

He's done this for weeks now, come in here alone to practice ride, since no one else shares his enthusiasm for bull riding. He needs real stock to ride. He needs a real teacher now. But it can't be Dane. There's too much tension between my brothers and Dane. Maybe one day they'll be able to work through the hard feelings, but for now, it's too soon after Cody's death.

Back at the house, I sit at the computer in the kitchen to Google bull-riding instructors in Texas. And the very first name that pops up is none other than Dane Kelly.

My fingers itch to click on the link to his website, but I don't. I refuse to be tempted. Dane broke my heart once, and he may be single again, but there's no way I'm going to let him get close enough to do it a second time.

Chapter Seven

———— ✦ ————

The next morning, I arrive at the newly built guesthouse on the McCurdy ranch just before eight-thirty and discover Blue already behind the desk inside the rustic great room.

Soft yellow sunlight dapples the limestone floor, and the house smells of freshly brewed coffee. The guesthouse, a two-story stone-and-log cabin with a vaulted ceiling, now serves as the office and ranch's welcome center, but Blue will one day convert it into a luxury residence to sell once the other home sites are gone.

Blue hangs up the phone as I walk in. "That was Brick. He's got the horses and is almost here. Will you give him a hand when he arrives?"

"Sure." I drop into one of the brown-and-white cowhide chairs facing his desk and stretch my legs out. "Are these horses for the photo shoot or the trail rides?"

"Both. Brick's hitched the big trailer to his truck, so he should have six or seven horses. He thought we'd want to use Sunny and Dandy for the shoot, and the others for the trail ride."

"Who's leading the trail rides?"

Blue squirms ever so slightly. "Brick."

"What?" Brick is not a trail guide sort of guy or the face of Texas tourism. "How did you get him to do that?"

"I promised him my tickets for the Cowboy-Giants game coming up in December."

"That's a big game this year."

Blue looks miserable. "I know. But I needed the help."

I'm still grinning when the Dallas photographer walks in, carrying a camera bag over one shoulder and a duffel bag of gear on the other. He looks familiar, and I wonder if maybe we've worked together in the past.

Blue gets up from the desk and crosses the floor to shake the photographer's hand. "Glad you made it, Mason. Looks like we're going to have a gorgeous day for pictures, too."

"I was thinking the same thing," the photographer answers before turning to me.

I'm still trying to place him, but he has no problem remembering me. "Shey Darcy," he says with a smile.

I rise from my chair, smile through my embarrassment. "I should know you. We've worked together, haven't we?"

"Not yet, no."

My forehead furrows as I try to figure out the mystery. "You're a photographer, though. And you know me."

"And I know your husband."

This feels awkward to me. "Give me a hint. Name the last time I saw you."

Mason smiles. "It was a party."

"A party?"

"I approached you, paid you a compliment, and then John walked up—"

"The *Vanity Fair* party!" I clap my hands. "You remembered me as a *Sports Illustrated* swimsuit model."

"Not knowing you were John's wife," he concludes. "John was pretty pissed off."

"You didn't say anything wrong."

"Just that you were my favorite *SI* model of all time."

Embarrassed, I shake my head, even as I'm suddenly aware that Blue is right next to me, hanging on every word. "You didn't tell me that," I protest.

"No, but it's true."

I can feel my cheeks grow hotter. "Well, thank you. I'm a lot older and look—"

"Exactly the same."

Blue looks from me to Mason and back. "So you already know each other?"

Mason gives me a smile that's definitely appreciative. "I'm a fan of hers, and I had no idea when you told me I'd be working with 'my sister, a former model,' that you were referring to the unbelievably hot, unbelievably gorgeous Shey Darcy." Then he turns back to me. "So how is John? Haven't talked to him since I moved back to Dallas."

I suddenly don't want to do this—be single, available, back on the market. I have too much going on, too much at stake. "He's good. Busy in New York, but that's John."

"So you haven't moved back to Texas?" Mason asks, disappointed.

I force a smile, ignore Blue. "Just visiting. Helping my brother out." And then I gesture to his camera bag and duffel bag of gear. "So what's the plan for this morning? Where are we shooting first?"

Mason takes the bait, begins to talk about our various shots and locations. Then, while he goes to set up his equipment, I retrieve my wardrobe changes from the truck.

Blue's waiting for me on my return. "Why didn't you tell

him about John? You made it sound like you and he were still together."

"I know."

"Mason's single, and successful, and obviously attracted to you."

"Too attracted."

"I thought he was being really nice."

"Then you flirt with him, but I'm not comfortable."

Blue just looks more bewildered, and I sigh. "Blue, I'm not the *SI* swimsuit model. Not the hot bod, calendar girl, or fantasy girl. That's just not me."

"What do you mean, it's not you? It is you. And I know I'm your brother, but you're beautiful and men are going to think you're beautiful—"

"But that's not how I see myself."

He's genuinely confused. "Why not?"

I see myself in my mind's eye, and I'm not the Shey Darcy of my modeling portfolio, or the Shey Darcy of Oxygen's *Model in the Making* show. I'm not smooth and taut, airbrushed and well lit. "Blue, I'm a mom. Hank, Bo, and Cooper's Mom. That's who I am. And that's all I need to be."

Mason's flattery may have made me nervous, but his skill as a photographer is immediately apparent as we start working.

I like his locations and love his lighting, and when he shows me what he's getting with the digital camera, I relax, realizing that Blue's going to end up with great pictures for his brochure and website.

The morning passes quickly, and when we break for lunch, I'm amazed that it's been four hours since we started shooting. Back at the guesthouse, I devour my chicken salad as Mason and Blue tuck into barbecue plates. A phone call pulls Blue away, and Mason and I discuss the afternoon shoot, which includes Brick. I've enjoyed working with Mason, and I'm reminded all over again how important work is to me and how much I need work, need a focus other than my marriage and kids.

The afternoon shoot with Brick is even more fun. We do the fishing and horseback-riding shots first, saving the couple shots for the very end. None of the "romance" shots will require kissing, but it's still awkward walking hand in hand with my brother and smiling up at him as if he's some lost love. "This is really weird, you know," I say to him, smiling to hide my gritted teeth.

"Let's just hope no one we know sees these," he answers.

The sun's just setting, painting the sky gorgeous, vivid layers of red and gold. It's perfect lighting for the romance shots. "You should have dragged Charlotte here," I add. "There's no reason she couldn't have done these pics with you."

"Or Dane with you," he retorts.

"Shut up. You're so juvenile."

"Me? I'm not the one who wanted to run away with him—"

"I never tried to run away with him—"

"Because we wouldn't let you!"

I swing around to face him. "What's this 'we' stuff? Mama and Pop sent me away, not you."

"You don't think I pulled Mama and Pop aside, told them you were sneaking out at night, chasing him all over the place?"

"Dane and I had a month of dates—that's it."

"But you were sneaking out at night." Totally unrepentant, he stares down at me. "I let Dane know that if he so much as laid a hand on you, I'd tear him apart limb from limb—"

"You didn't!"

"Shey Lynne, you were sixteen."

"You did talk to him."

"It wasn't much of a talk. I think I used my fists."

My stomach hurts. "You hit him?"

Brick doesn't even blink. "Don't feel bad for him. He got in a couple good licks, too. I think he was the one who burst my eardrum."

"I can't believe you fought your best friend."

"You were my baby sister. I had to make sure he respected you."

"Oh, he respected me all right. He never had anything to do with me after that."

"Good."

"Not good! Brick, I loved him—"

"You were a kid."

"Charlotte was sixteen when she met you. You were seventeen. Why were your feelings legit and mine weren't?"

"It's different."

"How so?" I demand.

"Dane's six years older than you. He was twenty-two to your sixteen and you were jailbait—"

"Okay, I've got it," Mason shouts, interrupting us. "The light's fading fast. Let's see if we can't get another ten or twenty frames in before it's gone."

"This isn't over," I whisper to Brick as we take position.

"And you, Shey Lynne, you need to move on," he responds, teeth gritted.

Our easy rapport is gone, and we stand stiffly next to each other. Mason works swiftly to take advantage of the little light that's left, and Brick and I drop the subject of Dane. But once Mason wraps up, I stalk off, still furious.

In the guesthouse bathroom, I wipe off some of the extra makeup and change into a long tiered black skirt, a black embroidered blouse, and a chunky silver-and-turquoise belt I wear low on my hips. My stomach churns as I brush my hair.

For the past twenty years I thought Dane didn't care and wasn't interested in me, but in truth, Dane was warned off.

Maybe we wouldn't have worked, but maybe we would have. What's upsetting is that thanks to Brick's overprotective instincts, we were never given a chance to figure it out for ourselves.

There's a pounding on the bathroom door. "Mom, we're here!" Cooper announces.

I put down the brush, open the door, and see my three dressed in jeans and boots. Hank and Bo are wearing collared polos, but Coop has on a western shirt. Coop's really gone country, hasn't he? "You guys look great. Ready for the party?"

"There are some hot girls here," Bo says, grinning. "And Uncle Blue said there would be more coming later. I guess they're still with their parents at the hotel but should be arriving in an hour."

"Hot girls, poor you," I tease, putting away my cosmetic bag and brush and turning off the light.

Tonight's party is for Blue's investors and prospective buyers, and he's gone all out for it, with an authentic Texas hoedown, a country-western band from Fort Worth, and a DJ and caterer from Dallas.

After stowing my gear in the truck, I follow the boys to the caterer's chuckwagon and smoker, where we inspect the slow-cooked ribs and tender beef brisket. Everything smells so good, and as we sniff around, mouths watering, the band begins to warm up.

Hank looks up at the colorful lights strung across the dining area and dance floor and then at the red gingham cloths and lanterns on the tables and grudgingly admits that it's pretty cool. "Uncle Blue went all out," he says. "They've even got real sawdust and everything."

"So do we have to hang out with you?" Bo asks, craning his head to keep an eye out for the girls.

I know where his interest lies, and I bite back my smile. "No. I'll hang out with Aunt Charlotte. You don't need to babysit me. Have fun."

I've just finished dinner and am chatting with Charlotte about the changes in her department at the hospital when Mason approaches and asks if I'll dance.

It's a line dance, and it's been a long time since I did the Texas two-step, but I laughingly accept. He takes my hand, pulling me to my feet.

"I'm going to look silly," I warn him. "I don't even remember the steps."

"It'll come back to you," he assures me as we take our place on the sawdust-covered dance floor.

And it does come back. Not immediately, but after a

few times through, I've got it down. I stop trying to think and remember, and just move.

It crosses my mind that John would have a heart attack if he saw me now. He hates country-western music, loathes anything western. But these are my roots. I grew up attending roundups, rodeos, and county fairs, and I loved the hot, muggy summers and the cold, crisp winters and the scent of hay and freshly churned earth. I might have spent the past twenty years living in Milan and New York, but the country has stayed in my blood.

My boots thud in the fresh sawdust and, turning, I sway my hips and catch sight of my boys' faces. They're watching me with avid interest, having only ever seen me dance at weddings and bar mitzvahs. I don't mind their grins and laughter, though. It's just part of being Mom.

I make a face at the boys and then ignore them by focusing on Mason and the warm night and the music. Dancing, I feel the swish of my full skirt against my bare calves and the weight of my hair spilling down my back. Looking up, I get a glimpse of the colorful red and yellow lights strung overhead. Beyond the lights are tree branches and the moon. It's such a beautiful night, and I feel an unexpected rush of pleasure.

I need to do this more. Dance. Laugh. Socialize.

I've become too isolated. I spend too much time with the boys or my brothers. I need girl time. I need positive girl energy.

Marta used to tell me I was so inspiring. She said I was the most positive person she knew. But the sunny, optimistic Shey has been gone a long time now, and I miss her.

I miss me.

I want the happy me back. The one who knew how to laugh and tell a good dirty joke and just be comfortable in my own skin.

I'm not sure what I need to do to get the happy me back, but I'm going to figure it out. I'll make Shey a priority for a change.

"You're a great dancer," Mason shouts to me over the amplified music.

"Not great, but I am having a really good time," I answer, flashing him a warm smile.

We do another spin, and as I turn, I see big shoulders on a big man, a man with thick honey blond hair. My breath catches in my throat.

Dane's here.

I lose track of what I'm supposed to be doing and step the opposite direction, bumping into Mason. He steadies me. "Gotcha," he says.

"Sorry. Got distracted," I say, flushing. I steal another glance in Dane's direction, and my skin prickles as I realize he's not alone, either. He has a date, a stunning brunette in snug jeans, an even snugger sexy western-cut blouse, and fancy dress boots. Despite the western threads, she screams city and money, and I'm reminded of Blue's wife, Emily.

Since I've already vowed that I'm not going to get involved with him, I don't know why I care that Dane has a date, but I do. I care very much, which just frustrates me.

Even more frustrating is that Dane's cane in no way diminishes his size or strength. I should find him less attractive now that he's injured. But he's still so big, and his thighs are so muscular, they stretch the denim fabric, making his Wranglers look as if they were painted on. Sinewy thighs. Lean hips. Perfect butt.

The song ends, and Mason walks me back to the table where I was sitting with Charlotte. I sit down, and Mason takes a seat near me.

"Thank you. That was fun," he says, running a hand through his dark hair. We're both warm and a little breathless from dancing. "Wish I didn't have to get back to Dallas. I'd love to stay another couple hours. Love to dance another dance."

"It was fun," I agree, suddenly self-conscious and knowing it's because Dane's here. But how can Dane give me butterflies twenty years later? How can he make me feel like a teenager all over again?

I glance up then, and as I do, my gaze collides with Dane's.

Dane doesn't look away. He holds my gaze, jaw squared, and I stare right back.

I'm not going to run and hide. Not going to back down. Not going to let him win this time.

I can hear Mason talking, but my attention is only on Dane, and we continue our little stare-down for another couple of seconds.

The edge of his mouth lifts. He smiles the smallest of smiles at me, as if he's somehow won.

But he didn't win. He hasn't won.

"I'm anxious to see how the last thirty frames turned out." Mason's still talking, and I force my focus back to what he's saying. "The sunset couldn't have been more spectacular, but I'm not sure about my lighting on you and Brick."

I'm listening to Mason, but my attention is still split and

it's a struggle to answer him. "I'm sure you'll have something Blue can use."

"I'll let you know," he promises. "And Shey, if you're not going back to New York right away, I'd love to see you again. Even as friends." He sees my expression and adds apologetically, "Your brother told me about John. I'm sorry. John's a fool."

I feel a sudden tightness in my chest. Don't want to think about John tonight. John's part of the past. I need to leave him there. "I guess we can't help who we love."

"You're a beautiful woman, Shey—"

"I'd love to be friends, Mason," I interrupt gently. I don't like cutting him short, but I'm not ready for compliments and charm. "Let's stay in touch. Okay?"

He pulls his business card from his wallet and scribbles a number on the back. "Here's my contact info. Call me the next time you're in Dallas. We could go to a movie, grab lunch, whatever."

"Sounds good." I take his card but don't offer one in return. I think we both know that it's going to be up to me to contact him, and I'm grateful he doesn't press for my number.

He gives me a quick hug and goes. I watch him leave and then turn my head a little to see where Dane has gone. But Dane hasn't gone anywhere. He's standing right where I last saw him—adjacent to the bartender's table—and he's looking at me.

I lift an eyebrow at him and he shakes his head at me, and just like that I get the crazy frisson of feeling. It's sharp and hot and electric. He makes me feel hungry and alive and reckless. So reckless.

"So Dane's here," Charlotte says, following my gaze. "That's interesting."

Charlotte and Brick have been together since high school, and like the rest of my family, Charlotte knew Dane was the reason my parents sent me to California.

"What is he doing here?" I ask.

"I don't know," she answers dryly. "Why don't you find out?"

"You think I should go talk to him?"

"Well, your brothers certainly won't."

"Not in a thousand years."

Charlotte is grinning too much like the Cheshire cat for my taste. "You always did have a soft spot for him."

Soft spot? Is that what she calls it?

I can see myself at sixteen, sitting on the top rail of the corral in my snug Wranglers and boots, wearing a tight pink T-shirt, trying to make the most of what God gave me while Dane takes a practice ride. I see me climbing onto his lap in his truck and kissing him with all the passion a sixteen-year-old can feel. I see me cutting the last two classes at school so I can jump in my truck and head to Fort Worth to watch Dane compete.

I would have done anything for him. Gone anywhere with him. But Dane didn't let anything happen. We came close a couple of times, but he stopped before we got carried away. And then suddenly I was shipped off, sent away to St. Pious.

The first month at the boarding school, I lost ten pounds because I was so worried he'd forget me, I couldn't eat.

It's been a lifetime since I attended St. Pious, but it still stings when I think about him marrying Shellie Ann. In my mind he was supposed to be with me, supposed to wait for me. I might have been a Stanford University grad, but my heart was holding out for a cowboy. I was never going to model, never going to travel the world. My dream was to be a bull rider's wife.

"I did like him," I admit, getting to my feet.

"Where are you going?" Charlotte asks.

I rap my knuckles on the table. "To find out what he's doing here."

He watches me approach, eyes hooded, arm draped casually around his date. I hate that he has a date. Hate that he never wanted me the way I wanted him. "This is the last place I expected to find you," I say to him before turning to his date. "I'm Shey Darcy, Blue Callen's sister."

"Lulu Davies," she answers. "Blue Callen's investor."

So this is Lulu Davies. I had no idea she'd be so young or pretty. Lulu is the widow of the late Hap Davies, one of Texas's original oil tycoons. She's his third wife and inherited billions after less than five years of marriage. And seeing as she's big, big money and one of Blue's investors, I suppose she can bring anyone she wants to the party, and that includes Dane Kelly.

"What do you think of the party?" I ask her, aware of Dane's scrutiny but unwilling to give him a reaction.

"Glad to see everyone having a good time," she answers, "but I'm not surprised. I sent Blue to my personal event planner, and I think they did a fine job."

I glance at Dane. "When we talked yesterday, you didn't mention the party."

His eyes gleam. He knows what I'm doing. Knows I'm deliberately stirring things up.

"When Lulu told me we had plans for Saturday night, I didn't know we'd be coming here," he responds, smiling down at me, "otherwise I'd have suggested we double-date."

So this isn't their first date. They may even be a couple. Dane Kelly, bull-riding champ, and Lulu Davies, Texas heiress.

Makes me want to throw up.

I smile grimly instead and gesture to the sawdust-covered dance floor. "The band's wonderful. Have you had a chance to get out there yet?"

Lulu's expression falters, and she looks at me as though I'm heartless. I sigh inwardly. I didn't mean it like that. I know Dane's been hurt, but if he can still ride a horse and drive a truck, he can dance, can't he?

"Dane doesn't dance," Lulu corrects me with quiet dignity. I imagine her using the same tone of voice when she ordered Hap Davies's dinner for him after his stroke. "His injury," she adds significantly.

As if she knows anything about him or his injury.

I glance at Dane's hip. "Giving you trouble, Dane?"

"Nothing I can't handle, Shey."

I hear the hint of laughter in his voice. He knows I'm annoyed that Lulu felt the need to correct me. He knows I didn't need Lulu's correction.

"Good to hear," I answer, smiling as pleasantly as I can considering the circumstances. I shouldn't have approached Dane in the first place. I'd imagined the conversation going so very differently.

"I bumped into Bo on the way in tonight," Dane says. "He didn't know I'd called yesterday."

"I forgot," I confess, taking a jittery step backward. Dane looks gorgeous in his black dress shirt and Wranglers, boots and big buckle, a buckle he was awarded in one of his many wins. "Things have been hectic, and Blue was there and I just got distracted. I'm sorry," I add sincerely, grateful for the kindness he showed Bo.

"It looks like he's healing."

"He is." I look up at him and our eyes meet, lock, and once again I'm hit by wildly conflicting emotions. Awareness. Desire. Curiosity.

I'm too warm, and I exhale hard. "I should go check on the boys. They've been on their own long enough." I look at Lulu. "Nice to meet you," I say to her, and then nod at Dane. "See you round," I say to him before moving on.

Dumb, I think, walking away.

That was so dumb of me.

I thought I was going to be clever and cool, show him just what he'd missed in life. But then I discover he's dating one of Texas's richest women and doing just fine.

A little too fine.

Chapter Eight

Two hours later, I'm rounding up my boys. It's nearing midnight, and I've had enough of Lulu and Dane playing kissy-face. Not that they kissed a lot, but even the one kiss I witnessed was more than my stomach could handle.

Although I say I'm not going to get involved with Dane, the fact is I'm already involved. I've always felt connected to him, possessive of him. I don't know why, either. He just feels like mine. As if he were made for me. I've never felt this way about any other man, not even John. I used to think it was because Dane was my first love, but now I think it's just the energy between us. That crazy chemistry that makes me feel fiercely alive.

And Dane does make me feel alive.

As well as hungry and passionate and physical.

Three things I never felt with John. With John I was sunny, stylish, and sophisticated. We were an elegant, fashion-forward, culturally sensitive, socially prominent couple. If there was an A-list party in Manhattan, we were inevitably on the guest list. Big party in the Hamptons? Of course we attended. Trunk show, fashion week, designers' darlings—check, check, check.

We lived a glamorous life filled with interesting people and exciting activities, and John was the ideal husband—handsome, charming, chivalrous. He respected me, even adored me, and even though our relationship was far from sexually charged, I never questioned the lack of passion because John was such great company.

But with Dane...it's all chemistry. I don't know if we're compatible. All I know is that when I see him, I want him.

The boys began arguing as we left the party and are still fighting as we head to my truck. Cooper is angry with his brothers for ditching him earlier, Bo's pumped because he got the phone number of one of the two hot girls, and Hank isn't saying anything, but I think he made out with the other one. But that wouldn't surprise me; girls have always had a thing for Hank.

"You're such a jerk," Cooper mutters as Bo trips him.

Bo whacks Cooper. "Don't call me names."

"Then stop pushing me!"

It never ends, does it? "Enough."

"He started it—"

"Did not."

"You're such an idiot."

"Well, you're an asshole."

"Boys!" I'm practically screaming. "Stop it. *Now.*"

"Kids giving you trouble, Shey?"

Of course it's Dane, and he's giving me a play on the very words I said to him earlier. *Hip giving you trouble, Dane?*

I turn my head, peer into the dark, and just make out his powerful silhouette. He's leaning against a sports car, legs extended. "Nothing I can't handle," I answer smartly, but in truth I'm humiliated that he overheard the scene. I find it embarrassing that my boys give one another—and me—such a hard time.

"Sounds like they're giving you a run for your money," he replies.

"Heck, no. This is our version of quality family time."

He laughs softly. "At least you still have your sense of humor."

"At least," I agree.

The moonlight plays on his face as he pushes off the car to join us. His lips are curved. Even his eyes seem to be smiling. I hear the crunch of his cane on leaves. I hate that he's hurt. Hate that I wasn't there when he was hurt. "What happened to Lulu?"

"She's having a word with Blue."

"Why? Is Blue in trouble?"

His husky laugh floats on the night. "She fires you up, doesn't she?"

"I have no feelings one way or another."

"Liar."

I blush and my cheeks grow hot, almost as hot as the rest of me. Because of course he's right. Lulu did fire me up, but then, I'd be fired up over any woman Dane dates.

"I don't think you've met all my boys," I say, aware of my boys there, listening to our exchange. I gesture to each of the kids as I introduce them. "Hank, my oldest. Bo you've met. And Cooper, my youngest."

"Hank, Bo, and Cooper," he repeats, looking at each in turn and studying them as intently as if they're the champion bucking bulls he raises.

I suddenly see my boys through his eyes. Tall, lanky, thin. The boys are in that awkward stage of adolescence where only a mother can find them beautiful. And some days it's hard even for me to see the charm in them.

Unsettled, I place my hands on Cooper's shoulders. "This is Dane Kelly, a friend of Uncle Brick's and a national bull-riding champion."

"Three-time national champ," Cooper corrects as he extends his hand to Dane. "I've read a lot about you, Mr. Kelly. You're the most famous person in Palo Pinto County."

Dane smiles, and creases fan from the edges of his eyes. "Follow the circuit, Cooper?"

"Yes, sir. I want to be a bull rider like you and Uncle Brick."

"You ride, then?"

"No, sir. Not yet. I'd like to get some training, but I don't have any roughstock experience yet. I was hoping you'd maybe teach me." Coop swallows nervously. "If you had time, that is."

"Coop," I protest in a low voice.

Dane is focused on Coop. "Your uncle won't teach you?"

"Haven't asked him."

"Why not?"

"He told me once that he wouldn't let my cousin Tyler do it, that bull riding's too dangerous."

"It's an extreme sport," Dane agrees.

"I know I'm skinny," Coop adds. "But I'm strong, and a lot tougher than I look."

"Cooper, I'm flattered you asked, but I'm not doing a lot of training right now. Lately my business has me on the road more often than not—"

"That's okay with me. We could work when you're

home. It'd be around your schedule, Mr. Kelly, whenever you have time," Coop interrupts, voice cracking. He's nervous and scared and yet so hopeful. "I can pay you, too. I have my own money. I've been saving for a while."

"Money isn't the problem, son. Time is."

Cooper is momentarily flustered. He digs the toe of his boot in the ground. "Will you at least think about it, Mr. Kelly? You're one of the best bull riders ever. I could learn a lot from you."

I didn't want Cooper to ask Dane to train him. I don't want to be indebted to Dane more than I am. But when I hear that pleading tone in Coop's voice, my heart aches. Cooper has never asked for anything before. He's never wanted anything like this before. And even though Dane isn't the one I'd have train him, I suddenly want Dane to tell him yes. I want Dane to make him happy.

Dane studies Cooper for a long moment. "As I said, I'm not working with cowboys right now, and I don't think it'd be fair for me to start training you and then stop because I'm just too busy. But let me sleep on it tonight. I'll give you a call tomorrow. How does that sound?"

Cooper lights up. "Good. Really good. Thank you."

A few minutes later, we're in the truck and heading home. The boys talk about Dane and bull riding, and every time Dane's name is mentioned I feel a little zing, a sharp shock of recognition. It's so strange to hear my sons discussing Dane Kelly. They have no idea that Dane and I once dated, that we had one month of clandestine meetings and stolen kisses and feverish make-out sessions before I got packed up and shipped off to Monterey, California.

For four weeks I was Dane's girl. For four weeks I thought we were a couple and we were going to make it work. At least, Dane let me believe we had a chance. But once I was sent away, it was over. Completely, totally over. I didn't understand it. Kept thinking it was a mistake. That once I was back home—during summer or Christmas vacation—Dane would see me and realize he missed me. But he never looked at me again, or took my calls, or sought me out. He showed absolutely zero interest, and it crushed me. Talk about unrequited love.

I was still hung up on Dane when I started Stanford, especially as he was beginning to make a name for himself. I was in the middle of my junior year when he won his first national championship, and he was leading the standings the following year when I graduated. It was a big deal in Palo Pinto County, as everyone back home followed Dane's career. Whenever I returned home, it seemed like Dane was all anyone talked about. That's why I headed to Europe after I graduated from college instead of moving back to Texas. I couldn't go back to Parkfield. Couldn't be in Dane's world but not be part of it.

Remembering hurts. It's bruising to know one can be so completely dismissed. So easily forgotten.

I'm still thinking about Dane when bits of the boys' conversation reach me. They're discussing the girls they met tonight, comparing them in terms of hotness. After listening to them analyze the girls' figures, I interrupt. "Give me a break, boys. They're still just little girls."

"They're fifteen, Mom," Bo answers.

"Not old enough to vote, drink, or drive, which makes them little girls," I answer. "And you guys have other things to think about. Like school. I haven't seen any of you do any homework yet this weekend."

"You weren't even around today, Mom. How would you know?" Bo protests.

"As if there's real homework," Hank answers sarcastically.

I stiffen and my hands tighten on the steering wheel. "If you're not being adequately challenged, Hank, then maybe it's time you challenged yourself. Do extra reading. Do your own research. Create your own projects. Not everyone gets to go to private prep schools that cost thirty grand a year!"

"What does money have to do with it?"

"Everything!"

"Jesus."

He'd said it beneath his breath, but I heard. And I'm sure he wanted me to hear, which makes me even more upset. Livid, I pull over to the side of the road and twist to look at him. "What are you doing?" I demand.

"What do you mean?"

"You know exactly what I'm talking about. You're deliberately pushing my buttons. Why are you picking a fight?"

He sighs with exaggerated patience. "I'm not picking a fight. You're picking the fight. I've done nothing—"

"Your school cost thirty-three thousand a year, and I paid that tuition for the past ten years. But things have changed and I'm not comfortable paying that kind of money for school."

"But we can afford the tuition. I talked to Uncle Brick and he said we could take a second mortgage out on the ranch—"

"You what?"

"Talked to Uncle Brick."

"Oh, my God."

"What?"

Bo and Coop are so quiet now, I'm not even sure they're breathing. But I barely give them a passing thought as I focus on Hank. "You would have me risk the family ranch, property that's been in the family for four generations, so you could go to your elite school in New York?"

Hank is unmoved. "If I graduate from Dyer, I'm virtually guaranteed a spot at any college I want to go to."

"That may be true, but you're not going to do it on Uncle Brick's back. This is your uncle's home—"

"This is my future!"

"Your future," I repeat, appalled and revolted.

"Yes. My future."

"When did you get to be so selfish?" My voice shakes. "Your uncle is one of the most giving, decent men you'll ever meet, and I'd rather you never go to college than do it by putting his home and security at risk. Now I don't want to hear another word about Dyer. You're not going back. You're going to make Mineral Wells High work. And you're going to find a way to be successful here. Understand?"

He glares at me in the dark.

"Henry William Darcy, do you understand?"

And still he stares at me, anger etched all over his face.

"Answer me, Hank, or you walk home."

I've pulled the ultimate power play, and he hates it. "Yes," he hisses.

I don't like fighting with him, but I can't back down. "Good. This discussion is now over."

I start the truck and drive the rest of the way home in heavy, suffocating silence. The younger boys don't dare to speak, and Hank seethes next to me. I can feel his anger. He hates me right now. He might still hate me in the morning. But I have to do what's right. I have to teach them, which means raising them to think of others.

I'm in bed a half hour later, but I can't fall asleep and end up watching the minutes change on the clock with its jumbo neon yellow numbers. Mama bought the electric clock for Pop because he had a hard time reading the numbers on the old one. But this clock is like a billboard, impossible not to see.

I have to talk to Brick. I know with Pop gone, Brick's become the head of the family and feels responsible for everyone, but it's not Brick's job to provide for my kids. I'll accept his time and his love, but we don't need his financial support.

I walk over to Brick and Charlotte's in the morning, determined to have a word with Brick. But he's already out on the ranch, checking on some missing cattle. Their house sits on the corner of the property, about a mile from Mama and Pop's house, but they didn't always have their own home. When Brick and Charlotte moved back to Parkfield after he graduated from college, they moved into Brick's old room for a year while they built the little house they live in now. Brick had promised Charlotte that once they had the money, he'd remodel the house to give her a proper home. He did remodel—adding on a bedroom for Carolyn and then another one for Tyler—but Charlotte never did get a big or fancy house.

Looking at Charlotte, who has just finished baking a large batch of zucchini bread with the last of the summer crop, I don't think she minds. She loves being a nurse, loves Brick, loves her kids, and is happy with life.

I find myself envying her. I want to be like her. I want to feel contented, too.

"Want a slice?" she offers, pulling the mini-tins out of the oven. "It's delicious warm."

"I just finished breakfast, but it does smell good."

"I'll send a loaf with you," she promises, motioning for me to follow her into the sunroom, which overlooks her rose garden. Charlotte's passion is gardening, and her roses are spectacular. "What's on your mind, Shey Lynne?" she asks as we sit in the wrought-iron furniture she and Brick got as a wedding gift from her parents more than twenty years ago. "Something's got you upset."

"It's a Brick-being-a-big-brother thing," I say, crossing my legs and swinging one foot. "Sometimes he helps a little too much."

Charlotte smiles sympathetically. "He can be a little overprotective, can't he?"

"He doesn't realize I'm an adult. I'm almost forty, Char."

"He just loves you. He wants what's best for you."

I flash back to my argument with Brick during yesterday's photo shoot. "I agree, and he has a good heart. And good intentions. But he can't fix everyone's problems, and he can't make decisions for us, either."

"Is he doing that?"

"When hasn't he?" I cry, exasperated. "Brick told me yesterday that he was the one who warned off Dane all those years ago. I thought it was Pop. Thought maybe he and Mama sat Dane down. But no, it was Brick, and he didn't just talk to Dane, he beat him up."

Charlotte shifts uncomfortably, glances out the window toward her rose garden, which is a riot of yellow, pink, and coral color. "You were sixteen, Shey, and I don't think Dane got beat up. Brick's a good fighter, but Dane's even better."

"The point is, you were sixteen when you met Brick. Why was it okay for you and Brick to be together and not Dane and me?"

"Because Brick was only a year older than me, and Dane was six years older than you. And Lord, Shey Lynne, this was over twenty years ago." She reaches up to tuck a pale strand of hair behind her ear. Charlotte's a natural blonde, too, although over the years she's let the color fade to its current ash blond shade. "Are you really mad at Brick about something that happened so long ago?"

She doesn't understand. She married her first love, found her soul mate, and has been with him for twenty-eight years. She has the life I wanted. She married her cowboy, and he gave her stability and security.

But there's no point in revealing that I'm envious of her life. She'd just tell me that I've lived an extraordinary life. How many girls from Palo Pinto become international models? How many girls from here publish books or put together a TV show?

I end up giving her a hug good-bye, and with the loaf of zucchini bread tucked under my arm, I walk home, kicking up dirt and gravel as I go.

I love Charlotte, I do, but talking to her isn't like talking to Marta or Tiana, my best friends. I don't have to be guarded with them, don't have to carefully pick my words or worry that what I say will be misinterpreted.

With the sun coating the fields golden, I take a deep breath and remind myself that my friends are just a phone call away.

I wistfully think back to last December when I flew to L.A., and Tiana, my roommate at St. Pious and then again at Stanford, met me at the airport and then drove us to Palm Springs for a girls' weekend of good food and massages and hikes and talks by the pool. The massages and hikes and meals were great, but it was the talks I needed most. The talks I need now.

Being with people who know you and love you is so healing. I know I can handle anything if I have my friends at my side.

Arriving back at the house, I find Cooper anxiously pacing the front yard. "What's wrong, hon?" I ask, taking a seat on the front steps.

He points to the open kitchen window. "I'm waiting for Dane Kelly to call. I can hear the phone from here, can't I?"

"Yes. But Coop, it's not even noon yet. He might not call until tonight."

He picks up a pebble and throws it at a tree, where it pings and falls to the ground. "I know. But I want to be ready."

He's so excited, so eager, which makes me worried that he's setting himself up for disappointment. "Coop, it may not work out. He's very busy—"

"But he was Uncle Brick's best friend. They traveled on the circuit together. You really think he'd say no?"

"Quite possibly," I answer honestly, then wish I hadn't

when I see the expression in Cooper's eyes. He looks so sad, it kills me. "But it's okay if he doesn't. We can find someone else to train you. This is Texas, babe—"

"But I want to work with Mr. Kelly. And he said he might."

"Might," I stress.

"So think positive."

"I am." I hold up the foil-wrapped loaf Charlotte sent home with me. "Want some zucchini bread? Aunt Charlotte made it this morning."

He makes a face. "It's green. Yuck."

"Green's good."

"On trees, yeah, but not in my mouth."

Grinning, I rise and head into the house but pause at the screen door. "I'm going to head into town, check the P.O. box and pick up groceries. Want to come?"

"I better not. Just in case he calls."

I do hope Dane calls soon, even if it's just to say he can't. Better to get it over with, or else it's going to be a very long day for everyone. "Okay. Text me if you need anything, otherwise I'll be back in an hour or two."

The next day passes and suddenly it's Monday night and I still haven't had a chance to talk to Brick about his offer to Hank because one of Brick's ranch hands crashed the work truck earlier in the day and ended up being rushed to Palo Pinto Hospital.

As frustrated as I am, it doesn't seem fair to unload on Brick now, and frankly, things aren't much better at our house. Monday rolls into Tuesday, and Hank is still upset with me. Bo is bummed that the girl he met at Blue's party no longer wants to talk to him, and twenty minutes after he arrives home from school, I find him in front of his laptop on Facebook.

"Bo. Homework," I remind him.

"It's all done," he answers without even looking up from the screen.

"How can it be done? You're reading a novel right now in English and I haven't seen you read all week. I haven't seen a math book, or a history book, or any other book, for that matter."

"It's because I've already done my work."

"Show me."

I've finally got his attention. "Are you serious?"

"Yes."

"Everything's fine, Mom. Don't be such a stress case."

I'm not a stress case, but I could be if I let my kids steamroll over me. "Are you telling me the truth? You're really on top of everything?"

"Yes."

"Because if you're not—"

"I know, I know. You'll take away my phone. Get rid of my Facebook page. Make my life a living hell. Got it."

I watch as he turns back to his computer and pretends I'm no longer standing there. Bo and Hank have become such different people. Moody. Aloof. Condescending. And friends say it's just going to get worse before it gets better.

God help us all.

Coop is quiet at dinner, and as soon as he's finished helping with the dishes he disappears back to the barn. I dry the counters and after hanging up the dish towel head down to the barn to check on him.

He's grooming Shady, one of Brick's horses and the horse Coop prefers to ride. I watch him run the brush down Shady's smooth flanks, each stroke of the brush long and steady. Coop is so comfortable with the horses. You wouldn't have known he'd never ridden until June.

"He never called, did he," I say, reaching in to pat Shady's neck.

Cooper shakes his head. "No."

He's so disappointed. "Do you want me to call him?"

"He said he'd call me."

"Maybe he just forgot. Maybe we just need to remind him—"

"He said he'd call. He'll call." His voice hardens. And then just like a man, he ducks out of the stall, ending the conversation.

Chapter Nine

—— ✦ ——

I don't sleep well that night, and I don't know why, but I keep waking up to look at the clock. Nearly every hour I check the clock and fluff my pillow and try to convince myself to go back to sleep.

Things are fine, I keep telling myself. Things are good. No need to worry. Don't be upset.

But I am upset. I wish Dane had called Cooper. It makes me want to call him, talk to him, make him realize how important this is to Coop. And I know my brothers have their issues with Dane, but that's their problem, not mine or Cooper's. Cooper is just twelve. He's falling in love with the whole Texas mystique, and I couldn't be happier for him.

I want him to pursue his dreams. I want him to have an interesting life. And if learning to be a cowboy is part of it, more power to him.

I'm grumpy as I drive the boys to school the next morning. I'm short on sleep and still drinking too much coffee. I need to cut down on the coffee and work on the food intake.

I'm just walking back into the house after dropping the boys when my cell rings. It's a local number, one I don't recognize. "Hello?"

"Mrs. Darcy?"

No one calls me Mrs. Darcy. Everyone around here knows

me as Shey, or Shey Callen, but not Mrs. Darcy. "Yes?"

"Bo Darcy's mother?"

It's the school, I realize. Bo's school. "Yes," I repeat with a sinking heart.

"This is Paul Peterson, Mineral Wells vice principal."

My heart sinks further. "Yes, Mr. Peterson?"

"We've had a little problem with Bo today and I'd like to meet with you."

"When?"

"Today. Now, if possible."

I pull out the little chair at the desk and sit down. "What's happened?"

"We believe he's been forging your signature."

"He's been cutting class?"

"No. But he's failing three classes and barely scraping by in the others, and we believe he forged your signature on his progress reports. Did you see them?"

"No." I swallow, hating the heaviness in my gut, a heaviness only Bo can put there. "When were they sent home?"

"Almost two weeks ago. They were due a week ago today, and Bo kept making excuses. He served detention last Friday and promised to turn them in today, which he did, but the signatures didn't match up with your signature on the paperwork we have on file. It's not the first time we believe he's forged your signature, either..."

His voice drifts off, and for a moment there's just silence on the line. I don't try to fill it, either, as I'm too disappointed to speak.

Bo promised me he was doing well. He promised me he was on top of his work. Promised me I could trust him, too.

The broken promises disturb me as much as the failing grades.

"I didn't know he had detention last week," I say.

"He'd just been home sick. At least he said he'd been sick."

Bo did miss two days after the fight.

"One of his teachers thought he'd been in a fight," the vice principal adds.

I don't say anything, afraid to commit one way or another.

Finally, Mr. Peterson clears his throat. "I have openings at one o'clock, two-thirty, and then I'm available after school at four. What time is best for you?"

I still have to do Brick's books. Need to grocery shop again. Clean house. Finish the laundry. But none of that matters. Bo comes first. "Two-thirty?"

"Excellent. I'll see you at two-thirty."

He's just about to hang up, but I have a question. "Mr. Peterson, you said he was failing three subjects. Which ones?"

"Math, English, and social studies."

"And the other classes? What are those grades?"

"A D in science. C's in Spanish and PE. But on the positive side, technology arts is a bright spot. He's performing well there with a solid B."

Bo was once a straight-A student. At a rigorous prep school, no less. My shoulders slump, energy draining. "Technology arts?"

"Typing."

Typing. Wow. Bo is really in trouble.

With six hours until I have to meet with Mr. Peterson,

I try to tackle Brick's books but can hardly focus, I'm so upset.

How can this be happening again? How can Bo be failing again? I've been down this road with him before. And this time his grades haven't slid just a little, they've plummeted off the map.

What the hell is that kid thinking?

I'm still stewing when Rae, one of the agents at the Stars agency, calls to say that Neiman Marcus is interested in booking me for their spring resort wear catalog, a job that would last from three to five days and would require me to travel to Puerto Rico, where they're shooting in Old San Juan.

The details sound too good to be true: I'd be paid at my rate for all the days I work, plus my two travel days, *and* they'd cover hotel, first-class air, and all meals.

Rae wants to know if I'd be interested.

Interested? Travel. First-class air. A four-star hotel. And meals.

I'd be thrilled to do it.

Lord knows I need a break, as well as a change of scenery. And even as I picture me hopping on a plane to the Caribbean, I hear Mr. Peterson's voice echo in my head: *We've had a little problem with Bo today.*

Oh, I want to go, I do, but how can I go now? Hank is barely talking to me. Bo is failing school. And Coop is still waiting for Dane to call.

It'd be irresponsible for me to head out on a trip, even if it's a business trip, when my boys so obviously need me at home.

"I'd love to do it—"

"Great!"

"—but I don't know if I can."

Rae's silence is heavy with disapproval. "This is an incredible opportunity. Most models would jump at the chance."

Tell me about it. But most models aren't single moms with three sons about to self-destruct. "I know, and I want to do it. Can you give me a day to work on logistics? Figure out child care?"

"Let me tell you more about the job, then. It's scheduled for the last week of October, and at this point I'm not sure which days they'll be booking you. I needed to confirm your availability first and then they'll finish scheduling the shoot."

As she talks, I dig through the pile of catalogs, junk mail, and unpaid bills stacked on the little desk in the kitchen, looking for my appointment book. I find it at the bottom and open the calendar to draw a line through the week leading up to Halloween. Fortunately, my boys don't do Halloween anymore, and maybe I can get Brick and Charlotte to help me with the boys, or maybe I can find a sitter.

"You'll be wearing a little bit of everything from swimsuits, to day wear, to designer evening wear," Rae continues. "They love your hair, so just make sure the color's fresh and it's in fabulous condition. Their makeup artists will be airbrushing you there, so they don't want you to tan or apply a fake one since they'll do it themselves."

"Got it. Anything else?"

"No body hair, of course." She hesitates and asks delicately, "Are you swimsuit ready?"

"I think so."

"Hope that means yes."

Me too. "I'll call you first thing in the morning," I promise. "Let me try to figure out child care stuff tonight."

I never return to Brick's books. Can't. They're boring as well as depressing. The ranch is in the red. Brick's paying everybody but not making anything himself. I have a feeling it's Charlotte's job keeping them afloat, but maybe it's just the kind of year we're having. I'm sure in past years the ranch has been more prosperous.

At one o'clock, I strip off my clothes to shower and dress for the meeting with the vice principal.

In the shower I let the water pelt down, hot, so hot until it's almost too painful to bear, and as I wash my hair, my mind races, trying to figure out how I can possibly make the trip to Puerto Rico when things are such a mess here.

But not everything's a mess, I remind myself. Hank's not in crisis; he's just mad at me. Cooper's waiting for Dane's call, but he can weather the disappointment. And Bo...well, Bo's the problem.

Bo is in trouble. I'm furious with him. Livid that he's been hiding the truth from me, pretending he's studying, insisting he's on top of things when he obviously isn't and hasn't been for weeks. But Bo's also a bright kid and he's in eighth grade, not high school. Maybe I can get him sorted out so that I could go.

Puerto Rico.

Neiman Marcus's resort catalog.

Shey Darcy getting booked for a big job at thirty-nine. Oh, yes.

Yes, yes, yes. I can make this work. I'll find a way to make this work. Rae's right. Opportunities like this are too good to miss.

I turn off the water and towel dry, then rifle through my wardrobe, looking for something appropriate to wear. Shouldn't show up to school in ratty jeans and old boots. Need to make a little bit of an effort. I settle on brown slacks, my brown Prada heels, and a tailored white blouse that looks crisp and fresh.

I start to leave my hair loose but am so aggravated that I end up scooping it into a high ponytail so nothing touches the back of my neck. While I feel cooler, I also look plainer and add a chunky red coral necklace to finish the look.

Anxious about the meeting, I arrive at school just after two and have twenty-five minutes to kill before the appointment. I sit for the first twenty minutes in my truck, head tipped back, eyes closed, as I work on clearing my mind and getting calm.

Bo's okay. Bo's just a boy. Bo's a teenager.

But what if his problems are more than teenage issues? What if he's going to turn out like Cody?

The fear claws at me, and as I think about Cody and how my mother refused to accept his diagnosis of bipolar depression, I can almost understand her denial. Almost, but not quite. Because I'm a mother, too, and if I were Cody's mother, there's no way I'd ignore his illness. His symptoms were all there, too. Mania. Depression. Then the suicide attempts. Someone had to do something. Someone had to act. And no one did, not for years. Not until it was too late.

I find myself recalling Cody's viewing and funeral. My

boys had never been to a viewing before, and it was painful taking them to see Cody, but I needed to. I needed them to see my beautiful brother who died too young. Remembering Cody's death and burial makes my stomach churn, and I practically leap out of the truck to escape my thoughts.

I arrive in the school office just as the office clock chimes two-thirty and take a seat in the waiting area across from two defiant-looking girls. The thin blonde with the pouffy bangs chews nonstop on her fingernails, while the brunette with the dark eyeliner sighs repeatedly with apparent boredom. The girls must be Bo's age—thirteen, fourteen—and yet their makeup and wardrobe look years older. They'd look so much prettier if they weren't trying so hard. When it comes to fashion and beauty, less really is more.

The thin blonde is staring at me now, and she leans over to whisper something to her friend. Her friend rolls her eyes.

"Are you a model?" the blond girl blurts. Her friend elbows her, but the blonde ignores her.

"Yes," I answer evenly.

"I thought so. You look like one." Her friend makes a scornful sound, but the blond girl gives me a hopeful smile. "I've always wanted to be a model. I watch all the shows, you know. *America's Next Top Model. Project Runway.* I know you have to be tall to be a model, don't you?"

"Usually five eight and taller," I say gently, aware that this girl is nowhere near tall enough. Nor does she have the frame or bone structure, but I'd never tell her that. There's no point. Kids need to dream. Sometimes dreams are all we have.

"But last year Tyra Banks's show was about short models." The girl nibbles on her lower lip. "I could be one of those. But I'd have to go to New York or L.A., right?"

"Probably New York," I say.

"But Tyra's show is filmed in L.A."

Suddenly a short, balding man approaches me. "Shey Callen!" he exclaims, moving toward me with an outstretched hand. "What are you doing here?"

I rise. "I'm here to meet with the vice principal, Mr. Peterson."

"That's me." He pumps my hand and looks at me as though he can't believe his eyes. "What can I do for you, Shey?"

I glance from him to the girls and back again. "I'm Bo's mom. You called me earlier."

He's still holding my hand in his. "Bo's mom?"

"Bo Darcy. He's an eighth grader here—"

"You're Bo's mom," he repeats as I slide my hand from his.

My awkwardness grows. Clearly I'm missing something.

The vice principal reads my confusion. "You don't remember me, do you," he says.

"No, I'm sorry, I don't."

"I went to school with Blue."

"Oh!"

He nods and, smiling, steers me away from the seating area to his office. "I had quite the crush on you," he confesses with a flush. "But your brother made it clear that he'd tear me apart if I so much as looked at you." His flush darkens, and he shakes his head. "He was serious, too."

Sounds like the common theme, I think, following Paul

Peterson into his office. I sit in the chair across from his desk, eager to get the meeting started so we can wrap it up. I hate stuff like this. I hate being confronted by my failings as a parent, because the boys' education is my responsibility and it's vital they succeed.

Unfortunately, Paul isn't eager to begin discussing Bo. He wants to know where I ended up going to school when I disappeared from Palo Pinto County. I quickly brief him on my two years at St. Pious and then my degree from Stanford before I headed to Europe.

"Stanford?" he repeats. "That's good."

I flash to Hank, realizing that I probably wouldn't have gotten into Stanford if I'd finished high school at Mineral Wells. The schools here are good, but they're not as rigorous as the private prep schools.

"About Bo," I say, deliberately shifting gears, thinking we've spent enough time catching up and need to focus on why I'm here. "I'm concerned about him."

Paul nods sympathetically. "Boys."

He says the word as if the single syllable covers it all. But I have three boys; Hank, although headstrong, and Cooper, although sensitive, have never been half as demanding as Bo. "I'm worried about him," I say carefully.

"No need for that. It's typical of boys this age to slack off in school. Hormones, girls, distractions."

I would love for it to be so simple. I would love for Bo to merely be distracted, but I'm beginning to see a pattern emerging and it troubles me.

How old was Cody when he first began showing signs of his illness? Was it at eleven? Was he struggling at thirteen? Or was it only later, near the end of high school? It's so hard to remember, as I was preoccupied with my life back then.

"He's normally a good student," I say by way of explanation. "For everything to tank like this, I can't help worrying. How's his behavior here at school? Is he participating in class? Are teachers having problems with him?"

"Teachers like him. They don't like forged notes, but he's a good kid. Polite. Tries hard."

I nod, even as I am awash with conflicting emotions—anger, shame, guilt, frustration, regret.

I should have been on top of this. I should have been aware that he was not turning work in. I should be paying more attention.

But even as the shoulds pile up, I feel a stab of resentment. I *do* pay attention to him. Every day I ask him about his work. I'm not an absent parent. I pick him up from school and am there at home when he returns from school. I'm around, available, accessible. And he's nearly fifteen. Shouldn't he start being responsible for himself?

But if it's depression...

Depression is another animal altogether.

Paul and I wrap up the meeting, spend another few minutes in small talk—he wants to know all about Budapest, where I was working when I was first discovered by a Milan modeling agent—and then I leave the front office with more questions than answers.

But maybe that's part of parenthood. Maybe it's not about having answers. Maybe it's just about being real.

Later, with all the boys in the truck, we head for home and I drive biting my tongue.

I want to demand an explanation from Bo, but I tell

myself I have to wait, I can't do it here in front of the others. But as the minutes pass, my frustration grows. I'm so mad, never mind frustrated. What is happening with him? Why can't he let me know when he's falling behind? I'll help. I'll do anything for him. He just has to ask. Just has to communicate.

We're a couple of miles from our ranch when I blurt out, "I spent a half hour meeting with Mr. Peterson this afternoon, Bo." I shoot him a hard look as my fingers tighten on the steering wheel. "Did you really think I wouldn't find out about your grades, or the forged signatures on the progress reports?"

He glances at me and then glances just as quickly away.

"Three F's, Bo. And the rest are nearly as bad. D's and C's."

He sinks into his seat. "I have a B in tech arts."

"Typing."

"Yeah, but it's still a B."

"You took keyboarding classes in fourth grade. That was four years ago. I'd hope you could pass a typing class."

Bo's mouth compresses, but he doesn't speak. I just want to scream. I'm trying to help him. I'm trying to save him. I'm trying to keep him from failing this quarter. But he makes me feel like the bad guy, as if this—his education—has nothing to do with him. "You're a smart kid, Bo. How can this be happening? How can you be failing? You told me just last week that you were on top of your work, that you do your homework at school—"

"I didn't want you on me, okay?" he interrupts flatly. "I

knew you'd freak out if you found out about my grades—"

"Yes, I would freak out. Yes, I am freaking out. You're so smart, so gifted. You've got a great brain, you really do."

"I'm doing the best I can," he answers defiantly.

"I don't believe it."

"Then that's your problem."

I swallow hard. Count to five. And then to ten. And my feelings still hurt.

Everyone told me that I'd rue the day my boys became teenagers. They warned me that they'd be difficult. They told me I wouldn't recognize my own kids.

And I didn't believe them. My boys were always good boys. Loving, thoughtful, respectful. But my good boys aren't my boys any longer. They're becoming part of the world, sucked into adulthood with this slippery slope of adolescence.

It's not pretty, either.

But I'm not going to disappear on them. Not going to quit. We're going to get through this even if it's by the skin of our teeth.

We arrive home to discover Charlotte on our doorstep. She's armed with an enormous tin of freshly baked chocolate-chip cookies and a tentative smile. "You have a few minutes, Shey Lynne?" she asks me as the boys pop the lid off the tin and dive in while still standing in the driveway.

I'm tense and tired and definitely not the best of company, but I always have time for Charlotte. "Of course." I hold the back door open so she can enter the house, even as I call to the boys to start their homework.

Inside the kitchen, Charlotte glances around. Following

her gaze, I see the sink full of the morning dishes, the kitchen table piled high with laundry I haven't yet folded, and the stacks of bills and paperwork on the desk, where I was attempting to do Brick's books before I got distracted by the calls from Rae and Mr. Peterson.

I'm embarrassed by the mess and chaos, embarrassed that I'm not doing a better job of juggling everything. "Sorry. Things aren't very tidy—"

"I don't care, Shey."

But Charlotte's house is never messy. I've never seen laundry on the kitchen table or dirty dishes piled in the sink. I drag stray socks and T-shirts into a mound to clear off the table. "But I do. I've never been so disorganized before. Can't seem to get anything done."

"Shey, stop. The laundry's fine."

But it's not fine. There's nothing fine about mess and chaos and a life that appears to be out of control.

And suddenly the mound of laundry feels like a metaphor of my life. Huge, sprawling, overwhelming.

My eyes sting and my chest grows tight. I'm trying so hard right now. I couldn't try harder, couldn't give or do more.

My frustration dissolves into fatigue, and it crosses my mind that I am overwhelmed, and a little blue, as well as lonely.

I miss my friends. I miss New York. I miss my old life.

I loved being married. I liked having a partner. I hate having to do it all on my own.

"Shey Lynne, stop," Charlotte says gently but firmly. "Just sit so we can talk. I want to apologize. I need to apologize."

I let go of the laundry and plunk down in the nearest chair. "Why?"

"I was thinking about what you said on Sunday. About how you were sixteen when you fell in love with Dane, and how I was the same age when I fell in love with Brick..." Charlotte takes a deep breath. "You're right. I never thought of it that way, and when I look back, I realize that my feelings for Brick at sixteen aren't that different than they are now. Our love's deepened over the years, matured, but it's the same spark, the same attraction. And I would have been devastated if anyone tried to keep us apart."

She looks at me, brown gaze somber. "I'm sorry. I am. You have every right to be upset with Brick—"

"It's okay. And you were right. It's been over twenty years. It's not an issue, not anymore."

"But it was high-handed of him. He's your brother, not your father." Charlotte's pretty face creases, and she suddenly looks years older than forty-four. Unlike my friends in New York, she doesn't do expensive skin treatments or visit a plastic surgeon for fillers and injections. "But as you know, he's always been so protective of you. You being the only girl and all."

I nod. I do know. All my brothers were that way, even Cody. They got it from my father. Pop was always gentle and chivalrous toward women. His father raised him to treat women with respect, and my father raised my brothers the same way. Girls weren't weak, just special.

Charlotte reaches for a pair of unmatched socks and spreads them flat on the table. They're similar but not a pair. "Have you filed for divorce yet?"

I'm caught off guard. "We've tried, but divorces in New York aren't as easy as other states. You can't get a no-fault divorce in New York. Someone has to be blamed."

"I certainly hope it's John shouldering the blame."

I nod. "The lawyers are handling it. It'll be a relief to get it behind me."

"I can imagine."

Charlotte reaches for another sock. "So have you thought about dating? Anyone you're interested in?"

"No." I can see that Charlotte's waiting for more, and I flounder about, searching for a good explanation when I don't have one. "I guess I'm just not ready."

"What about Dane? You still have feelings for him, don't you?"

"But everyone hates Dane."

"No one hates Dane. Brick and Blue are mad at him at the moment, but they don't hate him, and I certainly have no problem with him. I've always been close with him. Love him like a brother. And you know, Dane's been through quite a lot, too. You might find that you have more in common than you did before."

"Because he's also divorced?" I ask with a bitter laugh.

"Because he was also a parent, and he lost his only child. A child he absolutely adored." She sighs and looks at me. "I'm not saying you and Dane should be together, or are right for each other. What I am saying is that no one gets through life unscathed. Hearts get broken. Marriages end. Dreams die. But life goes on. And you have to find a way to go on, too."

I had no idea that Dane's divorce was so bitter. Can't imagine Shellie Ann keeping Dane's child from him. But then horrible things can happen when marriages end. Partners turn on each other. Hurt becomes hatred. I shiver a little. "Over the summer, Mama mentioned that you and Brick were godparents to Matthew. I didn't realize you were that close to Shellie Ann," I say, getting to my feet and reaching for the crumpled mustard-colored T-shirt near me.

"Shellie Ann and I weren't all that close, but we did spend a lot of time together. At least we did until near the end, when it became apparent that they weren't going to be able to work it out. That's when things got ugly."

I look up, interested. "Ugly how?"

"They were both in so much pain that by the time they separated they couldn't even be in the same room together. And I can't put all the blame on Shellie Ann. Dane shut down to the point that he wanted nothing to do with anyone. Not even Brick or me. I wasn't surprised when Shellie Ann moved to Austin. She needed to get away, needed a fresh start."

But when Shellie Ann left, she took Dane's son. I can't imagine that sitting well with him. "Was Dane a good dad?"

Char's eyes suddenly water. "The best," she says huskily. "He lived for his boy."

"I would have thought he'd try harder to keep Shellie Ann here."

"Shellie Ann was determined to go. You see, she'd met Brandon by then, and Brandon swept her off her feet. He was a big-name record producer, and Shellie Ann fell for him like a ton of bricks. There was no keeping her on the Kelly ranch when she could be part of Austin's music scene."

It blows my mind that Shellie Ann had everything I wanted—Dane, his love, his home, his son—and she let it all go. Left Palo Pinto. Left Dane. Started a different life with a different man in Austin.

For a moment I just fold clothes, struggling with the injustice of it all.

"You do still care for him," Charlotte says after a moment.

I fold the jeans, push them to the edge of the table, and look over at her. "I loved him, Char. I loved him the way you loved Brick. But I got sent away and Dane fell in love with Shellie Ann and eventually I met John. I have three great boys, boys I love with all my heart, so I'm happy."

"But Dane—"

"Isn't an option."

"Why not?" she asks, sounding genuinely disappointed.

I toss up my hands. "I'm done throwing myself at him. He had his chance and he passed on it and I'm okay with that." I see her expression and reach out to touch her arm. "Why does that bother you so much?"

She shrugs unhappily. "I just think you and Dane could be good together."

I give her a long look. "Char, I know you care about him, but Dane's not the only single man in Texas. This is a big state with plenty of available men. When I'm ready to date, I promise you, I'll date."

Chapter Ten

After Charlotte leaves, I force myself to put Dane out of my mind. It's time to return to mother mode.

I find Bo and we sit at the kitchen table to talk. He tells me he's sorry about his grades and wishes he'd asked for help. He doesn't know why he didn't, nor does he know why he can't get anything done. He just wants me to forgive him. And love him.

I do.

Together we work out a plan to help him be more organized. Turn in all missing work. Start going to teacher tutorials before and after school. Begin studying three or four days in advance for all tests.

Bo and I break for dinner and then pick up where we left off once the dishes are done. It's eleven before we're finished going through the mounds of crumpled school papers, tossing the old ones, sorting the current ones, and putting everything else in the proper section in the proper folder or binder.

Bo is happy to have me at his side, clearly relieved to have help organizing his mess. I'm happy to help him, too. I just wish he'd come to me before he'd hit rock bottom. But we're on it now, I tell myself. Things can only go up from here.

I kiss him good night, tuck him in, and then head to

bed. The two other boys went to bed a half hour ago.

I'm exhausted and think I'll fall right to sleep, but I don't. I can't, not with so much on my mind.

I relive the day, going over the events from Rae's call with the opportunity to model for Neiman Marcus's resort catalog, to the conference with Paul Peterson, to my confrontation with Bo, ending with my chat with Char about Dane.

I linger over my conversation with Char, thinking far too much about Dane and Shellie Ann, their marriage, their son, and the fact that Shellie Ann has remarried while Dane remains single.

Although how single remains to be seen. He was with Lulu at the party, and Lulu certainly seemed interested in him.

I guess what I'd love to know is how interested Dane is in Lulu.

Hopefully not a lot.

And then I groan into my pillow. I'm doing it again. Falling for him. Fantasizing. Creating impossible scenarios that will never come true.

Remember what you told Char, I remind myself sternly. Dane had his chance. Dane lost his chance. You've moved on with your life, and when you're ready to date, there are other men out there. Lots of men who'd love to be with you.

But as I breathe into my pillow, I know my heart. My heart doesn't want a lot of men. My heart still craves Dane.

Rae calls me early the next morning to say that Neiman Marcus would like me to come in for a go-see tomorrow before they commit to booking me for the shoot.

I'm still in my pajamas and haven't even yet driven the boys to school. The idea of rushing anywhere is far from appealing. "I thought they offered me the job," I say, propping the phone between my shoulder and ear as I refill my coffee cup.

"You've done a thousand go-sees in your career. What's one more?"

What I need to do is call Charlotte and Brick and see if they'd be willing to watch the boys if I did get the job. "Give me five minutes. I'll call you right back."

I phone Charlotte and get right to the point. Charlotte's delighted for me, thinks it's exactly what I need. "I don't have the actual days yet," I add. "They'll tell me after they make up the shoot schedule. That is, if I get the job. I have a go-see with them tomorrow at two—"

"Do you need Brick to pick the boys up from school tomorrow?"

I hadn't thought that far, but yes, probably. And Charlotte assures me that Brick would be happy to get them, that he enjoys his time with them, that they both love spending time with the boys. It feels as if Charlotte's trying a little too hard, but I'm grateful for the support. I thank her, hang up, and call Rae back to let her know I'll be at tomorrow's go-see as planned.

The morning's phone calls have eaten up more time than I anticipated, and I know we're going to be late as I drive the boys to school. Bo and Coop don't mind being late, but Hank's bummed because he has PE first period and the PE teacher will make him run a lap for every minute he's late.

"Sorry, bud," I say, pulling into the high school parking

lot and heading for the front office, where he'll have to go to get a late admittance pass.

Hank barely looks at me as he climbs out of the truck.

I roll down my window, call to him, "I really am sorry—"

"I know. It's okay," he shouts as he walks away.

So why don't I feel better?

The next day after dropping the boys at school, I return home to start getting ready for the appointment. In my bedroom, I strip off my white T-shirt and step out of my gray sweatpants and start to head for the shower when I catch sight of my reflection in the bureau mirror.

It's an old mirror and cloudy at the edges, but I have no trouble seeing me.

I'm thin. Quite thin. Scrawny and scary thin, and I pray they won't ask me to put on a swimsuit today.

But there's nothing I can do about my scrawny frame right now. If I get the job, I can definitely exercise and get toned again. I have three weeks. But first I need to get the job.

The brisk shower helps calm me, but my spirits remain low as I dry off and pull on honey slacks and a loose cashmere V-necked sweater. Dressed, I look at myself in the mirror and force a smile, then pose and smile. I can do this, get through this go-see, but I could use a little polish. Get that top-model sheen back.

Sitting at the desk in the kitchen, I'm able to book a thirty-minute massage followed by a manicure/pedicure and then a professional blowout at a midpriced spa in a not-so-ritzy part of Dallas. It's a chunk of change, but

I'm glad I spent it as I leave the spa feeling sleek and successful.

I arrive twenty minutes early at Neiman Marcus's corporate office at Marcus Square on Main Street for the go-see and breeze through the session knowing I look healthy and relaxed. I'm grateful that my long hair, one of my best features, hangs in a silken shimmer down my back.

The artistic director overseeing the resort catalog is pleased by what he sees, as Rae calls me ten minutes after I've left the appointment to say that everyone loved me and I'm confirmed for the shoot. Once my actual shoot dates are set, they'll have their corporate travel agent book my flight and hotel and then courier the details to me in a packet.

I'm thrilled by the news. Feel downright victorious. This is the sort of thing John and I used to celebrate, too. Whenever I'd get booked for a big job, John would make reservations at one of our favorite restaurants. We'd order a really good bottle of wine and toast the achievement and talk about the opportunity. I used to love how he made sure we savored the successes and celebrated the accomplishments. It's something I don't do anymore, but I should. There's no reason I can't celebrate on my own or with the boys. No reason I can't change it up and celebrate my way.

By the time I get home, the sun is sinking and the hills and trees are more gold than green. I park next to Brick's truck and head inside. Cooper's in a chair in the living room, watching the previously recorded Professional Bull Rider's Built Ford Tough Series from last weekend in Clovis, California, and Bo is flipping through *Sports Illustrated*.

"Mom, did you know that Guilherme Marchi got a ninety-two on his final ride on Sunday? You should have seen it. The bull was insane. Totally rank."

I smile at his use of rank. A rank bull is a tough bull, a fierce bull, a bull that riders love and loathe, because that's the kind of bull you get your big scores on. But it's also the kind of bull that injures you. "Good for Marchi," I answer, aware from Coop's updates that the Brazilian rider is one of today's big stars.

Dropping my car coat and handbag on the nearest chair, I ask if they're hungry.

"Starving," Bo answers, still flipping through his magazine.

The TV show has gone to commercial, and Cooper stands up to stretch. "Uncle Brick said you were taking us out, and we want to go to the Kountry Kitchen." As he stretches, his shirt pulls out of the waistband of his jeans, revealing thin ribs and hip bones. "Wednesday nights they offer a free slice of pie with every entrée."

"That's fine with me. But where's Hank?" I ask.

"In here. With Uncle Brick," Hank shouts from the kitchen. "And I'm hungry. When are we going?"

I head to the kitchen and find Hank hanging out with Brick. "I'm ready anytime," I answer, then look at Brick. "Are you free? Want to go with us?"

"Char's dragging me to a cocktail party being given by someone at the hospital."

"Next time," I say, checking my smile. Brick's a family man, dreads the social scene.

Coop hates to leave the televised PBR program, but he's hungry, too, so we leave a few minutes later for

Mineral Wells. Only a half dozen tables are filled at the Kountry Kitchen Café, a place that's been around as long as I've been alive.

Two waitresses are working tonight, and one of them knows Hank from high school. She comes to the door to greet and seat us. She's young and blond and cute—Traci is her name—and she chatters to Hank as she shows us to a table in her section. "Hey, Hank," she says to him, blushing and smiling. "How are you?"

"Good," he answers gruffly, shooting us an embarrassed look.

"Is this your family?" Traci asks, leading us to a big booth in the corner.

He nods, cheeks flushed.

Traci darts me a shy look as she passes out the menus. "My dad still has the *SI* swimsuit issues with you in it. You were his favorite swimsuit model."

"That's nice to hear," I answer, always amazed that people remember me. I enjoyed my work and still love it when I get the chance to be in front of the camera, but I never felt like a star or top model. I'm not sure if it's because John and I had the boys so early in our marriage or if it's my personality, but being a mom has mattered more to me than anything I've achieved in my career. "Tell your dad I'm flattered, and thank you."

My boys are turning red now. They hate it when they hear about me in swimsuits, particularly Bo, who loves *SI*'s annual swimsuit issue and can't stand to think that I used to be one of those hot girls in the skimpy suit and body paint.

"I've always wanted to go to New York. Did you like living there?" Traci asks, lingering at our table.

"I did," I answer. "There's so much to do, and everything's close."

"Did you ride the subway?"

"Every day."

"And you weren't scared?"

She's too cute, I think. So earnest and eager to know more about the world. "No. There's always people around, and most folks are pretty helpful."

She asks me a couple of questions, then rattles off the dinner specials before leaving to fill our drink order.

"She's pretty," Bo says, watching Traci walk away. "Does she have a boyfriend?"

"She's older than you," Hank answers.

"So?"

"So she's not going to want to go out with you."

Before things escalate into a full-blown argument, I change the subject and tell the boys about my trip to Puerto Rico, the days I'll be gone, and how Brick and Charlotte will be staying with them and making sure everything goes smoothly. Bo wants to go with me; he loves to travel. Cooper says he'll miss me. Hank asks if there's any way he can go stay with his dad.

"It's only for four or five days, guys. I'll be back before you know it, and maybe this summer we can take a trip somewhere together."

"Like where?" Cooper asks.

"How about a cruise," Bo suggests. "I bet there's lots of girls on cruises."

"Or Hawaii." Even Hank's interested. "We could go to a couple different islands. We've been to the Caribbean before, but never Hawaii."

They're still bouncing ideas around when I spot a big black truck park at the curb outside. Dane's truck.

I feel an icy tingle that's more pain than pleasure.

I hate that he does this to me. Hate that I can't seem to escape him. It'd be one thing if I didn't feel anything when I saw him, but I do feel. I feel so much that it makes me hurt.

This can't be normal, I think, watching him climb from his truck. Can't be healthy. Can't be good.

And worse, he let Cooper down. Cooper, who has never asked for anything or wanted anything or been a problem. Cooper, who just tries to get along and make things easier, make things better.

My eyes sting and I bite down into my lower lip, mad, so mad.

"I'll be right back," I say, voice rough as I slide from the booth.

"Where are you going?" Bo asks, but I don't answer. I'm too intent on getting outside to confront Dane.

He's heading into the taco shop next door when I physically put myself between him and the front door. He's big and so broad-shouldered that he practically fills the doorway. There's not a lot of room for both of us, and I lock my knees to keep from backing away.

"You were supposed to call," I say huskily, aware of the size and shape of him, the warmth of him, and the scent that's all his—hay, leather, spice, and man.

Love this man.

Hate this man.

Love to hate this man.

My throat seals closed and I swallow hard, swallow to

make the lump go away. "Coop waited all week for you to call."

Dane stares down at me, looks momentarily baffled, and then his expression clears. "It's been two days."

"Six. Today's Friday, and you said you'd call on Sunday."

His powerful shoulders shift. "I got busy."

The brusqueness of his answer stings like lemon juice on a cut. My spine stiffens, my shoulders square. "You got busy?"

There's no apology in his expression. He's a hard man, far harder than I remembered. "I run a big business, Shey. I travel. Meet people. Have appointments."

I look at him, shake my head a little. I know what big business is. I used to have that life and those responsibilities. But a promise is a promise, and anger whips through me. "You could have let him down that night. Just told him no then. Instead you strung him along—"

"I just met the kid, Shey. Don't put that on me."

I've known Dane my whole life, and he can be tough, but right now he's just ugly. *The* kid. *My* kid. No one talks about Coop like that. "Screw you, Kelly."

His eyes spark and his jaw tightens. It crosses my mind that if I were a man, he'd probably take a swing at me. I almost wish he would so I could swing back. Because there's so much I want to say. So much I want to get out.

But a glance over my shoulder shows me my three sons all watching from the café, their faces practically pressed to the glass. With another shake of my head, I turn around and walk back to the restaurant, my heart pounding with every step I take.

I hate Dane Kelly. I do.

But once inside the café, as I take my seat at the table, Cooper looks past me to Dane's truck. "What did you say to him?" Coop asks uncomfortably.

"Nothing," I answer, reaching for the sweetener to add to my iced tea.

Bo and Hank exchange glances. "Didn't look like nothing," Hank says. "You looked pissed."

I cringe at his word choice. Hate the word *pissed*. "It doesn't matter." I force a smile, will my pulse to return to normal, because I am still worked up, still fighting mad.

Cooper is still staring anxiously at me. "You didn't say anything about me, did you? You didn't tell him I was hurt or upset? Because that would just embarrass me, Mom."

I exhale slowly, silently. "I didn't do anything to embarrass you. You can relax. Okay?"

Every Sunday at one, Mama calls to catch up, which is her way of checking up on me. This Sunday is no exception. "What did you all do this morning, Shey Lynne?"

I know what she's asking. She's asking if I went to church, even though she knows I didn't. But she wants to make me say it. She's dying for the opportunity to point out my shortcomings. Again.

"Made the boys farmers' eggs and your sour cream coffee cake," I answer, trying to distract her from her goal. "The one with the cinnamon-and-brown-sugar topping—"

"I know which one."

"I haven't made it in a while, and I forgot how good it is. Really moist. I saved Brick and Charlotte a slice, but the rest is already gone—"

"Is that all you've done today?"

"Well, no. I did the dishes and I'm just about to mop the kitchen floor."

"Shey Lynne, this is the Lord's day."

"Yes, ma'am."

"Did you take those boys to church?"

"No, ma'am."

"Are you being smart with me?"

"No, Mama. But we do this every week, and every week I tell you that I'm not going to take the boys—"

"Then how about yourself? Because honey, I know you're struggling. You're not yourself. Not happy—"

"How do you know? You're not even here."

"I have ears and eyes."

And spies. Charlotte, I think. Probably Brick and Blue, too. Oh, why? Why do they all talk to Mama about us? I can't ever please her, have never made her happy. "I don't know who's telling you what, but I'm doing all right, Mama. I wouldn't call this my favorite year, but we're getting through it."

She doesn't answer, which makes me uneasy. If Mama's not talking, she's thinking something that's bound to make me miserable. "How's your day, Mama? What are your plans?"

"I'm going to come stay with the boys when you're on your modeling trip," Mama announces. "Don't worry about changing the sheets. I can do that myself. Just leave me the boys' schedule and I'll make sure they'll get to where they need to be—"

"That's sweet of you," I interrupt with a gulp, "but I don't want to put you out, and Brick and Charlotte are already planning on being here with the kids."

"Put me out? You're not putting me out. I'm your mother!"

"Yes, but Brick and Charlotte—"

"Both have jobs. They've got plenty of work to do without taking on more responsibility. And this is why you moved back home, to have family around to help you. So let me help, Shey Lynne, and stop treating me like a stranger."

I know when the battle's lost. With a silent apology to the boys, I raise the white flag of surrender. "Yes, Mama."

"So when do you fly out?"

"I don't have the final dates yet, but they were saying sometime around the twenty-fourth or twenty-fifth."

"Which would be three weeks from today."

My heart sinks. "That sounds about right."

"I'll arrive on Saturday the twenty-third, then. That'll give us time to get everything in order."

"Yes, Mama."

I hang up the phone and rub my face. I'm not happy. But the boys...they're really not going to be happy.

I've no sooner hung up from talking to Mama than the phone rings again. It's Charlotte. "Shey, I don't know how to tell you this, but Mama found out about your trip to Puerto Rico and she's planning on coming to stay while you're gone. She wants to help with the boys."

"She's already called with the good news."

I can feel Charlotte wince. "Sorry, Shey. Mama was trying to get us to come visit her in Jefferson for Halloween, and I told her we couldn't because we were helping you out. I should have known she'd see it as an opportunity to move in for a week."

I hear the distress in her voice. "Not your fault. Mama's strong-willed. If she wants to do something, she does it." And that's an understatement.

I hesitate. "Char, something happened last Wednesday that's been eating at me. I wanted to get your feedback, see if I was out of line."

"What happened?"

"I kind of had a run-in with Dane Friday night." I take a deep breath and quickly add, "I got so mad at him. Told him to screw himself."

"Why?"

"He's so different, Charlotte. He's not the Dane I knew. The Dane Kelly I knew would never have dated someone like Lulu Davies or forgotten a promise he made to a kid. What's happened to him?"

"He hasn't had an easy life, Shey. Things were never good with Shellie Ann, but losing Matthew pretty much did him in."

"But why did he lose custody of Matthew in the first place? I don't understand why a judge would award custody to Shellie Ann—"

"Matthew's dead," Charlotte interrupts.

"Dead?" I gasp, feeling as if she's just thrown ice water in my face.

"He died twelve years ago."

"No one told me."

"But I did. I told you he was gone. I said Dane had lost Matthew—"

"I thought you meant in the divorce! I thought he was

living with Shellie Ann in Austin." I feel sick now, sick and ashamed. I had no idea, and it changes everything. "How did he die? Was there an accident?"

"Matthew was born with special needs." Charlotte sighs, remembering. "He always needed a lot of care. His outlook was never good, but he lived a couple years longer than anybody thought. He died just before his fifth birthday."

Oh God. "I didn't know."

"Dane's never been the same since. He became reckless on the circuit, took stupid risks in the ring, or maybe he just lost focus. Either way he got trampled. It was pretty bad. Dane was out the rest of that season—must have been in 1998—had surgery, battled through rehab, returned the following year just to get hurt all over again. Yes, the man's wounded, but his hip isn't the problem."

As Charlotte talks, I feel worse and worse. I shouldn't have jumped all over Dane that way. Shouldn't have been so angry or aggressive. I was just feeling protective of Cooper. I hadn't realized that Dane's boy died.

No wonder Dane wasn't exactly jumping at the chance to work with mine.

My chest feels tight. My heart actually hurts. I don't want to feel sorry for Dane. Don't want to forgive him for being a jerk. But to lose a child...

I think of my boys, and I couldn't lose them. Not one. As it is, I don't know what I'll do when they move out.

But for one to die?

Unthinkable.

"I think I owe Dane an apology," I say in a small voice.

"He'll forgive you, Shey. Dane couldn't stay mad at you even if he tried."

*   *   *

The next morning, I'm still feeling bad for losing my temper with Dane. After dropping the boys off at school, I make an impulsive turn off 180, taking one of the back roads that cuts to Dane's property. I didn't plan on seeing him when I left home this morning, but guilt eats at me. I feel like a jerk for what I said to him.

It takes me fifteen minutes on the back roads to reach Dane's ranch. He has a decent spread of several thousand acres. It was once three times its size, but Dane's father sold off a couple of big parcels in the early eighties when beef prices tumbled and the cost of raising calves rose 15 percent. The early eighties were tough on Texas cattle ranchers, and many farmers and ranchers went bankrupt. Those who didn't struggled mightily owing to the shortage of winter pastures, high grain prices, and drought. Things turned around in 1988, and the cattle market became bullish for seven years, then struggled again in 1995. But that's the nature of cattle ranching. Up and down, down and up. It's all cyclical.

I haven't been to Dane's ranch in years and am shocked to see that the Kellys' simple ranch house is gone, replaced with a rugged two-story limestone mansion topped by a steep metal roof that glints in the sun. For a moment, I think I have the wrong place—maybe Dane sold these front acres—and then I see his big truck off to the side of the circular driveway.

The black truck's silver bed brightly reflects the morning light just like the roof, and I pull up next to his truck only to find a little red sports car already parked there.

The red sports car throws me. It's the same car Dane was leaning against the night of Blue's party, and I'm suddenly not so sure that appearing on his doorstep is a good idea. Maybe the apology would have been better made over the phone.

I let Pop's truck idle as I reconsider dropping in. It's not too late to go. I think I should go. But before I can reverse, the front door opens and Dane and Lulu step out.

She's talking to him and he's got his head turned, listening and smiling at her in a way he doesn't smile at me. She says something that makes him laugh, and my heart stutters to a stop.

He likes her. Maybe even loves her. The pain is shocking. The pain reminds me of the moment when John told me he was in love with someone else.

I'd vanish if I could. I'd snap my fingers and make Pop's dilapidated truck disappear with me inside. But there's no disappearing, not when the red rusting truck is right in the middle of the driveway, blocking access to their cars.

And now Dane looks up, sees me, and I give him a big hard smile so he won't know I'm feeling like the biggest fool there is.

Dane says something to Lulu, and she stops walking and he moves on alone toward me.

I fix my gaze on his cane as I fight to regain my composure.

"Hey," I say, cursing myself as I roll my window down. "How are you doing?"

He's definitely guarded. "Fine. You okay?"

"Yeah, oh, yeah, great." God, I'm stupid. I take a deep breath, inject a breezy note into my voice. "I was just in the neighborhood and thought I'd stop by."

He leans on my sill. "You were in the neighborhood."

Looking at him, I can see why I once loved him. He's big and tough and oh, so handsome with those eyes, lips, and jaw. "Yeah."

"Kind of a big neighborhood."

"Yeah."

His gaze travels slowly over my face, and I see something in his eyes, but I don't understand it. Don't understand him anymore. "Shey, what are you doing here?"

This is so awkward. I hate myself around him. Hate that he makes me feel so much, hate that I'm always so emotional. "I wanted to apologize for snapping at you Friday night. I was wrong. I'm sorry I didn't handle the situation better."

"You were pretty hot under the collar."

"Cooper was hurt and I, well…I went into my crazy mama bear mode. Protecting the young and all." I swallow hard, struggle to smile. "Kind of lost it, though. Sorry."

"Your boy was pretty hurt?"

My chest aches. I nod. "He's such a good kid. He never asks for anything."

"And I let him down."

"It's okay. I should have known…should have…" I look away, bite my lip, worried that the tears aren't far off. "I didn't realize—" I break off, unable to finish the thought.

"You didn't realize what?"

I shake my head. "I just wouldn't have let him impose. I wouldn't have let him ask you…"

"If what?"

"If I'd known about Matthew—" My voice breaks. "I'm sorry."

He doesn't speak. He just looks at me, and his eyes are

green, a beautiful bottle green. "You love your boys," he says after the longest moment.

"With all my heart."

"You're a good mom."

"I try," I answer, my voice husky. I glance to Lulu, who is waiting surprisingly patiently. "I don't want to keep you. I know you're on your way out."

"You take care, Shey."

My lower lip threatens to tremble, and I bite it hard. "You too." And then, because I'm terrified I'm about to fall apart in his driveway, I quickly roll up the window, back the truck up, and pull away from the house.

Chapter Eleven

I'm on my way home from Dane's when Pop's old truck dies, leaving me stranded on the side of the 180.

I call Brick, who comes to get me. After looking under the rusting hood, he calls Bern's Towing to have the truck taken to Manny's Auto Shop in Mineral Wells.

"We need to get you your own car," he says as we wait for the tow truck. "Something new and reliable—"

"I don't need a new car."

"Then a decent used car. But Pop's truck is as old as Moses and it's not going to get any younger."

I just shake my head. The last thing I want to do is buy a car, any car, especially if we end up returning to New York.

"Let's just see what Manny says," I answer. Having gone to school with Manny Ramirez, I know him and trust him implicitly. Manny was a running back on the high school football team when I attended Mineral Wells, back when Mineral Wells had a good team. And he's worked on our family cars ever since he took over his uncle's auto business fifteen years ago.

Since Brick needs his truck today, he drops me at the house and heads to Fort Worth, where he has meetings at the stockyard. But he has assured me he'll get the boys from school on his way home.

I'm frustrated being back at the house, though, especially without wheels. We're definitely isolated on the
ranch, and I don't like being trapped in the country without
wheels. It reminds me of being grounded as a teenager.

I zip through the house, gathering dirty clothes and
dirty dishes, and start a load of laundry before I tackle
unloading the dishwasher. The dishwasher's heat cycle
died years ago, so I dry every dish by hand.

I'm stacking plates when the kitchen phone rings. I
move to answer, only to trip over the open dishwasher door
and slam my shin against the side. I yelp in pain as I pick
up. "Hello?"

"Shey?"

I'll always know his voice. It's the pitch and the diction,
a little slow and very rich, like warm molasses. "Dane."

"You okay?"

"Noooo. Yes."

"So which is it?"

"Both," I say, laughing to keep from crying as I hop
around.

"Need first aid?"

"Can you come administer some?"

His chuckle is soft and sexy and makes me shiver with
delight. "How serious is the injury?"

"I might need a Band-Aid."

He laughs his sexy laugh again. "That is a call to action."

I stop hopping to rub my shin where it's tender. "So
what can I do for you, Mr. Kelly?"

"I wanted to apologize to Cooper personally."

"He's at school."

"I know, and I'll call him this afternoon. But I wanted

to talk to you first, let you know I'm sorry and you had every right to be upset. If someone slighted my boy, I'd feel the same way."

I'm touched and also flustered by the apology. "It's okay. Coop pretty much ambushed you."

"He's a boy. That's how boys operate."

"He'll appreciate the call," I say. "It'll restore you to hero status as well."

Dane is silent a long time, and then he clears his throat. "That's just it, Shey. I'm not a hero, and I get real uncomfortable when folks try to make me one."

"But you are a hero to folks who love the rodeo."

"You're not a hero because you last eight seconds on the back of a bull. Heroes are people who've done great things. I've never saved anyone."

He's angry. Angry with himself. And I don't understand it at first until it hits me—he's talking about Matthew.

He's never saved anyone. Meaning he couldn't save his own son.

"It's hard being a parent," I say slowly, trying to think of the right words but not sure what those words would be. I don't know this Dane. The Dane I knew was a gorgeous but rugged cowboy, an uncomplicated man who lived, breathed, and slept riding and competing. His focus was the chute and the eight seconds that followed, and I wanted him in the most simplistic, physical way. Now we're twenty years older and tested by life. "You end up questioning everything you do, as well as everything you don't do."

He exhales. "Isn't that the truth."

His voice has always been deep, but right now it vibrates with emotion. I don't answer immediately, struck by the changes in us, struck by the difficulty of life. We're not the same, but I take no solace in that. The spiritualists might say suffering is good for the soul, but I find it overrated.

"I am sorry, Dane," I repeat because I don't know what else to say.

We say good-bye then, and I hang up the phone feeling a hundred times worse than before he called. Dane isn't who I remembered. Twenty-three years ago he was young and physical and exuded sex. I loved his swagger and that delicious chemistry between us. All I wanted to do was look at him. Watch him. Listen to him. Be near him. It was a thrill. Heady, forbidden, exciting.

It didn't cross my mind that life would be any other way. That we could change. That love could disappoint. There were no layers to us, nothing to challenge us other than ourselves.

The phone rings again. "What are you doing right now?" Dane asks roughly.

My heart squeezes so hard, my breath catches in my throat. If I'm not careful, he could break what's left of my heart. "I'm standing in my kitchen."

I can practically feel his smile over the phone, and it gives me a jolt of pleasure. "How about lunch?"

"Now?"

"Yes."

God, I'd love, love, love to go—but I'm stranded. There's not another working vehicle on the property. "Pop's truck broke down this morning on the 180 on my way home from your place. Brick had it towed to Manny's, so I'm without wheels."

"That's not a problem. I'll come get you."

"You will?"

"Yeah. See you in a half hour."

I'm so excited that it's embarrassing, but since no one's around to witness my silliness, I turn on the iPod stereo next to my bed, cranking up the volume on the Faith Hill CD while I change. I sing as I wriggle out of my ratty Levi's and blue T-shirt and dance as I wriggle into a pair of less tattered Wranglers and a black peasant-style blouse with colorful embroidery at the collar and wrists.

It's absurd that I feel so happy just to be going to lunch with Dane, but it's been a long time since I felt this way— light, young, good.

Good.

Humming along to the song, I pull my hair into a pony- tail and then pull out bits to frame my face. With little diamond studs in my ears and mascara and lip gloss, I'm ready, which leaves me ten minutes to pace outside until Dane arrives in his hulking black truck.

I take a quick, nervous breath as his truck appears in the drive, the big tires crunching gravel and kicking up clouds of reddish dust.

Dane spots me in the shade by the house, and I jam my hands in my pockets, feigning nonchalance as he slows. Can't believe we're going to lunch. Can't believe he's driven a half hour just to pick me up.

He leans over to open the passenger door from the inside, and a lock of thick honey hair falls forward on his brow. He's not wearing his hat today, and his eyes are the deepest sea green. "Hope you're hungry," he says.

I'm hot and nervous, skin all prickly as I climb into his truck. "I could eat."

"How's Dixie's sound?"

"Great." Adrenaline's pumping as I shut the door behind me. I glance at him quickly, nervously. "Thanks for picking me up."

He smiles, and the creases at his eyes deepen. I don't know how it's possible, but he's better looking now at forty-five than he was at twenty-two. I don't miss the cockiness of youth, appreciating instead that he's a man in his prime—mature and comfortable in his skin.

"You're only a little out of the way," he says with that slow smile.

My insides do a free fall all over again, and I fumble with the seat belt. It takes me a few attempts before I'm able to get it buckled. I look at him from the corner of my eye to see if he's noticed. He has.

Relax, I tell myself. Come on, pull it together.

He shoots me an amused glance. "You okay?"

"Yeah."

"You sure?"

"I'll settle down. Just give me a minute."

"What's got you so jumpy?" he asks as we head down the lane away from the house, beneath the high canopy of seventy-year-old oak trees, the thick limbs gnarled, the sun poking through the leaves dappling the road.

I give him a long look. "You."

"Me?"

"Yes, you. You're a problem."

"*I'm* a problem."

I laugh at the way he repeats me, as well as his incredulous tone. I'd forgotten how he always made me laugh. "Yes. You've made me crazy since the first day I met you—"

"Shey, you were two," he answers dryly.

The laughter bubbles up in me again. "You know what I mean."

"Yes, unfortunately, I do."

"This is going to be a disaster."

"You just need some ribs. You'll be fine."

I can't help smiling at him. I'd forgotten that I could feel like this. Light and funny, clever and strong. Maybe that's Dane's magic. He's always made me feel special.

He glances at me. "It's nice to hear you laugh, Shey."

The hot, bright emotion rushes through me again, and it's overwhelming. "It's nice to laugh. It's been a while."

"I take it you're still modeling?"

"I wasn't doing a lot of work in New York lately—there are so many models to choose from there. But I've been able to get booked for some good jobs here. I guess I'm lucky."

"Not lucky. You're beautiful."

I close my eyes, fight the emptiness and the longing and all the needs that have gone unmet for so long. "You shouldn't pay me compliments like that. They'll turn my head."

"Good."

"Oh, Dane."

"What, darlin'?"

He sounds exactly like the man I fell in love with. Sexy and rugged and yet tender, too, and it makes my heart ache. "It's been a rough year," I confess huskily. "I miss how things were. I miss who I used to be."

"You're still the same Shey."

"Then why don't I feel like me?"

"Because you're hanging on to the negative stuff, lingering on the bad feelings. But you can't get hung up on the bad. You've got to let it go, otherwise you're toast."

We emerge just then from the dappled shade into the dazzling glaze of sunlight. "So you can let the bad stuff go now?"

"No. Not always. But it's the goal."

Dixie's is a little barbecue joint in Mineral Wells operating out of a converted A&W restaurant. The exterior is white. The interior is white with red picnic tables and benches. There's no artwork to speak of, just a huge menu handwritten on the wall. Dixie's serves ribs and brisket along with a choice of barbecue sauces, thick and tangy, hot and spicy, sweet or smoky.

In Texas, beef reigns supreme. Texas barbecue is synonymous with beef brisket, and the best pit masters don't even bother with sauces or rubs. They rely on time and wood smoke—up to eighteen hours in the pit. Tommy Johns, the owner of Dixie's, moved from Memphis and brought along his love of ribs, particularly the dry rib, a rack of spareribs cooked with rub instead of sauce, which is what we order today.

Dane pays for lunch, and I carry our plastic tumblers of iced tea to an open spot on one of the red tables. Fans whir overhead and from high on the walls. The air feels good on the back of my neck, and I tip my head back, exhale.

Dane joins me at the table, shifting his cane to the side to take a seat on the bench. I can see that he's not comfortable, at least not right away. He shifts his weight, extends his leg, and then catches me staring.

"Something wrong?" he drawls.

"Just watching you."

"You always were all eyes."

I smile. "I can't help it. You're nice to look at."

He shakes his head. "See? You haven't changed. You're still the same Shey. Beautiful, stubborn, and headstrong."

I study him, thinking I've loved his face for as long as I can remember—such strong cheekbones and jaw, with that straight nose and beautiful mouth. I love his mouth and the way his whole face is put together. "Are you and Lulu pretty serious?" I blurt.

He gives me a pointed look.

I push on. "She doesn't seem right for you."

"You don't know her."

"But I do know she married a man nearly fifty years older than her. What thirty-two-year-old woman wants to be with an eighty-year-old man?"

He shakes his head at me. "Nice southern girls are supposed to make polite conversation."

"I guess I'm not a nice southern girl anymore."

The edge of his mouth lifts. "Your mama won't want to hear that."

"Mama's never happy with me no matter what I do."

"So why did you come home, then?"

"When we came back for Cody's funeral in June, it just felt right. I was home. I was back where I belonged. And Brick and Blue were wonderful with the boys. It made me realize that I've missed having my family around, missed being part of the family. I thought that living here would be a positive change. It would give the kids time to adjust to their dad's new life, and allow me to spend more time with them as well. In New York I worked a lot, especially when I was younger. Here on the ranch I'm with them every day."

"So their dad has a new woman?"

"No. Their dad has..." I take a deep breath and plunge ahead, "A new man." I see Dane's stunned expression and try to ignore the sick feeling I get just talking about John. "It's been hard. The boys aren't sure what to think."

"Your husband's... gay?"

My smile isn't entirely steady. "Apparently so."

"Was he always?"

"He said he suspected, but he fought it, and thought with me he could be straight." I squirm a little, finding the conversation uncomfortable, knowing that everyone is wondering whether John and I had sex—and yes, we did, and yes, the sex was fine. Was it brilliant or mind-blowing? No. But did I enjoy it? Yes.

I glance at him, shoulders lifting and falling. "And no, I had no idea he might be gay. We had a normal relationship, a good marriage. A great marriage. He was my partner. My best friend."

"How many years were you married?"

"It would have been seventeen this year."

"Sounds like you were happy."

"I was. Very."

"That must have made your husband's announcement a shocker."

"A huge one."

The man at the counter calls our number, and I get our food.

We don't talk a lot as we eat. Ribs are messy and I'm doing a fair amount of finger licking, but Dane's doing the same thing. "Feel better, darlin'?" he asks after I've used one of the little wet towels to wipe my hands clean.

"I do. Guess you were right. I just needed some ribs."

He flashes a smile at me, and I get that wild adrenaline rush all over again. He's so damn hot. It's really not fair. "Were you happy with Shellie Ann?"

Dane had just started to rise, but he sits back down. He doesn't immediately answer, and then when he does, he picks his words with care. "We tried hard to make it work. But it was never an easy relationship. It was never like—" He breaks off, swallowing whatever else he was going to say. "Finished?" he asks instead, rising.

I look up at him, imagine how he might have finished the thought. But there's little point in fantasizing about us. There was never an "us"—we flirted for years and only had that one month of dates, which doesn't make a relationship.

We step out into the sunshine, and it's warm and the sky is a clear bright blue. It's a gorgeous day, and I tip my head back to take it all in. I love October, love this time of year.

Back in the truck, Dane asks me about my upcoming modeling trip. "Are Brick and Char watching your boys when you're in Puerto Rico?"

"No. Mama is." I see Dane's expression, and my lips curve ruefully. "I know. I feel the same way. And I'm worried. Hank and Coop will be fine with her for five days, but Bo...I don't know. He needs special handling. A little more patience. A lot more supervision. I'm worried Mama's not going to understand. I'm afraid there'll be a big blowup."

"Her or him?"

"Him. Then her."

"Does he blow up often?"

"No, not with me. But that's because I know Bo and I don't push him too far. When I see he's about to melt down, I back off, give him an out." I sigh, feel the weight on my chest, the pressure always there. "Brick says I'm too soft on him. Blue says the same thing. But Bo really struggles, far more than the other two, and I have to be careful with him, and vigilant."

"Don't worry about what other people say. You're his mom. He's your responsibility. Trust your instincts."

"That's what I'm doing."

"Then you're doing the right thing."

I don't know why, but that makes me feel so much better. I shift on the seat, pull one leg up under me, and we drive in companionable silence until we turn off 180 onto Turkey Flat Road, which leads to the ranch. We'll be home in just a few minutes, and I'm not ready for the trip to end. I loved being with him today. Loved talking to him. Looking at him. Just hanging out with him.

We hit one of the potholes in the road, and his cane slides off the seat. He reaches down and retrieves it, leaning it against the bench seat. His hand is strong, callused, and tan. It's also scarred. He's a fighter, not a quitter, and I can only imagine the fight he must have made for his son.

"I wish I could have met him," I say, the ranch house coming into view.

Dane glances at me as we pass beneath the shady canopy of the oak trees.

"Matthew," I say.

We pull in front of the house, and Dane shifts the car into neutral. "He was the best boy," he replies after a moment.

I look at him, wishing there were something I could

say, some comfort I could give. But I can think of nothing. His son has been gone more than ten years now, yet I can tell that the grief is still there.

I reach for my purse and then the door handle but then hesitate. "How do you bear it?"

He doesn't speak immediately, stares instead at the old barn and stables. Then, as the silence stretches to a breaking point, Dane looks at me. There's sorrow etched in his features, burned into his eyes. "The truth is, sometimes I don't."

The lump returns to my throat. "You still think about him a lot?"

"Every single day."

I sit for a moment, feeling his pain. Then, when it's too much, I open the door. "Thanks for the ribs."

The corner of his mouth lifts in a ghostly smile. "Anytime, darlin'."

I force a smile, lift my hand in a farewell gesture, and enter the ranch house knowing that Dane Kelly owns far more of my heart than he should.

Late that afternoon as I'm making dinner, Dane calls to talk to Coop, and they're on the phone for nearly ten minutes before Cooper hands me the phone. "He wants to talk to you," Cooper tells me, clearly anxious that this conversation go well. "Whatever it is, say yes."

I give him a look as I take the phone. "Dane, it's Shey."

"I had a good talk with Cooper and I've agreed to work with him three times a week for a couple hours each session. In exchange I expect him to pitch in around here, shadow my guys, learn what he can about raising livestock.

I thought we'd start next Monday. I've got the ropes, spurs, gloves, strapping tape, and so on. But he should have his own helmet, mouth guard, and face guard. Not everyone uses the helmet and face guard, but I think it should be mandatory, especially for juniors."

"We'll get them this week," I answer, grateful and touched that he's agreed to work with Coop after all. "What about chaps and vest?"

"I don't think he needs chaps for a while, but a vest, definitely. It's essential for upper-body protection."

"We'll get that, too, and I really appreciate it, Dane. You've made him very happy."

"I'm hoping he'll enjoy it. It's not going to be easy, though. He's a tall kid and coming into it late."

"He knows that. He's prepared." I'm about to say good-bye when I remember that the big State Fair of Texas opened last Friday in Dallas and I was thinking of taking the boys this weekend. "Are you around this weekend?"

"Yes and no. Why?"

"I was hoping to take the boys to the state fair. Wondered if you'd want to go with us." Part ag-fest, part carnival, the State Fair of Texas is a twenty-four-day party that even my boys would enjoy. "But there's no pressure, of course," I add quickly.

"I haven't been in years," he answers.

"Neither have I. I think the last time I went was the year I tagged along with you and Brick and Charlotte." I don't add that Dane was dating some redheaded rodeo queen at the time who surprised us all by showing up at the fair halfway into the evening. I was so bummed when she arrived, as it changed the dynamics. Dane had been talking to me and going on the rides with me, and then when she appeared, it all changed. Dane focused on her—Barb, I think her name was—and I became an awkward, and jealous, fifth wheel.

"I have plans on Sunday," he says now, "but could do Saturday."

"Then Saturday it is."

I promise to follow up with him on the exact time after I've talked to my boys, and then I hang up. It's not until I've replaced the phone on the wall that I realize what I've done. I've invited Dane to join us. Included him in our family outing. I smile nervously. This could be good. Or it could be a complete disaster.

Over dinner, I brief the boys on the plans for the weekend. Hank immediately opts out. He doesn't want to attend a gussied-up agriculture event. Bo tries to tell him that it's more of a carnival with the seventy-five rides and two hundred concessions, but Hank won't be swayed. Fortunately, Bo and Cooper are excited. And when I tell them Dane's going to be joining us, too, Coop lets out a whoop of pleasure. "Are you serious?" he demands. "Dane Kelly's going with us? To the fair?"

I laugh at his expression. "Yes."

"Are we all going together or is he meeting us there?"

"I think we're all going in one car."

"Wow. That's so cool."

Even Bo's impressed. "How did you get Dane to say yes?"

I realize the boys don't understand how close we all were and how much time we spent together growing up. Dane Kelly isn't just some cowboy. He was part of the family. He felt like my family. There are few people who meant more to me in my life than he did.

Manny calls the next morning to say he's got Pop's truck running and I can pick it up this afternoon. I phone Brick with the news, and he offers to drop me off in town.

Less than an hour later, Brick's picked me up and we drive in silence for a few miles. I stare out the window at scenery that's as familiar as my backyard. The 180 can be beautiful, but this section just looks neglected, the old highway marked by straggly trees, faded billboards, a rusting, abandoned car, and a gas station that was boarded up long ago.

"You're pretty quiet today," Brick comments, shifting gears as we approach the outskirts of Mineral Wells.

I lean back, extend my legs, study the tips of my scuffed boots. "Just relaxed. Happy."

He shoots me a quick glance. "You look happy."

"Yeah, I am. It's nice for a change."

A minute passes, and another, then Brick clears his throat. "Do those nice feelings have anything to do with your lunch with Dane?"

I get a sinking feeling in my gut. "What lunch?"

"Yesterday's date with Dane."

"It wasn't a date."

"At Dixie's," he continues, glancing at me, his expression inscrutable. "You had to know I'd find out."

"It was just lunch," I say, staring out the window. This isn't something I want to discuss with Brick.

"So you aren't going to the fair with him this weekend? And Coop's not training with him starting Monday?"

Sounds like Cooper was running off at the mouth this morning as Brick drove the boys to school. "Why can't we be friends with him?"

"Because you and Dane have never just been 'friends.' There's always been something more there, and the fact is, if you spend time together, whether it's you and him, or your kids and him, people are going to talk."

"Give me a break."

"Shey, you've been in New York too long if you think folks won't. This is a small town, and you and Dane are big celebrities."

"I'm not a celebrity—"

"No? Then why does your crochet bikini shot still hang in many a garage and tackroom?"

"That crochet bikini shot was a lifetime ago. No one normal would still have it pinned up—"

"Don't say that to Manny. He worked all night on the truck to get it fixed for you."

"Manny's got the photo up?"

"*All* your shots." He sees my shocked expression, shakes his head. "How do you think I feel? I'm your brother, for God's sake. I *know* what guys are thinking when they're staring at your pictures. Especially when they're in the men's room."

A few seconds pass, and I shift uncomfortably. "I take it someone called you after seeing us at Dixie's."

"No. Someone called Blue. Blue called me." Brick shoots me another long look. "*After* calling Mama."

"You're joking." I can't believe Blue called Mama. I slump against the seat. "Why would Blue do that?"

Brick shrugs. "Dane's seeing Lulu, Blue's biggest investor."

"And?"

"If you make trouble between Dane and Lulu, Blue's worried he'll lose Lulu's support."

"That's ridiculous! And what did Mama say?"

The edge of Brick's mouth lifts. "She told Blue to mind his own business."

I sit up straighter. "She didn't!"

His mouth quirks again. "She did. And then she called Charlotte to see if Char knew anything more than what Blue had told her."

Oh, my God. Gossip city. Everyone calling everyone. Everyone knowing everything. "Mama didn't call me."

"She wouldn't, and I doubt she'll say anything to you next time she calls."

"Why not?"

We've come to a red light, and Brick slows and shifts into neutral. We sit in silence, watching the traffic. A blue pickup passes, a silver SUV, a couple of white cars, and a guy on a bike, and then the light changes and Brick accelerates. "Because Mama always thought you'd end up with Dane."

"*What?*"

Brick shrugs and just keeps driving.

Chapter Twelve

———— ✦ ————

Manny's put on a good twenty-five pounds since high school and now sports a trim goatee and a couple of well-placed tattoos. He greets me with a big smile and pulls out his wallet to show me pictures of his five kids.

"Five, Manny?" I tease. "You've certainly been busy."

"I have a good wife and beautiful kids. I'm a lucky man."

Manny's always been a good guy, but I like him even better for the pride he takes in his family. "My oldest is a senior at Mineral Wells," he adds, tapping a shot of a serious-looking teenager in a football uniform. "He's in the ROTC program. Joining the army after school. They're going to help pay for college. Junior will be the first one in my family to go to college. I hope the others will, too."

I can't help comparing his son Junior with Hank. Junior's joined the army so he can go to college, while Hank expects the family to leverage the ranch so he can go to prep school. Hank's sense of entitlement mortifies me, and I find myself wishing Hank were more like Junior—willing to do whatever's necessary to go to school instead of asking everyone else to make the sacrifice.

I've screwed up. I haven't taught my kids personal responsibility. I haven't taught them well at all.

*   *   *

The rest of the week passes far more slowly than I'd like. I'm not normally a restless person, but waiting for Saturday makes me downright antsy.

I'm far too excited about Saturday. I have way too many hopes and expectations. I'm going to be disappointed, I know I'll be disappointed, and I try to temper my enthusiasm, reminding myself that just because I'm still attracted to Dane, just because I have lingering feelings for him, doesn't make him an option. The truth is, my life is complicated and my boys are demanding, and I should be focusing only on them. I should make them my sole priority.

Should...

Should...

Should...

The shoulds pile up in my mind, stacking like bricks, weighing on my conscience.

And then I push the shoulds away. It's just a family outing to the fair. I'm not abandoning the boys. I'm not having a hot, illicit date. I've just asked Dane to go to the fair with us. Big deal.

And then I get that little thrill of anticipation when I least expect it, and I know it's not just a big deal. It's a huge deal.

On Saturday, Dane picks us up at four to drive us into Dallas. Because it's been really hot the last few days, I'm wearing a long, slim coral spaghetti-strap sundress that should keep me cool, but I carry a jeans jacket in case I need it later tonight.

Dane's gaze lingers on my bare shoulders as we climb into his truck. "That's a good color on you," he says as the boys settle into the backseat and I take the front.

I see the expression in his green eyes—it's definitely all male—and my insides flip. He's physical and sexual. John was nothing like this. John was sophistication and elegance, but not sex.

Never sex.

And just like a moth drawn to flame, I look up into Dane's eyes again. The heat's still there.

In his eyes I'm beautiful.

In his eyes I'm still young, fierce, headstrong Shey.

Thank God.

Thank God someone, somewhere, still sees the real me. The me I lost. The me I miss.

"You look pretty good, too," I say, cheeks flushed, skin glowing sensitive and hot.

"You like my T-shirt?" he drawls, eyes resting lazily, provocatively, on my face.

I blush again and squirm inwardly. It is just a T-shirt, isn't it? "It's a nice one," I say weakly, thinking I'll never survive a night with him. Not when I feel this much. Not when I want this much.

I dig this guy.

I dig him a lot.

The edge of Dane's mouth curls as if he can read my mind. Then he shifts into drive and we're off.

We enter the fairgrounds at five after six, as it took twenty minutes just to find parking and then another fifteen to walk from where we parked to the main gate. Dane doesn't exactly spring to the entrance, but he does all right with his cane. The boys walk a little ahead of us, discussing what they're going to eat, see, and do. Corn dogs and fried

Twinkies are high on the eat list. Riding the roller coasters are a must on the to-do list. And maybe, just maybe, there will be cute girls here tonight, too. Bo's hands gesture animatedly as he talks. Coop laughs as he listens.

"It's nice to see them having fun together," I say, watching the two joke around. "More often than not, they fight."

"Boys do that," Dane answers.

"It grows old. All the posturing and competing."

"That's testosterone, darlin'."

"I know. Still."

We've reached the front and I move toward the long ticket line, but Dane stops me, shows me that he's already purchased them. "I'm impressed," I say, eyebrows arching. "How did you do that?"

"I'm connected," he answers with a grin, steering us into the fair with the fifty-two-foot-tall cowboy statue everyone calls Big Tex. It's been a fair icon since 1952, and the fair wouldn't be our state fair without it.

The boys want to go straight to the rides, so I hand them each a twenty to buy tickets and let them go ahead to purchase them.

"I was thinking about what you told me about Bo," Dane says as we watch the kids run to get in line at the little ticket booth. "Bo has a problem controlling his temper?"

I can see Bo laughing as he and Cooper jockey for position in line. "Not anger per se, but depression. He was diagnosed a couple years ago and we took him to counseling and it seemed to help, but he hasn't seen anyone since John's and my separation, and I just worry about him. If someone could just guarantee that he'd be okay, that the depression won't return, that he won't be bipolar. If someone could just make it okay..."

"But that's your job," Dane says. "No one can make it okay for you. You have to make it okay."

"How?" There's panic in my voice, panic and desperation.

"By making peace with life, and our lack of control. Because we have no control. We never have. Never will. Sometimes we think we do, but it's an illusion."

I hear what Dane's saying, but he can't be right. Maybe we don't have total control, but we have some, and that has to be enough. Enough to protect our families. Enough to allow us to live happy lives. "I refuse to believe I can't help Bo—"

"Oh, you can try, but you can't protect him, or save him. And sometimes all your best efforts to help won't change the outcome."

"I can't accept that."

"I couldn't either."

Bo has bought his tickets and Coop's purchasing his now. "I won't lose Bo," I say. "I can't. It'd kill me."

"It won't kill you," Dane answers after a moment as the boys run back to meet us. "But there are times you wish it would."

I look up at him. His expression is neutral, but there are shadows in his eyes.

I want to say something, but we're not the people we once were. We lack the easy familiarity of the past, and we haven't spent enough time together to have established anything new. Maybe one day, I tell myself as I take a deep breath to steady my nerves, before reaching out to touch his hand.

*   *   *

Monday after school, I drive Cooper to Dane's place. He's excited and nervous and doesn't talk much on the way there. "You going to be okay?" I ask him as we approach the big stone house.

He's dressed in Wranglers, boots, and a dark denim shirt and has the rest of his gear in a duffel bag. Coop nods his head yes.

I spot Dane's black truck parked down by the barn where he breeds his champion bucking bulls, bulls coveted by the professional rodeo association for their ability to kick, buck, spin, and move. A great bull doesn't kick or jump just in a straight line, but also from side to side. This is what every cowboy hopes to draw, as half the points in the bull-riding event go to the bull and the other half go to the cowboy's skill in sticking to the bull.

As we pull up next to the corral, a handsome red colt runs around the ring, shaking his head and kicking up his heels. I suspect he's not yet broken. I look at Coop and feel butterflies in my stomach. Dane may be an expert at breaking colts and riding bulls, but Cooper's only experience with livestock is with our mares, and they're old and placid and easy to lead.

"You want me to stay?" I ask him as Dane emerges from the barn.

Cooper shakes his head. "No. You'll just make it worse."

"How?"

"You know what's going to happen. I'm going to get bucked off, thrown, head-butted, kicked, and who knows what else. It's going to hurt. You're going to cry. And Dane's just going to get mad. So go home and come back in two hours."

I stare at this reed-thin boy of mine. Twelve years old and taller than most men. "Sounds awful. Are you sure you want to go through with this?"

He looks at me and his eyes are a bright, brilliant blue. There's fear in his eyes but excitement, too. "I never wanted anything half so much." And then he opens the door, jumps out of the truck, and heads toward Dane without a glance back.

Dane waits for Coop by the corral, a rope over his shoulder. I want to roll down my window and shout to Dane to be careful, to warn him that Coop's a greenhorn and still my baby. But I can see from Dane's expression that he already knows.

So I leave the window up, raise a hand in farewell, and drive away.

The sun is setting as I return to Dane's ranch to pick up my son. Coop is dusty and bleeding as he half hobbles, half runs toward the truck. "That was crazy, Mom," he pants, climbing into the truck. "Scary, crazy, and so much fun."

"What's bleeding?" I ask, tilting his head up.

"My upper lip. Oh, and I need to get a different mouth guard. This one was too big, and Dane says I could lose a tooth."

Great.

Dane walks to my side of the truck, and I roll down the window. "He needs a better mouth guard," Dane says.

I raise a hand to shield my eyes from the setting sun's rays to get a better look at Dane, who looks so tough and sexy that it makes my insides melt. "He just told me."

"But otherwise he did great. He's surprisingly comfortable.

Don't know that I'd go so far as to call him a natural, but he has a good center of gravity. Nice sense of balance. Today we worked on keeping his feet heavy and low and all his weight centered evenly in his thighs and hips."

"You didn't ride?"

"No, I had him on the mechanical bull and covered the basics. Showed him how to put on the bull rope, hold the rope with the riding glove, had him stand on the slats and lower himself onto the back of the steer—"

"What steer?"

"The one I rode," Coop explains with a swollen-lip grin.

I look at Dane, and for the first time it crosses my mind that John would not want Coop pursuing this. "He rode a steer today? His first day?"

Dane's powerful shoulders shift. "Thought we'd see how he'd do. And he did good. Better than I thought."

"It wasn't a bull," Coop pipes up. "Just a steer, Mom. That's what the kids my age compete on. Although next year when I'm thirteen I'll ride old bulls, ones that don't kick too hard."

I hear what Coop's saying, but I'm still looking at Dane. "Do you know what you're doing, Kelly?" I ask under my breath.

Dane's green eyes are flecked with yellow as he smiles faintly. "Usually I'd say no, but when it comes to bull riding, it's a yes. Your boy's tough. And smart. I think he's got a shot."

"So I'm coming back, Mom." Cooper leans forward to catch Dane's eye. "Wednesday, right?"

"We're going to go Monday, Wednesday, and Friday for the next month, schedule permitting," Dane explains. "But I know that's a lot of driving and you have three kids, so you drop him here and I'll get him back to you afterwards."

I immediately start to protest, but Dane cuts me short. "Cooper and I have worked it out," he says, voice pitched so low that I find myself looking up into his eyes. "If you can drop him here at four, I'll make sure he gets home after."

I glance at Cooper, who is cut and dirty and bruised, yet all lit up like a Christmas tree. "I can get him here," I agree huskily, thinking this is madness trying to pretend that Dane has no effect on me when all I want is to lean closer and smell his scent and feel his warmth.

"Done." Dane tips the brim of his cowboy hat at Coop. "See you Wednesday, Coop." And then he winks at me. "See you then, Shey."

See you then, Shey.

I replay his parting words over and over in my head as I drive Cooper home. I see the wink and the tilt of his mouth, and I'm flooded with yearning.

I want him. Want to be with him. But I don't know how to do this. I haven't been single in nearly twenty years. Haven't kissed another man. Haven't wanted another man. But now...

Now...

My libido is kicking in, and it's making me crazy.

I feel crazy.

I have just enough of Dane to know I want more, but not enough to feel remotely satisfied.

What would make me feel satisfied?

Sex.

Maybe I need to sleep with him. Maybe that would get

him out of my system. Maybe one good roll in the hay would cure me of my Dane obsession.

Maybe. But unlikely.

It takes me a week to work up my courage to ask Dane to stay for dinner. It's the third week of October, and the air is crisp and the leaves on the poplars lining Dane's drive are beginning to turn.

"Want to join us for dinner tonight?" I ask Dane as he approaches my truck. "It's nothing fancy, but we'd enjoy your company."

"Wish I could, but I have plans tonight. Taking Lulu to dinner."

Lulu. Ugh.

I must make a face because Dane shakes his head. "You're such a little girl, you really are."

"What?"

"You know what."

"I just don't understand the attraction."

"You don't have to. You're not dating her." And then he smiles at me, totally remorseless. "By the way, Wednesday's going to be the last day I can work with Coop for a week. I leave Thursday for Brazil. Won't be back until the twenty-seventh."

I force a breezy smile to hide my disappointment. "Sounds like we'll just be missing each other, then. I leave for Puerto Rico on the twenty-fourth."

"How long are you gone?"

"Six days."

"Looks like Coop's going to miss training for the next little bit. Sorry to hear that. He's making good progress."

He feels bad for Coop. He'll miss Coop. But not one word about me.

The next couple of days drag by. I hadn't realized how much I looked forward to those brief visits with Dane three times a week until I can't see him at all.

I miss him. And I find it maddening that I do miss him. I hadn't wanted to feel this way, not after he made such mincemeat of my heart all those years ago. But the attraction's still there. I'm still infatuated, drawn by his energy and charisma, hooked by the fact that being around him makes my heart beat a little faster and my imagination dance.

But I don't trust the attraction. I can't afford to be careless or reckless, not when I have three teenagers who are hormonally challenged.

I wake up Thursday morning and realize I'm down to three days before I fly to Puerto Rico. Mama arrives from Jefferson on Saturday.

I need to start packing and getting ready for the trip, but I wish I could see Dane before I go.

While coffee brews, I make a list of all the things I still have to do. Laundry, pack, hair, waxing, manicure, pedicure. That doesn't include the cleaning I need to do to get the house ready for Mama.

While the boys are at school, I zip into Fort Worth, where I get my hair done—a mix of lowlights and highlights as well as overall color to hide my few strands of gray. Hair a perfect gold, I see to the waxing and have it all done—eyebrows, underarms, full leg, and Brazilian bikini. When you're modeling swimsuits, there's no room for hair anywhere. Nails are last and easy, and with grooming behind me, I stop in at Barnes & Noble and buy a copy of Frommer's *Puerto Rico*.

As I thumb through the copy while standing in line for the register, I realize I'm finally starting to get excited about the trip. I haven't let myself get excited until now in case it didn't work out, but we're three days and counting.

Book purchased, I'm back in my truck, racing to get the boys. I pick up Cooper in Palo Pinto and then dash back to Mineral Wells to get Bo and Hank.

I'm just pulling into the junior high parking lot when I spot a cluster of girls standing at the edge of the lot. One of the girls is yelling at the other, and I slow as I pass, recognizing the girls who were in the office the day I met with Paul Peterson. The brunette with jet black eyeliner is screaming at the thin blond girl, who is crying.

My heart sinks. I don't know the situation, but I feel for the blond girl. She's so thin that I find myself wondering what her situation is at home. I glance back at the girls in my rearview mirror just in time to see the brunette girl reach out and slap the blonde hard in the face.

The air catches in my throat, and I brake hard.

"What are you doing, Mom?" Coop asks as I throw the truck into reverse and back up.

I don't answer. Instead, I climb out of the truck and approach the group. "Everything okay?" I ask, aware of the girls' hostile expressions but not intimidated. I'm not a prissy girl, and it helps that I'm nearly six feet tall.

"Yes," the brunette answers in a tough-girl voice, while the thin blonde looks away, the handprint livid on her cheek.

The other girls look at me with dislike. They don't know me, and they don't want me here.

"You want a ride home?" I ask the blond girl.

She glances at the others and then shakes her head.

"I don't mind," I say.

The blond girl looks as if she's going to refuse again, but then tears well in her eyes and she suddenly nods and moves to my side. "If you don't mind," she whispers.

"Where do you live?" I ask her as she takes the far backseat.

"On Northwest Third Street, near Fifth."

I nod. It's a town address not too far away.

Bo gives me an odd look as I pull up at the curb and he spots the girl in the backseat. "Hey," he says to her as he climbs in and closes the truck door behind him.

"Hey," she answers in a small voice as I head for her home.

Her neighborhood is an area of smaller older homes, many bordered by small patchy lawns and chain-link fences. Her house has white siding and a small covered porch. An older man in a white undershirt sits on the porch, smoking.

"That's my grandpa," she says with a sigh as I pull over in front of her house.

"It's a nice house," I tell her.

She looks quickly at me to see if I'm making fun of her. I'm not. "I grew up in a house that looks a lot like yours."

"Really?"

I nod, and Cooper scoots toward me to let Bo open the door and get out so she can escape.

"By the way, I'm Shey Darcy," I say as she grabs her books and climbs out.

"I know." She stands on the curb, clutching her books against her chest. Her cheek is still flushed where the other girl hit her. "I'm Delilah."

"That's a beautiful name," I tell her.

"It was after that lady in the Bible. The one that cut off Samson's hair."

I know the story well. Impulsively, I reach into my purse, grab a scrap of paper, and write down my cell number. "Call me if you ever need anything, Delilah," I say, holding the paper with my number out to her. "Or if you just want to talk about modeling."

Delilah's eyes light up. "Really?"

I nod.

She glances at the number and then up at me. "Thanks."

"Anytime, hon."

Bo climbs back into the truck, and we're heading to the high school to get Hank when Cooper asks, "Why did you do that, Mom?"

"Do what?" I ask.

"Give her your number."

I picture Delilah's thin face and lanky hair coupled with the teased bangs. She doesn't look like a girl who gets a lot of the right kind of attention at home. "I thought she might need it."

"Why?"

"I can't explain it, but my gut just said she needs to know someone cares."

Chapter Thirteen

———— ✦ ————

That afternoon as the boys do homework, I sit at the computer in the kitchen to begin typing up an outline of the week and where the boys have to be and when.

As I think about things Mama would need to know, I find myself dreading telling her about Bo's problems in school. Mama doesn't have patience with problems or special situations. Reluctantly I type: "Bo must show his homework nightly. He must be supervised while doing homework, not in his bedroom or on the couch in front of the TV. He must get his tests and papers signed and returned to the appropriate teacher."

And if he doesn't do his homework, I list the consequences: "He loses his phone, and the computer, as well as his games."

I feel like a prison warden as I start printing off the instructions for my mother. The pages are still printing when my phone vibrates with a text message from Tiana Tomlinson, Marta's and my other best friend:

Just returned from 3 weeks in India. And guess what? I'm married!!!!

Tiana got married? In India? I call her immediately. She answers on the first ring, laughing. "Marta's trying to get through, too."

"You did it?" I ask.

"Yep. We got married and honeymooned at Ajmer when Michael finished his Rx Smile mission in Andhra Pradesh. The mission itself is both tragic and miraculous, but the wedding and honeymoon...that was romantic. Ajmer is unbelievably beautiful."

"Who was there?"

"At the wedding? Just the two of us. We wanted it to be completely private—no paparazzi, no cameras, no distractions. The service was performed at the courthouse, and then we had such a blissful honeymoon. All we did was sleep, eat, drink, make love." She sighs happily. "He's so wonderful, Shey. I'm the luckiest woman alive."

I grin. Tiana can be a gusher, but I've never heard her quite this happy. "So are babies in the picture, too?"

"Almost forty. It's probably now or never."

"You're serious?"

"Shey, I'm so happy, and I'm so ready to be a mom. I've done everything else. I've had the big career, traveled the world, won awards and Emmys, and now I want to put family first. It's time."

I've known Tiana over half my life. She, Marta, and I all met as sixteen-year-olds at St. Pious in Monterey, and we've been through so much together—school and marriage and death and divorce. And in all these years I've never heard Tiana this calm or settled. Tiana is by far the most driven woman I know. She's had a successful career as a popular entertainment reporter, anchoring her own show. She's pushed herself relentlessly, yet since meeting Michael O'Sullivan, the famous Beverly Hills plastic surgeon, she's found love, slowed down, and changed her priorities.

"I'm so glad," I tell her. "You'll be a wonderful mom. Huge congratulations and heaps of love."

"Thank you, Shey. I couldn't wait to get back and share the news. Marta's on the other line again. I better take her call."

"Of course. Give Ta my love. I'll call you tomorrow for full details."

I hang up and stare at the phone. Tiana's married. *Married.* After eight years as a widow, she's found not just love, but peace. Joy. Whoever said there's only one person for each of us was wrong. There isn't just one partner or soul mate. The world is full of amazing people. We just have to be willing to take a risk to find new love.

Thinking of taking risks leads me to thoughts of Dane, but I don't want to do that. I can't make Dane the new love interest. It's too soon, and knowing our turbulent history, I wonder what makes him the right one now?

Later, as I turn out the lights and lock the doors, it hits me that I haven't yet told the boys that my mother will be coming to stay with them while I'm gone. They still think Brick and Charlotte are watching them, and I dread breaking the news that it's actually Gramma who will be here.

They're not going to be happy.

My fears were justified. The next morning when I announce the news over breakfast, the boys aren't ecstatic.

"Alone with Gramma for a week?" Coop exclaims in panic, his cereal spoon dangling in midair, milk dripping onto his quilted place mat.

Hank and Bo are staring at me equally horrified. I feel

their pain, I do, but I can't let them know. So I sip my coffee and focus on serenity. "She'll be here for a week, but she'll be babysitting only for five days—"

"Babysitting?" Hank interrupts. "Mom, I'm fifteen, not a baby, and not in need of child care."

Wrong word choice. Big mistake.

I take another sip of coffee, thinking I've made a mess of this already and I've only just delivered the news. They're going to hammer me the entire drive to school. I should have waited until I reached Mineral Wells. Dropped the bomb and then kicked them out of the car.

"This is the problem," Hank continues tersely. "You treat me like I'm still a baby, but I'm almost sixteen."

"You're not a baby. I don't think of you as a baby." I glance at the other two. "I don't think of any of you as babies. Gramma does."

It was a joke, just a little joke, but they explode with indignation. They're so mad and so fired up that it takes me a while to calm them down. It probably doesn't help that I keep laughing. "Guys, I'm just kidding. Relax."

"So Gramma's not coming to stay with us?" Coop asks.

"No, she is. She arrives tomorrow. But Uncle Brick and Aunt Charlotte will be around and they'll make sure Gramma doesn't torture you. It's only for a few days and I'll be back."

The boys are still fiercely, vigorously protesting as I drive them to school. I tune them out. There's nothing I can do at this point. My mother has made up her mind, and we are living in her house. And to be honest, it won't hurt the boys to have her here. In fact, it might even do them good.

*   *   *

I spend the day paying bills and organizing finances before turning my attention to packing. I won't need a lot for the trip—a couple of simple sundresses, sandals, an evening wrap, maybe a pair of linen slacks, and an easy top. I never check luggage and carry everything in a leather-and-tapestry tote bag I picked up in Turkey fifteen years ago. I add my iPod and camera to the bag and think it's probably time I broke down and bought an iPhone to handle all my music, picture, and cellular needs. But I'm funny about buying new things. I'm not a big shopper. I feel no need to upgrade every time something new is on the market.

Maybe this is one of the reasons I'm okay financially. I'm happy with old things, don't like splashy new things. And every time I can avoid making a purchase, I feel as if I've just done something wonderful.

With my bag packed, I tackle housework. Mama is the queen of domesticity, and I have to make sure everything is clean and organized before she arrives. I'm in the middle of vacuuming when there's a knock on the front door.

I head to the door, expecting Charlotte. Instead it's Dane.

I exhale hard, aware that I'm in short shorts and a baggy gray top minus a bra. I'm not one of those models who come sans boobs, either.

"I thought you were still in Brazil," I say, stunned to see him on my doorstep. I didn't expect him home for a few more days.

"Something came up on my ranch so I flew home early."

"And you missed me so much you raced right over to

see me?" I tease, folding my arms over my chest to hide the
jut of my breasts. I feel very naked right now and could
definitely use more clothes.

He's noticed the curve of my breasts, and he smiles.
"You look like a Dallas Cowboy cheerleader in those little
shorts."

It's all I can do not to reach down and tug my
shorts lower. "They're my yoga shorts. I wasn't expecting
company."

"I'm not complaining. You look like a teenager, all legs
and skin."

I blush, thinking I wore this outfit a hundred times in
front of John and he never said boo. But then, I'm beginning
to realize John wasn't a sexual dynamo. "So what brings you
to Parkfield? Were you just in the neighborhood?"

The creases deepen at his eyes. "There's not much of a
neighborhood," he answers, glancing over his shoulder and
taking in the mature oaks, weathered barn, and dilapidated
corral drenched in pale autumn sunlight. "In fact, I don't
think there's any."

My fingers curl into fists against my chest. "So you just
drove here to say howdy."

"And drop off a gift for Coop."

My giddy pleasure pops. He came to see Cooper.
"Coop won't be home for another two hours, and then he's
going with Brick to look at a horse."

"That's okay. I also wanted to see you."

The bubble returns. "Want to come in? I made some tea
earlier. I can pour you a glass."

"Sounds great."

I'm nervous as I lead him into the house and back to

the kitchen and catch a glimpse of my reflection in the oval walnut mirror that hangs above the dining room's sideboard. My long blond hair hangs loose, and my cheeks are a dusty pink, which just makes my eyes more blue. I look like a teenager instead of an adult, and from the way my heart's hammering, I might as well be one, too.

It's strange to feel so self-conscious. I'm rarely self-conscious anymore. Modeling has made me comfortable in my skin. I wasn't always so confident though.

In the beginning modeling was really hard. I felt painfully inhibited, constantly wondering what others saw and if I looked as ridiculous as I felt. Most photographers knew I was new to modeling and tried to work with me, but one day on a shoot for *Elle*—it was my first fashion layout with them and a big one—the photographer lost patience with me. I couldn't do anything right. Apparently I didn't even resemble a model. He said I was too chunky. He hated the way I posed. He mocked my expression, calling me a stupid cow, before he ordered me off the set.

But I wouldn't go.

I refused to leave.

That day will be forever etched in my memory. I can still feel my shame as I held my ground beneath the blinding lights, naked but for a Givenchy black lace wrap, shaking in my five-inch black heels. I kept lifting my chin to hold back my tears, terrified that if I did cry I'd ruin the thick black liner and shadow smudged around my eyes.

"I'm not going to leave. I can do this," I told him hoarsely. "Watch."

And somehow I did. I dug deep inside of myself for

courage, for strength, for self-respect. I focused on the camera. Tried to find a little magic to make the photo work. But nothing about that shoot felt good. I certainly didn't feel pretty. I knew the photographer loathed me. But I fought for every frame. I fought my fears. And I fought for my self-esteem.

That excruciating day became a huge turning point in not just my career, but my life.

I learned that there are people who just enjoy being ugly. I realized that if I want to be successful, I'm going to have to fight for it. And I learned that life requires growing some very thick skin.

I've grown that thick skin, too. I no longer let other people get to me. I let negativity roll off my back. And I'm never rattled by men.

But Dane appears to be the exception to the rule. Because right now he's rattling me big time.

My hand shakes as I pour the tea over ice, then grab the tin of jumbo molasses cookies I stashed in the freezer after making them last weekend and put several on a plate. As I arrange the cookies, I glance at Dane, who's leaning back in the chair at the table, eyes closed.

He looks tired.

I cast another quick glance his way as I cut up a lemon and add a fat wedge to each glass. Maybe not tired as much as in pain.

My nervousness gives way to concern.

"You okay, cowboy?" I ask, carrying the glasses to the table and pushing the sugar bowl toward him.

He opens his eyes and gives me a faint smile. "Just fine."

"Hurting?"

He shrugs. "It was a long flight. A lot of sitting."

"Sitting hurts?"

He starts to shrug again and then admits, "Everything hurts. The last surgery was supposed to make things better. Instead it seems to have just made things worse."

He's been in pain for months, then. Troubled, I sit down across from him. "Is there going to be another surgery?"

"Maybe. Unfortunately."

"I'm sorry."

His shoulders shift carelessly. "Occupational hazard. Can't complain."

"But you never complain. You never have. Sometimes I think you should."

His green eyes lazily examine my face. "And what would I complain about?"

"The things that have happened...things that have gone wrong. The end of your marriage. The loss of your child—"

"Matthew's the best thing that ever happened to me. I loved that boy. Every day I had with him was a blessing."

I think this is why I fell in love with Dane all those years ago, and this is why I still love him today.

He's a big, tough man with a soft spot for children. He would have been a great father, a doting, protective father. My chest feels tight. I ache for a moment. "You're a good man, Dane Kelly."

"Not that good. Just ask your Brick and Blue. Cody would probably be alive if it weren't for me."

"You're not responsible for Cody's addictions, or his overdose."

"But if he'd gotten the help he needed two years ago,

he might have been saved. He might be clean and sober and alive today."

The self-loathing in Dane's voice takes my breath away, and for a moment I don't know what to say.

Dane *hates* himself.

He blames himself. He honestly believes he should have been able to save both Cody and Matthew.

I exhale slowly, absorbing the realization that, yes, Dane's wounded, but it isn't his hip that's the problem. It's his heart.

"You're not being fair to yourself," I say, my voice husky, because of course he couldn't save Matthew. Matthew had severe, special needs. And there's no way he could have saved Cody, either. Cody refused to get professional treatment and medication for his depression, resorting to over-the-counter medicine and street drugs to soothe him when he was manic and lift him when he was depressed. "You're punishing yourself for things that were beyond your control."

"I know." And then he smiles a small, mocking half smile. "But it keeps me honest."

I know then that I will never stand a chance against him. I care too much, love him too much. Not that love solves everything. In fact, sometimes love is just one more problem.

When he leaves an hour later, I have a paper-wrapped bull rope for Cooper—a gift Dane picked up in Brazil for him—and the most ambivalent emotions.

I thought coming home would make things easier. Instead it's complicated everything.

*   *   *

It takes me a long time to fall asleep that night, and when I do, I dream of Dane. The dream starts out happy. We're together and talking and laughing as we drive around in his truck. But then the dream takes a strange turn and we get stuck on a train track and can't move.

From nowhere a train appears, whistle blowing, and there's no time to escape. For some reason Dane is hurt and can't get out, but he yells at me to jump. I won't leave him. He's shouting. I'm crying and the train is bearing down on us, and then Dane throws open his door and tosses me out of the truck just before the train hits us, exploding the truck into a fireball.

I wake up shaking. I'm nauseated and cold, and adrenaline is pumping. The dream was so real. I could taste the fear, hear the impact of the train hitting the truck, and feel the heat of the fire. So crazy. So awful.

Why would I dream a dream like that? What does it mean?

I get up and go to the kitchen, where I eat a bowl of cereal and try to get the dream out of my mind. I don't want to think about it anymore. Don't want to analyze what it could mean.

When I do go back to bed, all I want is for morning to come.

Mama arrives mid-morning, right on schedule, and I go through the file folder with her, letting her know that Brick will be driving the boys to school and covering the activities the boys have planned, including the high school dance. We all go to dinner Saturday night, and then Sunday morning I'm out of the house before it's even light in order to make my nine a.m. American Airlines flight from Dallas/ Fort Worth International to San Juan.

It's a relatively quick drive this morning, no traffic to slow things down, and I reach the airport in less than ninety minutes, park, and get through security just as easily.

I stop at one of the airport Starbucks for coffee and a pumpkin scone. I use the hour before we board to sip my coffee and read up on historic San Juan. I'll be staying at the Sheraton Old San Juan, which apparently sits in the heart of romantic Old San Juan, just steps from the wharf where the luxury cruise ships dock.

But everything sounds close in Old San Juan. San José Church, La Casa Blanca (the home of Ponce de León), Fort San Felipe del Morro, Fort San Cristóbal, the Cathedral of San Juan Bautista, plus several famous beaches and the El Yunque National Forest.

San Felipe del Morro (commonly known as El Morro) and El Yunque are both already familiar to me, as they're two of the locations Neiman Marcus is using for their shoot.

I'm still poring over the guidebook when they begin boarding the flight. As my row is called, I feel a little thrill of anticipation.

I am excited. Going somewhere new, doing something different. This is exactly what I need. I'm not depressed, I realize. I just needed a break.

Forty minutes later, as the jet taxis down the runway, I remember something I've forgotten—not glasses or phone charger or camera, but something pertaining to the kids.

Halloween. Halloween is Sunday, the day after I return, yet I completely forgot it, and so did the boys.

This is the first year none of them have asked to carve pumpkins or buy costumes or go trick-or-treating.

The first year none wanted to decorate the house or make our traditional rollout cookies.

I would have thought Coop still wanted to go trick-or-treating, but he never mentioned it, or about getting a costume.

Rather wistfully, I think of the days when selecting the Halloween costume was the big topic around the dinner table. Ninjas and Jedis and Power Rangers. But no more. They're getting too old.

The jet lifts off the ground, and I suck in a breath. I knew they were going to grow up, knew they couldn't be babies forever. But it's harder than I expected.

It's a four-and-a-half-hour flight to San Juan, and I fall asleep an hour after takeoff and am out most of the flight. When I first began modeling, I couldn't sleep on planes and showed up for jobs exhausted. Then I learned to take my own pillow, wear an eye mask, and put in earplugs. I don't need any of the above today and wake up just as we're making our final approach.

It's a reasonably smooth landing, and I walk to baggage claim, where I discover the driver holding the sign with my name. Since I didn't check a bag, we're able to head straight for the town car. It's warm outside, almost sultry, and I wish now I'd worn something other than gray slacks and a charcoal cashmere sweater.

Fortunately, he turns on the air-conditioning, and I fix

my attention out the window, curious to get my first
glimpse of Puerto Rico. It's late afternoon, and the sun sits
lower in the sky. Traffic snarls from the freeway.

"Lots of traffic for a Sunday," I comment a few minutes
later.

The driver looks at me in the rearview mirror. "Everybody goes to the beach for the day. Makes bad traffic."

"Are you from San Juan?"

"No, from Rincón." He smiles, flashes white teeth.
"Famous for surfing."

I read about Rincón in the guidebook, wish I were
here longer so I could explore properly, but vow to return
with the boys. This would be a great place to come
with them.

The next morning begins with a welcome orientation, followed by fittings to make sure there are no surprises with
wardrobe.

They're using six models for the shoot, four women
and two men, and it's a relief to discover that I am not the
oldest model. Adriana is fifty-two and a gorgeous silver-
haired model with a wonderful husky laugh and incredible
skin. I am immediately drawn to her, as she reminds me of
my friend Marta. During the morning fitting, we talk about
our families back home.

Adriana was widowed last year and is the mother of
twin boys and a daughter, none of whom live at home.

I tell her that I'm recently separated from my husband
and I've moved my boys back to my hometown in Texas,
but it's been a difficult adjustment so far.

"Change is always hard," Adriana sympathizes. The

stylist finishes with us then, and we're free for the next hour until we're called into hair and makeup.

This morning, we're shooting at the sixteenth-century fortress El Morro, built on the tip of the island overlooking the sea. The fortress boasts immense stone walls, lookouts, and fortified interior buildings, promising to be a dramatic backdrop for the designer skirts, blouses, dresses, and accessories.

Ellie, a stunning brunette and one of the thirty-year-old models, has been paired with one of the male models to pose as a couple. Adriana will be working with the other male model, a handsome man with unlined skin and a thick head of silver hair. Although Ellie gloats about being specially "selected" to work with Damon, I'm personally thrilled not to have been paired up for the shoot. There's only one man I want to talk to and only one man I want to smile at, and he's back home in Texas.

As the days pass, I fully expect to get a frantic call from home saying that Bo has run away or Hank's been rude to my mother, but I receive no emotional calls during the week. In fact, I receive no calls at all, which prompts me to start phoning home just to make sure things are going all right. Apparently, they're going so well that Mama tells me to stop calling and she'll just see me Saturday night after I fly in and drive home.

That last conversation with my mother has me phoning Charlotte to check in with her. "Is everything really okay?" I ask. "Because Mama just told me not to call again."

Char just laughs. "Mama's in heaven. She's making pralines and divinity. Quilting at the kitchen table. She loves being back in the house, taking care of boys, and being needed. Makes her feel like the queen bee."

"Mama always did love her boys," I say.

"And you do, too."

On the last night of the shoot, we're all treated to dinner at a small restaurant on the beach twelve miles outside San Juan. It takes forty minutes just to get across San Juan, and the moon is high and full by the time we arrive.

The hostess seats us outside at a long, linen-covered table on the deck overlooking the water. We're far removed from the lights and noise of the city, and the only sound we hear on the deck is our own conversation and the crash of surf against the sand.

The shoot's artistic director has handled the night's menu, and within minutes of being seated we're served icy cold mojitos. Mojitos, although a Cuban invention, are popular throughout the Caribbean, as rum is a Caribbean staple. Adriana and I clink glasses and then sit back to savor the tart, tangy cocktail.

"This has been lovely," I say, tipping my head back to get a better look at the moon. "I needed this break. Makes me feel almost sane again."

"Being a mom is the hardest job in the world," she answers. "Don't let anyone tell you otherwise."

"I thought the toddler years were hard, but they're nothing compared to the stuff I'm dealing with now."

Adriana's heard about my boys, knows their ages and stages, and smiles now. "I think that's why kids become awful in their teen years. It forces parents to step back, loosen the ties a little. Otherwise I don't think we'd ever let go."

"I don't know what I'm going to do when they're gone,"

I admit. "They give me a reason to work and wake up and get up every day."

"But being a mother is only one aspect of a woman's life. When the kids move out, we're supposed to move on."

"On to what? What can possibly fill our lives the same way?"

"I guess that's the challenge we face in our forties, fifties, and beyond. We have to rediscover ourselves. We have to figure out what will make life meaningful without our babies and men."

"It doesn't sound easy, or fun."

She sighs. "Oh, it's not always fun. There are times I miss the kids and the chaos so much, times when I'm so damn lonely I don't think I can get through the day. Dinnertime's the worst, too. That's when I wait for my husband to return from work and walk through the door." Her voice is husky, and she plays with the moisture beading her cocktail glass. "But he doesn't. And he won't."

Adriana looks up at me, dark eyes full of emotion. "And so I find ways to distract myself. I make it a game. I search out new activities and create new routines and plan for new adventures. Like coming here to model. And meeting you. And making new friends."

"You're brave," I tell her.

She shakes her head. "No, it's just called being a woman. We're all going to have to do it. It's not a choice. It's a matter of when."

Later, as we wait for the taxis that will take us back to our hotel, I find myself standing next to Ellie. She taps a cigarette out of the pack and slides the pack back into her purse. "Damon told me you're John Darcy's wife."

"Was," I answer cautiously. "You know John?"

"I worked with him on several occasions," she answers, digging in her purse for her lighter. "Brilliant photographer, but he definitely wasn't straight."

I feel the old, cold sinking sensation return. I wish I'd caught one of the first taxis back. Wish I were standing anywhere but here. "What do you mean?" I ask as she places the cigarette between her full lips and lights it.

She takes a puff and then tips her head back and exhales. "He had a thing for the male models, everyone knew it. You had to have known it."

I didn't, though. John and I were close, had enough, consistent sex that it never crossed my mind he might be interested in men. "No."

"Come on, Shey."

"I didn't." My voice is but a whisper. "How were you so sure?"

Ellie uses her cigarette to point to Damon, who's talking intently to one of the waiters who served us dinner. "Ask him. They had an affair off and on for years. It was apparently quite a torrid little thing."

I don't sleep that night. I lie in bed in my beautiful air-conditioned hotel room and hate Ellie.

Far easier to hate Ellie than to hate myself or John. I don't want to hate John. I loved him for so many years, and even though I'm discovering I never really knew him, it doesn't change what we once had.

And what we had was good.

And what we had was real. At least, it was real at the time.

But then Ellie's words return—*He had a thing for the male models, everyone knew it*—and I want to throw up.

I go to the bathroom and sit on the edge of the tub and pray I can be sick so I can get this awful feeling out of my gut.

And my heart.

And my head.

But I can't throw up and I can't forget, and after fifteen minutes of rocking back and forth like a madwoman on the edge of the tub, I jump up and grab my phone and call John's cell. It's two in the morning here, and New York and Puerto Rico are in the same time zone, so I know I'll be waking him up. But right now I don't care.

It takes him five rings, but he answers. "Shey, what's wrong? Has something happened to one of the boys?"

I hear his voice, and it's so familiar that it hurts. Hot tears fill my eyes. "Did you really have a long affair with the model Damon Lockwood while we were married?" My voice is thin with pain.

"Shey."

"Just tell me the truth. Were you sleeping with other men the whole time we were married?"

"Not the whole time."

Not the whole time.

Just part of the time.

I close my eyes, press the phone to my ear. "Did you love Damon?"

"It wasn't like that."

"What was it like, then?"

"Don't do this, sweetheart."

But a part of me has to. A part of me can't stop asking

the questions, demanding answers, needing to fill in all the gaps in the story. "So you were promiscuous."

"Not promiscuous."

"But you had multiple partners."

"There were a few, but it was over a number of years. And I was always careful."

"Jesus, John."

"Shey, we've been over this so many times—"

"And you're so, so very sorry." I can't help my bitterness, can't help that I want to tear him apart limb from limb. "You wish you could take it all back, undo all the hurt, make different decisions."

He's silent. I grind my teeth. Impossible. Unbelievable. And yet I don't hate him. I wish I could. It would make it so much easier. But he's a good person, a loving person, a fun person, and my best friend for the past seventeen years. "You should have told me sooner, John. You should have ended our marriage sooner."

"I loved you. I still do."

Fresh tears rush to my eyes, but I hold them back. "But I wasn't enough for you."

"I'm gay, Shey. I've probably always been gay, but I thought...hoped...I could live the straight life for you."

"You hoped." My voice breaks. "That's it? You hoped you could? But you didn't. Which made our marriage nothing but a lie."

"That's not true—"

"It is true. Just as for years you've hidden the truth about your sexuality from me. But it wasn't for you to decide. You owed me your fidelity. I deserved honesty. But you gave me neither."

*   *   *

It's raining as I land at Dallas/Fort Worth, and the rain just continues as I drive home. Maybe it's a good thing the boys hadn't planned on trick-or-treating, since the weather report said the rain would continue through the weekend.

I usually like the rain, but today's low gray skies just depress me and last night's conversation with John continues to weigh on me.

It strikes me yet again that it's easy to like yourself when things are going well.

But things aren't going well right now and I don't feel likable.

Don't feel lovable.

Don't feel good about myself at all.

I arrive home relieved to be off the wet roads, park the truck in front of the house, and dash inside to avoid getting wet.

The house is spotless. The laundry's done. And dinner is already prepared and waiting in the refrigerator to be reheated tonight. Unfortunately, the boys aren't there. It's just Mama to greet me.

"Where are the kids?" I ask her, trying to hide my disappointment. I was so eager to see them, and so in need of their hugs.

"Brick's got them helping him out at his stable. I think they're adding a new stall and repairing the others," she answers, shaking black sprinkles onto oversize frosted cupcakes. "He's good with them, firm, but patient." She sees me eyeing the dozen cupcakes, frosting tinted a vivid orange in honor of Halloween. "I promised Cooper," she adds. "I've never met a boy with a bigger sweet tooth."

I drop into one of the kitchen chairs and let her pour me a glass of sweet tea. She looks tired but satisfied. "You survived all right, Mama?"

"I enjoyed myself. We had a couple incidents in the beginning, but nothing I couldn't handle. And once the boys realized I wouldn't tolerate their shenanigans, they settled down."

"I'm sorry they gave you trouble."

She wipes a handful of black sprinkles from the counter into her palm and then dumps it all in the sink. "They weren't trouble. They're my grandkids."

I feel a rush of gratitude. My family might make me crazy but they also come through for me time and again. And after the last year, I need them, I need their love and support more than ever. "I'm glad. And I'm glad you came. Thank you."

She pats me on the shoulder as she crosses back to the stove to turn off the oven light.

My smile turns crooked. That brisk pat was Mama's way of saying "You're welcome."

Chapter Fourteen

———— ✴ ————

The next three weeks are busy with basketball practice beginning for Bo, and with Coop resuming his lessons with Dane. Hank is the only one with time on his hands, but he doesn't seem interested in spending any of that free time with me.

Hank isn't the only one avoiding me. Even though I'm still driving Cooper to Dane's three times a week, Dane doesn't always come out to the truck to greet me. In fact, more often than not, he doesn't come out at all. The first week I put it down to him just being busy, but as the second week melts into the third and I've spoken with Dane only a handful of times, I realize Dane is being deliberately distant.

I rack my brain trying to think of a reason why he should suddenly be so aloof, and I come up with nothing. The only thing I can think of is that he regrets being so open with me, and I tell myself to give him time. He'll eventually forget. We'll eventually get back to a more comfortable footing. But then on Thursday, one week before Thanksgiving, Coop announces at dinner that Dane's girlfriend has moved into Dane's house.

It's all I can do to keep my jaw from smacking the oak table.

"Who is his girlfriend?" Bo asks, his mouth full of meatball and sauce.

Coop twirls his fork in the spaghetti noodles, wrapping them around the prongs. "Her name's Lulu. I don't know her last name. But she's really nice. And really pretty. She always brings me a snack during training. Dane tells her not to, but she says I'm growing and I need it."

Bo hoots with laughter. "Maybe she likes you."

Cooper grins. "Maybe she does."

I choke on my mouthful of pasta. Lulu is now living with Dane? I had no idea they were so serious.

But an hour later, as I put away the clean dishes and wipe down the counters, I lose my temper and throw the damp sponge across the kitchen, where it bounces off the laminate counter and skids into the sink. *Why?* I want to demand.

Why Lulu?

Why Shellie Ann?

Why not me?

Two days later, I'm in the truck driving the three boys to Dallas to catch their flight to JFK to spend Thanksgiving week with their father.

I haven't talked to John since I called him from Puerto Rico, but John has phoned the boys a number of times. They're all looking forward to seeing their dad, although each one seems to have some concerns about staying with Dad now that he's living with Erik.

Fortunately, the boys are experienced travelers and know how to handle themselves at the airport. I printed off their boarding passes at the house, which means I can just drop them at the curb and say our good-byes there. It seemed like a convenient plan when I booked their tickets and then printed their boarding passes, but now that I'm just leaving them on the sidewalk, I feel like hell.

"Call me when you get through security," I insist, hugging each one in turn.

"Yes, Mom," Coop agrees.

"And then once you're on the plane," I say, pushing Bo's hair back from his eyes as I kiss him good-bye. Bo rolls his eyes.

"And once we land and find Dad," Hank concludes, giving me a brief hug. "Yes, we know. Got it. Gotta go."

I nod, jam my hands into my jeans pockets. "Have a good time."

"We will." Coop gives me one more hug, this one even tighter than the last. "Love you, Mom," he whispers in my ear. "I'll miss you."

I squeeze him back, hard. "Love you, I'll miss you. Travel safe."

"See you soon."

"Can't wait."

And then they're gone, walking into the terminal, and I return to my car even as airport police approach to issue me a ticket. "I'm leaving, I'm leaving," I say breathlessly, sliding quickly into the driver's seat and starting the truck to make a speedy getaway.

As I head toward the freeway, my cell phone beeps and I surreptitiously check the text message from Hank: *Thru security. At gate. Flt's on time.*

That's good. I'm grateful there are no delays. And yet my heart is heavy as I speed up to merge with traffic.

I will miss them.

I already miss them.

*   *   *

I expect Thanksgiving at Blue and Emily's to be excruciating, especially with Brick and Charlotte away at Carolyn's, so I bring two bottles of wine—one red and one white—along with the two dishes I was asked to make.

Blue answers the door and while hugging me, he mutters that Emily is feeling a bit tense, which is bound to be a huge understatement. He takes the wine and flowers from me and sets them on the round table in the middle of the marble foyer, and then together we walk to the truck to get the casseroles.

"Is this the sweet onion casserole or corn pudding?" he asks as I hand him one foil-covered dish.

"Baked onion," I answer, closing the truck door with my hip. "Although I don't know why I bother. No one ever eats it."

"But it's a Callen family tradition."

I grimace. "Mama already here?"

"She got in Tuesday night, spent yesterday baking pies and making the stuffing, and then woke up early this morning to do the cheese grits and sweet potato casserole."

"She's going to be tired," I say.

"She already is."

"No one needs this much food."

"But that's not the point," he says, glancing at me. "Is it?"

I follow him through the front door, down the hall, and into the kitchen. Blue and Emily's kitchen is the size of most people's living room, the result of an extravagant remodel several years ago. The remodel took six months, and the elegant cream cabinets were built on-site by a carpenter Emily flew in from England. The stone on the counter and floor is a French limestone. The backsplash is made of glass artisan tiles from Italy. It's a beautiful kitchen, but too grand for me. Even though I'm tall, I always feel a little lost in it.

"Where is everyone?" I ask, opening the refrigerator. I try to make room for the casseroles, but it's so packed that they end up on the counter.

"Mama's on the phone with Brick, and Emily's in the bedroom with her feet up."

"Why is she tense?" I ask, wondering if tense is a euphemism for tipsy.

He grabs a beer out of the fridge and then a chilled mug from the freezer. "Want one?"

"I'll wait for dinner."

He pops the cap off the bottle and fills the mug. "You know Emily. She wants everything just so, which contributes to the stress."

I lean on the counter. "How are you holding up?"

He takes a long drink, half drains the glass. "Today's a great day for football."

I go to the oven to peek inside. The turkey is just starting to turn golden. "And my nieces? Where are they?"

"Megan's out somewhere, and Andi is probably in her room on the computer."

"Facebook?"

"Or Twitter. Megan says Andi's a Twitter addict."

I've heard about Twitter but don't do it myself. In fact, I don't do anything online other than check my e-mail a couple of times a week. "What does she Twitter about?"

"Lord knows. But her thumbs are permanently attached

to her iPhone. She's either texting, Twittering, or posting updates on Facebook." He lifts his chilled mug. "Welcome to adolescence in the twenty-first century."

Emily emerges from her room a half hour later, appearing in the family room, where I'm watching the Dallas Cowboys get roughed up more than Blue would like. He isn't exactly hollering at the TV, but he's coming close.

"Blue, it's Thanksgiving," Emily complains from the doorway, a hand to her head. "Must you shout at the TV today?"

"We're only down by nine, but it might as well be thirty-nine the way the refs are calling the game," he growls, staring at the huge flat-screen TV that takes up most of the family room's dark-paneled wall.

"They're always blowing the calls when it's your team down," she answers dryly before glancing at me. "Welcome, Shey."

"Thank you, Emily." I rise from the couch. "How are you feeling?"

"Blue told you I was feeling poorly."

"He said you were putting your feet up. Is there something I can do? Toss the salad? Set the table?"

"Table's set. Salad's made. Mother's making the gravy once the turkey comes out."

"Girls," Blue says from his leather armchair, "can you take this to another room? I'm trying to watch the game."

I smile at the pain in Blue's voice, but my smile fades as I catch sight of Emily's face. She's livid. Her lips are compressed, her jaw set.

"You know, Blue," she says, "you might be more

successful if you cared about your job as much as you cared about football." And then she walks out.

I slowly sit back down, ball my hands in my lap.

Blue glances at me, shrugs. "I told you she was a little tense."

It's hard to hear my older brother take a tongue-lashing, and I gulp a breath. "That's tense?"

Blue laughs wearily. "Shey, hon, that's nothing."

I'd expected a rough Thanksgiving at Blue and Emily's, and it doesn't disappoint. The girls don't appear until dinner is on the table, and then it's a fight to get Megan to eat—she's borderline anorexic, Emily tells me with pride—and to get Andi off her phone. Blue pockets the phone when Mama catches her texting under the table after she's been told to wait until dinner is over. Andi's then mad at Mama, and Emily's angry at Blue. I just sip my wine and keep my head down so I can finish eating and run.

I'm back home by seven forty-five and totally content to stretch out on the couch with a blanket, a pillow, and the remote control. I flip through the channels until I find an HBO movie that I haven't yet seen.

I watch the movie, pausing it partway using our DVR to get a slice of the pumpkin pie I bought at the store yesterday and put in the fridge just for this occasion. Mama makes a better pie, but it was easier to buy my own than try to ask for a slice or two to bring home.

Movie finished, pie consumed, I head to bed. It's after eleven, and I know tonight I'll have no trouble sleeping. And I'm right. The moment my head hits the pillow, I'm out, dead to the world.

And then sometime in the night, a thud wakes me.

It's such a loud sound that even asleep I feel it all the way through me, jolting me awake with a vibration that hums from the floor, through my bed, and into my breastbone.

My first thought is that one of the boys must have fallen from bed, and I groggily push back the covers and struggle to my feet.

Then my second thought is, The boys aren't home.

They're in New York with their dad. There's no one here. I'm home alone.

Then I hear another bang and the sound of wood splitting. It's my door. My kitchen door. Someone's breaking in.

And just like that, I realize I'm not alone anymore. Someone's in the house.

A chill rushes through me. I freeze, rooted to the spot.

I've always thought in a moment of danger I'd be strong. Fierce. Quick on my feet. Instead, I'm made of cement. I can't even think clearly enough to move.

I need the phone. Where's the phone? The cell is in my purse. The only other phone hangs on the kitchen wall.

I long for a gun, not that I know how to shoot. But I feel so helpless, suddenly aware of how isolated I am on the ranch, how vulnerable I am if threatened. And with Brick and Charlotte at Carolyn's in San Antonio, our nearest neighbor is a good ten-minute drive away.

Glass shatters in the kitchen. The sound of splintering glass is followed by thuds as drawers are upended.

My knees go weak, and nausea rushes through me. I've got to get help. Have to get away.

And then I remember Coop's phone. He left it behind by accident, and his room is next to mine. I have to leave my room to go to his, but my legs are impossibly heavy and walking is a herculean task. Finally I reach his room and feel around his desk in the dark, careful not to make a sound.

Binder. Notepad. Pens. Stapler. Pencil sharpener. Phone. Phone. Thank God. Trembling, I punch in 911.

"Nine one one. What is the emergency?"

I nearly cry with relief. "There's someone in my house." I whisper the words, terrified of being heard. "And I'm alone." The fear rises up, bigger, blacker, colder than before. "Help me."

The female dispatcher verifies my address and promises that the sheriff has a car on the way. In the meantime, she tells me to find a secure location, lock the door, and stay low. I'm not to open the door until the sheriff instructs me to.

Chunks of ice freeze my blood. I can't move again. I can barely speak. "I don't have a safe room," I whisper.

"Go to a room that locks. Your bedroom. Your bathroom. Sit on the floor and stay there."

She stays on the phone with me until the first sheriff squad car arrives. I think she'll hang up then, but she remains on the line as the deputies search the ranch house, going from room to room and inspecting every closet and possible hiding place. Periodically she asks me questions about the house that the sheriff deputies are wanting to know. Are there any hidden closets, secret entrances, unsecured storage areas? No, no, and no. It's a seventy-year-old house. What you see is what you get.

But finally they're done, and the female dispatcher lets me know that the officers want me to unlock the door to my bedroom. I rise from the floor, my legs still shaky, and unlock the bedroom door.

Turns out they found no one. Whoever broke in left before he could be apprehended. The sheriff deputy who interviews me and fills out the paperwork speculates that the patrol car sirens must have scared off the intruder. Unfortunately, the house is no longer habitable. The kitchen door's been kicked in—the point of forced entry—and the living room has been ransacked. The kitchen is nearly as bad, with the refrigerator door left open and glass and Tupperware smashed and scattered across the floor.

After the deputy establishes a timeline, he accompanies me around the house, asking me to identify what's missing. The living room is in such a state of chaos that I can't even begin to figure out what's missing. We don't have valuables here other than the big TV, the boys' laptops—which they took with them to New York—and their various electronics. I've never been a jewelry person, and I have no cash stashed anywhere. However, my purse is missing from the kitchen, and that's scary because in it were my all my credit cards, ID, keys, and cell phone. Essentially my lifeline to the world. Replacing all of that will be a hassle and incredibly time-consuming.

But I'm not hurt. Just scared, just inconvenienced.

In the kitchen, I step over an upended lime Jell-O salad with its lonely bits of pineapple and the remnants of the pumpkin pie and walk the deputies to the front door.

Having finished dusting for fingerprints and documenting the crime scene, they're ready to go. They ask if there is anywhere they can take me. Someplace they can drop me off. I can't think of anyplace I could go, not at two-fifty in the morning the day after Thanksgiving.

"You might want to go to a hotel," the younger deputy urges me as he heads to the door. "It's not exactly safe to stay here."

I must be in shock, because I insist I'll be fine. I watch the four men pile back into the two cars and then head off down my driveway. It's not until the red taillights fade into the night that I'm hit by the reality of my situation.

My kitchen door is gone. I have no truck keys. No money. No ID.

What if the intruder comes back?

What if he's never left?

What if there's still something here he wants?

The nausea returns, even stronger than before, and I sit down heavily on one of the kitchen chairs.

I should have gone with them. Should have let them drop me at a motel. Why didn't I say yes? What was I thinking?

And then the thought comes unbidden.

Call Dane.

Cooper's phone has Dane's number saved as a contact. In fact, he's number 6 on Coop's speed dial, and I press the number.

My teeth chatter as the phone rings. I know it's three in the morning. I know it's Thanksgiving night. But Dane has to answer.

And then he does, his voice low and rough with sleep. "Hello?"

"Dane, it's Shey. Someone broke into the house tonight. The sheriff just left, but the door's smashed in and my purse has been stolen and Brick's gone—"

"Where are the kids?"

"In New York."

"You're alone?"

"Yes—" My voice breaks.

"I'm on the way."

Dane arrives in about fifteen minutes, which is damn near impossible from his property. But even fifteen minutes can feel like forever when you're scared out of your mind and jumping at every sound.

I almost cry as I spot his truck headlights shine through the night, cutting the darkness, and I'm outside, shivering on the front steps, as he pulls in front of the house.

I'm suddenly excruciatingly emotional as he swings open his door and steps to the ground. He looks me up and down as he approaches the steps. "You okay?"

I just nod, tears not far off.

"You don't know who it was?"

I shake my head.

"They dusted for fingerprints?"

I nod again.

Dane now looks past me, his gaze sweeping the house. "How'd he get in?"

"Kitchen."

"How did he get out?"

"Bo's bedroom window." My teeth are chattering. "Window's open and the screen's been cut."

Dane heads for the kitchen then, walking along the front of the house to the back door. He knows the house well. Growing up, Dane spent as much time in our house as he did in his own.

The kitchen door hangs from its hinges. It was never a big, heavy door in the first place, and decades of cold winters and scorching summers have weathered it to its brittle state. Even I can see it wouldn't have taken that much effort to break down the old door.

Dane doesn't even bother to hide his disgust. "Brick should have replaced this door years ago."

"Don't blame Brick. It's not his fault—"

"Maybe not, but someone should have taken better care of you." He jabs his cane into the floor, and the words come out in a hiss. "You could have been hurt—"

"I know!" I don't know why I'm shouting at him, because I'm not mad at him. I'm mad at me. I should have gone with the police, gone to a motel, done anything but called Dane. Turning to Dane is not the answer, never has been the answer. But I do it anyway. "I hope I didn't wake up Lulu."

"Shut up. Get your things. You're coming home with me."

"And Lulu?"

"God, Shey, you're a pain in the ass. Lulu's in Houston for the weekend, okay?"

Chapter Fifteen

─────── ✦ ───────

We arrive at his estate twenty-five minutes later, parking in front of the hulking house built from creamy Texas stone, the front facade marked with long shady porches and thick wood support columns. "This place always takes my breath away," I tell him.

Dane shifts into park and turns off the engine. "Biggest mistake of my life."

"Why would you say that?"

"Two years designing it, one year to build it, endless arguments over the stone for the kitchen floor, the color stain on the living room beams, the right material for the fireplace. For what? None of it helped Matthew. It certainly didn't improve my marriage."

"Was it supposed to?"

"Good question." He's come around to open my door, and I slide out of the truck.

"The house was for Shellie Ann," he adds. "The pool was for Matthew. I just wanted everybody happy." He closes the door behind me and gestures to the front porch. "It's late. I'll show you your room."

I don't think I'm going to be able to sleep in Dane's guest room at the opposite end of the upstairs from his room, but the queen-size bed has an amazing mattress and the softest sheets. I fall asleep almost immediately and wake up hours later to a dark, quiet house. It takes me a moment to remember where I am. Then, when I do, I snuggle deeper into the bed's warmth. For another few minutes I doze, trying to fall back asleep, but memories of the break-in return.

I shouldn't have called Dane. Shouldn't have turned to him just because I was scared.

A knock sounds on the door. "Shey, you awake?"

"Yes. Come in."

But Dane doesn't open the door, just talks through it. "I talked to Brick earlier. He wants you to call him."

This is news, as he and Brick don't talk. I slide out of bed and open the door. "He called you?"

"I called him." Dane's voice is flat, no-nonsense, making it clear that he didn't want to call Brick but didn't have an option. "He wanted to head back this morning and clean up things, but I told him we were handling it and that everything would be fixed by the time he arrived so there was no point in cutting his trip to see Carolyn short."

"I'll call him right now," I promise.

Dane nods and turns away. He's wearing work jeans, boots, and a long-sleeved thermal shirt the color of oatmeal, and as good as he looked from the front—the Henley-style shirt plays up his jaw and thick hair—he looks even better from the back.

"Stop staring and call your brother," Dane snaps over his shoulder as he heads toward the stairs.

"Can't help it," I answer. "You're still smokin' for an old guy."

He pauses at the top of the stairs to give me a reproving look.

I just smile, feeling a bit of the young, rebellious Shey rise up in me. He's hot, seriously hot, and maybe he's Lulu's, but I can still enjoy looking at him.

Dane isn't having any of it, though. "When are you going to grow up, Shey Lynne?"

"When are you going to get ugly?"

"Be careful, Shey."

"Why?" I flash, butterflies flitting wildly inside me. I love it when he's all tough and macho. Love the energy, crave the sexual tension. I never had this with John. We had companionship, friendship, comfort, but never this fierce, raw desire. And I like feeling this way. It makes me feel young and alive.

"Just saying, be careful. Don't start something you can't handle."

A shiver races through me. My eyebrows lift. "That *I* can't handle?"

"Just saying." He holds my gaze a moment and then disappears down the stairs.

I stand there after he's gone, feeling a delicious naughtiness that is so unlike me. These days I'm more maternal than sexual, yet the sexual part is pretty dang fun.

Returning to the bedroom, I replay the conversation, wondering if he really said what I think he said. Don't start something that I can't handle.

Interesting. And what exactly did he mean by that?

Still keyed up, I open the blinds at the window and am greeted by blue sky and wan November sunshine. From the upstairs windows, I get a glimpse of a shimmering dark blue pool surrounded by pale limestone pavers and shaded by two mature oaks that have been gracefully pruned.

This is a beautiful place. A dream estate. I could be so happy here.

I pull up an armchair to the window, then curl my legs under me and call Brick on Cooper's cell phone.

"Coop?" Brick answers immediately.

"No, it's Shey. I'm using Cooper's phone. Mine was in my purse and it was taken."

"You're okay?"

"Yes."

"Scared?"

"I was last night, but I'm good today."

He hesitates. "Dane said the guy got in through the kitchen door."

"Kicked it in. Made a mess of the door and frame."

"I should have replaced that door years ago. It's never been strong. Don't know why I didn't."

"Because it's not your house, and you've been raising two kids and working a big ranch without a lot of help."

"You could have been hurt—"

"But I wasn't."

"Glad you called Dane." He hesitates, his voice dropping and deepening. "Guess I owe him one."

"That's ridiculous. You don't owe him anything, and he doesn't owe you. And I do wish you guys would end this ridiculous feud. It's stupid."

"It's not stupid."

"Yes, it is, especially since Dane has been there for you—"

"Here for me? I'm the one who is always there for him. On the circuit. At the hospital. During rehab. When Matt was born and again when he died—"

"Because that's what friends do!"

"You haven't even been there twelve hours and Kelly's already got you brainwashed."

"Aw, Brick, is this really you saying all this? Because it's not the Brick I know. The Brick I know would give the shirt off his back for a stranger—"

"I'll be back tonight. Tell Dane thanks for everything—"

"No. Don't come back tonight. I don't need or want your help. I'm an adult. I've run a successful business, and I can manage to get the door fixed on the house I'm living in." And then I hang up on the big brother I've always adored.

Fifteen minutes later, I'm stepping out of the shower when Blue calls me on Cooper's phone. I wrap the towel tightly around my chest and pick up, knowing that Brick and Blue have just talked.

"Shey, it's Blue."

"I know," I answer tartly, hitching my towel higher and sitting back against the bathroom counter. "Coop's phone has caller ID."

"Why are you mad at me?" he asks, mildly surprised.

"Why do you think?"

"You women love your guessing games."

"So you haven't just talked to Brick."

"Lord."

"And he didn't just tell you I was staying at Dane's? And you haven't called to say you're on the way to pick me up?"

Blue is silent. And then he chuckles. "Mama said you didn't need saving."

"No, I don't. Not from you or Brick. Because I've had it with both of you."

"Is that a fact?"

"Yes, it is. And here's another one, Blue Callen. Dane's not the bad guy. He did nothing wrong by trying to help Cody, and I'm sick and tired of you and Brick turning Dane into the enemy. You two should be ashamed of yourselves. You've both got wives and kids and busy family lives. Dane has no one but us. We were like his family."

"Okay, sugar, got your point, now reel it back in."

"No." I'm even more angry now than when he first called. "I'm not going to reel it in. I don't need you making decisions for me. And I don't need you and Brick talking about me like gossipy old ladies with nothing else to do."

"Gossipy old ladies?"

"Yeah."

"Well, don't worry, sugar. You won't hear from this gossipy old lady for a while."

And then he hangs up.

I look down at the phone in my hand and exhale. This day isn't going well at all.

It's a clear but cold late November morning, so I dress in my favorite old jeans, boots, and a black long-sleeved turtleneck before heading downstairs to find Dane. I track him down in the kitchen, where he's pouring a cup of coffee.

"Got enough for me?" I ask, perching on one of the black wrought-iron stools at the counter.

"It is for you," he answers, sliding the cup my way.

"Thanks."

"I talked to the sheriff's department just a little bit ago. You didn't tell me that the guy got your purse, too."

"I did."

"Well, you've got a lot of calls to make. Cancel those cards, get new ID."

"You can be just as bossy as my brothers."

"Just looking out for you."

"I appreciate that. And just so you know, I made most of those calls I needed to make before coming downstairs. I froze my checking account. Closed one of my credit cards. I think I have a handle on everything."

"That's good."

My lips curve at his tone. He's definitely in a prickly mood, but I don't press because I'm curious about his house. I glance around, wondering if I can spot Lulu here. But the house is surprisingly impersonal. The architecture and interior are handsome, the furniture well appointed, the artwork expensive, but it feels cool, almost sterile, without plants or knickknacks or framed photos.

"I take it you don't like clutter," I say, noting that the granite kitchen counters are clear, the mantel in the adjacent great room is empty, the low trestle-style coffee table is clean. I'm reminded of a house that's been staged to sell, and it makes me sad. Dane isn't a money guy. He's never cared about personal possessions. Yet this house smacks of money and lacks love.

My hands circle the mug. "I thought you'd have pictures of Matthew somewhere."

I've caught him off guard. As he stiffens, I see such grief in his face that I wish I hadn't mentioned Matthew.

"I've put them in my study. They make Lulu uncomfortable."

My eyes sting and I blink hard. Screw Lulu. I dislike her even more now.

"Can you show me? I'd love to see pictures of him."

Dane nods and heads for his study. I pick up my mug and follow.

Dane's study is a small paneled room at the back of the house. Framed photos of bulls hang on the wall, but there are no trophies, award saddles, or buckles on the bookcase. But on his desk are a cluster of photographs, and Dane lifts one, hands it to me. It's Dane holding a newborn baby wrapped in a hospital blanket. Oxygen tubes are taped to the infant's nose, but it's Dane's eyes in the picture that hold me rapt. I look at the wonder in his eyes. Look at the love.

"He was just a little guy," I say, voice husky with tears I won't cry.

"Not quite five pounds." Dane hands me another framed picture, this of a towheaded toddler propped up on a couch, surrounded by stuffed cows. "Matt loved cows," Dane adds with a smile. "I think he said 'moo' before 'Mama' or 'Dada.'"

Dane is breaking my heart right now.

"Definitely your boy," I say, swapping photos with Dane as he hands me a third. Matthew's in a small wheelchair in this one, his head slumped to the right. But he's laughing and his eyes are a brilliant blue green and his baby teeth are white and straight and he's full of joy. Full of Kelly charm and charisma.

"Your mother must have doted on him," I say, aware that as an only child, Dane got lots of attention from his mother but not the right kind from his father. Dane's dad was a hard man, sometimes too hard. Growing up, Dane had it rough.

"She did. She'd do anything for him, and Mattie knew

it. My mom was probably his favorite person. Mom could always soothe him, even when he wasn't feeling well. She spent hours in the rocker, just holding him, singing to him—" He breaks off, takes a quick breath. "I've always believed that cancer killed her because Mattie was gone. If Matthew had lived, Mom could have fought the disease. But without Matthew, she didn't want to fight."

"What year did she die?"

"In 1999. Just before I won my third and final championship."

I can see he welcomes the change of subject. "She might not have been at the finals, but she knew you won. She was always so proud of you."

"My mom was a good woman," he agrees, taking the third photo from me and placing them all back on his desk so that they face his chair.

I follow him to the door, glancing at the eight framed bull photos lining the wall. "I take it these are your stars?"

He nods, turning out the light. "They're all rank bulls, and the basis of my breeding program. Each one has competed in the nationals, and Dark Angel there is my three-time Bull of the Year."

"Was it hard to switch from riding to breeding?"

"I'm a fourth-generation cattleman, breeding's in the blood. What's been a challenge is getting the PBR to protect the bulls as much as the riders. A good bull is upwards of fifty thousand dollars—Dark Angel was my first hundred-thousand-dollar bull—and they're as important to the event as the rider," he answers, closing the study door and continuing down the hall.

We return to the kitchen, where Dane offers to scramble me some eggs. I answer that I'd be just as happy with toast. Then, with toast and a refill on coffee, I head outside with him to start the day.

The poplars lining Dane's drive are nearly all bare now. Piles of yellow-and-brown leaves pillow the ground and crunch beneath my boots as I walk. I can't resist kicking one pile as I climb into his black truck and giggle as I send leaves flying.

Dane glances at me quizzically. "You're never going to grow up, are you."

"Hope not," I answer, closing the door.

He sighs, but I see a twinkle in his eye and know he's enjoying my silliness. I don't think Dane has a lot of people in his life who allow him to be foolish. But he needs the foolishness and silliness. He needs to laugh. We all need to laugh.

Dane is driving the back roads on our way to the building supply store on the outskirts of town. Since it's the day after Thanksgiving, the roads are empty, and I study the landmark trees and fences and ghostly gas stations with passing interest. I like small towns and old buildings and fences that are falling apart. They have character. I like character.

"There's something I want to say to you," I say as we approach Mineral Wells. "But you're not going to like it."

He shoots me a side glance. "That's never stopped you before."

"I know, but you're going to say it's none of my business. And you're right, it's not, but I care about you, Dane—"

"Just say it. I hate it when women beat around the bush."

Fine. I'll give it to him straight, then. "Lulu's wrong," I say bluntly. "Those pictures of Matthew should be all over the house where you can see them and enjoy them. She has no business telling you to put them in your office. And why would they make her uncomfortable?"

"Because he died."

I see red, and I just completely snap. "Lord, I hate her. I do, Dane. I realize I don't know her. I realize she might be a very nice lady. But she's not the right lady for you. You were Matthew's dad. You will always be his dad. And putting those pictures in your study changes nothing—"

"I know."

He's pulled into the store parking lot, parks in an empty space, and turns off the ignition. I just stare at him. "Are you in love with her?"

He swings open his door. "Let's just get the supplies we need and get to your house."

"Just answer me. Do you love her?"

His green eyes meet mine. His jaw is hard, expression flinty. "No. I don't love her."

"But she's living with you now?"

"No."

"Coop said she'd moved in."

He grabs his cane and steps out. "If you'd rather listen to a twelve-year-old—"

"I wouldn't. That's why I'm asking you."

We face each other on the asphalt. "Lulu's having her house remodeled. She needed somewhere to stay while they gutted and painted and whatever else they're doing to the interior."

"So she's just there temporarily."

Dane rolls his eyes. "Yes. That's what I've been trying to tell you. Now can we just pick up what we need and get over to your house?"

The lumberyard has the door and frame waiting for us, and while they're both being loaded into the back of the truck, Dane picks up new locks, hardware, and a couple of cans of primer and paint. With everything charged to his account, we return to his truck and start for my house.

By the time we reach the ranch house, it's almost eleven. I knew it would be a mess, but I'd forgotten just how bad it is.

Heart thumping, I step around the broken dishes in the kitchen and into the living room, where the upended drawers and scattered cushions remind me of the aftermath of a tornado.

"Glad the boys aren't here to see this," I say, picking up the sofa cushions and placing them back on the couch. "I don't want them to know about this, either. They're not used to being this isolated, and Bo's already jumpy as it is."

With the furniture returned to its rightful place, I tackle cleaning up the broken glass and straightening the kitchen while Dane pulls out the old door frame and hammers in the new.

He uses some pieces of wood he brought from his house to trim out the door, and once he's sanded it, he applies the primer. It takes most of the day to get the house cleaned up and the new door and locks installed. Dane doesn't just install a dead bolt on the new back door, he puts a new dead bolt on the front door and additional hardware on the windows, too.

"This poor house," I say as he finishes up. "It's in terrible shape. I really need to put some money and muscle into it."

"Well, the new door and locks are a start."

We're in the kitchen, where I've just made a pot of coffee. I pour him a cup. "I've got some pound cake and zucchini bread in the freezer if you're hungry. Charlotte's always baking something sweet for us."

"I'll wait for dinner. I don't have much of a sweet tooth." He carries his coffee to the new back door and checks his handiwork, making sure the knob turns easily and the dead bolt works well.

I like watching him work, like how he makes installing a door look easy. A man who can build things, make things, is seriously sexy. But then everything about Dane is sexy. His face, his body, his lips, his eyes, even his walk.

"How does the cold affect your hip?" I ask as he moves his cane out of the way while he jiggles the door handle harder.

"The cold makes everything ache a little more," he answers, satisfied that the lock will hold and the door is now secure.

"I know you were hurt badly twice. But it was the second time that ended your career. What exactly happened?" I see his smile fade. He doesn't want to talk about it. "Never mind. You don't have to tell me."

The corner of his mouth lifts. "You like asking a lot of questions."

I wipe the counter clean and then wash my hands at the sink, taking my time to dry them on the dish towel hanging on the oven door. "I've been gone twenty years.

I've missed out on a lot and am still trying to catch up."

He joins me at the sink and squirts dish soap into his hands, then scrubs them clean. "You didn't miss that much. Things around here don't really change."

I hand him the dish towel once he's rinsed his hands clean. "You've changed."

"I limp now. That's about it."

"Hardly. You've been married, divorced, a father, as well as a three-time national bull-riding champ. You run one of the most respected bucking breeding programs in the country, and you still know how to fill out a pair of Wranglers."

"You're always going to be shallow, aren't you."

"If you mean will I always be attracted to you, yes."

He tosses the damp dish towel at me. "Don't even go there."

"Why not?"

"You know why."

I snap his leg with the towel. "Because of Lulu?"

He sighs. "Lulu's not the issue."

"So what's the issue?"

"Your brothers."

"Are a pain in the butt."

"And they wouldn't like it."

"Since when did you care what people thought?" I snap the towel again but just miss his thigh. "You're Dane Kelly. Tough as nails. Fearless bull rider. National champion."

"Now you're just being ridiculous."

I'm getting worked up, not even sure why, but I want to rile him up, want him to feel as frustrated as I do. I twist the towel, about to snap him again when he reaches out and grabs the end as I snap it.

He doesn't let go.

Neither do I.

"You're asking for trouble, darlin'."

I lift my head and look up into his face to better see his eyes. They're so beautiful.

"Let go," he says.

Maybe I don't know him, but I have loved him anyway. I have loved him my whole life and maybe it's an imperfect love, and an impractical love, but it's still love. "You let go."

He pulls on the beige towel, hard. "Come on, Shey."

"No."

"You're not going to win."

"Maybe. Maybe not. But that doesn't mean I have to give up." My fingers ache from holding on to the towel so tightly, and even holding it as hard as I am, he's still able to inch me toward him, closing the gap between us. "There's something I've wanted to know for years," I say.

"What's that?"

My arm is beginning to tremble, so I use both hands to grip the towel. "Why Shellie Ann?"

He's pulled me to within a foot of him. "First Lulu, now Shellie Ann?"

"Yes."

"That was so long ago. Twenty years ago."

"I don't care. I'm still curious."

He's got me in front of him, toe to toe. My knees bump his, and with another tug on the towel, my chest touches, too.

"Why her? What did she have?"

Dane reaches out to touch my cheek. "You don't want to do this."

"Why not?"

"It's not going to make you feel better."

"But at least I'd know. I'd know it was her humor or her warmth or her quick mind that attracted you. I'd know you loved her intelligence—"

"Stop. She wasn't brainy like you, Shey. Or fiery. Or funny."

"Then what was it? What made her the right one for you?" I'm practically resting against his chest, and he's warm, so warm. I can feel the width of his ribs, the hard oval of his belt buckle, the sinewy strength of his thighs. He's definitely all man.

"She got pregnant."

I freeze, and he lets go of the towel to slide his arm around me and rest his hand low on my back. "She got pregnant, and that took care of that."

I never expected him to say that. Never in a thousand years. "You should have told me," I whisper, shivering at the touch. I love his hand on me. It makes me hot and cold and desperate for more.

"Why? We would never have worked."

"You made me hate you."

"That's probably a good thing. You're not a country girl, Shey Lynne. You were never cut out for this life."

"You don't know that." The warmth of his palm penetrates the worn-out denim of my jeans, making me aware of my body, his hand, and my skin. I'd forgotten that my body could feel like this, and it just makes me want more. The desire is raw and primitive and nearly all-consuming.

"You're still not cut out for this life," he adds, his palm sliding down my butt to my thigh.

I ache for him. I'm mad for him. I want him like a drug.

"You won't be staying," he adds. "You'll be gone within a year. Two if you're stupid."

I hear the word *stupid*, but I also feel him responding, and I rub up against his erection. I want him. Hot, hard, wild. His body in mine, taking me, possessing me, making me feel what I haven't felt in so long—good, beautiful, wonderful.

I never used sex as an escape before, but I want it now. I want him now, want to finally be his woman…even if it's only for one day.

"Your kids are city kids," he answers, taking my hips and holding them snug against him. "Your kids' father lives there. They need their father."

"I'm not going back."

"I don't believe it. Your kids are too important to you." He sets me back, pushing me gently away. "It's getting late. I still have plenty to do on my property, so we should probably head back."

His tone is flat and curiously detached, and I'm horrifyingly close to tears. For twenty years I believed Dane had fallen head over heels for Shellie Ann, and in the beginning I tortured myself by imagining them together, picturing her as his great love, his soul mate. Now I discover that maybe none of it was true.

"Maybe it's better if I stay here tonight," I say hoarsely. "You've fixed the door and changed the locks. I'm sure I'll be safe."

"You don't have your keys. You can't drive your truck—"

"I'll call Manny tomorrow. I'm sure he can send a lock-smith over."

"Sorry, darlin'. I promised Brick you'd stay at my place until he was back in town, and I'm going to keep that promise."

"So this is about Brick?"

"This is about you, and keeping you safe."

"But I am safe now!"

"The guy who broke in has your wallet, your phone, all your ID. If he didn't know who lived here before, he does now."

If his words didn't give me pause, his rough tone does. But Dane's not done. In fact, he's just warming up. "Your nearest neighbor is fifteen minutes away, and as you dis-covered last night, the sheriff takes even longer to get here. So no, I'm not worried what Brick will think. I'm worried Brick's right. We don't know who this guy is. We don't know what he wants. And yeah, things are complicated between us, but awkward and uncomfortable is a hell of a lot better than seeing you hurt."

Chapter Sixteen

Dane's not happy as we head to his house, and I glance at his profile illuminated by the green white light of his dash. His jaw's set. His mouth's hard. There's nothing remotely tender about him.

"You confuse me," I say finally, breaking the silence.

He doesn't answer, and I study the straight length of his nose, the angle of his cheekbones, the line of his brow. "I can't tell if you like me or hate me—"

He cuts me short. "You're being absurd."

"I'm not. I'm confused. Did I do something wrong back there? Say something? Push a hot button?"

His jaw tightens. "Things had gone far enough."

"But nothing happened!"

"It could have."

"Good. I hoped something would happen."

He shoots me a swift side glance. "In your mama's kitchen?"

"Yes."

He just shakes his head. "You scare me, Shey Lynne. You really do."

"You *asked*."

"Some things are better left unsaid."

"Are we back to the whole fake polite southern lady thing again? Good girls don't do this, good girls don't say that...Well, that's ridiculous and it's not me. I'm not your good little southern girl. I'm a Texas girl. Straight up. Honest. Strong." I shoot him a dark glance. "And I honestly can't believe you'd want me to be all fake and sugary sweet. Yes, Dane. No, Dane. How high should I jump, Dane?"

"Knock it off."

"Why should I? I'm tired. Tired of dancing around what's right in front of us." We've reached the edge of his property and pass through the gates, bouncing over the wide cattle guard. "I like you. You know I like you. And I can't figure out if the feeling is mutual—"

He slams on his brakes, and I put a hand out to the dash to brace myself. "You can't figure that one out? Well, let me clear up the confusion, then. I've been attracted to you since we were kids and you were just a skinny blond pipsqueak in pigtails and boots. Which is why *screwing* you isn't an option."

I cringe at his crudity. He's angry, really angry. But I don't understand why.

"If I could control myself around you at twenty-two," he continues, "I can certainly keep my dick in my pants now."

"Why are you doing this? Why are you talking like this? What's wrong with you?"

"What's wrong with me?" He drags a hand through his hair and gives his head a shake. "Hell, Shey, what's wrong with you? You might have filed for divorce, but it hasn't been granted, which means you're still married."

I lie wide awake in Dane's guest room, letting his words play over and over in my head.

You're still married, he said. *Married. Married.*

And if I weren't married, would it be okay for him to be with me?

If I weren't married, could we be together?

But I am still legally married, and in many ways, I still feel emotionally and psychologically tied to John. We might be living a thousand miles apart, but he's the father of my kids. He's my partner of the past seventeen years. It's hard to sever the tie completely so quickly.

Thinking of John makes me think of the boys, and I feel a rush of emotion. I miss my kids. Miss their faces, their big bodies, their noise, their chaos, even their attitude. They fill my life with activity and energy and conversation. I don't even remember life without them. I don't want a life without them.

And when they're home, you can hide behind them, a little voice whispers.

You can make them your world. Make them your mission and bury yourself in their wants and demands so you can pretend you don't need anything but them. But it's a lie. And you know it's a lie. Or you wouldn't still feel this way about Dane.

I throw an arm over my face, trying to hide, because that little voice inside my head is unfortunately usually right.

I'm still asleep the next morning when Dane knocks on my bedroom door. I hear it but don't open my eyes. It took me hours to fall asleep last night, and I'm not ready to face the day yet.

The knock sounds again, and Dane's deep voice rumbles through the door. "Shey, Brick's on the phone."

"I'll call him later," I answer.

"He thought you'd say that. So I'm to tell you that your mother is getting in the car and heading here this minute."

"Really?" I throw back the covers, march to the door, and open it wide.

Dane's in the hallway wearing nothing but jeans and dense, sculpted muscle. I know he's forty-five, but he's got the lean, hard body of a twenty-year-old.

"It's your family," he says, handing me the phone.

I put the phone to my ear, aware that I'm in one lousy mood. "Brick, if you're calling to see if I've been ravished yet, the answer is no."

Dane shakes his head at me in disgust and walks away, giving me an opportunity to check out his butt.

Brick's sigh is audible over the phone. "What's going on there?"

"Nothing. Unfortunately."

"What do you mean?"

"Apparently Dane, your archenemy, has scruples. He won't have sex with me because I'm still married."

Brick mutters something unintelligible before taking a breath and saying quite clearly, "You're out of control."

I return to my room and lie down on the bed. "I'm almost forty, Brick, I'm not out of control. You guys are just cavemen and it's pathetic and annoying and you're making New York look more appealing all the time."

"You tried to sleep with Dane?"

"It didn't get that far."

"Lord almighty, Shey Lynne."

I pull up the covers, nestle deeper into the downy warmth. "Am I never supposed to have sex again?"

"This isn't a conversation I want to be having, but no.

My sister doesn't need sex. You've already done it three times and that's more than enough."

"Is Mama really on her way?"

"No. Not yet, at least." He hesitates. "The sheriff's department phoned me a little bit ago. They've got a positive ID on the guy who broke in." He exhales slowly. "Shey, the guy's got an extensive record. He's a repeat offender with a violent history. Battery. Burglary. Worse."

Worse? There aren't many things worse than battery and burglary. Just rape and murder. "Thank God I was able to call for help."

"It could have been bad," he agrees. "I'm on my way home now. Char's going to stay with Carolyn for the next week and get a start on her Christmas shopping. I'm going to stay with you and the boys at the house. Hopefully they'll catch this guy soon."

I throw on jeans and a long-sleeved red T-shirt without bothering with a bra and race downstairs to find Dane. I search the house without any luck, which sends me out the front door. I spot Dane next to the barn, hitching a trailer to his truck, and race toward him. He's wearing a leather barn coat and hat and looks as though he's just about finished up.

"Did Brick tell you?" I ask, shivering. The temperature has dropped, but it's Brick's news that's chilled me.

He looks up from the trailer hitch, expression grim. "He did."

I rub my arms. "The guy has a violent history. A repeat offender."

"Now you know why I wasn't about to leave you behind last night."

"You knew about this guy?"

"No. Just that there's been a string of break-ins in Parker County," he says. Parker is just one county over. "Last time a couple got hurt."

"You think this guy would return to the scene of a crime?"

"Knowing what this guy's done...if he thought you were alone...maybe. That's why we both want you to stay here."

"You and Brick suddenly teammates?"

"I wouldn't say that, but we're both in agreement that it's better to err on the side of caution, and not just for your sake, but for your boys."

The boys. What if the boys had been home the night of the break-in? I shudder at the thought. "Let's not talk about it anymore. I have to live in that house, and I don't want to be scared. I've never been scared. I grew up there. I'm raising my boys there. I want to feel safe."

"I've got a security company out there today. They're putting in the same system I have here. Motion detectors, sensors on the glass, alarms, Pelco videocameras. If anyone tries to enter your house, the alarm company immediately notifies Brick and the sheriff. You'll be safe. I promise."

"Good." And I am reassured. I've seen Dane's security setup and it's impressive. It's what you'd expect to find in a Fortune 500 company instead of a country home. "Looks like you're heading someplace. Am I included or do I have to stay here?"

"I'm heading to Stephenville to pick up one of my bulls. Want to come?"

"Can we stop for coffee and pancakes somewhere?"

He smiles, eyes creasing. "You're in luck. Eggs'n Things is on the way."

It is nearly noon by the time we reach Stephenville, where Dane picks up one of his bulls that's been on the circuit but has just been retired. I stay in the truck while Dane and the cowboy load the bull and then stand around and talk. The cowboy's familiar, but I can't place him and wonder if perhaps he went to school with one of my brothers.

As Dane and the cowboy talk, I stretch out my legs and close my eyes, but my mind keeps returning to the break-in and how grateful I am that the boys weren't home. They would have tried to play hero, make a bold move, and God knows what would have happened then. I shiver just thinking about it.

A few minutes later, Dane climbs back in the truck, waves farewell to the cowboy, and we set off.

"You okay?" Dane asks as we drive away.

"Yeah. Just thinking about the guy who broke in. It's scary."

"It is. But Brick will be back soon and the security will be in place and you'll be okay, I promise."

"No, I know. And I'm not scared for me as much as I'm worried about the boys. I keep picturing Cooper confronting the guy—"

"Stop torturing yourself. It didn't happen. It's not going to happen. And the guy's going to get caught."

I nod and force myself to think about other things now. After a moment, I mention to Dane that the cowboy looked familiar. "I know I know him," I tell Dane. "Did he go to school with you? Was he friends with Brick?"

"He's five years younger than me, closer to your age than mine." Dane leans forward to get a better look into his rearview mirror before merging from Morgan Mill Road onto 281. Pulling a trailer, particularly a trailer with a thousand-pound animal, takes patience and skill. "But he should be familiar. That was Ty Murray."

"Oh, my God." I smile at my mistake. Ty Murray has to be the greatest all-around cowboy of all time. He won the national title seven times and in 1993 helped found the PBR, Professional Bull Riders tour, with Dane and a handful of other bull-riding champs. "How is he? Was Jewel around?"

"Apparently Jewel's somewhere recording." Dane turns off Murray's property onto the county road. "And now that you know it was Ty, do you wish you'd gotten out of the truck?"

"No. I'm a fan, of course, but what am I going to say? I watched you on *Dancing with the Stars* a couple years ago and thought the judges were a little harsh?"

Dane grins. "He did all right."

"Looked like you two were having quite the heart-to-heart talk."

"He's been trying to get me into the PBR broadcast booth for years. Thinks I'd make a good announcer."

"That's flattering."

"It is, but it's also a big commitment. It would involve a lot of time and travel. It would be hard to run my business here and be on the road for weeks at a time."

"But you're tempted."

Dane shrugs. "I love the rodeo, and the PBR has really

taken off. It's exciting to watch, and I'd definitely enjoy being part of it again."

"You miss competing?"

"Yeah. But there are no more comebacks for me. Nobody's Knight made sure of that."

I turn on my seat to face him. "That's the bull you were riding when you were hurt?"

He nods. "Rankest bull on the circuit that year. Not enough to buck and kick. He went for the rider every time. Nothing made that son of a bitch happier than stomping a cowboy's guts out."

"And he stomped yours."

"After rolling on me a couple times. Shattered my pelvis, hip, and thigh. Broke a bunch of other things, but it's the hip that's been tricky."

"Is that why you're having all the surgeries?"

"We've got fifty-two miles to go. Are you going to ask questions the whole way?"

He sounds so pained that I giggle. "We're just making conversation, Kelly."

"Maybe we should turn on the stereo. I've got some CDs in there. Tim McGraw. Rascal Flats. Brad Paisley."

I cross one leg over the other, swing my foot, totally amused. "You're trying to shut me up."

"You like country music."

"You know I do. But it's nice just hanging out and talking to you."

He grimaces. "Why do women like to talk so much?"

"Because we're women, and language is linked to estrogen." I lean my head back against the seat and smile at him. "Apparently you're lacking estrogen."

"Is that so?"

I laugh and, to keep him happy, turn on the stereo.

Brick swings by Dane's ranch to pick me up on his way home from San Antonio. I hadn't expected him for another hour and am not prepared, which forces Brick and Dane to make small talk while I run upstairs to gather my things.

As I toss my clothes and face stuff into my overnight bag, their voices drift up and I overhear bits and pieces of their conversation. Their conversation is so painfully strained, it's almost funny.

But after a few awkward comments about the cold front and crops, Dane mentions his trip earlier in the day to Ty Murray's ranch, which then leads into a discussion of the current PBR standings as the season draws to a close.

When Brick and Dane graduated from high school, they chose to join the Professional Rodeo Cowboy's Association rather than go to college. They paid their two hundred dollars and got their PRCA permit, which allowed them to enter rodeos where space was available. They wouldn't become full-fledged members of the PRCA until they earned enough money competing to buy their card. Back then it was around twenty-five hundred dollars, and Dane earned it his first year. It took Brick an extra year to earn his. But even then they stuck together, traveling from Pecos, Texas, to Eugene, Oregon, to Calgary, Alberta, and back to Prescott, Arizona. For four years they traveled together, roomed together, and competed against each other. And during those years, the injuries started to pile up.

In the end, the injuries were too much for Brick. He realized he'd be happier ranching than competing and retired from the PRCA. But Dane's career just kept getting bigger, and since Brick knew the business, he became Dane's manager, entering Dane in events, paying fees, signing sponsors, even as Brick began a family with Charlotte and took over the ranch from Pop.

Dane was doing well and making good money on the PRCA circuit, but it was the Professional Bull Riders that really cemented Dane's status as a star. And Brick was there the whole way.

This is the kind of relationship Brick and Dane have, and as they discuss the rankest bull on this year's circuit and the new young Brazilian riders, I feel a glimmer of hope that maybe Brick and Dane will eventually patch things up. Blood may be thicker than water, but you can't survive without water.

Once Brick and I are in his truck and he's heading to our ranch, he asks me about everything I'm missing. "Keys, phone, wallet, checkbook, you name it," I answer.

"Over Thanksgiving weekend, too." He shakes his head. "Terrible timing. Nothing's open. What can you do?"

"I haven't gotten anything done this weekend, other than try to clean up the house and help Dane get the new door and locks in."

"I'm pretty sure I have a spare key to Pop's truck at my house."

"That'd be wonderful. Otherwise I have to call Manny or a locksmith."

We lapse into silence, and Brick turns on the radio to a news talk station. Brick loves talk radio. He gets all his news and weather reports from the radio.

But a few minutes later, he turns down the volume. "I'm glad you called Dane. He and I might have our differences, but you'll always be safe with him." And then he turns the volume back up.

I look at him, eyebrows lifting. That's it? That's all he's going to say?

After a minute goes by, I turn down the volume. "You two were talking for almost twenty minutes," I say. "That's the first time you guys have really talked in years."

Brick's jaw hardens. "Don't go there."

"Don't go where?"

"You know. Just mind your own business and everything will be fine."

It's not the answer I want, but it's what I get. And at least they're talking. That's a start.

Back at our ranch, Brick and I go through the new security system together. The old house now has the security of Fort Knox, and I'm not sure if I should be worried or relieved by the hundred different ways we can trip the alarm.

With the security codes in place and all the doors and windows properly armed, Brick sees to his horses and I phone the boys to go over the arrangements for their arrival tomorrow. Bo and Cooper sound good on the phone— cheerful and happy—but Hank sounds depressed.

"Has it been a good visit?" I ask him, trying to understand why he's so down.

"Yeah. It was all right. Most of my friends were gone for the break, but I saw Cole and Paul and we tossed the ball around a bit."

"You played lacrosse?"

"It wasn't a game, but we ran around in Central Park."

"That's great. I bet it was good to see them."

"It was." Hank falls silent. "Mom...," he starts, then stops.

"What, hon?"

I can tell he's struggling with words, and I hold my breath, wanting to help him but not knowing how. He's fifteen. He's been pulling away from me for a while now.

"I love you, Mom," he says finally.

But he says it in a rough voice that just sounds sad, as though loving me were a bad thing. I swallow hard, and my eyes smart. "I love you, too. Can't wait to see you, baby."

"Me too, Mom." And then he hangs up.

I turn out most of the lights but leave one on over the front door for Brick, who plans to sleep in Coop's room. I'm heading down the hallway to my room when the photos on the wall catch my eye.

I pass down the narrow hall a hundred times a day and never pay the framed photos any notice, but tonight I stop. It's a gallery dedicated to the four Callen kids, with photos dating back to the mid-1960s.

There's Brick and Blue, towheaded toddlers in matching western shirts and cowboy hats, smiling for the Sears photographer.

Here's one of Brick on a horse, and then another of Blue in football pads, plus cheap oak-framed class photos that have already faded and yellowed.

Farther down the wall is Cody's eight-by-ten baby portrait, and he's a grinning, gummy-faced baby, completely bald but so smiley that his eyes glint with good humor. This is the Cody I know, this is the Cody I love.

When I was growing up, Cody was my best friend. We

were two years apart in age but just a year apart in school, and wherever Cody went I was sure to follow.

My gaze follows the cluster of framed photos—Cody as a Cub Scout, Cody as a football player, Cody holding a trophy after taking first at the state fair for his sheep. I remember how upset I was that Cody got to sleep at the fairground near his sheep and Mama and Pop wouldn't let me. I was so mad at Cody. But then the next day he won first place, and no one was prouder.

I reach out and touch the photo of grinning Cody and his trophy. My favorite brother. Gone far too soon.

Cody shouldn't have died. There's no reason for him to have died. We should have stuck together. Worked together. Helped him sooner. Helped him better.

Why didn't we? Why couldn't we? What's happened to all of us?

What's happened to *me*?

It's too late to bring him back, but it's not too late to get me back. The confident me, the strong me. The Shey who believed she could do anything. Be anything. Handle anything.

With a last glance at the photograph of Cody I vow to one day be that Shey again because I really liked her.

She was tough. Smart. Sexy.

Brave.

And on a good day, Lord, was she fun.

Chapter Seventeen

———— ✦ ————

The sky is a blustery gray as I drive to the airport, and for the first time this year I turn on the truck's heater. The weather forecast predicts rain in the next few days, and if temperatures drop much lower, we might see some snow. It's a very slight chance, but a possibility.

Although snow is beautiful, especially when it paints the fields white, I'm not ready for it. I have so much to do, and at the top of my list is getting a new driver's license and then opening a new checking account and pulling some cash from the bank to tide me over until my new credit and debit cards arrive. I also have to buy a new cell phone, as well as a new wallet. Such a hassle replacing everything, and sad to lose the boys' pictures.

I arrive at the airport with twenty minutes to kill. But then it's three o'clock, and as I wait at the appropriate American Airlines baggage carousel, the sliding glass door opens and my boys emerge.

Bo. Cooper. No Hank.

Where's Hank?

I count the heads again. Only two. There should be three. Where's my oldest?

Bo reaches me, hugs me hard, and blurts out, "Hank stayed behind, Mom."

He's so tall that his chin hits my shoulders. Automatically

I lift a hand, smooth the back of his hair. It's getting long again. "What do you mean?"

Coop shuffles up, his backpack hanging off his thin shoulder. He's built just like Cody. "He's not coming back, Mom—" Coop's voice cracks, and he flushes. "He said he'd call you..."

All I hear is the echo of Cooper's words—*He's not coming back*—before my adrenaline kicks in. Not coming back? How can he not come back? I'm his mom. He lives with me.

"What?" I whisper, my chest growing tight.

"He was supposed to call," Bo says flatly.

"He didn't say anything about staying," I answer.

Cooper looks nervous. "Sorry."

"When did he decide not to come?" I ask, reaching for Cooper's backpack so he can get a better handle on his rolling bag. But he brushes me off.

"I don't know," Bo answers evasively even as he and his brother exchange glances.

They know, I think, anxiety giving way to frustration. "Well?" I demand, seeing as I put three boys on a plane to see their dad for Thanksgiving a week ago and I expected three to get off.

"It got weird last night," Bo confesses as we head out through the exit to the parking garage.

"Weird how?" I ask, looking from one to the other.

"Just weird all the way around. You'd have to be there."

I see their faces as we step into the shadowy garage, and their expressions are grim. Reluctantly, I let the subject drop. It's Hank I need to talk to. Hank I'll call as soon as we're home.

*   *   *

It's a ninety-minute drive without traffic, but there's traffic today because of a horrific-looking accident that's turned the freeway into a parking lot. By the time we actually get home, we've been in the car close to three hours and my excitement over the boys' return has morphed into anger.

Hank should have called me, warned me. And if he wasn't going to tell me, John should have instead.

Inside the house, the boys head to their rooms and I use the kitchen phone to call Hank's cell. Part of me is thinking he won't answer, while another part of me is desperate for him to pick up. He picks up.

"Hey, Mom."

My throat suddenly closes. This is my firstborn, my baby. "What's going on?"

"I just...I mean, Texas, Mom, really?"

"So you're staying in New York with Dad."

"Yeah."

"You couldn't call me to warn me?"

"I did."

"You didn't."

"Check your damn voice mail. I left two messages on your phone, Mom, two."

And then I remember I'm missing my cell phone. It was in my purse, and since I always use my cell, Hank wouldn't think to call me on the house phone. "You didn't tell me when we last spoke."

He doesn't answer.

The hot band around my chest squeezes tighter. "I just wish you'd talked it through with me—"

"You wouldn't have listened. You would have just gotten pissed."

"No, I wouldn't have."

"Yes. And you're pissed now. You're always pissed—"

"*Please*. Don't use that word."

"See? That's exactly what I mean. It's like I can't do anything right—"

"Not true!"

"*Is* true. Besides, you still have Bo and Cooper. Dad has no one. And he loves us, and misses us, as much as you do."

And just like that, the anger goes, leaving a strange hollow place inside of me. "Dad does need you," I say quietly. "It'll be good for you to be there with him. He won't be so lonely."

"Yeah."

He says it halfheartedly, and I realize he's completely conflicted. As we all are.

I draw a breath to ease the hot, tight feeling in my chest. "Baby, I love you. I'm sorry you think I'm always upset with you because I'm not. I love you to pieces and I'd do anything for you. And if you'll be happier in New York, then it's good you stayed—"

"It's okay, Mom. You're doing your best."

He's right. I am. But my best in this case hasn't been enough. "Will you come see me at Christmas?"

"Of course. You're still my mom."

He says good-bye. I say something, and when I hang up, I put my head down on my arm and feel something break open inside me.

I've never lived without my kids. I knew I'd lose Hank in three years when he goes away to college, but I thought

I had three years. I need three years. I am not ready for it to happen yet.

I don't have favorites, but Hank's my first and so very dear to me.

Cooper appears at my side, wraps his arm around my neck, and whispers roughly, "Don't cry. Please, Mom."

I lift my head and wipe my eyes and give him a crooked smile. "Sorry, hon. I'm just tired. I was so excited you boys were coming home that I didn't sleep much last night."

"Neither did I." He makes a face. "I hate flying. Makes me so nervous. I just keep thinking that any minute the plane's going to fall out of the sky."

"Not a relaxing thought."

"No. But I don't have to get on a plane for a while, so that's good."

"Well, not until after Christmas when you go see Dad for New Year's."

He groans and drops into a chair at the kitchen table, burying his face in his hands. "That's only a month away!"

I try to distract him with a different topic. "Tell me about Thanksgiving. How was it? Where did you guys eat? Who was there?"

He sighs and listlessly rubs his knuckles across the table's scratched surface. "It was fine. Just the four of us. Dad cooked. The turkey was actually pretty good."

"That's good."

"Yeah."

"What did you like best?"

"The stuffing."

"Really?"

He nods and rubs his knuckles back the other way. "It

wasn't cornbread. But it was good. The mashed potatoes were only so-so, though. They were real lumpy, not fluffy."

"But that's good he tried."

He nods again.

"And Erik wasn't around?"

"No. He was supposed to be, but I think they had a fight. Because Erik left and didn't come back. Dad seemed really bummed, but he tried to hide it. You know how Dad is when he doesn't want anyone to know he's sad."

I do know. John has always tried hard to make everyone happy, even if he wasn't.

"When did Erik come back?" I ask, aware that I'm prying, but concerned.

"I don't know. He was there Friday morning when we woke up."

"Good." I reach out, ruffle Cooper's hair. "Hungry? It's way past dinnertime in New York right now. You must be starving."

"Yeah."

"What do you want?"

"Anything. As long as it's not turkey."

After dropping Bo and Cooper at school the next morning, I call Mineral Wells High to let them know that Hank won't be returning. The attendance clerk asks if this is a permanent or temporary move. "Probably permanent," I answer, although I don't really know. He's never lived apart from me. I don't know how this will go.

I do my errands then, hitting first the Department of Motor Vehicles, then the bank, and finally the Verizon store for a new phone. I plug the phone charger into the old cigarette lighter on the way home and check my voice mail for messages.

There's a call from Mama wanting to know if I'm okay, a call from Tiana saying she might have business in Dallas next month, and then two calls from Hank—so he did call—and a call this morning from John.

"Shey, we need to talk today, before Cooper's home from school. I don't want Coop working with this cowboy guy anymore. I don't care how good he is, these rodeo events are dangerous, never mind cruel to animals. Although I rarely put my foot down, I'm putting it down now. If you owe this guy any money, let me know and I'll send him a check, but otherwise, Coop's done."

Click.

I play the message again. And again.

Anger ricochets through me, anger and shame. Who is John to play the tough guy now? Who does he think he is, leaving the family and then laying down the law? He doesn't know the first thing about the rodeo or roughstock events, and he can't make these decisions on his own.

My hand is no longer steady as I delete the message.

I call John once I'm home, but he's not available. I leave him a voice message on his cell: "It's Shey and we do need to talk, because you can't make that decision for Cooper on your own. We're both his parents. We both have a say, and I support him learning to ride. He's not just a Darcy, he's a Callen, too." Click.

I try to work on Brick's books, which isn't easy as I'm on pins and needles waiting for John's call. I'm also beginning to feel overwhelmed by the ranch's mounting expenses, expenses that far outweigh ranch income. The ranch is in trouble. I've tried talking to Brick, but he keeps telling me it'll work out, that ranching and cattle is always cyclical. But God, it makes me nervous.

I work through lunch while keeping an eye on the clock. Then, just as I'm getting ready to leave to pick up the boys, my phone rings and it's John.

"Shey, are you serious?" he says by way of greeting. "You're going to fight me on this?"

"Coop loves riding, and wants to enter his first rodeo later this year."

"Absolutely not."

"John, you can't just dismiss his dreams—"

"He's never been interested in rodeos or country-western music until he arrived there a few months ago."

"Five months."

"*Five*. And he'll get over it. He's not that serious."

"You don't know that. You can't say that. You can't see his face as he talks about riding. You can't see his face when he walks through the door every day after he's trained with Dane. He's so happy, John, he glows."

"Bull riding is one of the most dangerous sports in the world. It's an extreme sport. Every fifteen rides a professional rider is seriously injured. Fifteen. And we're talking the pros, not kids."

"That's because the pros are riding tough bulls."

"But isn't that what Coop wants to do? Isn't that what you said his dream is?"

I'm silent now, and John seizes the opportunity.

"I love our boys, Shey, and there's no way I want one

to end up in a wheelchair or worse. It'd break my heart, and I know it'd break yours, too."

"I hear what you're saying, and I agree the sport can be dangerous. But can we please include Cooper in this discussion? This is the first time he's found a sport he loves. He's so into it, John. He knows the standings of the top ten tour leaders. He can tell you the strengths and weaknesses of the top riders as well as the bulls on today's circuit—"

"Shey, it's no. And you have to back me up on this. Don't make this get ugly."

Is he threatening me? I frown at the phone. "What does that mean?"

"You've moved the kids to Texas, a place they hate so much that Hank's now back with me. I'm beginning to think I'm the fit parent—"

"You better stop right there, John. You, the fit parent? The man who has been sleeping around with other men for God knows how many years during our marriage? You, the fit parent, when you lie and cheat on me for years on end—"

"Being gay isn't a crime. And at least I have the boys' best interests at heart."

"I don't care that you're gay! I care that you lied to me. I care that you slept around on me. I care that you married me when you must have suspected somewhere inside yourself that you weren't straight!"

"So you do care that I'm gay."

"Jesus, John. I loved you. I still love you. But don't you dare question my commitment to these children, and don't you dare imply that I'm not fit to be their mother."

"Then be reasonable and come back to New York. I'd

be able to see the boys regularly, and it'd nip Coop's rodeo obsession in the bud."

"I live here now."

"You're not a country girl, Shey. You're as urban and sophisticated as they come."

"I have to go."

"I'm serious about Cooper not riding. Don't make me take legal action."

I hang up with his ominous words echoing in my head.

I'm late to get the boys, and I grab my keys and purse and jump into the truck to race to Palo Pinto Elementary School for Cooper. He's the only one in the parking lot when I pull in.

"You're late," he says, climbing into the truck, "and now we're going to be late to Dane's."

"I know. I'm sorry." I glance at him, see his broad, thin shoulders, the intense blue eyes, the firm press of his lips. He's going to hate what I have to tell him. "I just talked to your dad."

"Yeah?" He looks at me, but he's barely listening.

"It wasn't a great conversation."

"Was it about Erik?"

"No. It was about you." I can see Coop's interest perk up, and I dread what I have to say next. "He's concerned about your safety, and the bottom line is that he doesn't think it's a good idea for you to continue bull riding."

"What?" His voice rises a full octave.

"He thinks it's too dangerous."

"Did you tell him I love it and that I'm not scared?"

"He's overruling you, Coop. He's your dad. He can do that."

"But didn't you tell him that he can't? You're my mom. You can overrule him."

"It doesn't quite work like that."

Coop just stares at me, and I struggle on. "I don't want to lose you, Cooper, and if I fight him on this, I'm afraid he'll try to get custody—"

"No. I'm not going to live with him. Not ever. It freaks me out being there. Freaks me out to see him sitting with Erik on the couch, holding hands, kissing."

"They kiss in front of you?"

He shrugs. "They kiss good-bye. No tongues, but still. It's gross. I don't like it. I mean, Dad used to kiss you!"

Yeah, there is that.

"Your dad really loves you," I say. "He's not gay to hurt you. He's not gay to hurt me. It's just who he is—"

"Which is why I'm not going back to New York. I'm staying here for Christmas break. I don't want to see him anymore. Don't want to be a kiss-ass like Hank just so I can get some money."

"Cooper!"

His blue eyes blaze at me. "It's true. Erik's rich. He's loaded. And he's buying Hank everything he wants. Why else do you think Hank stayed in New York? It's because Erik promised him all kinds of crazy shit."

"Don't swear!"

"Fine. But I'm not going back. I'm staying here and I'm going to be a cowboy. It's not up to Dad."

We drive for a few minutes in silence, and even though it's chilly in the truck, my hands are damp on the steering wheel.

By the time we arrive at Mineral Wells Junior High,

we're almost thirty-five minutes late. I find myself praying that Bo won't be upset, praying that when I pull up in front of the gym, Bo will be the boy he once was, the boy who woke up happy, and energetic, and excited about life.

I spot him as soon as I turn into the parking lot. He's the only kid there, and he's not smiling.

After pulling up at the curb, I shift into park, and Bo opens the door and climbs into the cab's backseat.

"Hey," I greet him as Bo slouches against the seat back. "How was your day?" I ask, shifting into drive and leaving the parking lot behind.

"Sucked." Bo doesn't even open his eyes. "Big-time."

I glance into the rearview mirror. "Why did it suck?"

"When doesn't it?" he answers, opening his eyes to fix his gaze on me.

I'm determined to keep my cool. Things are going to get better. Things are going to improve. "Something happen?"

"Just the usual. Some kid threw his sour milk at me. Another kid thought I'd like to get a close look at the inside of the garbage can." His eyes are burning, pink. "It was nice. Smelled real good, too."

My stomach rises and my heart falls at the same time. It's a good thing there isn't much traffic, because I'm barely aware of the road. "Did you go to the office? Did you talk to Mr. Peterson? What is the school going to do?"

"Nothing."

"What?"

"There's no one I can tell. There's nothing I can do."

"Yes, there is. Mr. Peterson will help you—"

"No, he won't. Yeah, sure, he can talk to the kids who do it, but then it'll just get worse. The kids will call me a pussy, a snitch—" He breaks off, jaw clenched. "God, I wish I was never born."

"Bo."

He shakes his head, stares out the window. "I mean it. I hate me. I hate my life. I wish I was never born."

We drive home, all three of us brooding in silence. As we reach the turnoff that would have taken us to Dane's, Coop yelps, "Aren't we turning, Mom?"

"Coop, we talked about this—"

"I can't ride roughstock. Fine. But I can still ride the mechanical bull. I can rope. I can do other things."

"I think you have to talk to your dad first."

"Why? You already talked to him and he said I can't ride roughstock. So, fine. I won't ride roughstock, but there are other things I can do. Other things Dane can teach me. Please, Mom. Please." His voice spirals up, panic and desperation making his tone sharp.

My hands are shaking so badly that I can barely steer. Heart racing, I pull over to the side of the road and press my head to the steering wheel. My heart's hammering and I'm sweating like mad and I can't help wondering if maybe I'm having a panic attack.

Cooper leans over, hugs me. "Don't cry, Mom."

"I'm not..." But my voice is muffled because I've got my face hidden.

"If you don't want me to go to Dane's—"

"But I do. You like going. You're happy there."

He falls silent, and neither boy speaks. After a moment, I take a deep breath. I taste salt on my lip, which is odd until I realize I'm crying.

I wipe the tears away with a fist and sit up and smile

at Cooper and then Bo. "You want to go to Dane's," I say to Coop, and it's a statement, not a question.

He nods.

"I'll take you there, but you've got to promise me you'll stay off broncos and bulls until your dad gives the okay."

Cooper's blue gaze holds mine. "You think he'll eventually let me?"

My shoulders rise and fall. "I don't know. I guess we're just going to have to wait and see."

Dane is waiting for us as we arrive at his ranch. It's cold enough that bits of wispy fog rise from the ground as he walks over to meet our truck. "We're late," I say, rolling down my window. "Sorry."

He looks at me and then leans down, forearms resting on the truck door. "What's wrong?"

"Nothing."

He reaches out, brushes my cheek with his finger. "I never see you cry."

Impatiently I scrub at my cheeks, not wanting to cry now. I'm frustrated, not sad. "I'm not crying. But I do need to talk to you. Could we take a little walk?"

He opens my door. I get out and step onto the ground, which is hard and cold. Shivering at the chill in the air, I walk with Dane away from the truck toward his fancy corral. "Has the burglar been found?" Dane asks, our footsteps thudding.

I shake my head. "No. No sign of him."

"What's wrong, then?"

"I had a call from John earlier and he flipped out about Cooper learning to ride. Doesn't want him training anymore."

I take another quick breath and stop walking to face Dane. "But Cooper's devastated. He loves working with you, loves the whole rodeo world, and he thought maybe there are other skills he can learn from you. Calf roping. Barrel racing. Timed events rather than roughstock events."

Dane's hat is low on his head, and it's hard to see his eyes. "I'm a rider, not a roper."

"I've seen you rope. You can lasso anything, anywhere."

"It's been a long time." Dane pauses, thinks. "Now if he wanted to learn bulldogging, I could teach him that."

I crack a small smile. "Somehow I don't think steer wrestling will make John any happier."

"So this is about making your husband happy."

"It's about making sure I don't lose custody."

Dane is silent now. He studies me, then glances at the truck where the boys wait. "I've already introduced him to roping. I suppose there's no reason we can't work on it more."

"And the mechanical bull? Coop could still practice on that. It's the live bulls John's worried about."

Dane snorts in disgust. "You married a fancy-pants city boy, didn't you."

"Aw, shut up, Dane."

"Can't have John worried."

I roll my eyes. "Please just help Cooper."

"I will. He's a good kid and he's got a big future."

Chapter Eighteen

———— ✦ ————

Cooper calls his father that night to tell him he's not going to ride bulls or broncos anymore but will focus on roping events instead. John immediately asks to talk to me.

"Yes, John?" I answer, striving to maintain civility.

"I thought we agreed Cooper wouldn't pursue the cowboy thing."

"You wanted him out of harm's way. He's out of harm's way."

"But he still worked with that Kelly guy today?"

"Yes, and with my blessing." It's obvious John isn't happy that Cooper's continuing to work with Dane, but this isn't my problem, it's his. "I understand you grew up in McLean, Virginia. I understand your family had different values, but I love my country roots and am glad one of my boys wants to follow in the family's footsteps. So don't make Coop feel bad for liking trucks and rodeos and country-western music, because I'm proud of him and can't wait until he's ready to enter his first rodeo."

"I thought you wanted better for the boys, Shey."

"Better than what? My brothers are stand-up guys. Dane Kelly's as solid as they come. This is a good place to raise the boys, and rodeos teach strength and mental toughness as well as practical skills."

"He's going to college, Shey."

"Of course he is. Cowboys and ranchers are also smart men." And then I hang up before I lose my temper with him.

But John's not the only one I'm fighting with. I've got my hands full with Bo, too. He's returned from New York short-tempered and withdrawn, and nothing I say or do seems to reach him.

I'm not sure what's triggered his latest blue mood, but it seems it started with Hank choosing to stay behind in New York. I didn't notice a big change in him the first day, as on Monday he merely seemed preoccupied. Tuesday he was emotional. Wednesday he just wanted to be alone. When he still wanted to be alone on Thursday, I knew we might have a problem.

It's such a slippery slope, juggling his need for independence with his need for support and stability.

All weekend Bo's been a ghost in the house, disappearing into his room, keeping lights off, speaking to no one unless he's communicating using his phone.

A month ago, I rarely saw him use his phone, but now it's a permanent fixture in his hand.

This morning, Mama called for her weekly Sunday afternoon chat. Her first question, of course, was about my spiritual life, and her next was about the boys. Apparently we're all still in danger of going to hell, but at least she said it nicely. I appreciate that, as I've kind of got a lot on my plate and burning in flames isn't a cheery thought.

Tonight we're having our Sunday dinner at Brick and Char's. Charlotte already has the house decorated, and Christmas carols play on the stereo in the background as we eat in the dining room.

Cooper talks a mile a minute throughout the meal, telling Brick everything he's learning at Dane's and how he's hoping to enter his first rodeo this spring. But Bo doesn't participate in the conversation at all. Instead he pushes his food around his plate, sighs loudly, and yawns repeatedly, as if he's never been so bored in all his life.

I'd kick Bo under the table if I could reach his foot. But I can't, so I content myself with glaring at him periodically instead. Where is my good kid? What's happened to Bo?

On the way out, I apologize to Brick and Char as Bo's already in the truck waiting for me. I'm mortified by his behavior.

"It's the teen years," Char tells me, patting my back. "We've all been there."

Maybe, I think, but it doesn't make me feel better.

Home, I send the boys to bed. Then, too keyed up to sleep, I tidy the house and start another load of laundry. I watch TV as I move the laundry forward, staying up until the last load is done. It's eleven-thirty when I quietly open Bo's door to leave his clean clothes on the chair at his desk and discover Bo's not asleep, but in bed, texting in the dark.

I turn on the light. "What are you doing?"

"I just had to answer this person."

"It's past eleven. You're supposed to be sleeping."

"I will in a second."

"Put it away, Bo."

"Let me just finish."

"Who are you texting at this time of night?"

"A friend."

"Your friend shouldn't be up this late, either. It's a school night. I want you off now."

"Can I just finish the message? I'll put the phone away then, I promise."

"Fine. But then I want the phone."

"What?"

"I want the phone. I'm taking it away for the next forty-eight hours—"

"Mom!"

"Fight with me and it's going to be a week."

"Fine." He rolls out of bed and practically slams the phone into my hand. "Happy?"

"Yes. Good night."

I think we have the phone situation resolved, but just two days later when I'm about to return the phone, I get a call from Paul Peterson. Bo is failing math and social studies. He's barely passing English and science.

After dropping Cooper at Dane's, I tell Bo I'm keeping the phone and he's off the computer until his grades improve. Bo goes ballistic.

He shouts at me that I'm ruining his life. Tells me he's going to run away. Keeps the drama going the entire twenty-minute drive home.

I give up trying to talk to him and just let him rant. He's not going to win. Not this time.

Back at the house, he goes to his room and slams the door shut. I let him stay there, too, because it's easier having him sulking in bed than throwing a fit in the living room.

But when it's six and time to head to basketball practice, Bo refuses to go.

Brick's been driving Bo to and from practice, and he hears Bo's answer. As he starts for Bo's room, I hold up a hand to stop him. "Let me handle this," I tell him.

"He's got to go, Shey."

"He's going to go, Brick. Relax."

But I'm not relaxed. My gut is in knots. I have a feeling we're about to have another scene, and Lord knows these scenes get old.

I walk to Bo's room and quietly open the door. The lights are off and the room is dark, but I can make out the shape of his legs and shoulders beneath the covers. "Bo, sugar, it's already six. If you're going to make basketball practice on time, you need to leave."

"I already told you, I don't want to go," he says, his voice muffled by the covers.

"Bo..."

"I'm tired, Mom. I just want to sleep."

"You can sleep tonight. You've got to get up—"

"No. Let me miss practice tonight. Just tonight."

"You missed practice once last week. Your coach won't play you if you don't make your practices."

"I don't care."

"Yes, you do." I flip on the lights, move toward the bed. "Let's get up. Get going."

"I can't," he groans.

"Why not?" I try to pull the covers back, but he's got a tight grip on them.

"I just can't. Now please, leave me alone."

"You heard your mom, Bo. Time to get up." Brick's not having Bo's attitude, and he's in the doorway to back me up whether I like it or not. "Your team's counting on you, son."

Bo lowers the covers. "They're not counting on me. Last game Coach hardly played me."

"You'll be played even less if you miss another practice," Brick retorts.

"I don't care," Bo answers, turning his face away. "I quit."

"You're not quitting. You're going to practice and I'm driving you there now."

I see tears tremble on Bo's lashes, and I grab Brick's arm and drag him out of the bedroom into the hall.

"I thought you were going to let me handle this," I hiss to my brother.

"You're not handling it—"

"I am handling it. My way."

"Your way seems to be letting him have his way."

"Bullshit."

"Nice mouth, Shey."

I reach behind me, grab Bo's doorknob, and close his door. "Don't fight with me. I can't fight both of you at the same time."

"I don't want to fight with you, but you're making a mistake here. You're babying Bo, and it won't help him—"

"I'm not!"

Brick's a calm man, but he's pretty worked up now. "Your little boy is fourteen years old, six feet tall, and quickly learning that he doesn't have to stand on his own two feet because Mama will do the work for him."

"That's not what's happening. I'm worried about him. He's struggling again, and it's getting worse. This isn't new. You know he's suffered from depression."

"Then help him. But don't let him quit, and don't let

him fall apart. This is a small town. Word travels fast."

"I'm doing my best."

"You don't want him to become Cody."

Cody. My heart falters. Interesting that Brick made the comparison. I do it all the time.

The bedroom door opens abruptly and Bo stands there in his long red-and-black basketball shorts and sweatshirt. His eyes are pink, but his jaw is set. "Let's go."

I reach for him. "Bo—"

He pulls away and walks toward the back door. "I'll be in the truck."

Brick follows without a word to me, and I hear the back door bang a second time. They're gone.

While Brick is driving Bo to practice, Dane drops Cooper off from training. It's dark now by six, and I walk outside to meet Dane's truck.

Cooper's cold and sore and starving, and he runs inside to shower and eat dinner. "How's he doing?" I ask Dane, shivering at the chilly temperature.

"He's doing great, but you're freezing," he answers. "Go inside."

I should have grabbed a coat on my way out, but now that I'm talking to him, I'm not going anywhere. I've missed him way too much. "How's your hip doing?"

"It's fine."

"But the cold snap—"

"I'm not an old lady. You don't have to fuss over me."

I laugh, picturing him as the Wolf in "Little Red Riding Hood," all dressed up in Grandmother's nightclothes. "You're nothing like an old lady," I say, still grinning. "Do you have somewhere you have to be? Want to come in for a bit? I've got plenty of dinner. It's just sloppy Joes, but it's warm and it'll fill you up."

"Sloppy Joes?"

"Mmmm, gourmet, I know."

"I happen to love sloppy Joes."

"Then park and come in. It's been a rough few days and I'd love some company."

"Sold."

He parks, and I lead him into the house through the back porch.

"How's it holding up?" he asks, stopping to examine the door he installed Thanksgiving weekend.

"Great." I head for the stove to adjust the heat beneath the bubbling meat mixture, then turn on the broiler to toast the buns. "So do you like cheese on your sloppy Joes, or just meat and buns?"

"Either way. Just glad for some home-cooked food."

I shoot him a quick glance and see that he's taken a seat at the kitchen table, almost in the same spot he used to sit as a teenager. "You should come in and have dinner with us the nights you drive Coop home. There's no reason not to—" I break off, remembering Lulu. "Ah, the girlfriend. Never mind."

He smiles at me, and it's such a sexy smile that it makes my toes curl. "Lulu moved out."

"Her remodel's done?"

"No. She met someone new. A pitcher with the Rangers."

I slide the tray of buttered buns beneath the broiler. "Are you upset?"

"No. I actually introduced them. Thought he was more

her speed, and it seemed nicer than dumping her."

"What's her speed?" I ask, keeping a close eye on the browning buns.

"Young, handsome, rich."

"But that's you."

His eyes crease with humor. "No, I'm handsome and rich. But not young anymore."

I grin, amused by the idea that Lulu would find some smooth-faced kid sexier than this rugged, beautiful man. "Not that it's any consolation, but I'd rather have old you than some young ace."

He snorts with laughter. "Thank you, Shey. That's very nice of you."

A freshly showered Cooper appears for dinner. After pulling the tray from the oven, I dish up the food so we can eat.

Dinner's fun with Dane there. Cooper and Dane have developed an easy, comfortable relationship, and they talk about everything—proposed changes in the PBR, school, the upcoming holidays. Dane gets Coop roaring when he asks Cooper if he'll be visiting Santa at the Weatherford Mall this year.

"I think I'm taller than Santa," Cooper answers. "Can you see me on his lap? My legs up to my chin. Hey, Santa, can you bring me a pony for Christmas, and a new saddle, too?"

I smile indulgently. "You want a pony for Christmas, Coop?"

Cooper rolls his eyes. "I was being funny, Mom."

"So what do you want?"

"A chance to ride a real bull."

I glance at Dane, whose expression is impassive, and

back to Coop, who clearly isn't expecting a positive response. "This one's out of my hands, Coop."

"It doesn't have to be. You have custody—"

"Temporary custody. There are a lot of things still to be decided."

"Like what?"

I don't want to do this with Dane here, but at the same time I don't want to act as though I have anything to hide. "Like if you can all stay here with me, or if we'd have to go back to New York."

Cooper flushes. "Why would we have to go back to New York? We live here now—"

"Well, that's still to be decided."

His eyes blaze furiously. "What do you mean? We moved here. I like it here. I'm not going back to New York. Ever."

I shift self-consciously. "It's not that easy, baby. I can't just move you away from your dad without a formal custody agreement, and right now we don't have one in place. That's something we're working on, and then we have to get a judge to sign off on it. But hopefully it'll happen and we'll stay and—"

Cooper jumps to his feet and walks out.

He's never walked away from me before. I sit back in my chair and weigh whether I should go after him or just let him be for now.

After a moment, I turn to look at Dane. "Sorry."

"He just needs some time to cool off."

I nod, but my insides churn. "He really does like it here," I say after a moment. "He's happy here."

"Is there going to be a custody battle?"

I take a deep breath. "Hope not. And this isn't about keeping the boys from John. John's a great dad, a very hands-on father. But I can't be in New York. I can't live there now. I need to be here."

"But he's not happy with the kids here, is he?"

I get up from the table, stack the dishes, and carry them to the sink. "No. He misses them."

"And you wouldn't let him have custody?"

My head jerks up. "God, no. I love them. I need them. I honestly couldn't survive without them." And then, realizing how that sounds, especially in light of Dane's loss, I add, "I mean, I guess I could if I had to, but I wouldn't want to. I love being their mom."

"It's obvious."

Turning on the hot water, I start filling the kitchen sink, feeling torn. I'm here with Dane, but I'm also worried about Coop. And yet this schism is part of motherhood. Once the first baby arrives, your attention is forever split. Husband and child. Work and family. "I'm sorry. I know I talk about them too much. The little buggers have a way of taking over—"

"It's okay."

"No, I need to learn to juggle better."

"You're juggling fine. I'd be worried if the kids didn't come first. And I like it that you're devoted to the boys. I find it sexy."

I nearly drop the bottle of dishwashing soap into the sink. "Sexy?" I croak.

"You've always been pretty, Shey, and I knew you were strong. But I don't think I realized just how beautiful you were until I saw you with your boys. When you're around your kids, you have this glow, this vitality, and it's a huge turn-on."

Did he just say "sexy" and "turn-on" in the space of thirty seconds?

"I wish Shellie Ann had been more like you," he adds flatly. "She always seemed annoyed by the demands of motherhood. Yes, Matthew needed a lot of care, but he was our son. I would have done anything for him, and yet I used to think that all Shellie Ann wanted was to get away from him."

"I'm sure she didn't mean it—"

"He had problems. He wasn't perfect. She hated it, you know. She couldn't get over the fact that he wasn't a pretty baby. She couldn't enter him in pageants and cute baby photo contests." Bitterness makes every word sharp. "I had no idea how shallow she was until it was too late. But what do you do? You make the best of it, right?"

"Right."

He stares past me, across the kitchen and out the window to the dark night. "I'm still angry with her. It's been years, but I can't forget the things she said, the things she did. Matthew deserved better."

I say nothing, and he turns to look at me, features hard, expression intense. "Do you know what Shellie Ann told Charlotte? She said she wished she'd aborted Matthew when she had the chance." His voice drops, deepens, and he grinds his jaw as he struggles to regain control. "The day she told Charlotte that, it was Mattie's second birthday. His *second* birthday. Lord." He draws a quick, shallow breath. "I would have died for that boy, and my wife, my *wife*, wished she'd killed him."

"I'm sure she didn't mean it. She was probably having a bad day. That happens when you're a mom. You say things you don't mean. You lose your temper."

He fixes his fierce gaze on me. "Have you ever said you wished your child was dead?"

"No, but exhaustion and depression can make women say things they really don't mean."

"Charlotte said the same thing. Shellie Ann was just depressed. She needed more time for herself. So I hired a nanny and Charlotte came over every night after work and my mother was here weekends. But it didn't help. Shellie Ann wouldn't be—couldn't be—happy, and we were this crazy miserable dysfunctional family."

"It had to hurt. You've always been such a family man."

He runs a hand across his face. "I wanted it to work. But, God, we weren't compatible. She loved the social scene and nightlife while I just wanted to hole up at home and chill out. Shellie Ann used to complain that I deliberately trapped her on the ranch. But I wasn't trying to trap her. I like living there. I enjoy the solitude. It's where I'm happy."

"That's why you built that big stone mansion."

"I didn't understand it was the ranch she hated. I thought it was the old farmhouse." Abruptly he rises, his forehead furrowed. "Let's not talk about this anymore. It's just getting me upset, and it all happened so long ago."

"Of course. Can I offer you coffee, dessert?"

He shakes his head. "No, I should go." But he says it reluctantly. "I have some calls I need to make tonight."

"I can make you a cup of decaf for the road."

Dane's expression suddenly eases, and he gives me a

crooked smile. "You're good company, Shey Callen."

"Shey Darcy."

"You'll never be Darcy to me," he says, crossing the kitchen to join me at the sink. "You're a Callen. My favorite Callen."

I can feel his warmth and smell that clean scent he wears, and it makes my insides turn to mush. "In that case, I don't suppose you'd want to do something this weekend?"

The corner of his mouth lifts and he reaches out, brushes hair from my eyes. "Is this a date?"

I shiver as his fingertips brush my skin. "It doesn't have to be."

His lashes drop, concealing his eyes, but I get the distinct feeling he's looking at my mouth. "But you'd like it to be?"

I squirm on the inside. "Not if it makes you uncomfortable."

"I see. You want me to be comfortable."

There goes my stomach again. I'm suddenly all pins and needles. "Of course."

"Of course." His mouth curves again in that faint, crooked smile.

"Or we don't have to have dinner. I'd be happy just going for a walk. Getting a coffee. Having a drink. I just want to see you."

He's still staring at my mouth, and the skin heats across my cheekbones. I wish he'd kiss me. I'd love for him to kiss me.

"Friday night, then?"

I exhale. "Yeah."

"I'll pick you up," he adds. "Six-thirty."

I don't know if it's his eyes or the pitch of his voice or just knowing we're going out this weekend, but I'm warm, overly warm, and overly turned on. I touch my tongue to my upper lip to wet it ever so slightly. "Great. I'll be ready."

He smiles at me. "See you then, darlin'."

He leaves just as Bo comes in, which means Brick and Dane must have seen each other's truck in the drive. I'm sure that didn't go over big with either one, but I put it out of my mind to reheat Bo's dinner plate and ask him about practice.

"Okay," he answers, taking a seat at the table.

I set his plate in front of him. "Still mad at me?"

"No. Well, a little."

I ruffle his hair. I guess I can live with that.

While he eats I tackle the dishes, energetically scrubbing the skillet clean as I think about Friday night's date with Dane. Our first date in twenty-three years.

I can't believe we're actually going to go out. Not for lunch. Not during the day. But on a weekend night.

I feel like a kid who's never been kissed, although I have been kissed, and kissed by Dane. And God, he was a great kisser. The best. Hands down. No one ever came close.

I wonder if he'll kiss me Friday night. He nearly did Thanksgiving weekend, and this time I don't want him to stop.

This time I won't let him stop.

Glancing at Bo still eating his dinner at the table, I feel guilty for even thinking these thoughts. It feels completely wrong to fantasize when I'm near my kids, but I suddenly have a one-track mind.

What would Dane be like in bed?

I haven't slept with anyone but John in eighteen years, and I haven't made love with John in over two years. I can't even imagine making love to anyone else. I'm not sure my body would even know what to do.

And then I picture Dane and feel a frisson of excitement and pleasure. He's so hot, and just thinking about how he fills out a pair of Wranglers makes my breath catch in my throat.

I'm such a liar. I know exactly what to do with him. I also know that I'd enjoy it.

I'm out with the boys doing some Christmas shopping Thursday night when I get a call from a number I don't recognize. I let it go into voice mail since my arms are full of bags and forget about the call until Charlotte calls two hours later to ask a question about this year's Christmas gift exchange. It's then I remember I have a message waiting. We've only just got home from town, and I check the message as the kids carry all the shopping bags into the house.

It's Delilah, the blond girl from Bo's school.

It's hard to understand her through her tears, but from what I can gather, her mom's boyfriend kicked her out of the house and she's walking somewhere and she needs a ride. Can I come get her?

I wish I'd checked messages sooner. I was just in town. I was just there. It would have been so easy to go get her.

I quickly call her. She doesn't answer. I leave a voice mail and hang up. For a long moment I stare at my phone, telling myself that it's been two hours and she's probably fine now. But what if she isn't?

What if she's still walking? What if she has no coat? What if she has nowhere to go?

My stomach hurts, and I'm sick with worry. With a shout to the boys that I've got to run back into town, I grab my keys and dash to the truck. As I drive, I call Delilah's number again and again, only to get her voice mail every time. I'm eight miles from Mineral Wells when I call once more, and this time Delilah picks up. "Are you okay, Delilah?" I ask, so damn relieved to hear her voice.

"I'm scared," she says in a small voice.

"Where are you?"

"Behind the train station next to the old meatpacking plant."

I know the area. We used to mess around the empty plant when we were kids. "I'm on my way."

Delilah's standing near the curb beneath a yellow streetlight. She's wearing a short skirt and a T-shirt and sneakers without socks, and her eyes are humongous in her white face. I pull up next to her, lean over, and open the door. She climbs in, teeth chattering. "Thank you," she whispers, closing the door behind her.

I pull off my coat and drape it around her shoulders. She's so cold that she doesn't protest but draws the lapels close to her thin chest. "How long have you been walking around?"

"Since before I called you."

Two and a half hours in a frigid, forty-degree temperature without a sweatshirt or coat. "What happened?" I ask, pulling away from the curb, anxious to be out of the warehouse district at night.

"My mom's boyfriend freaked out." She sags into the

coat. "When he drinks they fight, and then..." Her voice drifts off and her eyes close, her eyelashes inky against her pale cheeks.

"Does he hit you?" I ask, having seen this before when I lived in New York and worked with the girls at the YWCA. So many girls grow up with abuse. So many girls see things they should never have to see.

"Mostly my mom."

Mostly.

I hate alcohol. I do. I don't know why people need to drink. Don't like what drinking does to some people. Makes them mean. Makes them ugly. Makes them hate.

"Did you have any dinner?"

She shakes her head.

"Let's go get you something to eat."

She nods gratefully.

We end up at the Kountry Kitchen Café, and the place is deserted except for one old man eating lemon meringue pie at a booth in the corner. Traci was sitting at the counter studying when we walked in, but she jumps up to greet us.

"Are you still serving, Traci?" I ask, hearing no activity in the kitchen.

"Yes, ma'am. Just a quiet night." She grabs two menus. "Sit wherever you like."

I let Delilah pick the table—it's one of the small booths beneath the front window, where the glass has been frosted and painted with holly and wreaths. The inside of the restaurant has been decorated, too, with a miniature Christmas tree on the counter and a plastic Santa with a light shining through it.

"Order whatever you want," I tell Delilah. "Three

cheeseburgers, two French dips, four pieces of apple pie. My boys do it all the time."

Tucking lank hair behind an ear, she smiles shyly and orders just one cheeseburger, with a side of fries and a hot chocolate with whipped cream. I order a cup of herbal tea.

Delilah downs her cocoa before the burger even arrives. "Want another one?" Traci asks her.

Delilah looks at me hesitantly.

"Sure," I answer.

As Traci walks away, Delilah reaches for her water glass and gives it a little spin on the table. "Thank you for coming to get me."

"I'm just sorry I didn't get your call earlier."

"It's okay."

"So what happens now?" I ask her.

"I'll go home. Howie's probably passed out. And Mama's probably got a black eye, but that's how it is at my house."

I remember her grandfather sitting on the porch that day I drove her home earlier in the fall. "What about your grandpa? Where is he?"

"Sleeping. Watching TV. Staying out of the way." She looks at me, expression hopeless. "Because if he doesn't, Howie will whip his ass."

A half hour later, I'm dropping Delilah off at her house and feeling like a traitor.

Children shouldn't have to grow up like this.

Children should be protected.

I spend a sleepless night thinking about Delilah and all the other girls like her. Girls who don't get enough love. Girls who don't get enough support.

I have to do something to reach them, help them, especially those who live in Palo Pinto County. They need to know they're not alone. Need to know that there are women—mothers, sisters, grandmothers, friends—who care.

As the clock turns to four, I vow to look into the local community programs for girls. What kind of outreach exists here? What do the schools offer? What is the city and county doing? Where do girls go when things are bad at home? Who can they turn to who'll care?

As the questions go round and round in my head, I realize I'm starting to feel like my old self again.

The sunny Shey.

The positive Shey.

The Shey who believes in herself and knows she can do anything she sets her mind to.

Which means it's time to reach out to those who need a helping hand.

The next morning after dropping the boys at school, I call Paul Peterson at Mineral Wells Junior High and ask him about resources the school has for girls who need extra support. "Educational support?" he asks. "Or counseling?"

"Both. Is there somewhere our local girls can go for help? A teen center or club?"

"There used to be an after-school program run through the city that matched younger girls with high-achieving older girls, but it lost funding last year with all the budget cuts."

"So right now there's nothing for girls who are at risk?"

"No."

"There should be."

"I know."

Hanging up, I'm determined that now that I'm back in Parkfield, there will be. Because what's the point of being one of Palo Pinto County's most celebrated women if I can't give back?

What's the point of being successful if I don't lead or implement change?

Chapter Nineteen

Suddenly it's Friday night, date night, and Dane is dropping Coop off and picking me up as planned. He looks so good, too, dressed in jeans and a sage green button-down shirt that makes his eyes even more beautiful.

"Why are you smiling?" he asks, holding the truck door open for me.

"Just excited."

He shoots me a curious glance as he climbs behind the steering wheel. "It's just me, darlin'."

I look at him from beneath my lashes. "That's why I'm excited."

"You're dangerously good for my ego."

"I'm just dangerously good."

He lifts a brow. "Is that so?"

"Mmmm."

There are no streetlights or even traffic lights on most country roads, and tonight the moon is just a slip in the sky, which makes the night even darker.

I'm happy to be back in his truck. Happy to just let him drive. I don't even care about dinner. It's enough to be with him, near him. This is all I ever wanted. His company. His proximity.

Unlike Shellie Ann, I like the country and I like Dane for who he is. I don't want anything from him but his time and his attention. Having lived the posh life in Manhattan, having traveled the world as a model, flying first class and staying in four- and five-star hotels, I know all the creature comforts. I know the difference between a good champagne and a stellar champagne, but it's not the label of the champagne that makes the difference. It's who you're sharing it with.

I was happy with John, and it never crossed my mind that once we married and had our first baby, we wouldn't always be together. But now that John's moved on, I can, too. And I'd love the next phase of my life to include Dane. But I don't come solo. I'm a package deal. Shey and three teenage boys. That's a lot to take on.

"You look so serious all of a sudden," Dane says with a glance in my direction. "What are you thinking about?"

"The strangeness of life. How you and I are both single now. The fact that I'm back here. Who would have thought?"

His eyes gleam at me in the dark. "Who would have thought?" he echoes, teasing me.

I smile back. Can't not smile. He makes me feel good. He makes me feel like me. The old me, the strong me, the one who couldn't wait to wake up every morning and hated going to bed because I was afraid I'd miss something.

"So where are we going?" I ask after a bit. We've been driving for ten minutes, heading away from Mineral Wells and Weatherford.

"Taking you to dinner at a little place I love. It's kind of out of the way, though. You mind an hour drive?"

"Not at all. I'm perfectly content to just sit here and let you drive."

He reaches out, covers my knee with his palm. "Good.

Because I've been looking forward to seeing you all day."

I bite my lip and look down at his hand where it rests on my knee. I like his hand on me. It looks right there. Even better, it feels so good. I don't know why, but his touch is perfect. It's made for me. But then the physical between Dane and me has never been the problem. It's the logistics that hung us up. First I was too young. And then he was on the circuit and I was in college. Then before I could finish college, he was engaged to a pregnant Shellie Ann. But I don't want to think about Shellie Ann right now or any of the things that have kept us apart. I just want to be here, with him, happy.

We end up at in a small hole-in-the-wall restaurant on the outskirts of Stephenville. Dane says the restaurant serves the best Tex-Mex food outside San Antonio. It's a small building on a nearly vacant lot, tucked beneath a cluster of red oak trees wrapped in strands of green and blue lights. Our hand-shaken margaritas are made with fresh fruit juices and a special tequila the owner brings out just for Dane.

The radio's been set to a popular local station that broadcasts in Spanish and plays the top Latin pop songs. Dane's right about the fajitas—they're amazing, and I don't know if it's the marinated steak, the homemade tortillas, or the incredible chunky guacamole, but I eat two. And even though I'm stuffed afterward, I continue to pick the caramelized peppers and onions from the skillet, leaving the beef to Dane.

We're the only ones there when we first arrive, but by the time we're done half a dozen tables are filled.

As the place gets more noisy, Dane looks less comfortable. He'd been telling me about his breeding program and how his business was founded on the principles of ethical and humane treatment of all livestock, not just his famous bucking bulls, when he abruptly stands and picks up our glasses. "Let's go outside," he says. "It'll be quieter."

Colder, too, but I'd rather be outside with Dane than surrounded by noisy groups of people.

It is chilly outside, but we find a small outdoor heater by one of the scattered tables near a blue-lit tree and stand beneath that.

"Are you going to be warm enough?" Dane asks me, tugging the zipper higher on my wool coat.

My coat isn't particularly heavy, but I like the trees wrapped in strings of blue and green lights and am having a really good time. "I'm perfect," I say as I stomp my feet and rub my hands. "This is fun."

"Perfect? Even though you're freezing?"

I laugh and shiver at the same time. "Have you ever noticed how cold weather makes you feel so alive?"

"You look so young right now," he says, dropping onto a bench. "So carefree."

"Are you saying I don't normally look young and carefree?"

"I think you could use more fun in your life."

The wind whistles past our heads, and I shiver. "I wouldn't argue that point," I say. And then the wind whistles again and I shiver uncontrollably, which just makes me laugh. "Dang, it's cold!"

"We can go—"

"No," I protest, grinning down at him as I pluck a tangled strand of hair from my eyes and push it back behind my ear. "I'm so happy right now. I'm having such a good time."

"But you're freezing."

"This is the good kind of freezing. This is fun. I love this place and the lights in the tree and just being here with you. It's been a long time since I had a date night, so please, freeze with me."

He has that deep rumble of a laugh, and creases fan from his eyes. "I'll freeze with you any day."

"Thank you."

"You know, you're pretty easy to hang with, Shey."

"I've never been high maintenance."

"I like that about you."

I suddenly can't flirt or play. I can't pretend to care less than I do. Just being here with him hurts, and my heart aches, as my feelings for him are both bitter and sweet.

At twelve, I had a major crush on him.

At fifteen, I knew I wanted to marry him.

At sixteen, I was sent away to make sure I didn't do anything stupid like get pregnant or run away with him.

I have loved him my whole life. Loved him when I was still young and innocent, my love uncomplicated. Love is far more complicated now. Life is far more complicated. But it doesn't change how much I still want him and crave him and need him.

"I wish you liked me," I say.

"You don't get it, do you?" He stands and looks into my face, right into my eyes, and his expression is naked, almost vulnerable. "There's no one I've ever liked better."

"You mean—"

"No one," he repeats, reaching out for me and drawing me between his legs. "No one looks at me the way you do." He strokes his thumb lightly across my cheek, skimming the surface. "You're all eyes and need, and sometimes you scare me, Shey Lynne, but I've never not cared about you."

"Why would I scare you?"

His head dips ever so slightly, his mouth brushing my brow and then my nose. "You still want so much and I have so little to give."

"If that's true, what are we doing here?"

"I don't know, but I'm sure nothing good will come of it." He pulls me snugly against his hard thighs and rests his hands low on my back.

I want to touch him, to put my hands on the muscular curve of his thigh, but I'm afraid, so afraid to touch this man who incinerated my heart all those years ago. I am not a rock. Not strong at all. I'm so afraid that if I touch him, if I like touching him, I won't be able to stop. I'll want that connection again. I'll want that warmth and heat and love. It's been so long since I felt love. So long since I had sex.

"But then, it never has," I answer, fingers knotting into fists and my fists pressed to my own hips. "Liking you just got me in trouble, and then eventually sent me away."

"Your mama was afraid I'd seduce you."

"I think she was even more afraid I'd like it."

"You probably would have," he answers, his voice pitched so deep that it makes me shiver.

"So you seduced Shellie Ann instead."

"You were always the girl for me. Life just got in the way."

He sounds so sincere that my eyes burn and my heart beats double time. "You're not fair."

"No, I'm not. Because I knew how you felt, and I hoped you'd come home. But it had to be your choice. I wasn't going to ask you to come back, not when you had the whole world ahead of you."

"Oh, Dane. I would have come back. I would have, I missed you. Missed you like crazy. Missed you so much it made me crazy."

"Your brothers always made sure I heard about every new boyfriend you had at Stanford."

"Why?"

"They didn't want you hooking up with me."

"Why?" I repeat.

His powerful shoulders shrug. "You're the beautiful baby of the family. Gorgeous, and brainy, and sweet. They figured you'd go far as long as you stayed away from me. And they were right."

"No."

He nods. "You never did hide your feelings very well." One of Dane's big, callused hands slips up to my cheek, and he runs his thumb across my cheekbone. With curiosity. With warmth. With wonder. For a big man who's spent his life on broncs and bulls, he's so gentle that shivers race through me. I need this touch. I crave this touch. I want him as much as I did twenty-three years ago.

He turns his hand over and runs the backs of his fingers down my cheek to my jaw and to my mouth. "You really are too pretty for your own good."

"You can't see all the lines and wrinkles?"

"I just see woman."

I have to close my eyes at the heat exploding beneath the surface of my skin. He's making me burn, and when I burn, I feel like the girl I once was. So hungry, so wild, so alive. But that was long before I had other people to worry about, people who relied on me for everything.

"You broke my heart once. I don't want to get hurt again," I whisper, eyes still closed, knuckles still pressed to my hip bones. I'm made of glass, and he's the pressure that could break me.

"I never meant to hurt you."

"But you did."

"Life's like that, darlin'."

A lump fills my throat. "Maybe we should go. Stop now while we're ahead."

"That's probably a good idea."

But he doesn't let go of me, and I do not move away. Instead I wobble, lean forward just enough that my chest brushes his, and he inhales low and rough.

My eyes open and I stare into his eyes. They're green like the sea, and I reach for him then, pressing first my knuckles against his thighs and then opening my fingers to press the entire palm. His legs are hard, the denim fabric taut, and my belly hurts from the relentless surge of desire and adrenaline.

"You might still be married," he says, "but you'll always be mine."

And then he drops his head and his lips cover mine. And for an endless moment it is just that, the warmth of his mouth against my mouth, and I'm flooded with the smell of him and the feel of him and the hint of a taste of him.

If only this was real love.

If only this could last forever.

And like that, the pressure of his mouth increases and his lips move over mine, and I want this kiss. I want everything, and my lips part and I kiss him back. Kiss him the way I

wanted to all those years ago when he was too old for me
and too involved with other women.

I don't know how long the madness lasts, but it is madness. It's fierce and hungry and intense, and I feel his hands
in my hair and his chest hard against my breasts. My hands
are wrapped around the curve of muscle in his thigh, and
I'm pressed as close to him as I can.

And then one of us pulls back, not sure who, not sure
why, not sure it matters. Dane is looking down into my
face, and I can't tell if he's smiling or not, but his expression
is strange. A little wry, a little sad. "I should get you home,
sugar. You're going to get into trouble here."

"Too late," I whisper, digging my nails into the fabric of
his jeans. "I'm already in trouble."

We make love in his truck.

It wasn't supposed to happen, especially not this way.
We were just heading home with me sitting close to his
side, and then suddenly he's pulling off onto the side of the
deserted country road and we're kissing again.

Somehow my blouse comes off and then my jeans, and
I end up straddling Dane's lap in just my lace thong. And
then even that comes off.

There's always been chemistry and a strong physical
connection between us, but making love blows me away.
It's beyond good, beyond amazing, beyond anything I've
ever known physically, sexually.

I love him. It's that simple and that complex. I love him
and want him and need him more than I've ever wanted
or needed anyone.

I'm still straddling his hips, my breasts pressed to his

bare chest, and one of his hands rests on my thigh while the other tangles in my hair.

"I'm so crazy about you," I whisper. "So terribly, insanely crazy."

"As I am for you," he answers, lifting the hair from my neck to place a kiss at the base of my throat and then higher, just below the jaw. "I just hope this wasn't a mistake."

Our bodies are still warm and slick. With anyone else I'd feel self-conscious, but with Dane it's natural and right. I touch my mouth to his, kiss him gently and then hungrily, feeling famished and starved for him again already. "Why would it be a mistake?"

"There are still so many unknowns in your life—"

"Like what?"

"You're still married," he retorts grimly.

"But not for much longer."

I can see his jaw work, tighten. "But what does that mean? How long is that? Weeks? Months? Years?"

"I don't know. These things take time. There's the whole custody issue, and then in New York you can't have a no-fault divorce—"

"But are you pushing your lawyer to get things moving, or are you just letting it ride?"

"Well, I haven't pushed hard because I guess I worry about the custody stuff. I don't want to lose them."

"But wouldn't it be better to just know? To have it all settled rather than left in limbo?"

He makes a good point, as I think I do prefer the limbo. I'm nervous about having everything settled, nervous that the court could rule against me. Although I don't think it'll happen, it could...but then Dane's right. At this point, I don't know, and I can't really plan my future.

The truck's still running and the heater's on, but I'm beginning to feel naked and cold.

"You're right," I say faintly, carefully climbing off his lap and onto my side of the seat to begin putting on my clothes. "I need to make the divorce a priority. Need to get my lawyer moving things forward."

"You sound pretty reluctant."

I struggle to get my jeans up. "I'm afraid. Afraid a judge will rule that the boys need to be in New York, or living together, or split evenly between John and me, which would mean...it'd mean..."

"You'd return to New York," Dane finishes for me as he watches me dress.

"But it won't happen. I'm just being paranoid. Worst-case scenario and all," I add, tugging my navy cashmere sweater over my head. "And the bottom line is, John won't take the kids from me. He wouldn't do that. He knows I've always put them first."

"You trust him that much?"

"Yes."

"I don't. If he could deceive you all those years about his sexuality, I think he could deceive you about his intentions when it comes to the boys."

"John's not like that. He's not a threat."

"Of course he's a threat. He's the father of your boys and your partner for the last seventeen years. He's a huge threat until your divorce is final and the boys' custody is settled. Because otherwise he'll always have the upper hand."

He's made another good point, but I'm not about to tell

him so, and we finish dressing in silence. Once I buckle my
seat belt, Dane shifts into drive and we head for my house.
The drive home is so much longer than the drive to
dinner.

At the house, we sit in the truck, engine idling, but I
don't move to get out. I feel terrible, horrible, and I don't
know what's going to happen next.

"I don't know what to say." My voice is quiet, and I keep
my gaze fixed on the string of colored lights Cooper tacked
around the front porch yesterday. The Christmas lights are
crooked and gaudy, but they remind me of my kids and I
wouldn't have them any other way.

"I don't know, either."

"Are you ending things with me?"

He sighs and runs a tired hand over his jaw. "Shey, no.
But I also don't think we've even gotten started."

My stomach's in knots as I turn to face him. "I don't
understand what's happening. Things were going so good.
Dinner was great. Sex was great—"

"Yeah, sex was great. Damn fantastic. But that's because
I have feelings for you, Shey. And yes, you have feelings for
me, but my gut is telling me you're still not available. And
frankly, I can't share you. I won't."

"You don't have to!"

"I'm sharing you right now. John is still legally your husband. He has power over you. Your kids don't know where
they're going to live. And Cooper tells me all the time that
he's afraid you're moving back to New York this spring—"

"I've never said that!"

"You don't have to. You look like you're a short-timer.
You haven't bought your own car, fixed up this house, made

any friends. You're killing time here, not living here."

"You're wrong. I'm ready to settle down, ready to move forward, ready to make this my permanent home."

"I hope so, darlin'. I really do."

His voice is low and rough. I just stare into Dane's face. His gaze is intense. "You won't lose me, Dane. I'm nuts about you, and you have no idea how much I need you—"

"But that's just it. I think I do. Your kids are a handful. Your husband's gay. You're lonelier than hell. It's pretty obvious you've got some big holes in your life. But I'm not putty, and I can't be a rebound. Not with you."

The next morning, the boys help me haul Mama's Christmas decorations down from the attic. While we sort through the mismatched ornaments and old strings of lights, I find myself thinking about Dane and only Dane.

I want to see him. Want to hear from him. Want, want, want. But what is the proper etiquette for an almost forty-year-old woman who has just reunited with her first love? Do I have to wait for him to call me? And how long is he going to wait before he does call?

But he doesn't call. He drops by instead Sunday afternoon while I'm changing the sheets on my bed. I'm struggling to get the comforter back in its cover when I hear the engine of Dane's big truck. I know it's his and not Brick's truck just by the sound of it.

Goose bumps cover my arms as I drop laundry onto the bed in my room, and I glance self-consciously into the mirror above the 1930s dresser. Jeans, red T-shirt, long, straight blond hair. No makeup. Just me, the real me.

"Mom," Cooper shouts from the living room. "Dane's here."

And there goes my heart, I think, wiping my hands on the butt of my jeans before heading down the hall and out the front door to find Dane standing on the front walk. It's almost dark, and his charcoal coat blends with the twilight.

"Hi," I say, descending the front steps and walking toward him.

"Hello," he answers. "How are you?"

"Good. Just doing laundry."

He nods, glances past me to the house. "Any problems with the security system?"

I look at the house, too, and realize I haven't yet plugged in the Christmas lights. "Did you drive all the way here to ask about the security system?"

"No. But I'm curious."

"It's great, although very high-tech. I don't think NASA could install a more sophisticated system."

"NASA actually uses the same Pelco cameras."

"Yikes. That's going to be a big bill."

"It's already taken care of."

"You can't pay for it—"

"I didn't." He sees my expression and adds, "Brick and I worked out a deal. We bartered services in exchange for the security system. I get hay and grain. You get motion detectors and alarms."

"Thank you. It's very kind of you—"

"Not kind," he interrupts, the smile fading somewhat. "Concerned. I worry about you here all alone."

"I've got the boys."

"And they're getting ready to leave again."

"I've also got Brick."

"He's a mile away."

"Dane," I say, striving for patience, "I appreciate your concern, but I already have two big brothers who are over-protective. I don't need another one."

"Good. Because I don't feel the least bit brotherly towards you. Not once. Not ever." Then he turns and goes to his truck and opens the door. When he faces me, he has a wiggling brown-and-tan puppy in his arms.

He walks over to me and plunks the pup in my arms.

A German shepherd puppy.

"The final touches of your new security system," Dane says, ruffling the pup's head and scratching behind one small ear. "And a little more cuddly than motion detectors and cameras."

I've got the puppy against my chest, which is a mistake since she's determined to lick my chin. I love dogs, always had them in the family growing up, but it's been years since I had one of my own. But a dog now? A dog when everything is so chaotic? "Oh, Dane, this isn't a good idea. I've got my hands full as it is!"

"You'll be fine, and the boys can help train her."

"They don't even listen to me. What makes you think they'll be responsible—" And then my voice is drowned out as Cooper appears in the doorway and spots the puppy in my arms and shouts for his brother to come.

In seconds, both boys come bounding out of the house.

"A puppy!" Cooper exclaims, reaching my side first.

"Whose?" Bo demands, reaching in to give the puppy a welcoming pat.

"Yours," Dane answers.

"Ours?" the boys practically chorus, looking from Dane to me and back again.

"You've got to train her, and help housebreak her, but she's a very smart dog and she'll be a good watchdog for your mom when you guys aren't around." Dane looks at me, and that small crooked smile is back. "As long as your mom agrees that you can keep her, of course."

Dane is in so much trouble.

"We will, Mom, we promise," Coop pleads, sounding more like a six-year-old than a sixth grader. "Please, Mom!"

Cooper doesn't realize that I've already capitulated. The puppy's adorable, and her little lick of the chin sealed the deal. Besides, there's no way I can fight Dane. Against him, I've never stood a chance.

"Fine," I answer, avoiding meeting Dane's eyes. "But I will hold you two responsible for house-training her."

Dane smiles. "Figured you could use a girl in the house, Shey. You know, that whole estrogen thing."

The boys take the pup into the house, and I give Dane a long, level look. "A puppy, Dane?"

"You love dogs."

I don't think he's ever looked more rakish and rugged and appealing, but I'm seriously annoyed. "You can't give someone a puppy and then drop-kick them out of your life."

"You haven't been drop-kicked out of my life. If anything, I'm doing everything I can to keep you safe so you'll be in my life."

"But Friday night you were upset."

"I just think we both have to be careful. We can't rush things. We should take it slow so we can make it work."

"You're not a rebound."

"Good, because I don't bounce real well."

I grin and then remember the puppy. "But Dane...A German shepherd. She's going to become a big dog."

"You live on a big ranch."

"What if we have to go back to New York? What do we do with her then?"

And just like that, the energy changes and Dane draws back. His expression is strange, shuttered, even mistrustful. "You give her to me, then," he says in a curiously unemotional voice. And then with a faintly mocking smile, he returns to his truck.

At first, I don't understand what happened. He went from warm to cold as if a switch had been thrown. What the hell happened?

And then I hear my voice in my head: *What if we have to go back to New York...*

Weird. Why did I say that? Why would I say that? I have no intention of returning to New York...

Do I?

Flustered, I chase after him. "Dane. Wait. I'm sorry—"

"No apologies necessary." He cuts me off as he slides behind the steering wheel. "You said exactly what I needed to hear."

I watch him leave, more confused than ever. He took what I said the wrong way. He took it completely out of context.

But then as his tires kick up gravel and dust, I hear his voice: *You won't be staying. You'll be gone within a year. Two if you're stupid.*

And of course I just confirmed his suspicions.

Chapter Twenty

Monday morning after dropping the boys at school, I get a call from Dane. "I'm going to be in New Mexico for the next few days," he tells me. "Will you let Cooper know I'll be gone this week but I'll call him once I'm back and we'll resume training?"

"Of course." And then I bite the bullet and ask, "Do you have plans for Christmas?"

"I'm scheduled to be in Brazil."

"Brazil?"

"I've been working with PBR Brazil and agreed to participate in their big summer rodeo."

"How long will you be there?"

"One week. Maybe two."

I'm so disappointed. I've been looking forward to spending Christmas with him, picturing us sitting on the couch, sipping mulled wine and listening to carols. Hokey, sentimental stuff, but also romantic. "If I didn't have the boys for Christmas, I'd beg you to take me along," I tell him huskily, my chest tight, tears not far off.

"If you didn't have the boys, I'd insist you come along."

"Do you ever wish I didn't have them?"

"That's a ridiculous question. And no. Never. Ever. And don't ask that again."

"Okay."

"I better go. They're boarding my flight. I'll call you when I'm back in town."

Dane's gone, but the pup is here to stay. She immediately bonds with the boys and takes to sleeping with Bo in his bed. I warn Bo that she won't always be so small, but he loves the company and is adamant that Lacey, or Spacey Lacey, as they like to call her, is his dog.

Over the next few days, Bo spends so much time in bed with Lacey curled next to him that I begin to worry about him again.

He's very low, and strangely lethargic, but I'm determined not to project my worries onto him. Kids are full of hormones. Problems are part of life. I'll let Bo come to me when he's ready to talk.

But the week passes and he doesn't come to me. He just retreats further, living in his dark, cavelike room.

I open his door late Thursday afternoon and he's in bed, in the dark, just as he was yesterday afternoon. "What's going on?" I ask quietly.

"Nothing. I'm just tired."

"Are you coming down with something?"

"No."

"Do you want to talk?"

"No."

"You're okay?"

"Yes."

I leave him then and return to the kitchen to finish addressing Christmas cards. He passes on dinner and I don't press, but by bedtime when he doesn't get up, I'm really uncomfortable.

I return to his room, open his door, and find him texting in the dark. "Who are you texting?"

"No one."

"Bo, you're texting someone."

"Just a kid at school."

"Who?"

"Doesn't matter."

Suddenly, I've had it. With the phone. All his texting. Never mind his attitude. "You're taking a break from your phone. I want it for the weekend. You can have it back on Monday—"

"No!"

"What do you mean, no?"

"Take the computer. My Xbox. Take away TV."

"But the phone is the problem. I want the phone."

He loses it then, loses it in a way I've never seen him lose control. Shouting. Crying. Begging. I'm shocked. Horrified. But the more upset he gets, the more determined I am to take the phone. His attachment scares me. He's behaving like an addict who could resort to violence.

"What are you doing?" I'm practically yelling to be heard over him. "Have you lost your mind? It's a phone, Bo, not oxygen."

"It is to me. Just let me have it. Let me have it. Please, Mom—"

"No. Now give it to me." I hold out my hand, palm up. "Bo. Now."

As I'm talking he's wildly deleting messages, clearing out his in-box and sent folders. I try to snatch the phone from him, but he turns away. This has become a contest of wills, but I'm the parent. I cannot lose.

"You have to the count of three, Bo, or I tell your dad to cancel the service and it's gone forever. And I mean it. One. Two. Th—"

Bo thrusts the phone into my hand, and he's crying, sobbing as though I've just destroyed his world. "Just don't read any of the messages, Mom. Promise me you won't read them."

"You've erased them all."

"But if they come in. Don't read them. They're not meant for you."

"And they're so bad I can't read them?"

"Just promise me."

"I can't make that promise, Bo. I'm sorry."

He lets out an anguished cry and I walk away, desperate to escape. The whole situation is impossible. I go to my room, hide the phone in my nightstand drawer behind my sunglasses and pedicure kit, and then pace the bedroom floor, trying to process what just transpired.

Bo's totally out of control. His addiction to his phone scares me. How can any kid be so attached to a piece of technology? And what kind of messages is he sending and receiving that I can't see?

I wonder if they're about drugs or alcohol. Or are they possibly sexual? I can't imagine him engaging in phone sex, but you never know…kids are exposed to so many things now that I never was.

I wish I could call Dane, would love to talk to Dane about this, but I need to be able to handle my kids' problems on my own. I want him to realize that I'm with him not because I need him to solve my problems or handle the tough stuff for me, but because I love him and enjoy him and want to be with him.

I'm still worked up even after the boys have finally gone to bed. I read for a while to try to calm down, but my mind can't stay focused on the story.

Minutes pass and I'm still on the same page, rereading the same paragraph over and over. I give up on reading and turn out the light. I'm just starting to fall asleep when my bedside drawer buzzes and then, a minute later, buzzes again.

Bo's phone.

I look at the clock. Eleven twenty-five. That's so late for him to be getting messages. I'm tempted to look at the message, but it doesn't seem right. I've never been a snoop. It's not my place.

But Bo was so hysterical. So panicked that I'd see his messages. What could be so bad that I'm not allowed to see it?

I'm still debating what to do when the phone vibrates again. Another text message has come in. I glance at the clock. Eleven thirty-three.

That's it. I want to know, have to know. I turn on the light, open the drawer and retrieve the phone. It takes me a moment to figure out how to find his in-box and then how to read new messages. And when I do, the message is so strange that I read it once and then again.

You are so pathetic and ugly. No one likes you. No one wants you. Why don't you just kill yourself?

My hand shakes. My eyes burn. My heart feels as if it's going to explode, but I go to the next message.

Hey asswipe. Are you dead yet?

Oh my God. Oh my God.

How can any kid write that? How can any kid suggest such a thing?

I cover my face, press my hand hard to my mouth to stifle the sound, and scream.

I scream my rage, scream at the injustice, scream for my son, who has so much sadness inside of him and yet still has to deal with children who are driven to inflict pain.

How does this happen?

And where are all the parents?

I don't sleep.

I don't even try to go to bed. Instead, I call Verizon and turn off his phone. I uncover Bo's Facebook password and take down his page—noting as I do the number of put-downs that pass as "funny" comments.

I know I'm not cool; my boys tell me that all the time. But I always thought Facebook and MySpace were supposed to be for friends and friendship. This isn't friendship. This isn't socializing. This is just one more example of kids being given too much technology and a false sense of power.

Bo's going to be upset when he wakes up and finds out what I've done. He might even decide to return to New York to live with John, too. But if that's the case, fine. I'm going to do what I need to do, and that's protect my children while they live in my house.

In the morning, Bo and Cooper are at the breakfast table eating their breakfast when Bo asks me how long I am going to keep his phone.

I've been waiting for this moment since eleven thirty-five last night.

I drop the damp sponge I've been holding into the sink and go sit at the table in a chair next to Bo's. My heart's beating hard, and I flex my fingers ever so slightly, anticipating the scene that's about to unfold.

I look at him a moment, watch him eat, thinking he has no idea how much I love him. My emotional, awkward red-haired boy.

God, I love him. Love him with all my heart.

And then I think of Delilah and how she's fourteen, too, and struggling. But unlike Bo, she has no one on her side, no parent there to help her fight the good fight.

"I can give you the phone back, Bo, but you should know it's no longer in service. I called Verizon last night and had them disconnect your number."

His spoon clatters from his hand into the nearly empty bowl, but I just keep my eyes on his face. He has the darkest blue eyes, eyes so intense that they look navy, and the thickest lashes. If people only took the time to really see him, they'd realize he's beautiful.

"You had two texts come in late last night," I continue, praying I can keep my voice steady. "They were horrible messages. I'm sorry I snooped, but not sorry to know the kind of awful, hateful things kids have been saying to you."

His jaw works and I'm waiting for him to explode, waiting for the shouting and the anger, the rage and the blame. "What did they say?" he asks at last.

Coop's listening intently, and part of me thinks this discussion is best in private. But then another part of me thinks if we're going to make it as a family, then we need to act like a family, which means fewer secrets and more support.

"They were mean," I say, unable to repeat the messages word for word.

"Come on, Mom, tell me."

I can't look away from Bo's face, can't look away from the boy I made. He may be fourteen, but he'll always be my baby. "I can't repeat it." My eyes fill with tears, but still I hold his gaze. "They broke my heart."

Cooper gets abruptly to his feet, knocking the table and sending his juice sloshing out of the glass. I don't stop him from walking out.

I don't blame him if he's upset.

He's the youngest, but he worships his big brothers. He'd fight their battles if he could.

"How long has this texting stuff been going on, Bo?" I ask.

I don't think he's going to answer me, but then he looks at me and his eyes swim with tears. "Since October."

Two months. Two months of hate.

"Why didn't you tell me?" I ask.

"I guess I thought I could make them stop. Make them go away."

I reach out, brush his thick hair back from his broad forehead. "Who is doing this?"

"Just some kids."

"Which kids?"

"Does it matter?"

Yeah. It matters a lot. Everything that affects my kids matters. "Would I know any of them?"

"You might know some of their parents. I think you went to school with them."

And that just makes me crazier. Who are these parents

who let their kids text so much hate? "Do you know why they're doing this, Bo?"

"No." He looks at me, and I see from the confusion in his eyes that he's genuinely baffled. "I guess I'm just not cool."

Cool. Cool. Oh, my God, who is cool? And who gets to decide who's not cool?

This blows my mind.

I swallow back my fury, determined to keep focused on what matters most—Bo. But I'm going to look into this, to get to the bottom of it. "You think you can handle school today?"

He shrugs carelessly. "Sure. Why not? Things can't get much worse."

Coop corners me in the hallway just before we head out to the truck. "What did the messages say?" he demand, eyes bright with anger.

"It doesn't matter."

"Yes, it does, because I know who sent them. Carly and April, two girls in his social studies class. They've been mean to him for weeks now."

"You knew?"

He hunches his shoulders. "Bo told me it was just a joke."

"Telling someone to kill himself isn't a joke."

Cooper's jaw clenches. "They told Bo he should kill himself?"

"I thought you said you knew."

"I know what they were saying a couple weeks ago."

"And what was that?"

"That he was so ugly and stupid that no one would ever want to have sex with him."

I suck in a breath. These are eighth graders saying these things. Eighth graders. "You should have told me, Coop. You should have come to me—"

"Bo told me not to. He made me promise."

"I don't care. I'm the mom. This is something I needed to know."

I've just dropped Cooper at his school and am on the way to Mineral Wells to take Bo to his junior high when Bo says in a very quiet voice, "I want to die."

The words hang between us, and time seems to freeze so that I have a moment of stunning clarity. Bo slunk against the cracked vinyl seat next to me. The 180 shrouded in fog. The fields around us glittering with frost.

"Bo," I whisper in protest.

"It's too hard, Mom. I don't want to do this anymore."

The world has shrunk to just us. The truck is old and the heater coughs weakly and my son is exhausted by life.

My son has just said he wants to die.

I hold the steering wheel as if it were a dangerous thing, but it's not the truck that's dangerous. It's our hearts.

Bo doesn't realize I couldn't survive without him. He doesn't realize my world is him.

"How long have you felt this way?" I ask.

"A while."

The despair in his voice reminds me of the sea on a moonless night. Endless and dark and suffocating.

"When were you going to tell me?" My voice is gentle, belying my resolve. I love him.

"I didn't want to tell you. Didn't want to worry you. I wanted to fix it on my own."

And isn't that just like my family? Always trying to protect one another, even if it means burying the pain, denying the truth, killing the self? "I'm your mom. It's my job to worry."

I slow and then brake, pulling over onto the shoulder of the road. I leave the engine running so the heater stays on. "I'm going to help you," I tell him. "We're going to fix this—"

"How?"

"We'll get you help."

"Take me to another counselor?"

"Yes. A good one. And maybe talking will be enough, or maybe the counselor will recommend something else. We'll figure it out. All I know for sure is that we're going to do whatever we have to do to make you feel better."

He looks at me, and his dark blue eyes burn with a hell of his own. And I feel that hell, that fire, burn me. I reach out, touch his cheek. He flinches but doesn't pull away, and I trace the line of cheekbone to jaw. He's still baby-faced, still no beard despite his last growth spurt.

"Okay," he answers. "I'll go to counseling or take medicine or whatever I have to do, because I don't like feeling this way. It scares me."

It scares me, too. But I keep that to myself.

Bo goes to class, and I go to the school office to request a meeting with Paul Peterson. The front office is decorated with holiday lights and wintry décor. It's obvious today's the last day of school before break, as even the office staff are giddy and munching Christmas cookies and wearing earrings that light up and play music. I try not to watch as two of the office secretaries exchange gifts and open the packages in front of me.

I don't want to be here for this. I don't want to be feeling like this. It's almost Christmas, yet I'm absolutely panicked. My son is suffering. My son is talking of dying. How can anyone wear silly light-up earrings and a reindeer antler hat?

Paul Peterson finally ushers me into his office and closes the door. "You're upset," he says.

I nod and open my mouth, but nothing comes out. How do you tell someone something like this?

"I need your help," I whisper, my throat constricting, making it hard to get the words out.

"Tell me."

And I do. I tell him everything. The text messages. The bullying, including the sour milk incidents and the fight earlier in the fall. I tell him that Bo's depression has returned and I'm going to get help outside the school for it, but I need the school's support. I ask that he alert the teachers, and if he can't, then I will contact each of his teachers individually. "I don't want to turn Bo into a freak show, but people need to be aware that he's more fragile right now than we'd like."

"I will handle this," Paul promises me, "and I'll be discreet."

"Thank you."

"Are you already working with someone?" He pauses, reaches into his desk, digs through a file folder, and pulls out a sheet of paper. "If not, we do have a list of counselors in the county that work with children. I can't personally vouch for any of them, but I know families have been pleased with the top three names on this list."

*   *   *

The conversation with Paul at school is the easy one. Calling John is so much harder, and I put off phoning him until I'm back home.

"Hi," I say when he answers. "Do you have a minute?"

"What's up?"

"Bo."

"Is he having academic problems again?"

I sit on the edge of the kitchen table, my sadness weighting me down, making me feel as if I'm made of lead.

"The depression's returned and I'm looking for a good children's psychologist. The school gave me some names, but I'm going to check around and get some other recommendations."

"How do you know it's depression?"

"Bo's talking about dying." I say the words swiftly because there's no other way to say them. This isn't something you ever want to say at all.

"I'm coming out."

I nod. I expected he'd want to. "Do you want me to pick you up?"

"No, I'll get a rental car. You stay with Bo. I don't want him left alone."

"He doesn't know that you know."

"Well, you better tell him."

"What about Hank?"

"I'll just bring him with me."

"Do you need me to book the tickets?"

"No, we can handle it here. But I'll forward you our itinerary as soon as I get the flight booked."

We hang up, and I sit on the edge of the table with my

heart on fire. It burns. It burns something fierce.

I love my son. Nothing can happen to him. Hit me. Hurt me. But leave my boy alone.

Bo still sits at the kitchen table, helping me decorate the rollout sugar cookies I made earlier today. Cooper was helping us until half an hour ago, when he got bored and wandered away. But Bo's still carefully applying the icing and sugar sprinkles.

"Thanks for your help," I tell him, putting the last sheet of cookies in the oven to bake. "This wouldn't have been fun without you."

"It's nice to be with you."

"It's nice to be with you, too."

I fill the mixing bowl with hot, soapy water and drop in the spatula and mixer's beaters. I'm wondering how to broach the subject of his father coming out when Bo brings up the subject himself.

"Have you talked to Dad?" he asks.

"This morning." I turn to face him. "And he's concerned about you."

Bo stares at me without any emotion.

"He's flying out tomorrow," I add. "He'll be here by eleven."

"Erik can spare him?"

I'm surprised by his sarcasm. Bo has never said anything about his dad and Erik until now. "Why do you say that?"

"Because Erik's totally jealous of us. They had a big fight on Thanksgiving about the amount of time Dad was spending with us. Erik walked out and Dad was really depressed all day, although he kept trying to act like everything was fine."

Coop had said almost the same thing, and it troubles me because the boys don't need more chaos in their lives. But then again, merging families isn't easy.

"Do you not like Erik?" I ask.

"I'm sure he's okay on his own. But I don't like him with Dad. It's weird seeing them together, you know, like a couple. Makes me feel weird. Doesn't seem normal."

I study his face, reading the fatigue in his eyes. "Do you want to go back to New York?" I hate having to ask but realize it's what I might have to do. Send him back to New York. Send him to a place where he's happier. A place where he's safer.

"No."

"But you weren't so lonely in New York—"

"Not if it means living with Dad. I can't live with Dad. I want to be with you."

I dread the next question but have to ask. "Do you want us all to move back?"

He drops his gaze to the table. "I don't think it matters anymore."

"Why not?"

"You and Dad aren't going to get back together, and you like it here. You like being with your family."

I study his profile. His features are changing. Growing, thickening on the way to adulthood. "*You* are my family. You, Coop, and Hank."

"But Uncle Brick, Aunt Charlotte, and Uncle Blue, they're all your family. They're all here, and you never saw them when we were in New York."

"I know, but that's what happens in life. You grow up and go to school and move to where you can get a job, and sometimes it means you don't see as much of your family as you'd like."

"I'm not going to be that way—" His voice cracks, and he lifts his head to look at me. "I'm going to see my brothers. I'm going to live near them and see them all the time."

I nod, swallow, thinking I'd love that more than anything. No black sheep. No lost children. "But I thought Cooper drove you crazy."

The corner of Bo's mouth lifts, and it's Brick's small, wry smile and I love it. "Yeah, of course he makes me crazy, but that's because he's my brother."

"So you kind of like him."

"No. Yes. Well, of course I love him. I just don't always like him. But I don't have to. He's my brother."

Chapter Twenty-one

John hasn't been to the ranch since Pop's funeral, but with the help of the rental car's GPS, he finds us without much trouble.

I'm anxious about seeing him and even more stressed about having him here. I haven't seen John since last June when after the kids got out of school I packed up our apartment and moved us to Parkfield. I'm nervous as his car appears in the drive but excited to see Hank. It's been four weeks since he left for his dad's, but it feels like so much longer with everything that's been happening here.

Hank's the first one out of the car. "Hey, Mom," he says, giving me a tight hug. "Missed you."

Hank's now several inches taller than me, well on his way to six one, and I don't think he's done growing. "You're so tall," I say, reaching up to touch the back of his head.

John's out of the car now and walking toward me. He looks like the former model he is. Tall, dark-haired, tan, handsome. There aren't many men as handsome as John, and I feel so many different emotions as he leans down to kiss my cheek. "Where's Bo?" he asks.

"In the house," I answer, stepping out of the embrace. I still don't quite know how I'm supposed to feel when I'm around John. I remember his body. Remember our life

together. Remember how well we got along. It'd be easier
if we'd fought or had a stormy marriage, but we were
happy. I always thought we were one of the lucky ones.

"Did you find a therapist for him?" he asks, hands on
his hips.

I nod. "We have an appointment at four-thirty today in
Weatherford."

"Good." He glances at the house and then toward the
barn. I know they're looking dilapidated, know they could
both use paint and the yard could use tending, but I'm putting all my energy into the kids right now. There isn't time
to give TLC to everything.

"I'm going to paint the house as soon as it warms up,"
I hear myself announcing, "maybe enclose Mama's screened
porch and turn it into a sunroom. Charlotte has a sunroom
overlooking her rose garden, and it's lovely."

"This place needs more than a coat of paint."

My gaze skims the oak-lined driveway, the corral and
pasture. "I don't know. I like it." From inside the house, I
hear a whine and a scratch at the door.

John turns his head. "What's that?"

"Lacey. Our German shepherd puppy." I go to the
house to let her out, but John stops me.

"She's a cutie, Shey, but you better not. I'm allergic.
Remember?"

Now I remember why we never had dogs in New York.
"I'm sorry, John, I completely forgot. I better call the Mineral
Wells Hotel and see if they can't get you in there tonight."

Hank and Cooper wander around the Weatherford Mall
while John and I take Bo to see the child psychologist.

John and I are allowed to stay for the first part of the appointment and then are asked to wait out in the waiting room while Dr. Crosby meets alone with Bo.

We sit across from each other in the waiting room, tense and uncomfortable after listening to Bo describe his life to this stranger.

My parents separated last year after my dad decided he was gay. My mom then moved us to Parkfield, where we live in my grandma's house on the ranch. My older brother, Hank, now lives with my dad and his boyfriend in New York, and my younger brother and I live with Mom. The kids at school don't like me. They say I'm a freak of nature and call me a ginger. I'd move back to New York, but I won't leave my mom.

"You know it's not my fault," John says finally, breaking the silence.

My eyes had been closed, and I open them to look at him. "I never said it was."

"But he makes it sound like all his problems start with me."

I'd like to tell him that a lot of our problems do start with him, but I don't know that that's fair. And the blame game isn't going to help anyone. What I want is for Bo to feel better. "He's always been our sensitive one," I say. "He cares what people think, and wants others to like him. It leaves him open to be hurt."

John rubs at his forehead. He looks tired. I imagine he didn't sleep well last night. "I always thought Cooper was the emotional one."

"I think Coop's our strongest son. He's tough, John. Surprisingly fearless."

"I just don't see him that way."

I think about the two fights Cooper had in New York, fights to defend his dad. I think about how Cooper wants to be able to protect Bo. "He's growing up." I look at John. "They all are. And that's what we want."

He studies me for a long, uncomfortable moment. "You are coming back to New York, aren't you?"

I hold his gaze even as I search my heart. And then I give my head a slow, decisive shake. "No. I'm not."

"But the boys—"

"Will have to decide where they want to live, and we'll both have to be fine with that."

"How can you do that to them? How can you force them to choose?"

"You were the one who wanted out, and moved out. You left me to pick up the pieces, and I have. Here."

"But you hate the country! You hated growing up on the ranch—"

I flash back to my life in New York, a life dominated by the demands of the fashion industry and John's interest in art, culture, and photography. John was the sophisticated one, not me. John loved the arts. I tried to love them for John's sake. "No, you told me I hated the country. You tried to convince me that I hated life on the ranch. The truth is, I'm a total country girl. I've always been a country girl and have always been in love with a country guy."

"You're just saying that."

"I'm not. I love Texas. I love being back in my boots and jeans."

"So who's this guy you've always been in love with?"

"Doesn't matter."

"But it does. You always told me I was your one and only love."

I glance down at my bare hands, hands that once wore his wedding ring. "There was someone before you. My family didn't approve and sent me off to boarding school."

"How old were you?"

"Sixteen."

"Jesus, Shey!"

"Nothing happened—"

"Because your parents sent you away."

"—but I always loved him, and I never wanted to leave Parkfield. This was my home. This is where I was happy."

"And this guy you liked. Is he still around?"

I shrug. "It doesn't matter. Because I didn't come back for him. I came back for me. And it's been bumpy these past few months, but I'm starting to settle in now and this is where I want to stay."

"Even if the boys hate it here?"

I feel a prick of pain, because no, I don't want the boys miserable. They mean too much to me to have them upset. But Coop...I don't see him wanting to go back to New York. He's more Callen than Darcy, and he likes it here. And Bo...well, Bo's another matter. I'm not sure what he wants.

"I guess we have to ask them what they want," I answer.

"And what if they don't want to be here?"

I'm resigned. "Then they can do what Hank's doing, and live with you."

I see from his expression that he doesn't believe me. "You'd really let all three come live with me?"

I picture Bo and Cooper and how much I love having

them around the kitchen table. It would be a pretty lonely house without them. But I'd still have Lacey for company. Brick and Char are just up the road. And Blue's just ninety minutes away. "The boys aren't little boys anymore. They're growing up. Beginning to think about college and moving away. I think it's important for them to decide what they want, and where they want to live."

John is mistrustful. "But you've always wanted them with you."

"I have. I'm their mom. They're the best part of my life. But they're not toddlers, or little boys on bikes with training wheels. They're boys who will be driving soon and boys who like girls and boys thinking of colleges and careers."

My job when they were little was to protect them and nurture them so they could be confident adults. And while that's still my job, I also have to teach them to think for themselves and make good decisions and learn to stand on their own two feet. As much as I love them, the boys can't always live with me. They're not supposed to always live with me. The goal is to make them strong and loving and independent.

"And because I love them," I add quietly, "I realize it's time to support whatever it is they want to do."

After Bo's appointment ends and we've set up a series of appointments for the next month, we pick up Hank and Cooper from the mall and discuss where we're going to go for dinner.

Hank suggests the Kountry Kitchen Café, and the other boys agree since they love going there for dessert.

I'm disappointed when en route to the restaurant John

suddenly announces to the boys that they can move back
to New York with him. "Your mom's agreed," he says, dart-
ing me a swift glance while I drive his rental car.

Bo unbuckles his seat belt and leans forward. "You
want us to go live with Dad?"

"No—"

"Shey, you agreed," John insists, interrupting me.
"At Dr. Crosby's, you said the boys could come live with
me—"

"If they wanted to," I reply. "I don't want them to move
away, but I said I'd support their decision if that's what they
wanted to do."

John looks over his shoulder at the boys. "And it's what
you want, right? You told me at Thanksgiving that you
didn't like living here. Well, now you don't have to live
here. You can move back with me."

"I'm staying." Cooper's voice is flinty. "I like Parkfield. I
like the ranch. I want to be with Mom."

John turns to face the backseat. "Bo, I know you're not
happy here."

I glance at Bo in the rearview mirror. He's looking out
the window, forehead wrinkled, jaw clenched. He looks so
worried, so stressed. This isn't the time to be pressuring
him. He needs to unwind, settle down, start feeling better
again. "Maybe Bo needs some time to think about it," I say,
keeping my tone friendly, nonconfrontational.

"I think Bo knows," John says. "He's said he doesn't
have friends here. He's clearly bottoming out—"

"I'm staying with Mom," he speaks up, cutting his father
short.

John shoots me a sharp glance. "What if your mother

moved back to New York? Would you like that?"

Bo looks from John to me and back again, clearly confused. "Mom doesn't want to move back..."

"She would, though, if you wanted her to." John gives him a smile. "You just need to tell her what you want her to do."

Something snaps in me, and I exhale in a short, painful rush.

Men are still trying to make decisions for me. First Brick, now John. But I've had enough. I don't need a man to pressure me or push me. I'm smart and tough and grounded and I can make good decisions, great decisions, if given the chance.

"Bo's right," I say firmly. "I don't want to move back. I like living in Parkfield near my family. And I like having the boys here with me, but the boys are old enough to decide where they want to live. It's time we let them decide. That way we can tell the lawyers we've amicably worked out a custody plan, and we can settle this once and for all."

The boys are quiet the rest of the way to the restaurant. I park on the street, and as the boys head inside, John stops me. "You'd really give up the boys?"

"I'm not giving them up. I'm letting them decide where they'd want to live—with you, or me."

Inside the restaurant, I see the boys talking to Traci and I wonder if this is why Hank chose the Kountry Kitchen.

Traci's delighted to see Hank, and once John and I are inside, she leads us to a big booth, chattering animatedly about the end of the Rams' football season and the start of the basketball season.

John's still upset over our conversation, and the décor

of the restaurant isn't helping his mood. As we sit down, I see his gaze lingering critically on the yellowed walls, the brown vinyl booths, the long, lemon-colored Formica counter. It's not a cool or trendy place, and I'm sure the menu won't be to his liking, either. John's a sushi or Thai guy and almost never eats meat.

Traci's still talking as she passes out the menus. "I thought you moved, Hank," she says with the faintest of blushes.

"I did," Hank answers. "But I'm back for Christmas."

"You went to New York?"

He nods.

"When did you get back?" she asks.

"Just, uh, today. This afternoon." He flushes a little and glances down at his menu before looking back at her.

She only has eyes for him, and she smiles at him, dimples flashing. "Isn't New York a lot later?"

"A couple hours ahead."

"Gosh, you must be hungry."

"A little," he admits. "More tired than anything. We got up early to catch the flight."

"Let me get your order in, then." She tugs on her ponytail, rattles off the dinner specials, and then heads off to fill the drinks.

John watches Traci walk away and then looks at Hank. "She likes you."

Hank flushes again. "She's a nice girl."

John doesn't appear impressed. "You don't like her, do you?"

"I think she's sweet. She's always been nice to me."

"But not the brightest lightbulb—"

"Just because she has an accent, right?" Hank interrupts,

voice hard. "Well, you're wrong. She's in the honors classes at school and she's a peer tutor and she works here so she can save up for college."

John lifts his hands. "I'm sorry. You're right. You can't judge a book by its cover."

Hank says something under his breath and hauls himself from the booth. We all watch as he walks across the restaurant to the long counter, where Traci is organizing our drinks.

He says something to her, and she ducks her head. He keeps talking, and then suddenly she looks up at him, smiling and biting her lip and nodding.

Hank returns a minute later and slides back into the booth. "We're going to go out this week," he announces, looking at his dad. Then he turns his head toward me. "Mom, can you drive me into town Tuesday? Traci has the night off, and we thought that maybe we'd go to see the new James Bond movie."

"Sure." I do my best to sound blasé. "I need to do some Christmas shopping anyway."

A half hour later, we've finished our dinner and are waiting for our pie when Cooper nudges me. "Mom, Dane's here."

What? Impossible. Dane can't be here. He's in Brazil.

And yet jerking my head up, I see him, walking toward our booth. My pulse is now leaping like mad, acting like a colt first introduced to the saddle.

He's wearing a denim shirt and old faded Wranglers and a pair of brown boots. The tails of his shirt aren't tucked in, and the tips of his leather boots are scuffed and worn. Even though he hasn't competed in years, he still looks like a cowboy—earthy and tough, and sexier than hell.

"I thought you were in Brazil," I say, sitting tall.

"I leave Monday."

"You really have to go?"

"Unfortunately."

And then, aware of John seated across from me, I make the necessary introductions. "John, this is Dane Kelly, an old family friend and the one that's been working with Cooper."

John rises to shake Dane's hand. Put side by side, they're both the same height, around six two, and both handsome, but Dane makes John look slender in comparison.

"Nice of you to work with my son," John says, stressing the possessive as he extends his hand to Dane. "Although I'm sure he's told you that I have concerns about rodeos and the ethical treatment of animals."

Dane shakes John's hand. "I've enjoyed working with Cooper, and it sounds like you and I share the same concern about the treatment of animals." His green gaze holds the hint of a challenge. "Good to know we're on the same side."

I can tell from John's expression that Dane isn't anything like what he imagined. Dane isn't just some cowboy. Dane is big and rugged and charismatic.

"How long are you in town for?" Dane asks, arms folded across his deep barrel chest, making his broad shoulders and chest look even bigger.

"Not sure yet. At least a few days," John answers.

"Have to get you out to my ranch. Show you what your boy can do. He's pretty impressive for a twelve-year-old."

John's eyes narrow. "Cooper's not supposed to be doing any dangerous stunts."

"He's not. He's just working on his horseback-riding skills and roping skills. Things he'd need to know as a rancher." Dane smiles, but it's not a very warm smile. "Do you ride?"

John all but recoils. "No."

"We could get you on a horse, too," Dane offers. "Go on a trail ride with all the boys." He glances at me. "If you're free tomorrow, come on over. I'll fire up the grill, throw a few steaks on."

Traci arrives with an armful of dessert plates of the restaurant's famous homemade pies, and the slices are generously cut.

"Want to join us?" Cooper asks Dane as Traci passes out the dessert plates and tells John his coffee's on the way.

"No thanks, Coop, I'm just picking up a to-go order," Dane answers. "But hopefully I'll see you soon." He nods at John and the boys and smiles at me and then heads to the cash register to pay for his meal.

John sits back down at the table but doesn't seem to have much appetite for his pie. "It's forty degrees out," he says, pushing the prongs of his fork into the meringue topping. "Who'd want to go riding when it's this cold?"

"Ranchers do every day," Coop answers, taking a bite of his warm berry pie. "They have to."

"Yes, but a trail ride? Come on, what kind of clown does he take me for?" John looks up, stares at Dane's back as Dane talks to Traci at the register, then turns to me. "That's him, isn't it? The *old* family friend."

I hear the ridicule in John's voice, but strangely, it doesn't bother me. I'm happy here. If he doesn't like my life, he can get on a plane and leave. "Mmmm, love peach pie," I say, smiling at my boys. "How's yours?"

"You're not even going to answer my question?" John asks.

I look at the man I loved for so many years and wonder what it was that brought us together. I know what kept us together—the boys. But without the boys, what did we have in common? Has he always been this critical? Or is he just insecure at the moment because he's out of his element? Either way, I've just realized I'm okay with the divorce and definitely ready for the next stage of my life.

"Nope," I say, calmly as I take another bite of the warm peach filling, the flavor sweet and delicately spiced with cinnamon. I don't have to answer to him. This is my life.

And it's going to be a great life, too.

John ends up leaving the next morning, flying out alone, and when Dane calls to follow up on his invitation, I tell him that John's already left. "You and the boys are still welcome to come over," Dane answers.

"How about I come over without the boys?"

"And what would we do?"

I grin. "I don't know. I'm sure we'd think of something."

"We're supposed to be taking it slow."

"Oh, we will. Trust me."

He laughs softly. "You are so dangerous."

"I know. But you secretly like that," I sass back, feeling warm and sexy and very excited about seeing him again. It's been nine days since our date, and I miss him.

"What would you like to eat?"

"I'll bring groceries and cook for you. It's my turn to spoil you."

Chapter Twenty-two

———————— ✦ ————————

I arrive at Dane's house right at six, and he greets me at the door looking gorgeous in jeans and a black linen shirt and as he kisses me, I inhale quickly. "Yum," I say. He smells even better than he looks.

"Welcome."

"It's good to be back."

"It's good to have you back."

My eyes meet his. There's heat and awareness in his gaze, and I think this could be a very dangerous dinner.

"Would you like beer, wine, a cocktail?" he offers.

I lift the bottle of red wine from my shopping bag. "I brought wine."

"I'll open it."

I follow him to the kitchen. The lights are dim throughout the house, and I see a couple of big fat ivory candles burning on the wood mantel over the stacked stone fireplace. "The house looks nice," I say as he uncorks the wine. "I love the candles."

"I did it for you."

He sounds almost embarrassed, and I can't help teasing him. "So you don't light candles for yourself at night?"

"Not my style."

While he pours the wine, I unpack the bag of groceries.

As I set the filets on the limestone counter, I notice two framed photos on the edge of the counter.

Matthew.

Dane has brought the photos of Matthew back out from his office. I'm glad, so very glad. This is where Matthew's pictures should be. Out and visible, front and center.

Dane hands me my glass, and we lightly clink the rims. "Happy holidays."

"Happy holidays to you."

"So where are the boys?" he asks. "You haven't left them alone, have you?"

They're old enough to be alone, but with Bo's recent issues I didn't want to leave them. But I don't want to obsess about the boys tonight, so I simply answer that Charlotte's taken them to Weatherford to Christmas shop and then see a movie.

Dane's eyes gleam. "So what's your curfew?"

"I don't think there is one, although I probably can't stay out all night. That would definitely arouse suspicions."

"Don't want to do that," he answers as I finish unpacking my bag. I've brought everything I'll need from skillet to seasonings. I've even partially baked the potatoes so they won't take too long here.

"Anything I can do to help?" Dane asks, watching as I set up shop in his beautiful modern kitchen.

"Nope. I'm good. I just need to get the oven on, the filets in the skillet, and we'll be good to go."

While I heat the olive oil in the skillet for the filet mignon, Dane crouches before the massive hearth and lights a fire.

I lean on the counter, watching him. He's such a big,

handsome man, and everything he does seems sexy to me. He also happens to be great at laying a fire. The kindling ignites right away, and soon he's adding a small log and then another to the flames.

"Can't you stay for Christmas, and then fly out to Brazil on the twenty-sixth?" I ask impulsively, picturing old-fashioned Christmas with everyone I love together under one roof. "I want you to be with us. I think you'd have fun with us."

He glances at me over his shoulder. "You're not going to Brick and Char's?"

"No, we are, but you could come, too."

"Yeah, right. That's not going to happen."

I frown at his back. "I don't want to have to pick between you and my family."

"You don't have to." He rises carefully. "You can have us both, but just not at the same time."

We end up eating on the big suede couch in front of the fire, and I don't remember when wine or food tasted so good. I eat everything on my plate, too—steak, potato skin, and every shred of lettuce. "I'm stuffed," I groan, setting my plate on the iron coffee table and stretching. "That was a huge steak, too."

Dane's been finished for a while and he smiles at me. "I'm impressed. You really put away that steak."

I lean my head against the couch. "Did everything taste okay?"

"Everything was great. I'm a happy man."

"I like to hear that."

We sit in silence, listening to the crack and pop of the fire as the flames dance and throw shadows on the living room ceiling. "I love your house, Dane. It really is beautiful."

He stares hard at the fire, brows drawn in concentration. After a long moment, he answers. "It is, I won't argue that. But it's a lot of house for one person. Sometimes it's hard being the only one living here."

"Is that why you let Lulu move in?"

He grimaces. "I shouldn't have let her, but I like having company. Makes me feel a little more human."

I hate the idea of Dane being so lonely here. It's just not fair. He's always been a family man. Even growing up, when he wasn't with his own family, he was with mine.

"I'm glad to see Matthew's pictures back out," I tell him.

"Me too. I shouldn't have ever put them away. It just felt wrong...So how's Bo?"

I hesitate. "The last week has been pretty brutal. Friday it all came to a head, which was why John flew out. But Bo's going to be okay. I have such faith in him."

"I'm glad to hear you say that. That's such a good attitude, because I wasted so much of my time with Matthew worrying about all the things I couldn't change, and anticipating the bad things that hadn't happened but might."

He draws a slow breath, his broad brow furrowed. "It wasn't until after he was gone that I realized that I was so preoccupied with him dying that I missed out on him living." Dane looks at me. "I wasn't ever supposed to fix him—there was no cure for him, there was never going to be a solution. All I could do was love him."

I move toward him and lean in to touch my mouth to his. "You're amazing, Dane Kelly," I say gently.

He kisses me back, and in seconds the tenderness

explodes into fire. I'm hungry for him, desperate for him, and I end up on his lap again—seems to be my favorite place to be—and he's tugging at my sweater.

As I sit up to peel the top off from over my head, he tells me, "You know how I bumped into you all last night at the Kountry Kitchen? It wasn't by accident. Coop texted me. Told me to come check out his dad."

"He didn't!"

The edge of Dane's mouth lifts, and he reaches around to unhook my bra. "I was already in town so I thought, Why not?"

The bra falls away, but I cover my bare breasts with my arms. "You came to meet John."

"He was rather ridiculous."

"Because he wouldn't go on the trail ride?"

"I knew he wouldn't go riding. Coop had already told me his dad was afraid of horses. But I thought I'd make the offer anyway."

"Just to make him uncomfortable."

Dane laughs, enjoying the memory. "It was fun."

"Dane!"

He's completely unrepentant, and his hands circle my waist, his fingers so warm against my skin. "You're the one who's married to him."

"Not for long. Yesterday we agreed on the boys' custody and we're having our lawyers file the custody plan the first week of January. Shouldn't take long for the divorce to be granted now."

His green gaze grows speculative. "Sure you've had enough time? Thought this through?"

"God, you're horrible!" I drop my hands to begin

unbuttoning his shirt. I have to have him out of his clothes, too. I want skin to skin. Need skin to skin.

He drags a hand through my long hair and pulls my mouth back down to his. He kisses me slowly, leisurely, thoroughly, until I'm squirming on his lap.

"Your shirt must go," I pant against his mouth. "Now."

He makes a rough sound deep in his throat as I finish unfastening the buttons and then push the offending fabric open and off his thickly muscled shoulders. His skin is warm and smooth, and I run my hands across the shoulders and deltoids and then down over the hard planes of his chest. The man's body is beyond beautiful, and I want him naked.

"Are you on the pill?" he asks, his palms against my breasts, his hands so warm that I can't think straight. "Last time we didn't use anything... can't do that again. That was stupid."

"No, I'm not on the pill, but I don't get pregnant easily. I had to work hard to make each of the boys."

"That's not exactly reassuring."

I lean against his hands, arch my back. "You don't have a condom?"

"I don't carry them around in my wallet."

"How about in your nightstand?"

"Maybe."

I laugh. "You do."

"I am a man."

I rock on his hips just enough to create some friction between his body and mine. He's got a great erection. Be a shame to let it go to waste. I lean against him, rub my breasts against his bare chest, and whisper in his ear, "Go get them."

He grabs my hips, pulls me down hard on him, and I gasp. "Why don't we go upstairs? It's a big bed and very comfortable."

"But the fire's nice," I whisper before kissing him slowly, erotically. Once I find his tongue, I suck on the tip and feel him practically jump beneath me.

"I have a fireplace in my bedroom, too," he growls.

"So what are we waiting for, cowboy?"

In the bedroom, Dane knows how to please. I feel as if we're kids exploring as we try a little of everything. And it's the sexiest sex I've ever had in my life.

I love this man. I just hope this man loves me.

I arrive home at one in the morning and creep into the house, careful to reset the alarm behind me. I'm smiling as I slide between the sheets of my bed and still smiling when I wake up the next morning.

We're four days from Christmas Eve, five from Christmas, and nothing can dampen my mood. I shop and wrap and bake and whistle.

Whistle.

How ridiculous is that?

I'm still wrapping and baking and whistling when Dane stops by with a box full of wrapped gifts for me and the boys. "What are you doing?" I say, flustered. I haven't bought anything for him. I've wanted to, and started to, but I wasn't sure we were at that point in our relationship.

"I'm just on my way to the airport but thought you needed some gifts under your tree," he answers, carrying the box into the living room and carefully placing each gift beneath the tree boughs.

I see all the little tags with our names printed on them: Shey. Hank. Bo. Cooper. Lacey.

Even Lacey gets a gift.

I bite my lip, checking my smile. "That's so sweet of you, but Dane, I don't have anything for you yet—"

He stands, shrugs slightly. "I'm not expecting anything. I did this because I wanted to."

"When will you be back?"

"I don't know yet. But I'll stay in touch, I promise."

It's the first Christmas the boys have spent away from New York, and I don't think their first Texas Christmas is one to forget. We have tamales and enchiladas at Brick and Charlotte's on Christmas Eve, and then coming home, I let the boys open a gift from me before bed. Christmas morning they have stockings, even though they're getting too old and it's getting harder and harder to find fun stocking stuffers for boys their age. Then later, around noon, we head back to Brick and Charlotte's for more presents and Christmas dinner.

Once all the gifts are open, I clean up torn wrapping paper and strewn ribbon and find myself thinking about Dane.

I wonder what he's doing in Brazil for Christmas. I wonder how he's celebrating, or if he's even celebrating. I wish now I'd sent a small gift with him. Just so he'd have something to open.

I carry an armful of crumpled paper outside to the garbage can, and as I smash it down, Charlotte comes out with an armful of her own.

"You okay, hon?" she asks me, pushing her paper on top of mine.

"Yes. Why?"

"You seem kind of down."

"Oh, I'm good. I'm not down. I'm just thinking about Dane."

"You two have been seeing a lot of each other. Is it getting serious?"

I can see us from the other night, having dinner at Dane's house, sitting on the couch in front of the fire. It was a cozy dinner. Fun and romantic and real.

It feels right when I'm with him. I feel right. I feel like myself. I don't have to pretend with him. I don't have to project anything or sell anything. I just have to be me—Shey—not the supermodel or the glamour girl.

Charlotte's still waiting for an answer and her expression is so sweet and hopeful it makes me want to hug her. "I hope so," I say, smiling crookedly. "I'm still pretty crazy about that guy."

The next morning, I print the boys' boarding passes and am trying to get them to close their luggage and load the back of the truck, but Lacey senses that something's up and keeps climbing into Bo's open bag and lying down inside. Even Hank has to laugh at Lacey's antics, but finally the bags are zipped, packed, and the boys are in the truck. Lacey's in the truck, too, coming along for the ride.

At the airport, I hug and kiss each of the boys goodbye while Lacey whines from the truck. "Love you," I tell each of them. "Call me when you can."

Bo gives me an extra hug. "Love you, Mom. Thanks for helping me."

"Always, baby."

And then they're off, and I hold my breath as I watch them walk into the terminal, the air bottled inside me until they disappear through the tinted glass doors. It's then that I exhale.

My boys.

My heart.

On the drive back to the ranch, Lacey lies with her muzzle on my thigh. Every now and then she sighs heavily, and I reach down to rub her ears and pat her back. "I understand, girl," I tell her after yet another sigh. "I feel the same way you do."

I'm on the outskirts of Mineral Wells when I realize I don't want to go straight home. Leaving Lacey in the truck, I stop in at the Kountry Kitchen for a quick French dip sandwich.

It's noon and the café is crowded, and I end up taking a seat at the long counter since I don't want to wait for a table. Traci sees me and comes over to take my order.

"I thought you worked nights," I tell her, surprised to see her in the café now.

"Phyllis wanted off to hit the sales, and I'm trying to pick up all the hours I can during vacation. It's easier working holidays than during school."

"You work a lot."

"I have to. I want to go to FIDM—Fashion Institute of Design and Merchandising. It's in California. Have you heard of it?"

"I have."

"It's supposed to be good, and moving to California doesn't sound as scary as New York."

"Good for you. I'm proud of you for setting such clear goals."

"My mom laughs at me. She doesn't think I can do it."

"Does that upset you?"

"It used to, now I just see it as a challenge." Traci smiles. "I can't wait to prove her wrong."

The week without Dane and the boys doesn't pass quite as slowly as I expected, since my gorgeous niece Carolyn is home and Charlotte's taken the week off to spend it with her. Carolyn and Charlotte include me in their girl fun.

Monday we go shopping. Tuesday we meet Emily and her daughters for afternoon tea at the Rosewood Mansion on Turtle Creek. Wednesday I plan to stay home, but I get a call from Rae at the Stars of Dallas agency with a job offer.

"I know it's last-minute and New Year's is just two days away, but the fashion director for Neiman Marcus personally requested you and I'm hoping by some miracle you're free."

"When is it?"

"Tomorrow."

"I can do it."

"It's in Seattle. Well, Bellevue, actually. Neiman has a new store there—and they're celebrating their one-year anniversary with a huge party and fashion show, and their big-name model fell off the catwalk during rehearsal this morning and broke her ankle. Can you fill in for her?"

Marta lives in Bellevue. I haven't seen Marta since last December, when I attended Zach's baptism. I'd love to see Marta, but even if she's not there, it's still a great opportunity.

The kids aren't here. Dane's gone. There's no reason not to go. "Yes," I answer decisively.

"There's a six p.m. flight. Can you be on it?"

"Definitely."

As soon as I hang up I call Marta, hoping against hope she's home and free. I've gone a year without seeing her, but now that I know I'll just be minutes from her house, I have to see her.

She answers just before the call goes to voice mail.

"Ta, it's Shey," I say. "I've just been booked for a job in Bellevue. Are you home right now, or are you away?"

"I'm home, definitely home. When would you arrive?"

"Tonight. I'm catching the six o'clock flight to Seattle. I'll land around nine."

"Luke will come pick you up."

"Let me just grab a cab."

"Absolutely not. And you're staying here." She pauses. "You don't mind the kids, though? Because it's one noisy house."

I laugh. "I don't mind, Marta, and I can't wait to meet the twins."

My flight's delayed and I don't arrive in Seattle until ten-thirty, but Luke is there as promised. He's an imposing-looking man—six seven and all muscle. The first time Marta saw him, she was sure he was a professional football player. Instead he's a businessman with a soft spot for nonprofits.

It doesn't snow often in Seattle, but snow glitters on the big trees and the side of the freeway as Luke drives to

Bellevue. "When did it snow?" I ask, enjoying the clear night with the luminous sweep of stars overhead.

"Two days ago. But it's been really cold, so it hasn't melted yet."

Marta's waiting up for us when we arrive at the house. She's still slim, but her long dark hair is shorter now and hits just below her shoulders with some blunt pieces around her face to frame her eyes and cheekbones.

"Your hair!" I exclaim. "When did you cut it?"

"This fall. Do you hate it?"

"No. It looks great. Very stylish."

"I couldn't cope with all the hair and the babies. Something had to give," she confesses as we sit on the oversize couch in the living room.

"Pretty brutal, huh?" I sympathize, as she's really been slammed. Three babies under the age of two.

"It's been a lot harder than I expected, and maybe it's because I'm still nursing and they're not great sleepers, but I crave sleep like it's a drug."

"Soon they'll be sleeping through the night. Hang in there."

"I'm trying."

"Do you need more help?"

"Can you reproduce me?" she answers with a laugh. "Because I don't know how to do everything anymore."

"I don't think we're supposed to do everything," I say.

"I know, and I've cut back at work for the next six months. I've handed all my big accounts off to others and only appear in the office two mornings a week."

"Do you miss work?"

"I'm a workaholic, you know that. But being a mom is

nonstop. It's brutal. We don't get enough credit. We really don't."

We stay up talking until midnight, when Marta confesses she has to go to bed or she won't be able to get up for the two o'clock feeding.

I do not miss middle-of-the-night feedings.

I frankly don't miss the baby stage at all.

The fashion show is in the lobby of the beautiful new Bravern shopping center, which is also home to the sparkling Neiman Marcus. The store itself will host the glamorous black-tie afterparty.

Upon arriving at the Bravern, I'm whisked to a final fitting and then join the others in the final run-through before this afternoon's fashion show.

Most of the models are really young—late teens and early twenties—girls half my age, but I'm comfortable being older. I like being older. At twenty-two, I worried about freckles and pimples and if my stomach pooched. I don't anymore. Today when I walk, I own the runway, and I don't walk, I strut. I love my strut, too. It's my signature walk—it's a little high in the knee and heavy through the heel, and it makes my hair bounce.

As I hit the bottom of the runway to pause and pose, I can see the younger models watching from the wings. I don't mind that, either. I'm a lucky woman and a happy woman, and I've achieved more than I ever dreamed.

The fashion show goes off without a hitch, and I have an amazing time, particularly as I've managed to sneak Marta's twelve-year-old daughter, Eva, into a front-row seat. She beams at me throughout the show, and as I pass her on my final walk, I wink at her and she loves it.

I might be a mom to boys, but even I know that girls rule.

I stay in Bellevue until New Year's Day, and then hop on a flight midafternoon to coincide with the boys' return to Dallas. My flight arrives an hour before theirs, and I hang out at their gate waiting for them.

I'm flipping through *W* magazine in a great mood as I think about the past three days spent in the Pacific Northwest with Marta, Luke, and kids. It was a rushed trip and New Year's Eve was spent with Marta and her gang at home, but Eva had Luke buy us all party hats and noisemakers and we watched the Times Square ball drop together. Well, Marta, Luke, Eva, and I watched. Zach and the babies were asleep. Thank God.

Now, as I flip through the magazine and pause to study a sleek navy wrap dress, I wonder what day it is. New Year's Day, yes, but what day of the week? Thursday? Friday? Saturday?

I count backward to Christmas. Christmas Day was Saturday. Today's New Year's Day. That's a week. That means today is Saturday.

My pulse beats a little faster now, and I close the magazine and count the days again, making sure I have it all right.

Saturday's the key. For the past however many years, my period always starts on Saturday. Every twenty-eight days without fail.

I count the weeks again. My last period was in November. Thanksgiving weekend, the Saturday following the break-in. I was staying at Dane's house.

My period was due Christmas Day. It's five weeks since my last period.

I'm seven days late. I've never even been two days late.

Except the three times I was pregnant.

Oh, my God. The oversize *W* magazine slides from my lap to the ground.

I'm pregnant.

Chapter Twenty-three

━━━━━━━━ ✦ ━━━━━━━━

Bo and Coop return to me in high spirits. They had a good time with their father and entertain me with their stories as I drive us home. I smile and nod at all the right places, but privately I'm in agony.

Can I really be pregnant when I don't feel remotely pregnant? I rack my brain trying to remember my previous early pregnancy symptoms and come up with none. I don't get pregnant easily, but once pregnant I've always felt good and had easy pregnancies at that.

But this...

This was not supposed to have happened this way.

We arrive home, and the boys are thrilled that Brick has dropped Lacey off already. Brick and Char kept Lacey while I was gone, and now Bo rolls around the living room floor with her while Coop checks the fridge for something to eat.

"Mom, look what Aunt Char did," he shouts from the kitchen.

I join him at the refrigerator and see that she's made us a welcome-home dinner of fried chicken, mashed potatoes and gravy, and her famous baked beans. A note is taped to the casserole dish of chicken: "Call me, Char."

I call Char immediately to thank her, thinking she's

eager to hear all about my trip to Bellevue. But she's bursting with news of her own.

"Shey, have you heard?"

"Heard what?" I ask, pulling out a kitchen chair to sit down.

"Blue's left Emily."

I'm suddenly glad I'm sitting down. "He what?"

"He moved out. And Mama's moving home."

"What?" My voice rises an entire octave.

"She's here now, staying with us, and she's going to tell you tomorrow but I thought I should warn you first."

I feel positively faint now and put my head into my hand. "Where's Mama going to live?"

Char hesitates. "With you."

"Sweet Jesus." My mind is completely boggled. Mama back on the ranch. Mama living here, with us?

"Shey," Char adds in a small voice, "that's not quite all."

How can that not be all? What else can possibly go wrong? But then I remember the old adage, that things happen in threes. "What?" I ask.

"Dane's a big story in the news today."

"Dane?"

"He just signed what's being called a lucrative deal with FOX, joining the announcers in the PBR booth for the next five years."

I'm stunned to silence.

"He's their new star," she adds. "At least in the broadcasting booth. Didn't you know? I thought he might have told you about it."

I know Dane had a conversation with Ty Murray

Thanksgiving weekend about broadcasting, but I didn't know he'd decided to do it. "No."

"It's going to involve a lot of travel. He'll spend up to five months at a time on the road."

I don't know what to say. I'm shocked. And scared. A five-year contract, to travel five months of each year? What am I going to do? What are we going to do? I'm two months shy of forty and I'm having a baby and Dane's not even going to be around. "I can't believe it."

"You're not happy," Charlotte says.

"No. Yes. Oh, I don't know." My voice quavers and I jam my hand against my mouth, imagining a life with a baby without him. And then I imagine him giving up this job when I break the news about the baby. And then I imagine living with my Southern Baptist mama while I raise a baby on my own...

It's a nightmare, no matter how you look at it.

Sex was supposed to be sex. We weren't supposed to be making a baby.

"What about Dane's business?" I say after a moment, struggling to absorb everything. "How can he manage his bulls and the travel?"

"That's the blessing. Dane talked to Brick in early December about forming a partnership with him if he took the broadcasting job, but Dane hadn't made up his mind at that point. Said he wanted to talk it over with you." Charlotte pauses. "But I take it he didn't."

"No." I swallow the lump in my throat. "I have to admit I'm surprised Brick agreed."

"I'm not. It's been a hard year on the ranch. As you know from doing the books, we're in the red lately more than the black." Her voice suddenly thickens with emotion, too. "Dane's doing us a huge favor."

"But things have been so strained between them."

"And things are still strained. I don't know if it'll ever be the same, but hopefully working together will keep them from being at each other's throats—"

Another call is coming through, and I check to see who it is. Dane Kelly.

My stomach does a quick rise and fall. "Char, it's Dane."

"Talk to him, and fill me in later."

I click over to take Dane's call. "Hey, Dane."

"Happy New Year, darlin'."

"Happy New Year to you, too."

"How's your day?"

"Interesting. I've just arrived back from Seattle to all kinds of news."

"Yeah?"

"Blue's left Emily. Mama's moving back to the ranch. And you've just signed a big contract with the PBR to join FOX's broadcast team."

"So you've heard already. I'd hoped to tell you myself."

"Char said it's been all over the news."

"I've been in meetings all day. I'd hoped to reach you earlier." He pauses. "What do you think?"

What do I think? I think it's overwhelming. Not just his news, but mine. I take a deep breath. "So you'll be traveling a lot."

"That's a definite drawback, but I thought with your kids getting bigger, maybe you could join me on the road now and then. It could be fun."

He doesn't sound excited, he sounds tired. But I'm not

surprised, as it's probably been a long day with endless meetings and press conferences. "Have you managed to crack open a bottle of champagne yet?"

"Haven't had a chance. It's been nonstop here all day."

"Where are you?"

"Pueblo, Colorado, at PBR's headquarters. I've been here all week hammering out the deal and am scheduled to return tomorrow."

"I've missed you."

"I've missed you, too. How was your New Year's in Seattle?"

"Good. Low-key, but nice."

"Sounds like mine." He hesitates. "So when do I get to see you?"

"Is tomorrow too soon?"

"I'll come by as soon as I land."

After hanging up, I go get my purse and car keys. I have one more thing to do before I can call it a day.

I hit the convenience store in Palo Pinto. It's closer than Mineral Wells, and even though it's New Year's Day, convenience stores are always open.

The heels of my boots click on the linoleum floor of the 7-Eleven as I search the aisles, looking for diapers, feminine hygiene products, and pregnancy test kits. I know they'll carry them. Where else do teenagers go to buy theirs?

I pay and stuff the box into the bottom of my purse.

Back home, while the boys watch TV, I slip into the bathroom and take the pregnancy test. It comes up positive right away.

I am pregnant.

I'm having Dane's baby. Now I just need to tell him. And the news will change everything.

Morning arrives cold and dark, and I go to the kitchen to start my coffee. Leaning against the counter, I shake my head.

This is crazy. I'm a mom to three teenagers. How can I be having a baby?

And Dane...Dane will say we have to get married. Dane will want to be honorable. Respectable.

He'll want to do the right thing by me, but I don't want a chivalrous gesture. I want romance and love and a happily ever after that comes in the right place at the right time.

This isn't the right place or time.

We've gotten all the steps out of order.

Too agitated to stay inside, I bundle up in my winter coat and pace outside between the house and barn. What do I do? What can I do? I have to tell Dane, but God, oh, this isn't what any of us wanted. I mean, a baby...

A baby...

I haven't had a baby in so long, I don't even remember what it's like.

Not true. I was just at Marta's. Babies are so much work. They cry. They eat. They sleep. They cry some more.

I try to remember my own boys as babies, and I see flashes of each of them. Hank was serious. Bo was bald. Coop had a shock of red hair. And each of them loved me so much. All I ever had to do was enter the room and my baby boy would light up.

How I loved them.

How I love them still.

And of course I'd love this baby, too. Dane's baby. *Dane's*. It's wonderful, and horrible.

Magic and tragic.

Creating this little life means destroying the old one. The life I knew with my children. The life I had before.

"Mom?"

It's Bo, and I turn and face him. "What's up, hon?"

He's standing in the driveway, his eyes intense. "You okay?" he asks, running a hand through his short auburn curls.

"Yes."

"You look upset."

"I'm not. I'm good."

"Are you?"

"Yes."

He digs the toe of his shoe into the cold ground. "I haven't been easy, and I'm sorry—"

"I couldn't love you more."

"But I know I'm a lot of work, and I hope you know I appreciate everything you do for me, and if there's any-thing I can do for you..." He gives me a small, hopeful smile. "I want to."

Love rushes through me, love so strong that it brings tears to my eyes. "You're doing it, baby."

"How?"

"Just be yourself. And learn to like yourself because I absolutely adore you."

He gives me a hug, and I hold him tight because he was once my baby, just an infant in my arms, and even though he's now fourteen he will always be as dear to me as the day he was born.

We walk back to the house, and when I offer to make him breakfast, he accepts, telling me French toast sounds good.

I'm just whisking the eggs when Mama appears on my doorstep with her big 1972 Cadillac parked in the drive. "You going to church today, Shey Lynne?" she asks me, her navy coat buttoned to her throat.

My mother is a tall woman, but I still have a couple of inches on her, and I don't know whether to laugh or cry as I realize my mother is never going to change. My mother will be worrying about my spiritual well-being for my entire life.

"No, I'm not, Mama," I answer, leaning forward to kiss her forehead. "But you go and have a really good time for me, okay?"

"Shey Lynne!"

"I'm serious. Go, and when you're done, come home and tell me all about it."

Mama wastes no time getting back, either. She must have run straight from the church to her car and driven at breakneck speed to get here. So now we sit like two proper women at the kitchen table, having a cup of hot tea and a chat.

"I'm thinking of moving back," Mama announces after a few minutes of small talk, unaware that I already know her big news. "I miss the house. Miss my friends and my church and, of course, you kids."

I pretend to be surprised. "I thought you liked living in Jefferson."

"I take care of Mamie," she answers, using the name we always called her mother. "And I've made friends there, but it's not home. This here, this is home."

"Then come home. I only moved into the house because it was empty—"

"I'm not chasing you out, Shey Lynne. There's no reason we can't all live here together. If Bo and Cooper share a room, that still leaves two bedrooms. You keep the master bedroom and I'll take Cooper's room."

"No, Mama. I'm not having you in a kid's room. This is your house. You should be in your bed. I wouldn't have it any other way."

And hell, I probably won't even be here then. Dane's not going to leave me here. When he finds out I'm pregnant, he'll marry me and move me into his house.

Just as he did with Shellie Ann.

My stomach heaves.

This is not a storybook ending, I think, clutching my china cup painted with bluebonnets, Texas's state flower. But then, this hasn't been a storybook life.

Mama and I are still at the kitchen table when I hear Dane's truck outside. "Someone's coming," Mama says.

I nod, suddenly so nervous that I want to throw up. "It's Dane, Mama," I say.

I rush to my room to check my hair and face, then return to the kitchen to grab my coat from the peg by the back door. "I'll be gone for a little bit," I tell her.

The wind whips at my hair as I slide on my coat and hurry toward Dane's truck.

"Hi," I say, stopping him before he can climb from his truck. "Can we talk out here? Mama's in the house."

He looks at me intently as I climb into the truck and close the door behind me.

"What's wrong?" he asks bluntly, his green gaze searching my face.

I open my mouth, pray for the right way to tell him, but nothing comes. So I just say it. "I'm pregnant."

He stares at me for the longest time. "There was only that one time we weren't protected."

And it only takes one time. "I'm sorry. I'm so sorry." And God, do I mean it. I want to be with Dane, but not like this, not ever like this. To trap a man like Dane...to use a baby to make him mine...

"You've seen a doctor?"

I shake my head. "Just taken one of those home tests, but they rarely give false positives. And to be honest, I knew. I knew before I took the test. I'm so regular, Dane, twenty-eight days on the dot. I would have noticed sooner, but the holidays and the last-minute job in Seattle...It took me a few days to remember what I'd missed."

He just looks at me. I can't see anything in his eyes, and the lack of all emotion terrifies me.

"I won't get an abortion," I say swiftly, determined to say what I must say. "But I also don't need you to make any rash romantic overtures. I'll be forty in February. I've got a home, and income, and a supportive family—"

"Is it my baby?"

His voice is so deep and rough that it's like nails against a chalkboard. "Yes. Of course it's yours."

"Then why cut me out?"

I wince. "Because you've been through this before, and I won't do it to you again—"

"But I haven't been through it before. Not with you. Not with this child." He draws a quick, deep breath. "I loved

Matthew, but as you know, he wasn't here long. I didn't have a lot of time with him. But I'd love to have that experience again. To be a dad. To be someone's father."

We're still sitting in the drive in front of my house, and the wind howls outside his truck and the sky's a dark, stormy gray. "But it wasn't supposed to happen like this. It wasn't supposed to happen until we were ready."

"Maybe we wouldn't have ever been ready."

I glance at him sharply. "Why not?"

"My career. Your children. Our history."

"So I've trapped you."

"No, the pregnancy wasn't planned, but you didn't trap me." He sees my face, shakes his head. "Why are you so upset? Help me understand."

Suddenly I'm suffocating in his truck, suffocating sitting here. I fumble with the door handle and open the door, swinging it wide. I step down and move away from the truck but don't know where to go next. Don't know what to do. I love Dane, and once upon a time I wanted his baby more than anything. But not now, not like this.

Dane opens his door, climbs out of the truck. "It's cold, Shey. Let's get back in the truck, go for a drive."

I shake my head.

"Then let's go inside the house. Your mom is standing at the kitchen window watching us."

I glance over my shoulder toward the house, and he's right. There's Mama at the window, watching us as intently as though we were her favorite reality show.

"Let's walk," I say, shivering.

"Where?"

"The barn. Brick's house. I don't care."

We set off down the driveway, and as we walk I notice Dane's limp becoming more pronounced. I hate that I notice, hate that I care so much. "Your hip," I say as we approach the barn. "It's bothering you, isn't it."

"It's the cold," he admits, leaning on his cane more heavily than usual. "But I'm fine. I'm used to it."

But I'm not fine with him hurting. I don't want him hurting. The whole point of loving someone is that you want to help them and protect them.

"Stop it," he says quietly. "Stop whatever weird masochistic scenario you've got going on inside your head. You and I made love. We didn't use protection. We're not teenagers. We had to know there could be consequences. And there are. So we deal with it."

"So what do you propose?" I ask, bundling my coat closer to my body.

"We get married and move you and the boys into my house and raise the baby together."

He makes it sound so simple and so very practical. But I might as well be Shellie Ann. He spoke no words of love, just words of duty, responsibility. He'll provide. He'll take care of us. He'll do the right thing. But that's not what I want from him. I need his heart.

"This isn't how it was supposed to be," I say, pushing open the weathered barn door and stepping inside. It's musty but warmer, and I fumble on the wall for the light switch. The single bulb overhead clicks on, illuminating a rail of saddles and a broken-down tractor parked in the corner. "It's not. I've waited so long to be with you, and then this…this…"

He waits.

And my hysteria builds. "This isn't right, Dane. You must see that. You must realize. But this baby, this baby is—"

"A miracle," he completes my thought.

I turn to look at him sharply.

Dane has taken a seat on the wheel of the tractor. "You're giving me a miracle."

I've never heard anyone say anything so beautiful. And some of my pain and fear eases. "What if... what if there are what ifs?... I am almost forty..."

"I'd love him or her no matter what."

Just as he loved Matthew.

Just as he always loved me.

"Dane—" I choke, and I reach out to him. "This just feels wrong. It's not the way I wanted it."

He takes my hand and draws me toward him. "How did you want it?"

"I wanted us to have a proper romance and a proper courtship, and then if it all worked out, a proper wedding—"

"Just like a storybook," he says, holding me captive between his thighs.

"Yes," I answer huskily. I don't know where to put my hands. It doesn't seem right to rest them on his legs. Too much muscle there. Too much intimacy. "All pretty and shiny with a tidy, happy ending."

"But that's not real." He pushes hair from my cheek and tucks it back behind my ear. "Life isn't pretty and shiny and tidy. It's chaotic and ever changing, sometimes intense, sometimes damn boring. And sometimes just perfect, which is pretty incredible when you consider how imperfect we are."

"Dane, I'm scared."

"Good, so am I."

Dane Kelly, the man who's ridden some of the world's rankest bulls, is scared? I crack a wry smile. "Why are you scared?"

"Because you don't have to do this…marry me, or raise a family with me. You could decide you're going to do this all on your own."

"That scares you?"

"Hell, yes. God knows I need you." He drops his head and presses his lips to my forehead. "God knows I've been lonely. That house of mine needs you and I need you, and together we can fill it with the boys and the baby and love."

I want the love part most. I need the love part, too. "You love me."

"Since forever."

"That's a long time."

"And I'm a really old man."

I shake my head, determined to hold myself rigid against the warmth of his lips on my skin. I can't let myself feel. Can't let myself cave in. Mustn't be seduced by the physical.

Be strong.

Be strong.

Be strong.

His lips move to my temple and press another light kiss there. "I do love you, beautiful girl," he whispers. "Won't you come live with me? Won't you come be a family with me? Won't you please be my wife?"

I squeeze my eyes against the tears. "You're just saying that because you knocked me up."

"I'm not saying that because I knocked you up. I'm saying it because it's true."

"Huh!" I sniff, trying to wrestle free, but his hands are locked on my lower back. His thighs hold me immobile. I put my hands against his chest and push, and push, but he doesn't let me go. "You can't trap me into marriage, Dane."

He's smiling into my eyes. "I think I just have."

"You don't want to marry me!"

"Oh, but I do. That's why your folks sent you away. Brick told them I wanted to elope with you, and your watchdog of a brother wasn't going to let it happen."

"You're just making this up."

"And you're ruining our romantic moment. How can I make it like a storybook if you won't cooperate?"

I crack a smile even as tears tremble on my lashes. "I don't want a storybook. I just want you."

"You've got me, darlin'. That's never been in doubt."

I lean into him, rest on him. "So what do we tell everyone?"

"That you seduced me. Couldn't keep your hands off me—"

"Dane!"

"Well, it's true."

I look into his eyes, eyes I've loved nearly all my life. "It is true," I admit. "And I guess I knew that sooner or later it'd get me into trouble."

Epilogue

Blending a family is far from easy, and keeping Cooper, Bo, Hank (when he visits), Dane, and baby Sophie happy under one roof—even one as big as Dane's house—is difficult and sometimes downright impossible. But we're trying.

Sophie was born two and a half months ago and is pretty perfect if you can overlook the colic, which isn't always easy to do. The boys thought they'd love having a baby sister, but her hours of screaming have seriously tested their devotion.

Dane's on the road more often than home right now, but come the end of December he won't be traveling until he begins his stint again in August. In the meantime I have Mama, and she's been a huge help. That's right. My mama is practically my new best friend. Why?

She's got the magic touch with Sophie. It doesn't matter how long Sophie's been crying, the moment my mother picks her up, Sophie calms down, nestles into Mama's shoulder, and goes to sleep.

I don't think I ever truly appreciated my mother until now.

Mama's a great woman, and I'm proud to be part of this family. Yes, it's been a tough couple of years. John leaving. Our move from New York. Bo's depression. Cody's death. And then the unexpected pregnancy. But all those negatives also have positives. All that change brought growth and hope, strength and love.

Like the girls' program I run now in Mineral Wells, where I offer free classes for eleven-to-eighteen-year-olds on fashion and modeling, self-esteem, and goal setting.

And the monthly column I've begun writing for *Teen Cosmo* on how it's beautiful to be strong.

Sure, it's hard juggling all the different roles, and sometimes it's a little messy, but my messy life gives my mama a purpose, makes her feel needed, and makes me realize how much she's always loved me. Me, Shey Lynne, her own baby girl.

Here's to the girls. We rock.

We really do.

Reading Group Guide

1. In Chapter 1 we meet Shey's mother. How does knowing about her relationship with her mother give insight into the inner battle that wars inside Shey's head—the battle between Shey's former young girl self and the woman she wants to be?

2. How do Shey's three sons factor into that battle? How does Shey feel about being a mother? Do you think Shey is using her boys and her "duties" as a mother to shield herself from moving forward?

3. We find out that Shey's husband is no longer in love with her and is having an affair with a man. Do you agree or disagree with Shey's statement "...I can compete with another woman, but how on earth do I compete with a man for my husband's affections?"

4. How are Shey's deceased brother, Cody, and her son Bo alike? Their "condition" affects the relationships of many characters in the story. Shey tries to reassure herself by saying, "Bo isn't crazy. Bo isn't like my brother Cody. Bo is going to be okay." Do you believe her? In your opinion does Shey's response to her son help or hurt him?

5. Dane Kelly, who Shey hasn't seen since high school, was the love of her life until she was sent away to boarding school. Do you think her immediate strong

feelings for Dane are normal or a "rebound" reaction
to the recent split with her husband?

6. Many women think about their first love. Do you have
a "Dane" you wonder about now and then? What
would you do if you ran into him?

7. Shey drops in on her sister-in-law Emily in the morning
and smells vodka on her breath. What were your first
thoughts about Emily and her picture-perfect life? What
were your thoughts after finding out that she might
have a drinking problem?

8. After Dane brings Bo home when he sees him walking
alongside the road after a fight, Brick has a man-to-
man chat with him telling him, "...go for the nose.
Draw first blood. It's the only way to win a fight." Do
you agree with this advice from his uncle? Who do you
think gives the boys the best advice, Shey or the "men
of the village"?

9. Shey is surrounded by men in her life—her brothers,
her three sons, her ex-husband, and her ex-love Dane.
What does this say about men and their place in a
woman's life? How do they all affect Shey's world?

10. Do you agree with the saying that "blood is thicker
than water"? Do you think Brick should have given up
his friendship with Dane to support his brother Blue?

11. Cooper wants to be a bull rider and take lessons from
Dane Kelly, three-time national bull-riding champ, but
Shey is uncomfortable with that. Why? What outside
influences are affecting her decision?

12. Shey finds out that Dane's son died and that opens her
eyes to understanding Dane better. How did this vital
piece of information change their relationship?

13. Shey is home alone on Thanksgiving night and someone breaks into her house. She calls Dane and he takes
her back to his house until she's safe. What does Shey
find out about Dane during her time with him after the
break-in?

14. Hank doesn't return to Texas after spending Thanksgiving with his dad; Shey's soon-to-be-ex-husband is
demanding that Cooper stop his bull-riding lessons with
Dane; and Bo is being bullied at school by his class-
mates. This is almost more than Shey can handle. How
does having a strong support system, whether it be family
or friends, help people survive the toughest of times?

15. Dane brings gifts for Shey and her family to put under
the Christmas tree. What gift does Shey share with
Dane? How does he respond? What are your thoughts
about the ending of the story?

16. How difficult was it for Shey to move back home? What
are the issues and difficulties that can arise from returning to the place where you grew up? What are good
reasons for going back home?

About the Author

I'm a mom and a writer, in that order. I love being a mother, too, particularly a mother of sons, as it's made me look at men differently. I've always been drawn to strong men—the classic alpha hero—but the process of turning little boys into men is bittersweet and sometimes downright painful.

Men enter this world as babies—helpless infants, gorgeous infants—and mothers dote on their babies, kissing and cuddling and cradling. Our beloved babies become toddlers and the toddlers become boys and with each new phase and stage, our boys learn new life lessons. Hard life lessons. Lessons about what being male means and how real boys don't cry and aren't sensitive and don't go running to Mommy for comfort.

I've watched the confusion in my boys' faces as they've been told to "suck it up" and "take it" and "deal with it." I've seen their expressions as they glance at me and then turn away, having finally internalized that they cannot continue to come to me. To become a man they must break away. Must shoulder life and responsibility and pain on their own.

And now I have a new baby, a third son, and we start the process all over again even as my oldest son enters his sophomore year of high school and my middle son begins middle school.

It's a tricky thing being a mother, a series of balancing acts and risks and challenges, but it's also the best and greatest thing I've ever done. Not every woman needs to be a mother. Not every woman should be a mother. But I wouldn't be me without my boys.

My favorite author when I was growing up was Louisa May Alcott and my favorite Alcott novels were *Little Men* and *Jo's Boys*—novels about raising boys. My mother said I was destined to be a mother of boys, and she was a right. My boys are my heart. They own it completely even as they wrestle and tussle their way into adulthood.

I realize now it was inevitable that I'd write a novel about raising boys, and I loved Shey's busy, complicated life made even more challenging due to her three sons, three brothers, and first love, Dane Kelly. But strong Texas men aren't fictional. My grandfather was a Texan, a cattleman, and a very handsome man. He died the year I was born but his portrait dominated my grandmother's family room as did the paintings of the ranches he once owned. After he died my grandmother sold off the cattle and two of the three ranches but kept his favorite, the one closest to where we all lived. Growing up, I spent every Easter on that ranch, and during Easter week we rode horses, played in the corral, picked wildflowers, and generally ran wild.

I love that my family raised me to love the land and fields and big sky. I love that they gave me confidence and taught me courage and pushed me to succeed. And maybe that's what's important. Not that we have boys or girls, but that we make sure we raise confident children who aren't afraid to take risks and are encouraged to dream.

5 Ways to Go Country

1   Swap the designer jeans for good old-fashioned Wranglers.

2   Kick off the high heels and slip on a pair of cowboy boots.

3   Trade the four-door for a pickup truck.

4   Dine on ribs and beef brisket at a real barbecue joint.

5   Spend the night two-stepping at a honky tonk bar.

If you liked
SHE'S GONE COUNTRY,
here are two more books that will hit the SPOT